Praise for Wild Spinning Girls

'This book is stunning. Haunting. There are ghosts at the window. There is wild weather. There are lost dreams and found people. The _____ House with stopped clocks and sec_et bureaus and all the answers. _You don't mess with w___ _____ _e not, but it makes for a heck of a yarn if you do. *Wild Spinning Girls* has all the Welsh magic you'll find in the land's poetry and music. Just beautiful and utterly unforgettable.'
– *Louise Beech*

'More folkloric than fantastical, this is a timeless tale of grief and belonging. The ties between mothers and their daughters unfurl with particular sensitivity, and come alive with a wild old magic. I tried to spin the book out as long as possible, but Ms Lovekin makes that hard! Haunting and hopeful and highly recommended.'
– *Mags Phelan Stones*

WILD SPINNING GIRLS

Also by Carol Lovekin
and available from Honno

Ghostbird
Snow Sisters

WILD SPINNING GIRLS

Carol Lovekin

HONNO MODERN FICTION

First published in Great Britain in 2020 by Honno Press
'Ailsa Craig', Heol y Cawl, Dinas Powys,
Vale of Glamorgan, Wales, CF64 4AH

1 2 3 4 5 6 7 8 9 10

A catalogue record for this book is available from the British Library.
Published with the financial support of the Books Council of Wales.

ISBN 978-1-912905-09-6 (paperback)
ISBN 978-1-912905-10-2 (ebook)

Cover photograph © Arcangel.com/Tania Benito
Cover design: Graham Preston
Text design: Elaine Sharples
Printed in Great Britain by 4Edge

For Natalie
my own wild spinning girl

Acknowledgements

My thanks to Caroline Oakley, editor extraordinaire, for your astute eye, essential questions and another incomparable cover. To the brilliant staff and committee at Honno, thank you for your expertise and dedication to making our books the best they can be.

To Janet Thomas, my love and gratitude for your unfailing kindness and wisdom.

Endless appreciation to Juliet Greenwood whose author-encouraging, knowledge-sharing skills are *nonpareil*. Thanks to the other side of the sky to Janey Stevens, my constant writing other half who encouraged me to call on my dormant dancing past for this book. Special thanks to Eve Merrick-Williams for your ongoing loyalty and support.

I remain indebted to Book Connectors and a bevy of book bloggers. Heartfelt thanks to Anne Williams and Anne Cater. You are both magical women with no equal. To the marvellous, intrepid gang at the Savvy Writers Snug, thank you for the space to be real.

Boundless love to my family, because you are mine.

And to you, dear reader, my constant, heartfelt appreciation. Writers are nothing without readers and book buyers.

To Lola and Phoebe: love and cwtches, pooches.

If it wasn't haunted before she came to live there, after she died, Ty'r Cwmwl made room for her ghost. She brought magic with her. And the house, having held its breath for years, knew it.

Before I was old enough to read a book, I roamed the moor.

My sister stayed home, dressing dolls and preening in mirrors.

One day I stood on a stool and lifted the latch on the door. Nain tried to stop me but Mam said if I was clever enough to work out how to open the door, I was smart enough to stay safe.

Mam was a wise woman. She made medicine to heal wounds and soothe hearts, and she sent me off gathering: searching for sloes and self-heal, burdock root and asphodel.

Out on the wild moor near the stone where the black birds watched, a woman dressed in grey came spinning out of the mist. She held a finger to her lips and handed me an owl pellet. I broke it open and inside found an acorn, a tiny shrivelled shrew's heart and a cluster of bones.

The black birds followed me home and I sang to them.

When I told her about the woman, Mam said she was from the Wild Edges and if I came across her again I should take note of what she told me.

I was fourteen the next time I saw her. The sky was the colour of a broken heart and this time she whispered in my ear that tainted love marked me. Her breath, near my mouth, smelled of apples and I inhaled her like a spell.

I never saw the spinning woman again.

Wandering across the heather-clad moorland, I sang for the birds and they followed me again. I collected every owl pellet I found, split them open and kept the bones, made them into a necklace.

When I asked my mother about love, she said it was a losing game.

Part One

Prelude

2004

Ida Llewellyn doesn't have a reckless bone in her body.

Which makes it ironic when a simple misstep on a *chaîné* turn ends her dancing dreams forever.

In the light, airy studio, the dust motes are made of rosin. They rise, in invisible clouds, each time Ida's pointe shoes glance against the wooden floor. She has done a brief warm-up – too brief and she knows it. Less than fifteen minutes at the barre: *pliés, tendus, dégagés, frappés, développés...*

In her head she can hear Margeaux's voice, high and sharp.

Heels out! In, in, in and side! Shoulders down... And change!

Ida has been taught by Margeaux Anson since she was seven years old. Her mother, Anna Plessey, the famous ballerina, was taught by Margeaux too.

It's a tradition. The Margeaux Anson Academy is small but prestigious; her reputation for preparing young, talented dancers for acceptance to an elite company school, is legendary.

Without Margeaux's circling, correcting presence, Ida drifts. She moves to the centre of the floor, facing the mirrored wall. Her reflection is dishevelled, too much loose hair, grubby tights and month-old shoes, softened by overuse, the satin fabric sweat-stained and worn.

Make sure you change your shoes, Ida... The voice in her head is her mother's now, redolent with repeated urging. *At least once if you're going to dance for more than an hour...*

Ida knows this pair of shoes is dead. She may not be rash, she is lazy, and reluctant to change them. Her feet are blistered and painful, two of her toes are taped, and these shoes are perfectly worn in. She bends, checks the ribbons, straightens up, and pushes a stray lock of dark hair behind her ear.

Ida is alone in the studio. Somewhere along the hall, a class is in progress, the thump of a piano muffled by solid walls. Ida shuts it out until the only thing she hears is the dull echo of her feet, the darned toes of her shoes on the smooth boards. And her breathing, measured and focused. She can feel every bone in her body, each muscle as she inhales and begins to move, diagonally across the floor, in a repetitive series of turns.

She counts the beats to the music in her head, picks her favourite focus point: a mark on the wall between two high windows.

Spot, Ida, you must remember to spot … focus your eye … watch your arm placement … concentrate… And…

Ida concentrates.

Chaînés are deceptive. Fast, travelling movements, they give the appearance of being the simplest of steps. Ida has had hers criticised since she was eleven years old. Five years later, she's still struggling to master them.

On this particular afternoon, there is no class in the small studio. Ida, the ballerina's daughter on whom expectations have been heaped, can come and go as she pleases. Today she has decided to please both Margeaux and her mother, and practise her *chaîné* turns.

Margeaux may be her teacher, but Ida's mother has always coached her, picked at her technique, offered the benefit of her superlative expertise. At sixteen, Ida is close to being considered for a coveted place at the company school where her mother's name is revered.

Anna Plessey's talent is rare. Her presumption for her daughter is a shadow attached to Ida like the feathered headdresses worn by corps of dancing swans.

Pale bands of sunlight turn the blonde wooden floor to speckled gold, float across the dark patina on the grand piano. It's alchemy, and as Ida watches, her frown softens. She flexes her left foot. Her ballet shoe bends, too easily.

Ida extends her arms, shapes them, makes bird's wings of her hands, attempting to echo her mother's impossibly elegant placements.

Come on, you can do this.

From fifth position, into the turns as they unfold like quick heartbeats.

And spot...

The fall, when it comes, seems to Ida to happen in slow motion. Her shoe gives way, her balance falters; she stumbles, spreads her arms to halt her body's trajectory, and still she falls.

There is no sound when the fragile bone in her foot snaps. It's tiny and relatively insignificant.

Unless you are a dancer.

Ida lands hard. The pain in her foot is excruciating. Tears spring into her eyes.

The voice in her head is her mother's again, caught in the motes made of rosin, in the particles of light glittering across the floor.

How could you, Ida...? How many times? You're a dancer, you can't afford to cut corners...

One

2017

Bad things happened in threes, everyone knew that.

Ida Llewellyn, as superstitious as her mother, certainly did. When she lost her job, and within a fortnight, both her parents died, she decided either someone couldn't count, or the worst was still to come.

On a fine day in September, Ida focused on pay day, and enough money in her bank account to pay her car tax. She tried not to feel anxious, even though it was her default setting. The bookshop had been quiet all day. It was quiet every day and it didn't take a genius to work out the place was hanging on by its fingertips. Since opening up that morning, Ida had sold only three books.

It was late afternoon now. The sun, fading into the west, still cast lines of light through the shop window, reflecting off the book covers. Glancing at her watch, Ida saw it was twenty minutes to five.

The door opened and a young man in a Hard Rock Cafe T-shirt strolled up to the counter. People didn't usually do this. Even if they knew what they wanted, they tended to browse first.

'Do you have anything on Welsh fairies?'

Ida looked up. 'Beg your pardon? Did you say, Welsh fairies?'

He nodded. 'Yes. Please.'

'That's a new one. I'm a bit Welsh myself as it happens.'

'Only a bit?'

'Half. My father.'

'You can't be "a bit" Welsh.' His voice didn't tease. He sounded curious. 'It's like being Irish or Scottish – it's all or nothing.' His voice held a hint of a Welsh accent, lyrical and low and Ida found herself smiling.

'If you say so.'

'It's bloodlines.' Light glinted in his eyes. 'So how Welsh are you then?'

'I haven't lived in Wales since I was a little girl.'

'Never been back?'

'No.'

'You should. Magical place. Full of ghosts and mad poets.'

Now Ida thought he might be mocking her. She hated it when anyone told her she "should" do something. And the idea of ghosts terrified her.

She changed the subject. 'Do you have an author in mind?'

'Afraid not. Stab in the dark really. It's for my sister's birthday. She's mad about folklore and fairies. Ghosts and whatever. This looked like the kind of place that might have something of that ilk.'

Who the hell used a word like "ilk"?

'Okay – Welsh fairies it is.' Ida stepped from behind the counter. 'If you hang on a moment, I'll check with my boss.'

'No problem. Thanks.'

Ida made her way to the back of the small shop, through the tall shelves of books, wincing slightly as her left foot gave off a twinge. Sitting around was bad for her. Walking too far wasn't an option either. Ida sometimes wondered if she would ever get the balance right.

She tapped the door of the office.

'Yes?' A woman in her early fifties with curly brown hair and an enormous pair of red spectacles opened the door a few inches, peered through the gap. She looked startled, as if she'd never seen Ida in her life.

'Sorry,' she said. 'Ida. Yes. What is it?'

'Are you okay, Gina?'

'Yes. No, not really. Sorry. What do you want?'

Ida explained and as usual, Gina knew exactly where to direct her.

'*The Welsh Fairy Book*,' she said. 'W. Jenkyn Thomas. Classic. Try the bottom shelf of kids' non-fic.' She glanced at her watch. 'Closing time in ten?'

'Sure.'

'Okay. When you're done, lock up and then can I have a word?'

Before Ida could answer, Gina waved her away, turned into the office and closed the door.

'Wow, this is amazing.' The young man flicked through the pages of the book, nodding and smiling. 'My sister will love it.'

'You're welcome. My boss, she's the amazing one. If Gina Fellowes hasn't heard of a book, it probably doesn't exist.'

'Skills.' He looked around. 'Cool place.'

'Yes, it is.'

Fellowes Bookshop had been established by Gina's grandfather in the fifties. It was one of the oldest independent bookshops in the county.

'I like to think, the world,' Gina had said when Ida applied for the job, straight out of university with a history degree she could see no obvious use for.

Eight years later, the shop still felt like a second home, and her degree not entirely pointless

'I hope your sister enjoys the book.'

'I'm sure she will. Thanks again. Really appreciate it.' He turned to leave. 'Maybe you should buy yourself a copy. Reconnect? See if the Welsh *bit* still recognises you?'

Ida smiled and shook her head, closed the door behind him, locked and bolted it, turned the sign round. She opened the till and began balancing the meagre takings when Gina appeared.

'Leave that, Ida, I'll see to it later. I need to talk to you.'

This time, Ida felt a flutter of unease. Gina had been preoccupied for days now, weeks even and Ida put it down to the fact that her husband had recently been diagnosed with vascular dementia. Ida had been running the shop practically single-handed for weeks. On the occasions Gina was there, she was anxious and distracted.

This time it felt different. Gina hadn't made eye contact with Ida all day.

'Sit down.'

'Gina, what's wrong. Is it Pete?'

'No. Not Pete. Although in a way it is.' Gina's shoulders sagged. 'There's no easy way to say this, Ida.'

'You're sacking me.' Her heart lurched.

'I'm afraid, I'm sacking us both.'

'What?'

'I'm closing the shop. I'm so sorry, sweetie, I can't tell you how much, but it's no use. The bank is on my back. We've had no customers for months now. Not so you'd notice. I can't compete with online. And what with Pete.' She stopped, placed her hands in front of her mouth and let out a long breath through her fingers. 'He's not going to get any better, Ida. I have to face it, and I need to be at home for him.' Her face quivered. 'I'll give you a glowing reference. You're the best employee I've ever had. You're my friend and I feel terrible.'

Ida swallowed, fought the tears. 'It's okay.'

'No, it isn't.' Gina looked distraught. 'It's a nightmare. I've tried every which way to make the books balance and I can't. And now Pete.' Her voice cracked and tears bloomed in her eyes. 'I'm done, Ida. It's over. Door's closing. Move on, nothing to see here.'

Tears welled in Ida's eyes too, and they were in one another's arms.

On her way home, sitting on the top deck of the bus, Ida sent Liz a text.

Shop's closing. Am almost unemployed. Later at mine? Bring wine. x

Liz replied, reminding Ida she was away until Sunday, on a school trip with her class. *That's awful. Billion hugs. See you soon, def with wine. x*

The words skittered in front of Ida's eyes, caught in the cracked screen of her battered phone. Alone on the bus, the day fading around her, she felt her heart under her clothes, a quickened beat, and the phone against her lips, it's tiny imperfect window clouding and clearing as she breathed.

Out. In. Out.

Door's closing … nothing to see here…

The job in the bookshop was the one Ida had always wanted. Losing it was more of a blow than she cared to admit. Fresh from university Ida found booklovers comfortably engaged in their obsession, which soon became hers.

It was safe too: a world away from dancing, and after the accident, satisfied her need to be less visible. With her small dreams dashed, even a career as a teacher evaporated. In the real world, what parents would entrust their budding ballerinas to a teacher with an obvious limp?

And in any case, dancing was a calling.

By the time she was twelve, the rigours of regular practice had begun to disabuse Ida of the notion that ballet was a weekend treat for princesses. She resented giving things up: food, friends, and living with a body that hurt all the time.

Accepting her foot was too damaged for serious dancing, Ida disguised the early relief she felt in pseudo-regret. She was never sure if her mother was convinced by it. Any leftover wistfulness she buried in academia, in books and a newfound freedom to please herself.

'You could try physio.'

Anna's relentless hope had only made things worse.

'There's no point, Mum. We both have to accept the fact that I was never meant to be a dancer. I never fitted anyway – you know I didn't.'

From the start, Ida had had her own ideas about what being a ballerina entailed. When they had shopped for her first pair of soft-toed shoes, she had demanded red ones.

15

'Like the lady in the film,' she said.

Her mother protested. 'You're much too young for red shoes, darling. And for class, it's always pink.'

'Please, Mummy, I *need* the red ones.' Ida's uncharacteristic stubborn resistance had surprised her mother and reluctantly she agreed, so long as Ida consented to the more conventional pink for class.

Her feet were tiny, and Ida wore the red ballet shoes for years. She danced around the house and sometimes out into the garden, and after they began to pinch she still forced her feet into them, dancing until her toes and heels were blistered.

'You'll ruin your feet for pointe work,' her mother scolded.

Even after they were worn to shreds Ida wouldn't allow Anna to throw away the red ballet shoes. She knew they still had life in them.

Red shoes had magical properties. They were made of daring and rubies and flames, of summers lasting forever. Red shoes knew the way and took a dancer wherever she thought she wanted to go.

Ida was too young to know red also stood for danger.

Two

Anna stood in the doorway to the sitting room, a bottle of wine and two glasses in her hands.

Observing her languid beauty, Ida was struck by how impossible it was to mistake her mother for anything other than a ballerina.

'It's not the end of the world, darling,' Anna said.

'No, but it's the end of something.'

Soft, evening light caught in the comfortable furnishings, glinted on mirror glass, the open wine bottle as Anna placed it on the low table in front of the sofa.

'I know,' she said. 'But don't fret, you'll get another job.' The wine glasses chinked together.

The unsaid drifted like old cobwebs in a breeze.

'Do you wish you still danced, Mum?'

If Anna was surprised by the question, she didn't show it. She poured them both a generous glass of wine. 'I have my memories. I have you. And Dad. What more could I ask?'

That I was still dancing, in your place?

'I'm sorry I had to stop.' For once, Ida meant it.

Her daughter's terminated career as a dancer was something Anna rarely mentioned. Children like what they're good at and she had made sure her child was good enough. She refused to acknowledge that what had been missing from Ida's repertoire was obsession, which wasn't the same as being starry-eyed.

She smiled, the bright, fixed one she saved for deflecting purposes. 'We don't have to talk about that.'

Ida persisted. 'Mum, we never talk about it. Shutting it out won't make it not have happened.'

'Neither will dissecting it.'

'I was never going to amount to much, never make a career of dancing and we both know it.' Ida's eyes filled with tears and she wasn't sure for what or for whom.

Some things, once they're taken apart can't be put back together again. However Ida and her mother pieced together that day – that moment – the truth was, Ida had committed the ultimate dancing sin. She had failed to pay attention to the detail, and it had ruined any chance she had of entering her mother's world.

'I was never going to be as good as you, Mum, even though I wish I could have been. I know how happy it would have made you.'

Anna made a dismissive gesture with her hand. 'What's done is done. It's the past. Let it be. I have!'

I don't think so.

Ida gulped down her wine. 'And I'm sorry to dump myself on you. I didn't want to be on my own in the flat. I don't mean to open old wounds, or sound dramatic.'

'Losing your job *is* dramatic, darling. And you're welcome here any time you like. This is still your home.' Anna topped up the glasses. 'I don't know why you ever moved out.'

Because I needed to grow up? Because Dad wanted me to?

Oblivious, her mother carried on chatting. 'The good news is, while we're in Paris – and since you're determined not to come with us – you'll have ten days to yourself to search for something else.'

'Mum, stop it. Paris is Dad's gift. The last thing you need on a second honeymoon is a gooseberry.'

'Oh, he wouldn't mind.'

Ida and her father had an important trait in common. Their devotion to Anna. His was rooted in a passion for his wife, and a self-absorption that, much as he loved her, sometimes blinded him to his daughter's presence. He spent his weekdays in Cardiff, at the history faculty of the university where he taught. At weekends in Warwickshire, apart from Sunday lunch at Wisteria Cottage, Ida made herself scarce, wondering if her father even noticed her absence.

'Say no, Ida.'

He'd sought her out at her flat. The tone of his voice cajoled. He ran his hands through his dark hair; fixed Ida with an intense gaze.

She'd recognised the look, heard the irritation he tried to disguise.

'I did, but she went on, and—'

'No!' He'd raised his voice and Ida flinched. Her tall father, with his limbs splayed like a broken umbrella, paced the small room. Ida never liked it when he shouted, when his mood changed and his normal, quietly modulated voice tipped into exasperation. 'Don't be selfish.'

She knew better than to argue. It was a game they played and Anna, the glittering third side of the triangle, adored her entire life by everyone, smiled and drew her beloveds to her, barely registering how they vied for her affection.

'I know, and you're right,' Anna said. 'But you can still change your mind. There's enough time to get another ticket.'

Ida's heart beat faster and she wanted to say yes, and for her mother not to leave her behind. Instead she told her it was the most romantic thing she'd ever heard. 'There's no way I'm agreeing, and you must make every moment matter.'

'Then I shall miss you each second we're away.'

'No you won't. You and Dad will fall in love all over again and neither of you will give me a second's thought.'

Her mother tucked a strand of Ida's long dark hair behind her ear. 'Will you be okay?'

'Mum, I'm twenty-nine.'

Twenty-nine and still single, with no hint of romance in her life. Not since an abortive two months spent with a man Liz's boyfriend had introduced her to. Ida almost blushed, thinking about him. Men, with sex on their minds, gave her the creeps. Fastidious and wary of their rough natures and rougher voices, Ida found almost everything about young men alarming.

She'd lost her virginity in her second year at university, to a quiet, earnest Classics student. It was an act of curiosity – as much for him as for her – devoid of passion and only confirmed what Ida already suspected. It was the softness of girls she was drawn to.

Knowing she preferred women was something Ida still didn't have the courage to publicly own. None of her friends were gay. Not that she was aware of. She was safer by herself. Being alone held a kind of certainty. When it was just her, she knew who she was.

She reached for her wine. 'Mum, do you ever regret leaving Wales?'

'What an extraordinary thing to say! You're full of tangents today. No. I hated the place.'

'There was a guy in the shop. Looking for a book about Welsh folklore. I told him I have Welsh blood.'

Her mother frowned. 'Well, technically, yes. But—'

'Do you suppose bloodlines mean anything?'

Ida sensed her mother's discomfort. The few years she'd spent in Wales was something else Anna rarely mentioned. And when she did, her reminiscences were fraught with tales of loneliness and isolation. A remote, stark stone house with an unpronounceable name, and the black birds she said reminded her of witches.

'No. Not really,' she said. 'I mean, yes, your father was born in Wales but it's not a thing. It's not like he identifies as Welsh, is it?'

Ida knew this was what Anna preferred to believe, and not wholly true.

It's a land of fairy.

Her father's voice slipped into her head, his uncluttered, historian's mind rarely given to flights of fancy. And wanting to be enchanted, she'd believed him, about the magic.

'Yes, I suppose so. I'm curious, that's all.'

'Well, I'm sure if you ask him, Dad will tell you what he does remember.'

No he won't, he'll be too busy adoring you.

Ida smiled to herself. Adoring Anna was easy.

'Don't you remember anything about being there?'

'No.' Her mother's voice adopted an edge. 'The only good thing about Wales for me was you. And your father of course. If I hadn't met him, I'd never have had you.'

'Now that was romantic.' All at once, Ida longed for the certainty of childhood, when class was still for princesses and her friends had been impressed that her mother was Anna Plessey: the famous ballerina whose beauty and talent had mesmerised her father. 'Tell me the story.'

'What? Again?'

'You love talking about yourself!'

'Cheeky!' Chuckling, her mother drew Ida into an embrace. 'I was principle dancer, on tour with the company and your father saw me perform *Giselle* in Cardiff.'

'And fell in love with you across a darkened auditorium.'

'It was destiny.' Her mother's laugh rang round the room. 'The proverbial whirlwind romance.'

'And you talked yourself into believing you were ready to give up your career for domesticity.'

'Oh, I thought I was. Be the perfect wife, live in Wales – even in that hideous house – and have a baby.'

'Me.'

Her mother's features softened. 'I told you, you're the best part.'

When Ida was born – her wedding bouquet barely wilted – Anna had smiled at her child, danced in her dreams until her heart began to wilt too.

'And then the company asked you back.'

'Yes, and I couldn't believe it. I thought they'd forgotten about me.'

'As if.'

'I was lucky – it happens to some dancers. No matter how famous you are, once you begin to fade, you're soon gone.'

'You were Anna Plessey.'

'It was still an honour.'

'And Dad didn't mind?'

'No.'

The weight of her need had let him know, if he wanted to keep her, he must agree. Don't leave me, he'd whispered. And she told him she wouldn't. Only not here, not any more, my love. Not in this dark house, and then it will be perfect.

Ida leaned into her mother. 'It's a lovely story.' She yawned.

'You must be exhausted,' Anna said. She patted Ida's hand. 'What you need, my girl, is a good night's sleep.'

There were moths at the window, drawn to the light from the lamps. Ida hugged her mother, sensing, deep down, she probably thought losing a job in a bookshop bore no comparison to throwing away a vocation as a ballet dancer.

At the weekend she drove her parents to the airport, waved off the plane through the glass on the concourse.

Have the best time! Be happy! See you soon!

Don't say 'good luck' theatre people insisted. The actors called, 'Break a leg!' – dancers whispered, '*Merde.*'

Ida drove home, overwhelmed by the silence and the image of her mother smiling and blowing kisses.

'*Au revoir, ma chérie!*' Already a Parisian.

'*Merde*, Mum, *merde…*'

Three

'I'm sorry,' the policewoman said.

On a night as cold as sorrow, hunched in the doorway, Ida wondered if bad news was always broken at night. There was a circle of glass in the front door, frosted with chestnut leaves and it made the two police officers look as though they were inside a tangle of foliage. When she opened the door, Ida refused to look at either of them, only up at the sky, so clear the stars were close enough to touch.

Once inside, the woman officer guided Ida to the sofa. With infinite kindness she explained. A freak accident. A driver, over the limit, the train crashing through an ancient wall, crushing her parents who had been walking along the boulevard adjacent to the railway station.

'Are you sure?' As though there was some sort of a mistake.

It wasn't a mistake.

'We're so *very* sorry, Miss Llewellyn,' the male officer said.

Was this *very* sorry more than the regulation kind, reserved for a particular kind of tragedy? Were there degrees of sorrow? If her mother and father had been murdered, would an alternative version have been used?

Once the words were said, Ida tried with all her might not to cry. In those few moments she knew if the words were true, anything was possible. She could step outside the front door and find the street turned to sky, find herself walking on dead stars.

In the space of a few moments, what was best in her life turned bad. And from that day she stopped believing anything would ever be good again. However blue the sky, however beautiful a garden full of yellow roses, however sweet the songs the blackbirds sang at twilight, Ida's world turned to grey.

'Is there anyone you'd like us to call?'

My mother?

The funeral was a dull affair. Outside the crematorium people hovered, shook their heads in strangled disbelief.

Gina, dashing between crematorium and a hospital appointment, laid a hand on Ida's arm and whispered, 'If there's anything at all, call me.'

Numb, Ida shook her head, turned away.

'You don't have to talk to anyone,' Liz said.

Kind, pragmatic Liz – her oldest friend, whose belief that all people were essentially good, meant there was always somewhere for Ida to turn to when she felt bad. Liz, doing her best to take charge and alleviate Ida's incomprehension.

'So why don't you leave me alone?' Ida's misery ripped a hole in both their hearts. Liz held her friend close, felt her rigid body, her thin bones shaking.

'They mean well.'

'They mean nothing.' Ida pulled out of Liz's embrace and went back to Wisteria Cottage alone. No wake had been planned, the idea of any kind of gathering too much for her to bear. When Liz, refusing to be rebuffed, called by later that evening, Ida had the grace to apologise.

'It's all right,' Liz said. 'It's your grief, you're allowed to choose how you deal with it.'

It didn't help and Ida said so.

'Like you'd know,' she snapped. 'No one you love has died.'

Refusing to take offence, or point out how much she had loved Anna, Liz said, 'You need to take care of yourself.'

'Why would I even care about myself?' Ida shot back. 'You need to look out, Liz. Disaster's everywhere you look.'

'You're being absurd.'

24

'Am I? I lose my job and then my parents die? What's next, huh? How horrendous is the third bad thing going to be?'

Liz, used to Ida's superstitions, pressed her lips together.

'And don't you dare cry,' Ida said. 'I can't cope with your grief on top of mine. Don't tell me everything's going to be all right either. Or not to be sad.'

'I wasn't going—'

'Being anything else isn't an option.'

'Ida, stop it. I know.' Liz took Ida's hands in hers, uncurled the knotted fists and stroked her cold skin. 'You don't have to pretend with me.'

People's kindness appalled Ida. When they offered condolences she translated them as pity. She stayed indoors and Liz tried to persuade her to get out for some fresh air.

'You can't stay indoors forever.'

Ida thought she could, but to stem the flow of Liz's concern, agreed to go for a walk, so long as it was after dark. She wore an oversized beret pulled low to hide her face and a dark blue coat that had belonged to her mother.

She lay in the bath until the water went cold, but forgot to wash her hair. She stopped eating, lay in bed for hours and didn't sleep.

'If you don't sleep soon,' Liz said, 'or eat something, you'll be ill.'

Urged by Liz to see her GP, Ida finally agreed.

'But only to shut you up.'

Liz made the appointment and made sure Ida turned up.

The doctor explained it away as PTSD.

'Isn't that what soldiers get?'

'It's what can happen to anyone who's experienced a deep trauma.'

Ida scowled at him. 'The wall didn't fall on me though, did it?'

The doctor didn't say anything else. Instead, he scribbled on a pad, handed Ida a prescription she knew she would never fill. She hadn't been there, what did she have to feel traumatised about?

'Bloody quack,' she muttered, sweeping past Liz, perched on a bench in the waiting room.

Back at Ida's flat, Liz made coffee and suggested a holiday.

'I don't want a holiday.'

'You need something, lovely.'

'I need my mother.'

Ida wore a long black frock.

It clung to her sadness like a thin shroud. Since the funeral she'd lost so much weight, people with no manners asked if she had an eating disorder, when what they ought to have realised was, she had a heart condition.

If your heart doesn't give a damn, you stop caring about yourself.

Ida's heart was so small it had space around it. For weeks, she walked around holding onto her shrivelled heart for fear it would die too.

The hem of her frock flapped round her ankles. What had seemed appropriate clothing for a conversation with a solicitor, now struck her as ludicrous.

'You will have to decide how to proceed.'

Ida tried to concentrate. The solicitor perched on the edge of Anna's sofa, shuffled papers on his lap.

'Proceed?' Ida frowned.

He smiled, a professional twitch, the semblance of a raised eyebrow and Ida was reminded of a caterpillar. 'I'm appalled that your father never explained that this cottage is a leased property. If you were thinking of moving in—'

'I'm not.'

Ida didn't want to talk about the business end of death. But bleak though they were, she knew she must at least have the facts.

She cleared her throat. 'The house in Wales, tell me about that.'

'Rented out for years. Left to you, as his only surviving relative.'

Why would you say that? Like I don't know my own father is dead?

'Your father gave me few instructions. He had another solicitor apparently. In Wales.'

He made it sound like Ulan Bator and Ida wanted to hit him.

'Anyway, er, Ty'r…' He tapped the papers on his lap. 'I'm sorry, the Welsh defeats me.' He didn't sound defeated – he sounded disdainful. 'Cloud House is yours now and—'

'Is he still there? The tenant?'

'She. A woman.' A caterpillar eyebrow jerked. 'And no, she died about a year ago and the house was shut up. When I questioned him about it, your father was vague about finding another tenant. Said to leave it to the chap in Wales.' He tapped his fingers on the paper. 'I advised him to sell. He wouldn't hear of it. A childhood attachment I suppose.' He gazed at Ida and her irritation mounted. 'It's all very irregular.'

Ida thought him impertinent. It wasn't in this bumptious solicitor's remit to criticise her father. He had been a client and now, so was she.

She stretched out her hand.

The will was written on heavy paper, its surface textured, giving an impression of age. Ida half-expected it to creak. She stared at the words: *Last Will & Testament* and felt the looped, embellished weight of them. There was a photograph too, which she knew she was meant to recognise: a dark, louring house, a band of cloud threading between thick chimneys protruding like stunted turrets at either end of a steep roof.

The solicitor's voice intruded. 'Goodness knows what state it'll be in by now. I'll send someone…'

'No, don't do that.'

'My dear—'

'It's my house now, right? And this place – Wisteria Cottage – isn't?'

'No. I'm afraid not. Although I'll see that you have time to settle things. Your parents' belongings…'

'Well, that's something to be grateful for.'

He coloured and Ida didn't care.

'As I said—'

'Is it worth much? The house in Wales?'

He looked taken aback, as if talking in monetary specifics was beneath his dignity. 'Depending on the market there, I imagine it would fetch a reasonable price.'

'Enough to buy small flat – so I don't have to go on renting?'

'Yes, I'd say so.'

'In which case, these are my wishes. Do whatever's necessary regarding this place. Buy me some time if you can, please. I'm not ready to clear it out yet. I'll drop by your office in a day or two, collect the keys to Cloud House, or whatever it's called.'

'With what in mind, may I ask?'

By now his manner was beginning to seriously rattle her.

'Putting it on the market I imagine.' Getting to her feet, Ida gave him what she hoped was a firm handshake. 'I assume you approve.'

'Well yes, quite, but—'

Ida cut him short again. 'I'll let you know my decision once I've seen the house.'

'You're going there? To Wales?'

'I may as well – see what's what.' See what a house she barely recalled looked like. 'It's where I was born, after all.'

You can't be a "bit" Welsh…

It was the last thing she would ever have imagined herself doing. 'Tie up loose ends?'

'If that's your wish.'

'It is. But I don't expect to change my mind. I will be selling.'

Four

Liz stood too close, with the concerned expression on her face: the one that was supposed to be nonchalant and had worry written all over it.

The phone shop was hot, too loud. Piped music hummed in the background and Ida had to take short breaths to stop herself from screaming.

'You can't go off to the wilds of Wales without a proper phone,' Liz said. 'It's got everything you need.'

Eying the impossibly thin device, Ida replied that it had very little she wanted.

The young man behind the counter spoke: bright, practised words. 'It's top of the range. Lots of great Apps. You name it, this phone's got it.'

Does it have an App for grief?

A tear pricked in the corner of Ida's eye. She turned her head, poked the tear away, snatched her credit card from her wallet, and slid it across the counter.

'Welcome to the twenty-first century, sweetie,' Liz said. 'You won't regret it.'

'You might, though,' Ida said. 'You have to show me how it works.'

Out on the pavement, Liz took Ida's arm. 'Lunch? My treat.'

'No. I want to go home.'

Home … but for how long?

'Can we? To the cottage.'

Liz drove slowly, through the small town, out onto the main road. 'You okay?'

Ida could barely speak.

'Sorry – it's a reflex.'

'It's fine.'

'No it isn't.' Liz changed gear, picked up speed. 'Every time I open my mouth the only words that come out are "okay" and "sorry".'

'What else is there to say?'

Inside Wisteria Cottage, amongst her parents' belongings, the books and mirrors, paintings and photographs, Ida paused, unable to take another step, her body shaking.

'Sit.' Liz steered her into the sitting room. 'I'll make coffee.'

Ida would have preferred gin. She lay back against the sofa cushions, breathed in the scent of her mother's rose perfume. Outside, it began to rain and Ida watched the window, changing from clear glass to a Jackson Pollock painting.

Grey period.

Liz reappeared with two mugs of coffee.

'How did I not understand my mother needed me, Liz?'

'Now, come on, not that again. You're being irrational.'

'That's what Gina said.'

'She didn't mean it unkindly. Neither do I.'

'I know. And I was vile to her – I've been horrible to everyone. Even you.'

'No you haven't.'

'When Mum invited me, I ought to have agreed. I tempted fate.'

'No, you didn't.'

'You don't understand, Liz. I let her down. I've always let her down. Ever since the accident … I broke her heart.'

'It wasn't your fault.'

'Yes it was. I was stupid and careless, and I failed her.'

'Ida, there's no law that says you had to be a dancer. And you told me – you never had the killer instinct anyway.'

It was true. Liz wasn't a dancer, but she didn't need to be.

'Your insecurities don't come from not being able to dance, Ida. They come from not having lived up to your mother's impossible expectations.'

'That's not fair!'

'It is, and you know it. You didn't fail anyone.'

Ida rocked back and forth, her hands squashed between her knees. 'But Paris was such a small thing. He shouldn't have stopped me.'

Liz gave an exasperated sigh. 'Ida, no right-minded person would have agreed to go. Your dad was right. It was their second honeymoon for heaven's sake.'

'But—'

'No.' Liz was adamant. 'It really was an odd request, sweetie. I know you and your mum did everything together, but it wouldn't have worked.'

'It would have been different.' Ida's head was aching and her breath came in gasps. 'We'd have done other things at different times, not been on that particular street – when the train…'

Her voice broke and she started crying.

Liz knelt on the floor in front of her friend, stroked stray strands of hair away from her face. 'Ida, you're grieving. And you don't go round grief, you go through it. Everything you're feeling, these muddled emotions – they're all normal.' She reached for the tissues and stuffed a few into Ida's hands.

Ida blew her nose. 'Including wanting to run away to Wales?'

'Is that what you're doing?'

'I don't know.' Ida sniffed. 'But there's only me to consider now. Even if I could stay here, I'm not sure I could bear to.' She blew her nose again. 'I can live anywhere.'

The image of the young man from the shop made her blink.

Maybe you should see if the Welsh bit still knows you…

'Wales is as good a place as any, for now. And I do need to see the house. I mean, it's mine, and I was born there.'

'It's a long way.'

'It's Wales, Liz, not India. And it won't be for long. If the house is in a reasonable state, I'll put it straight on the market.'

'And if it isn't?'

'Put it on the market anyway?'

'You might like it. You might want to stay. You can go anywhere now, Ida, do anything.'

Ida's hold on normality was still slender. Liz was saving her, one kindness at a time and Ida couldn't have been more grateful. She swallowed another deluge of tears threatening to choke her.

'Yes,' she whispered. 'I suppose I can.'

'And if nothing else,' Liz said, 'it'll be a break.' She nodded at the new phone, poking out of Ida's bag. 'If my number's the only one in that thing, at least you won't be entirely friendless.'

'Thanks for today,' Ida said. 'You've been brilliant.'

'I've been a nag. Now, run that bath, have a good night's sleep and tomorrow, we'll get your packing done.'

'I'm not taking much. I told you, I shan't be stopping. A week or two at most.'

'Whatever. It's turned cold. Have they even discovered fire in Wales? You'll need socks, and all the jumpers.'

Ida managed a grin.

Liz left, and in her wake, Ida felt slivers of cold where her warmth had been. She imagined her mother calling, somewhere in the house, and when she went to look, the cold spots followed her.

Ida pushed open the door to her parents' bedroom. It hummed with their presence: the sense of him, in a tie draped on a chair, and of her mother – in a tangle of tights and frocks rejected as unsuitable for Paris on the bed. The bed itself, half-made before they left, had its covers flung carelessly to one side, indentations on the pillows.

In the bathroom she ran her fingers through a film of dust on a small white-painted dresser. Her mother had been addicted to talcum powder. On the ledge above the washbasin, an empty china pot, where toothbrushes ought to have been. And next to it, a hairbrush with a few dark strands of her mother's hair caught in the soft bristles.

Ida turned on the taps, sat on the edge of the bath while steam filled the room. Her own hair, long and so like her mother's people remarked on it, fell in a loose knot over her shoulder. Without Anna to brush it, Ida had stopped taking care of her hair. It had formed snags and the weight of her grief lay caught in it.

Snatching up a pair of scissors, she hacked at it, watched as it fell to the floor, tangled up with the fragments of her broken heart.

Five

Smoke-coloured sky stretched for miles.

Mid-afternoon and still at least a hundred miles to go. Instead of stopping at one of the numerous motorway service stations, Ida turned onto a slip road, pulled into a lay-by next to a stone bridge, snacked on bananas, nuts and a chicken wrap she'd picked up in a supermarket before leaving. (Years of not eating, in order to stay thin, meant she'd had to learn not to be afraid of food. She was still working at it.)

As she listened to a trickling stream beneath her, Ida tried to work out if it came from Wales or, like her, was trying to find its way back.

On the motorway once again, crossing a different bridge, she saw how this one rose in a majestic ripple of slender metal lines. Its elegance was lost on her. Ida saw only bars and their towering vastness stunned her.

Croeso i Gymru.

Welcome to Wales.

She may as well have been driving into Patagonia.

Fumbling in her purse for the toll fee, the sense of separation was complete.

'Sorry, I don't have the right money.'

The man in the booth reached down to hand her the change. 'No worries, *bach*. There you go. Safe journey.'

After a couple of hours, the motorway narrowed to dual carriageways and lanes. Towns gave way to villages and eventually to scattered countryside beneath careless skies. As she drove closer to her destination, Ida returned to the mental list she'd been compiling since she'd set off: things she'd need to do once she reached Ty'r Cwmwl.

She tried the Welsh name again out loud, tripping over the lack of vowels.

'Bloody silly language.'

Cloud House it would have to be. And top of the list would be cleaning. The house was bound to be dusty and neglected. As for the contents, she couldn't imagine wanting to keep anything. The furniture would be older than she was. Possibly older than her father. Ida frowned, but her dismantled memories revealed nothing. She would get essential repairs attended to and sell the house as seen.

Pulling onto the side of the road again to check the map on her new phone, Ida squinted at the screen, zooming in. The house still appeared like a dot in the middle of nowhere, a mile from the closest village and another twenty from the nearest town.

There was a text from Liz. *Are you there yet? x*

Ida shaded her eyes, watched as lines of edgeless curving land merged into an illusory vanishing point. For a fanciful moment she could believe that reality and myth had become interlaced. Flicking off the phone, she looked up again, for a connection, a moment of recollection.

I'm a bit Welsh…

It didn't come and a sense of unease enfolded her. What memories she did have were her mother's cast-offs.

Horrid place … I hated it.

Finally, her uncertain memory led her, more by luck than good judgement, to the right road. Too narrow and insignificant to warrant a number, it uncurled through the imprecise light, finally arriving at an open gate flanked by broken, intermittent drystone walls.

A solid metal sign bolted into a stone upright bore the legend: Ty'r Cwmwl.

Twenty-nine years ago, she had been born here. For five years it had been her home. The last time she'd driven down this track she had been barely big enough to see through the back window of her father's car as it jolted away from the house.

Ida had a vague memory of her mother tucking her into her arm, as if she hadn't wanted her daughter to see what they were leaving behind, and make a memory.

She needn't have worried.

Gazing around her now, Ida recalled very little of either the house or her surroundings. Other than the sky, wide and endless and, regardless of the season, always with an edge of winter, nothing was familiar. The marbled, changing glare of it reached for miles.

And in each direction, falling away in a palette of washed-out colour, a landscape out of legend.

There were no landmarks, only barren moorland and rocky outcrops. Skinny blackthorns with witch-finger branches fought the prevailing wind, making it hard to believe they could ever grow leaves. Ida blinked, searched her fragmented memories, anything to reassure herself being there was a good idea.

Houses are said to look smaller when we grow up.

At the end of the track, the house loomed large, austere and squat, with no redeeming features. No porch to deflect the wind. No roses round the door, only a stone façade broken by black windows reflecting the rapidly fading light and offering no clue as to what might be inside. Coloured in shades of grey it appeared to rear backwards, as if it strained against the force of gravity, equally at the mercy of the wind.

A number of larches, taller than the house, framed it. Trees as old and dark as the building itself, their needles sparse, thwarted by the effort to hold on to them.

The light was losing its lustre, fading to a stain behind which the sun had now disappeared. Cloud was beginning to descend, coiling like ashen candyfloss. And arranged on the tree branches, along the ridge tiles on the house's roof, several black birds crouched, shapeless and silent.

The car came to a halt and a shiver ran through her. Winding down the window, Ida listened. Other than the mew of a buzzard it was silent. A strip of breeze lifted the edge of her short hair. It caught on her mouth and she touched a finger to it, flicking it away.

Ida let out the clutch, negotiated the gateway and drove tentatively along the rutted track, stones popping under the wheels. The small Peugeot struggled and she winced as she heard something catch on the exhaust pipe. Cutting the engine and hauling on the handbrake she eased her weary body out of the car. Her boot caught on a protruding rock. Ida let out a short gasp of pain. Hours of driving had made her foot ache.

A noise erupted and a crowd of black birds rose into the air in a crack and snap of feathers. She shrank back, her mother's face in front of her, laced with fear as she recounted her mistrust of the large birds. Ida eyed them, watched as several landed on the low stone wall surrounding the house.

'Scat!' Her voice sounded pathetic and the black birds ignored her, flouncing and gleaming, before flinging themselves skyward like torn black flowers falling upwards into the gathering cloud.

Ida stumbled against a low gate: raw wood bisecting the wall, most of the paint stripped by wuthering winds. Fumbling for the latch, she glanced over her shoulder.

The last patch of sky seeped into the hills, the stratus cloud curtain drew closer and lower. Pushing open the gate, in the uncertain light, Ida's peripheral vision picked up a shape: a shadow, near a stone outbuilding. Blinking, she peered into the damp air, swallowing a quiver of apprehension.

Ida had never liked the dark – in the dark you saw things that weren't there. Now it made her nervous because she could have sworn she saw something that was.

'No, you can't see anything,' she whispered. 'You're spooking yourself.'

She was exhausted, hungry and thirsty. Probably dehydrated

and possibly delusional. The ache in her foot was becoming acute. Reaching for a logic she was barely confident of, Ida told herself whatever she thought she'd seen was an illusion.

She slotted the key into the lock of the solid, wind-whipped door. The hinges creaked and she pushed, stepped into a square hallway. A dark newel post the size of a small tree guarded an uncarpeted staircase. Wallpaper patched with faded flowers no garden had ever seen, vanished up into the shadows.

Fumbling along the wall for a light switch, Ida found one, flicked it up and down to no avail. She remembered the solicitor handing her a heap of instructions, including one about a generator.

Ida had no idea where a generator might be. Outside, most likely. In the outbuilding. The light was too poor to see properly, and in any case the instructions were in the car. In the gloom there were too many disguised spaces. At the front of the house there were two doors, one each on either side of the hall. A dim passageway lead to the rear of the house and another room.

Kitchen?

Ida walked towards it, pushed open the door. Inside the air was chilly, laden with shreds of old conversations and older arguments.

Like most families, they'd had their best quarrels and conversations in the kitchen. Ida was transported to the one at Wisteria Cottage, too far and too many hours away now, ringing with her mother's laughter. And left behind because in the end, it hadn't been Ida's to lay claim to.

I'm appalled that your father never explained … this cottage is leased…

Nothing about this dull room looked familiar. There was a little more light than in the hall, insinuating through a large window above a crock sink. Treading on fractured flagstones Ida took in a heavy painted dresser holding oddments of crockery, a set of cast-iron scales with brass weights, and a green tin tea caddy.

A small, sagging sofa, and a table set against the wall beneath the window with chairs pushed underneath it. None of them matched – another thing her mother had disliked: nothing matched and nothing fitted.

Apart from a rough pottery bowl, the table was bare and Ida had another vague memory of china cups decorated with violets, gold lines adorning the rims. Once again her mother's face swam in front of her. Luminous blue eyes, features as fine and delicate as a bird's. Her ballerina hands made of feathers – and Ida reached out too, touching air, touching nothing.

Other than a handful of hours on either side of days spent working, or with her mother, Ida hadn't been by herself for years.

Checking her phone she discovered it was dead. Either that or there was no signal. She allowed herself a wry smile.

So much for smart phones and keeping in touch.

Six

Night clamoured at the window.

Falling faster than Ida could believe, it eliminated everything both indoors and out. It hung outside the room like tattered curtains. She couldn't resist flicking the light switches again. The sound echoed round the room and still nothing happened. On the windowsill she discovered an old-fashioned oil lamp and a box of matches. After a few fumbling attempts she realised she had no idea how it worked. In any case, the wick was black and dried out, the matches damp. She replaced the smoke-stained glass chimney.

'Useless.' Her voice echoed in the still room.

There might be candles in the dresser only she couldn't see well enough to find them. Ida fiddled with her new phone, searched fruitlessly for the torch and gave up.

'Stupid smartphone.'

Smarter than her for sure. Frustrated, she fumbled in a drawer at random, located a bundle of candles and a dry box of matches. A kindlier light ought to have comforted her. All it did was enhance the shadows. The ones outside were deeper still. Ida knew she must settle in before the light disappeared completely.

Opening the front door, she paused. The dark was as deep as a pit. She hesitated. The world beyond the house impressed her as dangerous; she didn't recognise the scents drifting on the sharp air. The car was less than two metres from the gate. Stumbling across the uneven ground, she pulled open the door and too exhausted to unload the box of food, gathered the remains of her lunch.

Her phone, tucked in the back pocket of her jeans, buzzed, making her jump. She peered at it, at the single bar of connection.

It was another text from Liz: *You were supposed to tell me when you arrived. x*

Ida tapped a reply: *Safe. I'm fine. Lousy signal. I'll be in touch. Don't worry. x*

Not waiting to see if the message sent, Ida grabbed a large, rubberised torch from the glove compartment. A ghostly sound that may have been an owl punctured the darkness. Her heart stopped in her mouth. Swallowing, she turned on the big torch and retraced her steps to the house. Shivering, her coat pulled close, Ida ate the second piece of chicken wrap and a banana.

She considered a fire. The kitchen was dominated by a vast mantelpiece subduing a small range. Ida eyed it with suspicion. It looked ancient and complicated. Retracing her steps down the hall, she spotted a longcase clock standing in a shallow niche in the wall, softly ticking and, according to her watch, dispensing perfect time.

'Is someone winding you?'

A brief flash of the half-glimpsed shadow made her heart twist. *Stop it.*

Ida wondered if the clock chimed and if it did, would it keep her awake. Next to it, on a small wooden table, sat a beige, rotary dial telephone. Ida lifted the receiver and to her surprise, heard a dialling tone.

Who, after a year, was paying to keep the phone connected?

The torch gripped in her hand, Ida opened a door into what must have been the room she recalled her parents calling the parlour. In the wavy light more frayed shadows flickered and large pieces of furniture loomed like sleeping animals.

The unexpected scent of mildewed apples caught in her nostrils. Her throat constricted, the odour fetid and Ida swallowed hard to be rid of it. As the torch beam touched a fireplace, in front of it, an ugly metal heater materialised and Ida was reminded of a robot.

'R2-D2?' She hadn't talked to herself this much in years.

As she heaved it to one side, the heater groaned on soot-clogged castors. Ida looked at the bare fireplace and sighed. Even if she had the energy to set a fire, there was nothing to make one with. No kindling or coal, no paper. Setting the torch on a small table, she dragged the dustsheet off an ancient sofa and slumped down. She took off her boots and one of her socks, massaged her aching instep. She didn't look at it – her ugly foot revolted her. Kneading some warmth into it, she replaced the sock.

A woollen rug, neatly folded, lay over the back of the sofa and she pulled it round her, grateful for its warmth. It smelled odd – a trace of apples again – and underlying it, the stale whiff of roses, her mother's favourite scent. It was as if a shred of Anna still existed in the house she'd tried so hard to erase from her memory.

Was it possible? Could anything of her mother still be here? Ida doubted it and the tears she was desperate not the shed for fear of being overwhelmed, burned her eyes.

'What do I do, Mum?' she whispered into the shadows. 'How do I make sense of this?'

Shivering, Ida considered the robot heater. Letting the rug fall she lifted a small plate in the top and played with the controls. Nothing she did worked, her efforts producing little more than a splutter.

Frustrated, she swore under her breath. 'Come on R2, how hard can it be?'

She tried again, pressed buttons and twisted a knob. A spark and a flash; but within seconds it died, leaving a poisonous stink polluting the air.

Overcome by weariness, and on the verge of tears again, Ida unlaced her other boot, curled into the sofa, the musty rose-scented throw pulled close. The only things she had extricated from her bag were a pair of shabby red ballet shoes and a slender doll dressed in a silk gown. Ida tucked the shoes under a cushion and hugged the doll close, her mouth pressed against the sweet face.

'Giselle, what am I doing here? I didn't need to see this dump to know I want rid of it.'

Out of habit, she began chewing a fingernail.

Sweetheart, please don't … think of your extension…

Gazing at her bitten nails, Ida knew her fastidious mother would have been horrified. Anna's elegance had been effortless, like her body when she danced, pleating the air, her perfect feet in their impeccable, pale satin ballet shoes.

Uncomfortable on the lumpen sofa, Ida folded into herself, into the scent of the doll, the red shoes and her no-longer mother.

You don't go round grief, you go through it…

With the windows shut tight she could still hear the ebb and flow of the wind, the creak of the stunted trees; otherworldly, and so unlike the more urban sounds she was used to, they might have come out of a supernatural dream.

Only Ida never dreamed, and undreaming she slept, without moving, and in the morning her body was stiff and heavy and haunted, possessed by memories of her mother.

Don't become a ghost, Mum. I need you to be a memory.

From the roosts in the dark shivery trees flanking the house, the black birds blinked at the cloud as it ambushed the moon, skittering in shreds around it.

Practised in grief they recognised the truth of it: the silent, one for sorrow cry of it.

They felt the rattling feathery wind under their inky wings, hopped and hunched, branch shuffled and settled into ancient dreams.

The black birds had their ways, and weren't afraid of anything.

Seven

Reaching for her watch, Ida squinted and remembered where she was.

Twenty past nine.

Hearing a noise she blinked. Light fell through a gap in the not quite closed curtains and it took several seconds before she realised what she was hearing was a bird. A small bird singing its heart out.

Ida shivered with cold, her clothes clung, the feel of them gross against her skin. She was in a different country, her old life in outline.

I'm a woman with no job, no family, and I'm stuck in a horrible house I hate.

With a grunt she swung her legs off the sofa. The rug, cold under her feet, exacerbated the numbness in her foot.

Reluctant to open the window, she tugged a curtain open and peered out. There was no sign of a bird. Ida turned away and around her the room came into focus. It had the preserved, pulled-together look of old money and older taste. Another, larger more elegant dresser from a bygone era, holding a collection of fine china and a gilt-edged platter. An ancient radiogram that must have been more than fifty years old. She looked around but could see no records. There were serviceable carpets and rugs on the floor, and here and there, cushions and touches of threadbare Bohemian colour, which she didn't at all associate with her mother.

A woman … she died about a year ago…

Her eye landed on a shawl, hand-knitted and delicate, discarded on a button-backed armchair. It might have been her mother's only it was an uncertain memory. A paperback book, the cover creased, lay on top of the shawl. She glanced at the title: *Wide Sargasso Sea*. None of these objects prompted memories Ida could trust. It was easier to dismiss them. The personal things could be disposed of – charity shops took anything these days. The rest could stay, and be sold with the house.

She closed the parlour door behind her and at the foot of the stairs, took in the hallway. In the morning light it looked bigger. Opening the front door Ida blinked up at the immense sky. It looked as if it had an opinion, and behind her the house stirred in response.

Beyond the confines of the low stone wall and a stretch of scrubby grass, mist shivered in the wizened trees. Ida gathered her cardigan round her body and backed into the hall, pushed shut the heavy door, turned the key in the lock and pocketed it. Desperately thirsty, she walked down the passage to the kitchen and spotted the bottle of water where she'd left it on the table the night before. She drank down what remained.

Looking around, she was surprised how clean the kitchen appeared. Only the grate at the bottom of the range was dirty, full of dead coals. A gust of wind scurried down the chimney disturbing a heap of grey ash. Tidy or not, the room had a damp chill to it and there was a whiff of vegetation and old drains. Before she put the house on the market she would need to get that looked at.

'You need to at least open a window.' No one answered her and Ida wondered how long it took for loneliness to drive a person mad. 'You've only been here five minutes and you won't be here long enough to find out,' she told herself. 'Get a grip.'

The sofa filled the wall opposite the fireplace. Like the one in the parlour it was covered in cushions and throws in shabby colours that must once have been bright as jewels. A low chair draped with tatty sheepskins slumped in the corner.

In a drawer in the dresser she found a pile of thin tea towels, neatly folded. In another, carefully arranged cooking utensils: a collection of worn wooden spoons, an old-fashioned whisk and an egg slicer, several things she couldn't identify. And a collection of cutlery, some of it old and good quality, with bone handles, the silver heavy and hallmarked.

Ida had a strong desire to make a mess. She had inherited her mother's dislike of housework and this room was too neat. Anna, for all her elegance, had been disorganised. As a family, the Llewellyn's had been careless. No one put anything away and it was left to the woman her father insisted on employing once a week to pick up after them, to dust and tidy and organise.

Realising she was still thirsty, Ida crossed to the sink and reached for the tap. It refused to turn. The downpipe juddered; she twisted the tap with more force and finally it turned. There was still no water, only a brief spit followed by a splutter of rust.

Pulling out a chair Ida sat at the table, ran her finger across the surface of the wood. There was no dust here either and again it struck her as odd. There ought to have been a film on everything. In the centre of the table stood a heavy bowl, rough-glazed in shades of blue containing three small apples. Ida touched one of them and the flesh gave slightly. She took them out, set them on the table.

Who would have left apples?

Ida turned the bowl over. Hand thrown by the look of it. She ran her finger over a mark scratched into the clay.

A circle? Or the letter 'O' perhaps.

Replacing the apples, she picked up her car keys deciding she needed to get her priorities in order. She must track down a plumber and perhaps an electrician – a handyman at the very least. The village, a mile away, seemed the likeliest place to start.

As she reached for her coat, a knock on the front door made Ida jump out of her skin. Before she could call out or make an attempt to answer it, she heard a key turning in the lock, a creak of hinges and the deep swish of the door as it opened.

Shaking, Ida gripped the edge of the table. She stared through the open kitchen door, down the hallway to the front door.

A girl stood on the threshold.

Weak sunlight streamed through the door. Held in its aura, her face partially hidden, the girl walked down the hallway and into the kitchen, with purpose, pushing the door shut behind her.

As it blocked the light, Ida saw her clearly. Her stare was so intense the air between them fizzed. Ida started – a question running away – and she frowned. The girl's eyes were a colour impossible to describe: the colour of rain, if rain had a colour.

She smelled of apples and opportunity.

Her clothes were a disguise: layers of grey and peat, green so drab it was almost black. Over a billowing skirt she wore a dark sweater and a shapeless jacket. She had a dishevelled look, the edges of her skirt were muddy and Ida caught a glimpse of bottle green boots, loose-laced and clogged with dirt. A woollen hat was pulled low over a mass of brown hair. Her skin was the colour of a nut and overlaying her face was a scowl of irritation.

'*Pwy ydych chi?*'

Welsh?

In spite of her obvious youth, she spoke with authority and when Ida shook her head in apology a slight look of disdain crossed the girl's face.

'Who are you?' she said, slow as you like, with spaces between the words and the kind of emphasis one reserved for a child.

'Ida Llewellyn. And you?'

The girl threw her a look capable of withering a stone wall.

Ida swallowed, acutely aware how dry her mouth was. 'How did you get in?'

Through the front door. Clearly.

The girl's face changed to a smile: an enquiring affair with little warmth and a hint of entitlement. 'With my key?'

Her key?

'I only came in the front because I saw your car. Normally, I'd go round the back.'

'I see…'

47

'I don't think you do. You still haven't told me who you are and more to the point, what you're doing in my mam's house. And don't try anything funny. I'm stronger than I look.'

Her voice was melodious, rippling away like unravelled knitting. She stepped closer and Ida saw herself reflected in pale irises.

Who are you?

'There must be some mistake,' she said. 'This is my house. I told you, I'm Ida Llewellyn. My father is – was – David Llewellyn and…'

'I don't care if he was Owain bloody Glyndŵr,' the girl said, 'this house was my mam's and you've no right to be here.' Her impossible eyes scanned Ida as if she was memorising her. 'And my name, for your information, is Heather Esyllt Morgan.'

She said it like it was a title.

A woman … she died … The house is empty…

Through the window, clouds layered across the sky like lace.

Mr Caterpillar eyebrows didn't say anything about a daughter.

Ida shook her head and coughed, knowing the instant she did how nervous it made her appear.

I am bloody nervous…

'Listen,' she said, determined to regain control. 'There's obviously been some sort of mistake. Both my parents died – recently as it happens…' Her mouth dried to bark. She released her grip on her coat, reached under it for her bag. 'My father's solicitor said the place was empty. Look, I have papers.' She fumbled with the flap. 'I can prove the house is mine.'

For the first time, the girl looked wrong-footed. Ida saw how young she was and how the bluster was probably part of an act. She guessed she had ten years on this odd, hostile creature. It was bad enough to lose a mother at twenty-nine, how much worse when still in your teens. Whoever she was and whatever she was doing here, Ida felt a flicker of compassion.

The girl's chin lifted. She pulled off her hat and shook out a

48

mass of flagrant hair. Her jacket fell open revealing a necklace. It looked to Ida to be made from bones and she shuddered. Her fingers hovered at the place beneath her sweater where a gold chain and a tiny diamond heart lay. A twenty-first birthday gift from her parents. She rubbed her forehead in an effort at distraction even though she sensed, if this wild girl wanted to, she might see through walls.

'That's as maybe, Ida whoever you are,' Heather said. 'This was my mam's home, mine too until she died. No one's ever said I couldn't come here.'

Come here?

'So you don't actually live here?' Relief flooded through her. Not a squatter.

'I never said I did—'

'Well actually, you did; or you implied it. You asked me what I was doing in *your* house.'

'Same difference. Me and Mam – this was our place. I was born here.'

So was I.

Ida glanced at Heather and once again met her eyes, bright with challenge in her questioning face. She attempted a smile and it didn't work.

'And since she died, I've taken care of things,' Heather said and her voice lowered, as if she was imparting a secret. Her eyes didn't leave Ida's face; they held scorn and Ida felt unaccountably young, as if their roles had abruptly become reversed.

Did this explain why the place was tidy, why there was no dust? Why the clock in the hall was fully wound?

'I live in the village, but I'm up here all the time, to see to things.'

Heather held the space in the room and she owned it. The stillness of her body belied the rapid movement of her eyes which flickered with such speed round the room, Ida wondered what she might be looking for.

Was she nervous or simply nosy and a nuisance?

'Right,' Heather said, and there was neither nervousness nor fear in her voice. 'What's going on then? You better explain. Did your dad really own this house?'

'Yes. He did.'

'So what you're saying is, he was my mam's landlord.'

'Yes. Exactly. This was my father's house.' Ida tried to stand up straight and make herself tall, taller than this wide-eyed, belligerent girl whose skin gave off the scent of apples, and whose presence filled the kitchen as if she, not Ida, had the sole right to be there.

Eight

Hypnotised by the stillness of the room, Ida's mouth was so dry now, if she didn't have something to drink soon, she thought it would turn to dust.

'I'm not stupid,' Heather said with a touch of asperity. 'You don't need to go repeating yourself. I got you the first time. It's your house.'

'I hope I didn't suggest you were.' Ida licked her lips. 'Stupid that is.'

'You look like you need a glass of water.' Heather crossed to the sink, turned the tap, banged it with the side of her hand and after a couple of splutters, the water ran clear. She found a glass, held it to the light, shrugged and filled it with water. 'There you go.'

As she set down the glass Ida noticed her nails were bitten to the quick and her hands were covered in scratches.

She downed the water in a single gulp. 'Thanks, I...'

'It's a knack.'

Ida wiped her mouth with the back of her hand. 'I'm sorry – I'd offer you a coffee, only the electricity's off.'

'No thanks. But if you're stuck, there's a camping thingy in the cupboard under the sink.'

Ida followed the girl's gaze. Opening a door, Heather pulled out a small Primus stove.

Thank you, God and Buddha and all the angels!

She didn't believe in God – or Buddha – but under the circumstances, it seemed like a good idea to cover all bases.

'Thank you. If I don't have a coffee soon, I'll die.'

'Really?'

Heather clearly didn't do rhetoric.

Ida summoned a smile. 'It's kind of you to take such good care of the place, but honestly, it won't be necessary now.'

'Meaning?'

'Meaning, I'm here so…'

Heather's eyes ceased their restless perusal, landed on Ida as if she suddenly found her fascinating. 'Ida did you say? Are you Welsh? You don't sound Welsh.'

Determined her child wouldn't have a Welsh name, Ida's mother had reached for one both quintessentially English and simple. A neat, old-fashioned name, with no embellishments. One that would go well with Plessey.

Ida Plessey.

A ballerina's name.

'Well, I wouldn't would I? Seeing as I'm not. Not entirely. My father was.'

You need to find out if the Welsh bit recognises you…

'My mam was totally Welsh.' The girl snatched the glass and refilled it. She thrust it back into Ida's hand. 'Too much coffee will kill you. You're more likely to die from lack of water.' She took a step back. 'Her name was Olwen.'

'Whose name?'

'My mam. You aren't listening.'

Ida wanted to stop the girl talking.

'What about *your* mother? She have a name?'

Don't talk about my mother…

'Look,' Ida said. 'This is getting silly, I…'

'Well yes, a dead English mother, a daft English name and a dead Welsh father doesn't exactly make you Welsh.'

It was an extraordinary thing to say: callous and thoughtless. Before Ida had time to arrange her thoughts, the girl was wandering around the room, touching, inspecting, her manner proprietorial.

52

'Mam loved this room. It was her favourite.' Heather stopped by the low chair in the corner, stroked the dull sheepskin. 'This chair's special. It belonged to Nain.' Heather ran her fingers along the arm. 'Don't move it, Mam wouldn't like that.'

Ida had had enough. 'Heather.' She cleared her sandpaper throat hoping her voice wouldn't falter. 'This is making me very uncomfortable. I've barely arrived and I'm sure you appreciate, I have things to do. I'm sorry if I seem rude or if this is difficult for you but I'd like you to leave now.' She paused. 'And I'd like your key. My key. If you don't mind.'

Heather ignored her. 'Did you see the clocks have stopped? They did that when Mam died. Twenty-five to four in the morning.'

Ida waited.

'The one in the hall keeps time – I wind that one – Mam wouldn't like the house to be totally silent.' Heather's voice was a monologue. 'This table always had a vase of flowers on it: wild ones – I picked them for her. Apples in the bowl. We lit candles in the evening. She didn't like too much light at night.'

Ida didn't mind that the clocks had stopped. They could stay that way forever for all she cared. She didn't need or want to know when Heather's mother had died, or what time it had been. Time stopped for Ida on a starlit evening in Paris, when a wall collapsed as an out of control train crashed into it, and both her parents had been killed.

A freak accident.

A rushed flight to Paris had culminated in a cacophony of words Ida's schoolgirl French failed to make sense of.

Reposez en paix…

She opened her eyes, let out a few jerky breaths and she was back in the room.

'You look like a ghost.'

'I'm fine.'

53

'I'll show you round if you like.' Heather opened the door to the hall.

The girl raised her eyebrows in a questioning gesture. Her possessive air made Ida's hackles rise.

Heather stepped to one side, still managing to take up space. 'Landlady first.'

Was she still trying to claim rights to be here?

Ida said she didn't need showing round. 'And I told you, I have things to do. I'd be grateful if you'd leave now.'

The girl's eyes narrowed. 'Think a lot of yourself, don't you? Ida Spider or whatever your name is. Well, I don't care who you are, I know my rights. You can't chuck me out, just like that.'

'And you can't barge in here like you own the place.'

'Because you do, right? And you think it gives you some kind of power over me? Well, think again, lady. My mother was a wise woman, and this was her home.'

However you dressed it up, "wise woman" was just another way of saying witch. It was Hansel and Gretel, a gingerbread house and an old hag with an oven. It was Baba Yaga and Snow White's wicked stepmother.

The stories that had frightened Ida as a child were all at once vivid in her mind. Anna, the famous ballerina, knew the terrifying tales, the ones so many ballets she'd danced in were based on. The one with the girl in a pair of enchanted red shoes that wouldn't allow her to stop dancing: her obsession and ultimately, her demise. The price for vanity – cutting off her own feet.

Ida tried not to shiver. Tried not to notice the sudden ache in her foot. 'You mean she was a witch?'

'Do I?' The girl's eyebrows shot up and her eyes glittered. 'Well, there's a thing. You don't mess with witches either.'

Her words came out fast, slightly mocking, as if she couldn't be bothered to listen to them or how they fell, only Ida knew she did both. If Heather Esyllt Morgan missed anything, it was because it was of no interest to her.

Before Ida was able to come up with a suitable reply, a loud clattering interrupted them. Behind them, on the other side of the kitchen window, something dark landed with a thud against the glass. Ida's heart leapt into her mouth and she let out a small yelp.

'It's only a bird.' Heather's eyes widened. 'Bloody hell, you won't last long here if all it takes to scare you is a crow. And don't get me started on the rats and mice.'

'Rats?'

The girl laughed. 'God, your face.'

Ida bit back a retort.

'It's a bird,' Heather said again.

'I don't like them.'

'Don't like birds? Scared of rats and poor little mice. And birds.' Her voice was mocking now. 'Well, whatever will Mam make of you?'

The air shifted, an imperceptible movement, yet enough to make the hairs on the back of Ida's neck stand on end. Without thinking, she turned her head, certain someone else was in the kitchen, watching them both.

Behind her, Heather gave a soft snigger.

There was no one, just this tiresome girl and Ida had an answer in her head, only the words wouldn't come out.

'What?' Heather smiled.

Ida's heart clattered against her ribs and the already volatile air rippled. 'I thought…' Her voice was scratchy. 'Who…?'

'There's no one else here, just you and me, Ida.' The way Heather said her name sounded like a challenge. 'You'll be telling me next you're scared of ghosts.'

She stared now, and in her eyes Ida saw a sly intelligence – her best guess.

'It must have been my imagination. Lack of sleep I expect. I'm still exhausted and I hardly slept last night.'

'Maybe. Maybe not. It's not a bad idea to be wary of ghosts mind.'

'Meaning?'

'Nothing. Except…' Heather paused, and her eyes – eyes Ida couldn't look away from – were bright as glass. 'All I'm saying is, don't go out at twilight.'

Nine

The door, as it closed behind Heather, trembled.

Too shaken to consider driving anywhere, Ida pressed her hand to her palpitating heart, waited while her breathing calmed. At this rate, her lungs would explode. When she licked her lips they tasted of fear.

What the hell was going on? Why hadn't the solicitor told her a crazy girl believed she had a right to be in the house? There had been no mention of a daughter. Only the mother, the dead tenant who, it now turned out, had been a witch and one who might possibly have it in for Ida.

Whatever will Mam make of you?

What would her mother have made of a ghost woman haunting the house? Ida was as credulous as Anna had been. She suspected the idea of a ghost would have scared her mother half to death the way it did her.

Like most theatre people, Anna had been highly superstitious. No one whistled backstage or wore blue or allowed a peacock feather into a dressing room. And in the theatre or out of it, Anna had been terrified of the dark.

Last one out don't forget to leave a light on!

The spirits which were said to hang around an empty theatre followed Ida's mother home, and she always crossed her fingers and threw spilled salt over her shoulder. She avoided ladders and black cats, and didn't own an umbrella for fear she might forget and accidentally open it indoors. She didn't put her shoes on the table, and carried two rabbits' feet for extra luck.

And still, none of it had been able to save her.

A single moment, a pause to exchange a second honeymoon kiss, a train driver over the limit, an ancient wall tumbling out onto the boulevard…

The weight of Ida's grief was all at once more than she could bear. Huddled into herself, tears blocked her throat. She was like a dried up pond, stagnant and pathetic.

How assured Heather had seemed.

As a child, Ida had been the way she was now: stand-offish in lieu of confident, blushing and quiet, not caring to impress. Her teenage self hadn't been much better. In contrast, Heather was a hurricane in muddy patchwork, reminding Ida of a smouldering bonfire, a hint of something wild and explosive emanating from her. Her ownership, reasonable or not, had filled the room.

Tomorrow Ida would telephone the solicitor and find out what her legal rights were. Regardless of its state, she would tell him to go ahead and place the house on the market. That would take care of the interloper.

In the meantime, she would explore.

'I don't need permission to look around my own house, or an escort, do you hear me, Miss Heather whatever Morgan?' Even to herself she sounded like a petulant fool. And she half-expected the crazy girl to reappear, laughing in her face.

As she opened the door into the room opposite the parlour, Ida was startled by the echo. It was empty. The bookshelves built into the alcoves on either side of the fireplace were bare.

What had happened to her father's books?

He had owned hundreds of books. Ida had another indistinct memory: books being delivered to Wisteria Cottage, her father's pleasure as the boxes piled up in the hallway, and her mother's fluttering protest.

'There's no room, David. Please, no more books!'

Ida supposed the surplus must have been disposed of – perhaps to the university in Cardiff. One less thing for her to be concerned with. She spared a wistful thought for her own books, in the flat. The couple she'd brought with her were still in the car.

She closed the door and stood at the bottom of the stairs.

Under her socked feet, the wooden stair treads were solid. The bannister was worn with polish and hands and time. Ida's fingers stroked the wood and she wasn't sure if it was out of respect or apprehension. She trod tentatively, expecting creaks and when none came, the silence hung like old breath.

Turning on a half landing, she pulled aside a flimsy curtain hanging at a wide window, saw how the land stretched, unfolding into the distance towards the edge of the world. The sombre hills were a book falling open at different pages, each one telling a story in a secret language.

Ida had no language anymore. And the new story she had deliberately chosen scared her. She knew she was probably depressed, although it was hardly surprising.

When your parents died in horrible circumstances, how else were you supposed to feel?

On the first floor, she hesitated. A piece of threadbare carpet, rucked at its edges, covered a square landing. Ida slid her foot forward, straightened it with a toe, paused, and tried to get her bearings.

The landing was flanked by four doors. She looked to her right. Bathroom? No, the bathroom was opposite. This must be her old bedroom.

Turning the knob the door swung open with the slightest of noises, as if it slid on runners. Inside it was brighter than she expected. Light ricocheted off the windowpanes casting pale lines across the walls.

Ida searched for a sensation, however small, carried across the ether from her five-year-old life. Her memories were blurred: clothes folded in drawers, piles of story books, a Snow White lamp and a primrose-yellow quilt.

As she stepped into the room the watercolour moment faded.

The room contained only two tangible memories: a white-painted ironwork bed devoid of anything other than a mattress, and curtains hanging motionless, their sun-faded blue stars nearly invisible. There was nothing else she recalled – a chest of drawers and a wardrobe, neither of them memorable. Nevertheless, the room was gentle with no sense of intrusion. If Heather had been sleeping in the house, it wasn't in this room.

It overlooked the back of the house and Ida had a good view across a scrubby yard patterned with stones and weeds. Dandelions grew in gaps between broken paving slabs and led to the ramshackle outbuilding she had glimpsed the night before. In daylight she could see how the rusted tin roof sagged, and Ida thought how dangerous it looked. A strong wind would surely lift it.

To the right lay a small garden. It looked to be completely overgrown, derelict and wild, set on the land as if it was an isolated afterthought.

Her mother's garden at Wisteria Cottage had had a swing and a pond with goldfish. Anna had a hammock with cushions, strung between two trees. This garden appeared ugly and threatening, and Ida didn't remember anything about it.

Leaving the door ajar, she crossed the landing and opened the door to her left. Confused, she couldn't recall if this or the remaining one had been her parents' room. There were marks on the door, shallow scars in the wood and another memory – her father telling her how he'd been told off for trying to carve his name.

His bedroom, not the one her parents had shared.

Inside, it bore no evidence of a boyish childhood. Another, larger wardrobe, and a dressing table with nothing on it. A double bed with an ornate wooden frame took up most of the space. It was covered with blankets, a dark green velvet pillow and a heavy brocade bedspread. An old angle-poise lamp bent over a couple of books lying on a wicker table next to the bed. Ida ran her finger across the cover of the top one.

Little Women.

As a child, she'd loved this story. This was an old edition and she wondered if it had belonged to Heather's mother. Lifting it, she read the title of the second book.

It was a book on herbal medicine and it too was old, the covers worn. Ida opened it, a fraction, and read the inscription: Olwen Morgan. Nervous and wanting to leave them as she'd found them, she straightened both books.

You don't mess with witches.

Or their daughters.

A set of lace curtains hung at the window like bridal veils. Ida slid one open with a single finger, making a gap.

She felt like a spy.

Across the lichen-pocked stone sill, she looked down on the scrubby patch of ground masquerading as a front garden. Below, she saw the roof of her car, small and travel-stained, hunched against the gate. Beyond the wall, where a few of the ubiquitous black birds sat, the track stretched away and on either side, rough, reedy bog lumbered into the distance. Ida could see where the track curved and disappeared; at this angle, the gateway was hidden from sight. She had a sudden feeling of being trapped, with no way to the road and no escape.

Her fingers bumped against something solid. On the windowsill sat a wooden bowl filled with stones, some of them with holes and threaded together on string. Running her fingers across them, Ida picked up a large white one, and as she placed the stone to her eye, a sliver of cold stroked her spine. Through the hole she saw dust motes and they looked like flying insects. She tried to blink and couldn't. Her finger and thumb prickled and dropping the stone back into the bowl, she rubbed her hands together to be rid of the itching.

Backing out of the room, she couldn't take her eyes off them, and Ida knew, as surely as she knew her own name, the stones belonged to Heather.

61

Ten

Now she was outside the last bedroom, Ida found herself shaking.

The brass doorknob caught a spark, bright as fire through the landing window, and Ida thought if she touched it her skin would catch alight. What would she find if she opened it? Had Heather cast a spell?

Had Olwen?

This room was also at the front of the house and would have the same view. It was the one her parents had slept in. There was nothing to be afraid of. And yet the sense of apprehension crept around her like a damp cloak. Unlike the rest of the house, which felt bland and inert, she half-expected this door to open on a roomful of bats, or the shadow of some terrifying ghoul.

Don't be stupid. It's an old house, it's bound to feel spooky.

Under her hand, instead of burning her, the knob was cool as ice. She turned it, pressed the fingertips of her other hand to the wood and gave it a push.

The moment she opened the door a far more pungent scent assailed her, richer and redolent and with no trace of roses. Only the strong aroma of old apples. And with it, the creeping feeling she wasn't alone.

She looked round – had the girl come back?

The room was empty. It was grubby too; the wallpaper stained and dull. Save for a wooden bureau under the window, and a heap of faded cushions on the floor, the room was devoid of furniture. No sign of occupation or that her mother and father had ever been in it. Her parents' bed, Ida realised, was the one now occupying the room with the stones. For whatever reason, someone must have moved it – along with the rest of the furniture – shifted it into the room Heather must sometimes occupy.

An old-fashioned metal candlestick holding a stub of candle sat on the windowsill amongst the husks of flies. In the corners of the window frame, shrivelled spiders and a desiccated bee lodged in dry, dirty cobwebs. Heavy, yellowed lace curtains, the old-fashioned kind that excluded light, hung half-open. And on the floor, withered brown leaves added to a sense of decay.

The room was thick with silence, and the certainty someone else occupied it was absolute. Ida stopped, turned, and as she did, something brushed her face, as if the cloud had insinuated its way through the window frame.

Or someone breathed against her cheek.

The hairs on her arms lifted and the smell of apples intensified. Reaching behind her for the doorjamb, Ida swallowed hard. A dense chill infused the room and she felt it like the touch of cold, goose-fleshed skin.

This room was a mirror image of the one next door. On the outside end wall sat a small fireplace, the tile surround embossed with stylised flowers. Soot had fallen from the blind chimney space, silted and black as crows, spilling into the tiny hearth.

Gathering what courage she could muster, Ida stepped unsteadily into the room. The apple scent smothered her and for a moment an irrational resentment, mixed with an emotion impossible to explain, coursed through her.

My mother's room ought to smell of roses.

Unlike the other rooms, this one was shadowed, lace curtains partially covered the window, holding back most of the light. A room held in time, suspended in dust and an ambivalent ambience.

Ida took another step, steadied herself and listened to her heart thumping under her ribcage.

And she was falling, leaning into space and the room tilted. Ida blinked and it filled up with furniture – the big wooden bed, a white-painted cane chair, a marble-topped table, pictures on the walls, and a wardrobe with a violet silk frock hanging on the door.

The air rippled and the inert dust particles came to life, coiling in the thin bands of light. For a moment the spinning stopped, the not-there furniture froze and Ida was certain if she turned round Olwen would be behind her. She was falling again, until she wasn't, and as quickly as it had begun, the toppling stopped and there was no furniture, no pictures – only the wooden bureau.

It was old. In the dull light it had a gleam of oak, as if it was alive and Ida managed a smile because she knew wood was always alive. Old wood remembered where it began and if you took a piece of furniture apart and forgot to keep an eye on it, it might well turn back into bark and twigs.

Another memory, unreliable at first, because it took her by surprise.

Blinking, Ida held her breath.

Her mother used to write letters at this desk. Ida could almost see her, sitting on a straight-backed wooden chair, a pen in her hand. Dressed in a cotton wrap, exactly like the ones she'd worn in her dressing room at the theatre. Pale green and scattered with roses.

Ida blinked again and the image was gone.

The bureau had three drawers, each one elegantly carved with leaves, acorns and flowers, and finished with discoloured brass handles. As Ida opened each one in turn she discovered they were empty. The fallboard was also carved, the leaves forming circles with more acorns at the centre. Ida reached out to pull it down and it resisted. It was locked and she felt ridiculously out-smarted. Hooking her fingers over the lip, she pulled harder and a chill ran down the back of her neck like ice slipped under her clothes.

I will tie my truth to the wings of birds…

It was a whisper, clear and concise inside her head and Ida was rendered motionless, her hand on the fallboard frozen in place. She couldn't move – dared not – she held her other hand to her mouth, blew in and out into her cupped fist.

Wind rattled down the chimney and it sounded for all the world like a woman singing – in harmony with the whisper in Ida's head – and it frightened her more than if a ghost had materialised in the room with her. The last reliable vestige of her courage failed and she let out a moan, sure she was going to faint.

The song ended, the whisper faded and shadows as thick as wool stretched into the gloom. Through the window Ida saw what little sun remained was fast disappearing, slanting away through the gathering cloud. It was as though rather than barely beginning, the day was ending and now all she heard was Heather's voice, mocking her.

Don't go out at twilight.

Eleven

Ida closed the bedroom door behind her, creating a barrier, scanning the lock for a key, to make sure.

There wasn't one.

The faintest hint of apples lingered on the landing. Still shaking, she went back into her old room. She wanted to cry and yet she was afraid to in case her emotions overflowed. It disturbed her, her crying. She had no control over it. For other people's sake, after her parents died she had tried to behave as if things were normal, until she realised there was no point and less reason.

She lingered at the landing window, drew the curtain to one side again. There was a bare, wintry cast to the countryside; it was still afternoon and yet it might as well have been much later. Everything – the narrow lanes, the isolation, the relentless cloud and the wild black birds – leant itself to notions of ghosts.

In her hand, the curtain felt limp against her finger. She let it go, shutting out the view and her imaginings, and made her way downstairs.

It didn't take long to unload the contents of the car: a small suitcase, a rucksack and a sleeping bag. Returning to the car, she grabbed a box containing basic food essentials, plus a cafetière and several packets of coffee. Hungry, Ida threw together a meal from cold baked beans, bread, cheese and an orange.

Wandering into the hall, at the foot of the stairs, she glanced at the longcase clock. It was a few seconds before nine o'clock. Ida watched as the long hand crept to twelve and when it hit, there was only a click, and the soft ticking as it continued.

She'd read somewhere that the chiming mechanism in longcase

clocks could be switched off. She tried to recall if she'd ever heard it chime – another lost memory.

In the little bedroom Ida made a half-hearted attempt to unpack. She made up the bed with a duvet and linen she found in the airing cupboard. It was clean and layered with sprigs of lavender and rosemary and although the sheets were cold they weren't damp. Her delight, when she discovered the primrose-yellow bedspread neatly folded on a low shelf, was disproportionate. Hugging its weight against her chest, once again she fought tears.

With the bed made, Ida arranged her clothes, folded jumpers and shirts, underwear and jeans into drawers and hung a single frock in the wardrobe. She sat Giselle on the pillow, the red ballet shoes underneath it, and placed a photograph of her mother on the bedside table.

It was a rare shot, unadorned by the trappings of dance. In her suitcase, Ida had an album filled with pictures of her mother performing, and posed studio shots in which Anna looked ethereal and unobtainable, her face and neck classically proportioned, like a swan.

Ida ran her finger over the photograph: her mother's lips smiling, her hair slightly adrift. 'Here we are, Mum. Back where we began. Who knew?'

Her instinct was to throw open the window. It was a thing her mother did first thing each morning regardless of the weather. Ida tried to recall if she had done it here and couldn't. Small children don't concern themselves with domesticity. Very little in this house was the same in any case. And now it had a ghost. If Ida opened the window would she let it in?

Stop it!

If she didn't believe in ghosts, she had nothing to fear. Only she did, and she was scared stiff. Anna's superstition was imprinted on Ida's psyche. Now the fear was palpable and if there was a ghost Ida didn't want to see it.

'Just open the bloody thing,' she told herself.

The sash was stiff and unwieldly and Ida had to exert all her strength to shift it. As the window opened, a breeze touched her face and she watched as it caught in the curtain. The sky had turned to dark blue, low and oppressive, and a score of black birds wheeled above the house. Her hand shook on the sill and abruptly she slammed the window closed.

Lifting the doll, Ida held her against her nose, inhaled the scent of her.

Giselle smiled her bland smile and Ida placed her back on the pillow. 'Sit tight. I'll soon find us somewhere else to be.'

Her mother had bought the doll in Paris, a gift for Ida. At the moment of impact she must have clutched the box to her chest because they said, when they found the bodies, David's arms were around his wife; Anna's were wrapped around the box.

Although it had been damaged by falling masonry, inside, the doll was intact and perfect. Wrapped in cream tissue paper she was slender, with sweet painted features. Her golden hair was twisted into plaits, wound in looped buns on either side of her head and dotted with tiny roses. Her arms and legs were long and her pale rose silk gown had tight sleeves, billowing at the wrists over tiny hands.

Her shoes were carved from wood and painted red.

She was the most beautiful thing Ida had ever seen. She named her in honour of her mother's favourite ballet.

Although she knew she would never go to France as long as she lived, Ida took comfort from the fact that until a moment of horror overtook her, Anna had been happy there, on her second honeymoon with her dearest David, stealing a kiss under the moon.

Weary to her core, Ida lay on the bed, her eyes drooping. She fell into a deep sleep for an uninterrupted nine hours.

And because she didn't dream, she missed the one in which her mother came back and told her it had been a terrible mistake. Ida didn't dream the scent of roses or see the broken building fall in reverse – the way things do in dreams – or see her mother smile and dance through a Parisian *jardin*, or how people stared in amused wonder, not knowing whether to be delighted or shocked.

In the morning, thwarted by the lack of electricity and longing for coffee, Ida got the Primus going. It took ages. The water didn't boil properly and the resulting coffee tasted grim. After a breakfast of cornflakes and the last of her milk, Ida fiddled with the radio, trying to find a station between the crackling. There was no television. Right at that moment she would have given anything to be flipping through the *Radio Times* with her mother, picking out their favourite programmes, marking them with a highlighter pen. Ida would have liked something to look at – pictures to lose herself in, ones she didn't have to make up. Would it be worth buying a small television?

Digging a notepad out of her bag, Ida tried to make a list. She needed to be practical. The pen hovered over the paper and she realised other than candles, she didn't have the first idea where to begin.

Calor gas for the heater in the parlour?

Yes, because the kitchen range daunted her and it was far too cold to go for more than another day without heat. Only where was she supposed to go for gas? The bottle would need connecting. How did she do that? She guessed there would be someone in the village who would know.

Heather will…

She dismissed the girl. Nothing would induce Ida to ask favours of her.

As well as candles, she needed fresh food and probably rat poison. She wanted to believe Heather had been joking, trying to frighten her about the rats. Only, what if she was telling the truth? Ida didn't trust her. At the same time, she reasoned a house this old probably did have a few rats.

Mice at the very least.

Traps?

Thinking about Heather reminded Ida of the locked bureau and her anger resurfaced, edged with a residual fear and some curiosity. No one had locked doors or desks in Wisteria Cottage. No one had secrets.

Ida set the list aside. Would the key to the bureau be in the house somewhere? She hesitated. If she started searching, did it mean she was somehow buying into whatever game the girl was playing?

Ida's unease, her fear of the ghost of Heather's mother remained real. She resisted it, determined not to be cowed. She would have a quick look for the key and if she couldn't find it she would ask Heather. And while she was at it, demand her house keys too.

In the kitchen, she opened more drawers in the dresser, lined with yellowing newspaper, found only junk and the detritus of a house abandoned. In the parlour, she investigated cupboards, and in the study swept her hands along empty shelves where books had once stood.

Closing the doors on both rooms she returned to the kitchen and continued searching. She climbed on a chair to reach the top shelf of the dresser. It was dusty and she suppressed a small smile of satisfaction.

'You missed a bit. Not so perfect then, Miss Clever Heather.'

As she stepped down, her foot gave way and Ida recoiled in pain. Sitting back on the floor, she massaged her instep.

'Sod you, Heather,' she muttered.

The girl was absurd, believing she had some crazy right to trespass. One way or another, Heather would have to be dealt with. No one would buy a house with a squatter, even a part-time one.

Ida recognised saying the words out loud was a pathetic attempt at imagining she was in control and could ignore Heather, or that the situation might change itself without her having to intervene.

The life Ida knew was over and for the time being, this was the alternative she had chosen. Chance and horror had led her here, to a place where the past was filled with other people's memories, a house to which a strange girl she didn't know anything about, had a set of keys.

A girl whose dead mother hovered in the shadows.

Ida didn't care about logic. She knew exactly what had happened earlier, in the bedroom her own mother had once slept in.

Heather's dead one prevailed.

Ida could pretend as much as she liked, tell herself for a hundred years that it was all in her imagination. She wasn't fooled.

The ghost of the wrong mother haunted Cloud House.

Twelve

Abandoning her search for the key, Ida decided she may as well go to the village after all.

She was still unsettled by the eerie room, and needed to be in a different place, breathe different air. Before she set off, curious to see the rear of the house, she unlocked the back door and peered around. Outside the door, a black dustbin stood next to a weathered wooden chair. A washing line sagged between two metal posts.

Across the weedy yard the outbuilding was more of a barn, and a ramshackle affair at that. Beyond it lay the garden, bounded by the broken, perimeter wall and random bits of wooden fence, its detail obscured by shreds of misty cloud.

It didn't look in the least bit inviting.

Ida made her way round the side of the house to the front door. Making sure it was locked, she turned to walk down the path to her car.

A large black bird perched on the gatepost, steely-eyed and watching her.

'What are you gawping at?'

The bird immediately set up a vile racket, shrieking and pecking at the stones in the wall, picking one up and flinging it into the air. Ida watched, horrified, as the bird bent its head, cracked open a snail shell, dug out the glistening body with its beak. It looked like entrails and she gagged. Shaking, she pulled open the gate. The bird cocked its head, its jewel eye unbothered.

As Ida approached her car, a different noise made her turn. Heather appeared, from the other side of the garden, pushing an ancient bicycle with a basket fastened to the handlebars.

There must be another, hidden path, leading to the village.

Pink and red plastic flowers decorated the basket and the strap of a cloth bag dangled over the rim. Heather's hair hovered like brown wings on either side of her hat and this time, she gave off the scent of rain and lichen. Mesmerised and slightly annoyed, Ida stared.

'I assume you're spying on me for a good reason?' Searching the girl's face for subversion, Ida saw it was innocent of all but a slight query.

'What's your problem? I told you, I come here all the time. I look after the place.'

'And I told you it won't be necessary.'

'Well, I beg to differ. Yes it will. It'll always be necessary.'

Taken aback, Ida stared, trying to work out what this strange girl wanted. Her jacket hung loose and unbuttoned. Ida saw the bone necklace, pale against her brown jumper. She wasn't particularly pretty – not conventionally so – she was striking, with an air of confidence Ida couldn't fathom. Her tanned skin was flawless, and outside in daylight Ida saw she was probably younger than she had first thought.

'What is it you want, Heather?'

They held one another's gaze.

'Sorry if I'm disturbing you.'

No you aren't. You're doing it on purpose.

'Well, I'm afraid you are,' Ida said, 'and since you're here, I'd like my house keys, please. And, while we're at it, do you have the one to the bureau in the front bedroom?'

The girl's eyes widened. 'Have you been in my mam's room?'

Ida could hardly believe her ears. 'For the last time, Heather, it isn't your mother's room. Not any longer. All the rooms are mine.' The girl's stare was hostile now and Ida immediately sensed the shreds of her confidence slipping away. 'Look, I'm sorry, but you'll have to get used to it.'

'And I'm telling *you*, you'll have to get used to *me*.'

73

Angry now, Ida persisted. 'There's a locked bureau in one of the front bedrooms. I need the key.' Surprised by the force of her words, she gave herself a mental pat on the back.

The feeling was short-lived.

'You better not have touched anything.' Heather flung down her bicycle, sending the back wheel spinning, and before Ida could stop her Heather was running towards the house. In an instant, she unlocked the door and was inside.

'Stop!' Ida yelled and the air caught her words and one of the black birds hurled itself into the air, swooped down again, in front of her. 'Go away, you horrible thing!'

The bird screeched – *kraa!*

Ida ran into the hall and climbed the stairs calling to Heather to wait. On the half landing, she saw a flash of red beneath the girl's dun-coloured skirt, her booted feet clattering and raising puffs of dust.

Heather stood in the centre of the room, transformed by the light from the window into a silhouette. Ida stopped on the threshold, her hand on the door frame. The faintest whiff of apples hung in the air.

'There's nothing *to* touch,' she panted, 'only the bureau. And even if there was, this is still my house.'

The girl didn't move; only her fists clenched and unclenched.

'Listen, Heather, I—'

'No, *you* listen!' She stepped forward, out of the disguising light, and Ida saw how her anger blazed.

'I'm sorry if it's hard for you, I—'

'You don't get to talk!' Heather spat the words, took another step and Ida flinched. 'And you don't get to touch anything.'

'Just give me the key, Heather.'

'I don't have it. I've never had it.'

'So where is it?'

'How do I know, and in any case, why do you want it? What do you need it for? That bureau was Mam's. It was here when she moved in and nobody said she couldn't use it. She paid rent for it, like everything else in the house. It's none of your bloody business what's in it.'

'Everything in this house is my business, you stupid girl!'

Heather's eyes shone now: limpid and pale, as if she had stared too long at the moon.

'There you go again,' she hissed, 'making out I've no right here. Calling me names. Thinking you're cleverer than me.' She was close now and her breath was scented with peppermint and a sly rage.

Before she thought to avoid it, Ida inhaled and the taste was dangerous.

'This was *my* mother's room.' Heather's rage was barely suppressed. 'She made medicine in here, her best healing and no one, not you, not any bloody solicitor or any bits of fancy paper can change that.' Her eyes were so bright and sharp, they were ready to sear flesh. 'You don't know what you're messing with, Ida the spider.'

Did she mean spells? Or was she babbling more euphemisms?

'And if I did have the key to that bureau,' Heather went on, 'which I don't, I wouldn't give it to you. Not in a million years. If she locked it, it means Mam didn't want anyone poking around inside it and if you do, I'm telling you, it won't end well.'

There was something explicit about her arrogance, as if she was emphasising a hidden ability. Ida didn't want to believe her. She didn't want to hear what sounded like manipulative, scary rubbish.

A threat…

'That bureau was here long before your mother came, Heather. Mine wrote her letters at it. This was *her* room – my parents' *bedroom.*'

As she said the words she wanted to take them back. Didn't want to start a conversation with Heather about her parents. About how they slept together in this room, made love, made *her*.

She didn't want to reveal anything to this furious, bellicose girl. She knew if she closed her eyes tight enough she might see the room again, the way it had been when she was a little girl. How her mother's beautiful frocks had floated on the wardrobe door, how the pillows on the bed smelled of roses and love.

Ida didn't want to talk about the way this made her feel. She didn't want to be made to look inside herself and discover there was nothing to see: how her memories had dissolved, and all that was left was a bleak room with moth-eaten curtains, ragged cushions, an old locked bureau, a dead candle and soot spilling out of an antiquated fireplace.

She wanted desperately to understand it was the same for Heather – she was mourning her mother too. Olwen was dead and although Ida didn't want to know how she'd died, she was kind enough to experience a moment of sympathy. 'I'm sorry—'

'Don't you dare be sorry for me!'

Heather's fury was heating up the room, and the wallpaper threatened to catch fire. Her face was a mask of misery and Ida saw beneath the anger, to her anguish.

'How old are you, Heather?' she asked.

'Seventeen.' Heather scowled. 'Why? What's it to you?'

Oh god, she's younger than I thought.

'Okay,' Ida said, 'here's the thing. I understand. You don't want me in this room.' She sighed. 'It's not like it has much to recommend it, frankly. It's filthy. And why is the rest of the furniture not here?'

'Mam got Dan to move it. She liked the room empty – a quiet space, to work in.'

What kind of work? And who's Dan when he's at home?

'I left it the way she had it. It's not been touched. I don't want it touched.'

'All right.' Ida eyed the dead flies and the battered candlestick with distaste. 'While I'm here, until I decide what I'm going to do, I'll be sleeping in the back bedroom, so you can calm down.'

Heather didn't say anything.

'But as there's no reason for you to be here anymore, maybe you can take your bits and pieces from the room you've been using? When you're ready?'

Still Heather didn't say a word.

'I'm trying to be reasonable here, Heather.' Ida felt a knot in her stomach and a chill ran down her spine. As she flinched, as her eyes darted round the room, she knew the girl had noticed.

'You feel something now, don't you?'

Ida shook her head, half out of anxiety and half in exasperation.

'Yes, you do,' Heather said. 'I can tell.'

'Do *you*?' Ida's voice cracked. 'Feel something?'

'Oh yes, she's here all right.'

Ida tried to imagine what it must be like to sense the ghost of your own mother. Wisteria Cottage, bland and suburban, hadn't leant itself to ghosts.

'Your mam's here too.'

'Don't be ridiculous. My mother hated this house, why on earth would she still be here? She left years ago. And in any case, I don't believe in ghosts.'

If she said it often enough, she might eventually believe it.

Heather offered Ida a look she was beginning to recognise.

'You don't understand how it works one bit, do you? You can't destroy a person's spirit, however hard you want to deny its existence.'

'My mother—'

'Part of your mother will always be here. Anywhere she spent enough time to make it matter. Any place she loved, any place she hated. Anger's the most powerful kind of energy there is, as powerful as love.'

Ida didn't want to give credence to anything Heather said. Hopeless at confrontation, she wasn't a person who lost her temper easily, for fear she would end up looking foolish. She had no capacity to rise to the girl's hostility.

'Look at you,' Heather said. 'Closed up, scared of the dark and your own shadow.' She laughed and the sound grated. 'You wait until winter, then you'll see how dark it gets.'

It sounded like another threat. Ida took comfort from the fact that she would be long gone before winter set in.

'And you need to open a few windows – otherwise you'll choke on your own disbelieving breath.' Heather wrenched open the window, and turning on her heel, she left the room, her boots clattering on the stairs.

Ida listened for the sound of a door slamming.

Silence.

Not wanting the girl to see how unnerved she was, Ida mustered as much dignity as she could and made her way to the kitchen, knowing Heather would be waiting for her.

Thirteen

Still shaken, Ida tried to regain a semblance of control, smiled as she entered the kitchen.

'Still here, then?'

Heather didn't answer. She sat at the table, one foot propped on a chair. Ida caught another glimpse of red.

'We don't have to be enemies, Heather.' Ida reached for the kettle before remembering there was no electricity.

'Say what you have to, Ida. Then I'll go.'

'I just want things to be clear.'

'Fill your boots. I'm listening.'

'Can I ask you a personal question?'

Heather shrugged. 'Depends.'

'What do you do? I mean, are you still at school? College?'

'School's for losers.' Heather made a dismissive noise.

'You've never been to school?'

'Of course I've been to school – when I was a kid.' She ran her finger round the rim of the blue bowl, picked up one of the shrivelled apples. 'They're not nice places, schools. Not if you're a bit different. And they don't teach you the right things. I can count and read. Mam taught me the important stuff.'

Ida sensed another benign challenge.

Heather smiled and caught her gaze.

'If you're born to the Old Ways,' she whispered, 'there's no hiding. A brush is enough to mark you.'

As non sequiturs went, it was impressive.

Ida had no idea if what Heather said was serious or if her words were meant simply to unsettle. 'You'll be telling me next you really do believe in ghosts.'

'I will. Because I really do.'

'You're just trying to scare me off.'

'You think that's what I'm doing? That I haven't anything better to do than frighten you? Believe me, Ida, there are ghosts everywhere. And they're right here, in this house. Loads of them, going back hundreds of years.'

Ida leaned against the counter to steady herself.

'How many people have lived here do you suppose? In the old days, most folk died in their beds. Stands to reason this place has seen its fair share of death. And long before you fancy Llewellyn's came to live here.'

Ida knew the house had been in her father's family for at least three generations. That David's grandfather had sold off tracts of land to neighbouring farmers. Beyond that, she knew nothing and felt at a keen disadvantage, having so little knowledge about her own heritage. She tensed, knowing the girl was waiting for a reaction.

'You may not believe in the old ghosts, Ida … you better believe in my mother.' She searched Ida's face. 'She's one of them. The last person to die here in fact.'

'Don't.' Ida held up her hand. 'Please. I don't want to hear this.'

Heather wouldn't give up. 'You need to leave a candle burning in the window.'

'Which window? Why?'

'The one upstairs. Mam's room. And open, like I said. So she can find her way back in.'

Ida snorted. 'That's your superstition, not mine.' Hers were made of backstage whistles, perfect dress rehearsals and putting on her ballet shoes in the wrong order. She tried to push her mother's fear of witches to one side, keep the tremor out of her voice. 'And I don't like the idea of naked candles in an unoccupied room.'

'An unoccupied room.' Heather repeated the words and they were an incantation, her fleeting smile a question.

'I'm sorry about your mother, but this spooky stuff is getting on my nerves,' Ida said, as much to reassure herself as anything else. 'When you're dead, you're dead.'

Ida knew she was being unkind and didn't care. Heather didn't have a monopoly on grief. Expecting to be challenged, she was surprised when the girl's face softened and a flicker of understanding crossed her face.

'Call it what you like, Ida. You'll see.' She leaned back in the chair again, an arm slung across the back. 'You think your family's old – Mam's goes back to a time you can't find in history books. And the knowledge always passes – like blood.'

Knowledge?

Ida lowered her eyes, torn between apprehension and curiosity. *Is she right in the head? How can she believe this nonsense?*

When she looked up and scanned Heather's face for subterfuge, Ida saw only a direct challenge in her eyes. Consternation momentarily gave way to more anger. There was something shrewd, even unscrupulous about Heather, and Ida was no longer in any mood to be made a fool of. And what kind of a person deliberately sets out to scare another half to death?

A bereaved teenager, that's who. Ida chided herself for her insensitivity. Heather was little more than a kid.

'It's true.' Heather's voice was sharp.

Ida reminded herself that grieving or not, she wasn't a child. Heather may not have spent much time in school, but a lack of formal education wasn't a barrier to integrity, or a knowledge of the difference between right and wrong.

Why would she go to so much trouble to frighten me?

Ida leaned forward, placed her hands on the table. 'Just stop it, Heather. If trying to scare me into leaving is your plan, then it won't work. I'm not going anywhere, at least not until I'm good and ready.'

'Imagine.' The sly look was back and Heather pushed her hair out of her face. 'Makes two of us; I'm not going anywhere either.'

She scooped the shrivelled apples out of the bowl, set them on the table. 'You can chuck these. I'll bring fresh ones next time. Mam liked her apples.'

Ida recalled the whiff of apples, in the parlour and on the landing.

In the empty room.

Imagination, Ida. Keep it real.

Refusing to rise to the bait, or question why a dead woman would need apples, Ida looked straight at Heather. 'Fine. Now, before you go, can I ask your advice about a couple of things?'

'Like what?'

'The telephone in the hall still works. Who's paying the bill?'

'Mam paid bills once a year – a thing with the bank.'

'Direct debit?'

Heather shrugged. 'I guess. I don't know.'

'Okay, thanks.' Ida nodded. It was something she could deal with at a later date.

She said she needed a plumber. 'And someone who can get the generator working. Do you know where it is by the way? I don't…'

'No, you don't, do you? You don't know anything.'

Ida sighed. 'For goodness sake, just tell me.'

'The generator doesn't work.'

'So how do I heat water?'

Heather shrugged. 'Dunno.'

'Are you saying you've never had a bath here?'

'Of course, but after Mam died, the boiler broke.' She shrugged again and Ida tried to hide her irritation.

'What about washing your clothes?'

'There's a machine at the cottage, where I live.'

When you aren't pretending you live here.

'Well,' Ida said, 'where's the boiler located? Can you at least tell me that?'

Heather opened a tall cupboard next to the sink. Inside sat a massive, unwieldy looking contraption. 'It's no good without the generator.'

'Obviously.'

'There's a gas heater in the front room. If it still works.'

'Thank you, yes, I saw it.'

'It won't last long mind – the bottle will be running out, if it hasn't already.'

'I think it has. Where can I get another one?'

'Garage. And ask in the village shop if you want a handyman. Dan will come.'

Ah… Dan's the handyman…

'And the oil lamp?'

'You really are a townie, aren't you?'

'Yes, I am and it's why I'm asking for your help.'

'Before you tell me to sling my hook? Charming.'

'I…'

'Don't bother.' Heather took the oil lamp off the sill. 'I'll trim the wick for you.'

'Thank you. I appreciate it.'

Heather made short work of the trimming. Removing the glass chimney, she examined the wick. It was black and charred. In the dresser she fished out a pair of scissors from the clutter. They were surprisingly sharp and she made a straight cut, exposing the clean white wick. In a cupboard under the sink she located a bottle of oil and refilled the lamp base.

'There you go.'

Ida thanked her again. 'Listen, I'm sorry if we've got off on the wrong foot. I don't want to be awkward or make things difficult. I can see it must be hard for you.'

'You don't have a clue what it's like for me so don't pretend you do. I know when I'm not wanted, only it isn't going to be that easy.'

'Meaning?'

'Meaning nothing.' Heather ran her finger along the dresser, picked up a small glass jug and stared at it. 'Here, you better have my number. In case you're really stuck.' She replaced the jug, picked up a pen from the table, and scribbled a landline number on Ida's notepad.

'Don't you have a mobile?'

'Why would I want one of those? If I'm out, I'm out.'

Ida hid a smile. There was no way she was going to admit to having even the vaguest thing in common with this exasperating girl.

Heather flicked the pen across the table. 'What you planning on doing then?'

'Excuse me?'

'You're the one who owns the place. What are you going to do with it?' Heather waved her hand, drew the room to her. 'With all of this? The things in the house?'

She sounded like an official custodian, or a retainer waiting for instructions and Ida felt a sudden reluctance to disclose her plan to sell up. She realised she had no idea what belonged to her and what might belong to Olwen. It was a conversation for another day.

'I made her a promise,' Heather said. 'My mam. About the house. Said I'd take care of it. And I can't break my word to my mother, can I?'

'I'm not asking you to do that.'

'So what are you asking?'

Heather was by the door now, and Ida thought she would leave and it would save her replying.

'You need to understand about Mam,' Heather said, her voice low. 'She was special. This house knows her. Knows who she was.'

The confusion closed in again and Ida looked down, not wanting Heather to see her apprehension.

'Her legacy is all that's left. I don't have any choice.' Heather's face held a mutinous sadness and Ida experienced a shiver of fear.

What might happen if you broke a promise to a ghost?
Or a witch?

Fourteen

Down by the gate one of the black birds sidled along the wall, pecking away at the stone.

Ida peered out from the front door. 'You don't scare me.' Pulling on her coat and beret, she stared at the bird.

It dipped its head. *Kraa*.

Ida locked the door, hunched into her coat and made for the gate. As she approached, the bird shouted again and in her anxiety to escape, Ida stumbled. She reached the car and almost fell into it.

She was cold and miserable. In spite of extra blankets piled on top of the duvet, she'd spent a wretched night. Lukewarm coffee hadn't helped, although it was better than nothing.

Out on the ribbon road there were few hints of human activity. The starkness was overwhelming. It was cold and she turned the car's heater up to maximum. The road was narrow and as she drove, slow as a learner, round a blind bend a huge tractor loomed, filthy and threatening. Ida braked hard, on the verge of panic until she saw how the driver, high in his cab, peered down at her, offering a stilted salute. He mounted the verge, passed her with ease and in a flash, was gone.

'Bloody agricultural oaf!' she yelled. She gripped the steering wheel and carried on. A mud-spattered Land Rover rumbled by leaving barely an inch between the two vehicles.

'Maniacs. I'm surrounded by maniacs.'

The moorland fell away in all directions and she was certain, were she to stop the car and step off the road, she would be lost in an instant. A few wrong turns and she would be in a bog, floundering amongst reeds and stagnant water, tripping over broken stone hedges. Or she would be taken – swept off to some dark version of her father's fairyland.

She caught her breath. Heather's nonsense was still playing on her mind.

According to her paper map, the village was about a mile away. Ida hoped Heather was right and there would be someone who could direct her to a decent plumber. As she drove she was reminded of her father again, earnestly academic and the least practical of men. He'd known nothing about plumbing or electrics and always called people in. His car had been serviced at a garage and although her mother had loved to garden, another man came regularly to mow the lawns.

At a junction, Ida stopped, peered at the signpost and turned left. The car climbed a winding stretch of road, ambled past a stand of thin trees out onto the moorland once more. When the road dropped into a valley, the land became a little greener and Ida wound down the window. Ahead of her she saw a sign announcing the village, and a half-moon stone bridge marking its boundary.

She pulled onto the side of the road, turned off the engine, wound up the window. Locking the car, Ida walked across the bridge, past a straggle of houses and a few cars parked at the kerb. She tried to see the village through five-year-old eyes. How often would she have come here? Once a week with her mother to buy a newspaper, bread and sweets?

Ida glanced from the side of her eyes. The layout was odd giving the village the appearance of being triangular, with buildings on three sides. Ahead of her, a dismal garage boasting a single petrol pump sat semi-detached from a brow-beaten grey house. At an angle, an ugly pub leaned against a small shop, a bicycle propped in front of the window.

On the third side, Ida's eye was drawn to a bus stop, a solitary stone cottage and a row of slightly larger ones, huddled next to a squat chapel. Blank windows scowled at her. A woman in one of the doorways studied her. An elderly man, sitting on an upturned crate outside the pub, did the same. Both of them watched her, and Ida, who hated being the object of anyone's scrutiny, scurried towards the shop.

The windows were smeared and the interior dim. A few faded leaflets clung to the inside of the glass. The name over the door – Pritchard Stores – did nothing to jog her memory. She pushed open the door. A bell sounded above her head, jangling and loud. As Ida started, her elbow snagged on a stand of postcards and she grabbed it.

'Sorry. Oh god, I'm so sorry.' Her default response – apologetic – and the words were out, announcing her. She held onto the stand, willing it not to fall over.

The cramped shop was held in a dejected, shadowy light. Stacked and random, the contents seemed to be caught in a crease of time.

Two women – on either side of the wooden counter – were deep in conversation. They spoke in Welsh and as the door closed behind Ida, and the bell clanged again, both women fell silent. Ida held her hand against the card stand, still not trusting it. Not trusting herself.

'Don't worry,' the woman behind the counter said. Her mouth twitched in a semblance of a smile. Her teeth were framed by sugar-pink lipstick. 'It's a menace that rack. Top heavy. If I've asked my Dan to fix it once, I've asked him a thousand times.' Her voice was husky as if she smoked too many cigarettes.

'So sorry,' Ida said again. The vinyl floor was sticky underneath her boots.

'Oh, *dim* problem. Now, what can I do for you?'

Ida kept her hand in front of the cards. 'I was wondering if anyone knows of a handyman. I need a plumber actually, but a general handyman would do. I…' She was babbling and her face flushed.

The other woman stared. Her face was nearly the same shade of brown as her coat, making her dyed blonde hair appear bright as butter.

'You're from the old house aren't you?' she said.

'I beg your pardon?'

The woman behind the counter opened a wooden flap and emerged, brisk on slippered feet. 'Well of course she is.' A cardigan made for someone twice her size accompanied her. She shoved the sleeves over her wrists, exposing stick-thin arms. 'We heard the owner was coming back.'

For a ridiculous moment, Ida thought the woman was talking about her father. She let go of the card stand. 'Oh no, you're mistaken. My father's dead.'

The woman's eyes narrowed. 'Well, yes, we know that, and we're sorry for your loss I'm sure. We heard the new owner had moved in. We've been expecting you.'

Expecting me?

'It stands to reason you'd be wanting groceries. We've got everything you need here.'

Ida doubted this.

'Well, I do need bread,' she said, 'milk, potatoes and fresh fruit if you have any? Candles?'

The woman produced a cardboard box and began loading it with items. A loaf, a litre of milk, a packet of butter, a bag of potatoes, a bunch of spotted bananas and an assortment of wilting greens. She added various tins Ida failed to identify, and a box of candles.

Ida was about to protest, explain how she didn't need the tinned vegetables, when the woman started speaking again. 'I'll set you up with an account, you can pay monthly.'

'I doubt if—'

'How are you finding it? Being back at the old house?'

'What old house?' Ida said, like an idiot, forgetting where she'd been born and spent the first five years of her life. 'Oh, you mean

Cloud House, er, Ty'r … Cwmwl?' She struggled with the pronunciation.

'Where else would we be talking about?' The blonde woman moved closer. 'You'll be the professor's daughter.'

'No. He's not – wasn't – a professor.'

The woman's face gave nothing away. 'You are a Llewellyn though?' She squinted up at Ida's face. 'It's in the eyes.'

Momentarily nonplussed, Ida offered her hand. 'Yes. Ida Llewellyn.'

The woman ignored it. 'From the old house,' she repeated. 'Well, good luck with that then.' She snatched up a loaf of bread. 'I'll be on my way, Catrin Pritchard. *Da iawn.*'

As the door clanged shut behind her, Catrin shook her head. 'No manners, some folk.'

Ida considered pots and kettles.

I'm getting used to it. And speaking of rude, I wonder if either of you know Heather bloody Esyllt Morgan.

'Now then,' Catrin said. 'You need a handyman, you say.'

'Yes.'

'I'll send Dan.'

The famous Dan.

'My husband. He hasn't fixed a thing for me in forty years of marriage but he's useful. He'll see you right.'

'That's great. Thanks. Mostly it's the water. The taps in the kitchen stick and there's no electricity.'

'What about the generator? There's a big generator in the barn.'

'It doesn't work.'

'You sure? Dan's dad helped install that generator.'

'Well, it isn't working now. Perhaps, he could take a look? Mr— er … Dan?' Ida rummaged in her bag for a pen. 'Here, I'll give you my number.'

'No need. I'll send him.'

'Maybe call first, to make sure I'm in?'

'I'll send him.' Catrin's voice hovered, precise and impassive.

There was nothing wrong with the words, only the way they were said. 'I'm closing up now.' She followed Ida to the door. 'You'll be needing Calor gas too I expect. Bring your old bottle next time. You can change it at the garage.'

Even if she had been inclined to respond – or thank Catrin – Ida knew the woman didn't want or expect her to.

She had demanded the last word and Ida was dismissed.

Fifteen

Outside, on the strip of pavement, Ida paused.

You'll be the professor's daughter.

Is that what they'd called him? Her father had been a senior lecturer – nothing as grand as a professor. She supposed, to the uninitiated, it was the same thing. She didn't care to be recognised, even though it was inevitable, and tried to dismiss the queer women with their false smiles and odd manners.

It's only words.

Words could be sorted to suit and Ida could choose to take no notice of any of them. She didn't have to listen, the same way she didn't have to listen to Heather.

Balancing the box of groceries, Ida walked back to her car, suspecting the entire village must know who she was. They didn't know her and yet already she sensed judgements being made, conclusions drawn: about her, her parents and probably the accident.

Her intention for the house.

The street was deserted, the old man and the woman no longer anywhere to be seen. It didn't mean she wasn't being watched. She eyed the contents of the box. Tinned peas? Really? At least the bread looked fresh.

Cross for being so easily intimidated Ida made a deal with herself. Forget the hostility and impertinence of two random strangers and as soon as possible take herself off to the nearest town. It wasn't that far and there would be supermarkets and people minding their own business. She could buy decent food, not tins of disgusting vegetables months past their sell by date.

It wasn't much of a deal. One way or another, the village was a part of where, in the short term at least, she now lived.

She tapped her phone, saw she had a signal, found the solicitor's number. The sooner she rectified matters, sorted out the issue of Heather, the better. His secretary informed Ida he was away for a week. If it was an emergency she could pass on a message.

'Thank you, it'll keep.'

With access to a signal, she dashed off a text to Liz: *Making plans & progress. All good. Will call soon x*

White lies didn't count, not if they were text ones.

Driving back across the moor, Ida watched as it unrolled, flecked with scraps of green, dull yellow and purple. She pulled into a lay-by, turned off the engine and wound down the window. In the distance she saw a house which, were it not for a skein of smoke curling from the chimney, she might have thought deserted. The land looked abandoned, lost in time.

And now she was becoming as fanciful as Heather. Ida closed the window, started the car and drove away.

The big trees stood watchful and shadowy. A few black birds perched in the highest branches. As the Peugeot inched its way up the track, Ida thought how naked the house looked, starkly fitting in the bleak, monochrome setting; leaning back, its dark mirror image under the earth, black foundations held fast, embraced by the bones of prehistoric creatures. Dragons perhaps. This place, in the long ago, must surely have been home to dragons.

Had her father told her dragon stories? She stopped the car by the gate, tears pricking her eyes. She wanted to suspend this life she'd had thrown at her and retrieve her old one where, for all his faults, her father filled the house with his tall, reliable presence. The one in which her mother still existed, and told her stories about princesses and happy ever after.

I want to wear her like a lovely gown, sense her under my skin, her heart beating beneath my ribs. Move like her…

She would never move like her mother – she couldn't even walk like her.

Ida no longer danced. There were no more daily classes; her muscles had weakened and stiffened until only a semblance of flexibility remained.

To confirm the point, her foot twinged. And now the wind was picking up and the rhythm of it echoed her shallow breathing. Ida's grief clawed at her and all at once she had no braking system for her thoughts. Squeezing her eyes tight she willed them away.

Get a grip. Unless you do, this nightmare is going to get a whole lot worse.

Ida wondered about her elusive grip – she suspected it was lost, accidently thrown out with rubbish.

Grabbing the box of groceries, she kneed the car door shut. She pushed open the gate, unlocked the front door and stood on the porch half-expecting to find Heather inside.

The house was empty.

Behind her, the sky, which ten minutes earlier had been bland and dull, was changing fast. Ida couldn't believe there were so many variations on the colour grey. As she watched, plumes of cloud unfolded like cloth, and threads of mist inched their way through the skinny trees.

Indoors, she cut slices of bread, slathered them with butter and stood at the window, eating and watching two of the black birds on the wall, picking between the stones with their pale beaks.

They looked ancient and she shuddered. Somehow, in the space of three days, she had become older too and she didn't know how. Ida no longer called what had happened to her unfair; she wasn't a child. She was twenty-nine years of age and she may as well have been a hundred. Was it the place? The house? Had time shifted, and without her old life to anchor her, had she fallen into one in which even the sky could fool her?

The shadows beyond the edge of her vision might well be ghosts.

A ghost.

You may not believe in the old ghosts, you better believe in my mother.

Was it a joke? Some kind of test? Heather was surely too old for games – the kind guaranteed to frighten a person. Until recently, there had been nothing in Ida's life to be truly afraid of. Now, her nerves were getting the better of her and she was on the verge of becoming stupidly scared of an empty house, a few black birds, and a ghost she couldn't even see.

The scary witches from her childhood lurked on the periphery of her mind again, along with other, more calculated cruelties. She could see the image on the cover of the book, the fearful girl in her ragged dress and wilful red shoes. She heard the pages of the book turning, her mother's voice, mellifluous and low.

Dance she did and dance she must...

Ida pressed the heels of her hands into her closed eyes, tried to banish the images. She stood up, shook her head and shouted into the silent room, 'Fuck off, Heather! Olwen too and yes, Mum, you as well! It's all just stories and I refuse to be scared. Go away, the lot of you!'

Dusk fell, unreliable and redolent with things half-imagined. Craving light, Ida turned her attention to the oil lamp. She removed the glass, fiddled with the brass wheel until a lip of wick showed. Shaking the base she heard oil sloshing, lit the wick and replaced the chimney. The flame rose and flared, illuminating the room with a wavering light. Turning the wheel until the flame settled into a gentle glow, Ida was ridiculously pleased with herself.

For a moment she saw her mother again, gentle now, insisting how kind to women soft light was. Shadows flickered on the walls. Ida pressed her forehead against the windowpane. She tasted oil and smoke on her lips. A moth, drawn to the lamp's light, hovered on the other side of the window and she thought how Welsh daylight disappeared too quickly.

She looked up and saw the moon shimmering through the

cloud. And for a few seconds, a pale face peered down at her. As the dark stole the last shreds of the day, Ida snapped the curtains shut. She rested her arms on the table, one hand folded over the other, and lowered her head. Closing her eyes she felt utterly empty.

Her limbs and body were made of pollen and, for two pins, a sigh of wind would blow her away.

Sixteen

Since her return to Ty'r Cwmwl, all Ida had accomplished was compiling a vague list of the contents of the house.

After five days, it seemed like a poor effort. If she wanted to sell the place, she needed to buck up her ideas. Needed to ask Heather what, if anything, had belonged to Olwen and if there was anything she wanted.

It was the trivia that bothered her. What was she meant to do with mismatched crockery and the contents of the kitchen? The worn soft furnishings? She thought she could donate some of it to a local charity shop. The good china, on the dresser in the parlour, might be worth something. She supposed she could get anything that belonged to her valued.

Ida, who didn't particularly care for old things, planned on taking only the primrose bedspread and maybe some of the pretty china. She considered the longcase clock. It was elegant and she liked it.

Today, sitting up in bed, still in her pyjamas with a blanket round her shoulders and sipping tepid coffee, Ida frowned at the list. When the pounding sounded on the front door, she flew out of bed, only just managing to stop the coffee spilling everywhere.

She crossed to the window and stood behind the curtains, shifted it to one side and sneaked a look through the gap.

A man stood on the doorstep. He was short and broad and she saw the top of a flat cap, a large metal toolbox on the step beside him and next to it, a blue gas bottle.

He looked up. 'Anyone home?'

Leaping back, Ida tripped on the rug, stubbing her toe on the chair.

Damn.

She peered out again. A maroon van was parked behind her car. She hadn't heard a thing.

'You there, Miss?'

Dragging on her jeans and a jumper, Ida made her way downstairs.

'Who is it?'

'Who do you think? Dan Pritchard of course.'

Of course.

He was as amiable as his wife was dour. As Ida opened the door he offered a smile, before edging his bulk through the gap. 'Wife says you need the taps fixing.'

'Well, yes—'

Dan made his way into the kitchen. He clearly knew the way. He hefted the gas bottle into the room. 'Wife says you need gas.'

'I do – thank you so much. There's a heater in the parlour.'

'Soon have it hooked up. Bring it in here until you get the range going?'

Ida nodded, thanked him and in the space of minutes, the robot was wheeled into the kitchen, the bottles exchanged and a hiss of heat began permeating the room.

Dan fetched his toolbox from the step, dumped it on the table and regarded the taps. 'You can leave me to it, *bach;* you get yourself sorted.' He looked down at her bare feet and Ida blushed.

In her bedroom, she dressed properly, pulled on thick socks and combed her hair. Clanking noises reverberated through the floor, together with a tuneless whistle. After about ten minutes, Ida crept downstairs again, lurked in the doorway.

'Almost there.'

She watched as Dan tightened something, knelt down, head in the cupboard under the sink, and turned the stopcock back on.

'There we are.'

Ida painted on a smile and walked into the kitchen. Dan heaved his bulk upright, turned the taps on and off, testing them.

'Good as new,' he said. 'As new washers at any rate.'

'Goodness, how quick. Thank you so much. I'm really grateful.' Ida snatched up the kettle. 'Would you like a cup of tea? I think the Primus still has enough paraffin, although it takes an age.'

'Tea can wait, *bach*.' Dan was putting his tools back in the metal box. 'Until I fix the generator.'

'Oh yes, of course. And I'm sorry, I don't know where the generator is.'

'Good thing I do then, isn't it?' He hoisted up the toolbox. 'It's in the barn. Come on.'

Dan unbolted the back door and Ida followed. The rain had stopped and they were greeted by a breeze and a dusting of birdsong. The sound rose through the air like musical confetti.

'Skylarks.'

'Skylarks?'

'All over the moor,' Dan said. 'You'll hear them, even this close to the house but you won't see them. Clever bird, the skylark.'

The barn loomed like a ruin and he disappeared through the door. It hung off one of its hinges and inside it was in a state of worse disrepair. Ida thought again how a few fierce gales would see off the roof. An old wooden manger, broken and rotting suggested animals must once have inhabited the place. Dried mud smudged the cobbled floor. In the corner, a stack of wood rose in a neat pile. In front of it, next to a large chopping block, a pile of fallen logs lay in disarray.

Dan was already examining the generator. 'Sound as a pound. Sturdy old girl. Needs a bit of TLC, that's all. Don't judge a book by its cover.'

Ida had no idea what a generator was supposed to look like. The thing loomed, a rotund unwieldy looking metal contraption, with wires and dials meaning nothing to her.

Dan took off his jacket, hung it on a nail.

'Me and this monster, we're old friends, Miss. Now you know where it is, you can take yourself off back into the warm. Fill the kettle and before you know it, you'll be making us both a cup of tea.'

'I have good coffee, if you prefer it.'

'Tea's fine, *bach*.'

As she retraced her steps, Ida glanced at the little garden. A broken wooden gate tied with a piece of rope, and on the other side a bristling tide of fading green. Two of the black birds flew down to the gate and Ida recoiled, scurried back to the house.

In less than twenty minutes Dan was back.

He wiped his feet on the mat, pushed back his cap. 'All sorted.' Groping along the wall he flicked the switch. Light flooded the gloomy room. 'There you go.' Opening the wooden door next to the sink, he turned his attention to the boiler. He adjusted the dials and nodded with satisfaction. 'It'll take a couple of hours. You'll have hot water before you know it.'

'That's wonderful. I'm so grateful, Mr Pritchard…'

'Dan.'

'Ida.' She filled the kettle, found the teabags Catrin had put in the box. 'Thanks, Dan. And I'm thrilled to bits. About the boiler. The heater. I can't tell you. And the lights.'

'Some people are easy to please.'

'I'm not good in the dark.'

'Not scared are you?'

'No, not really.'

Terrified.

Dan lowered his bulk onto one of the wooden chairs, laid his strong arms on the table. 'The dark won't hurt you, *bach*, and you had the lamp.'

'Yes. A girl dropped by; she fixed it. Heather? I expect you know her.'

'I do. Morgans. Trouble, the lot of them.'

'Really?'

'You'll know about her and her mam.'

Ida busied herself with the tea.

He carried on. 'What with them being your dad's tenants like.'

Ida didn't want to admit she'd had no idea about Heather Morgan's existence, or that she'd known nothing about Olwen. She didn't want to give anyone any more cause to gossip about her.

'I never met her – Heather's mum, I mean. I left here when I was five.'

'Ah, right.'

'Did you know her? Olwen?'

'Kept to herself. Like her mother.' He took a slug of tea. 'Lived over by Henbryn, three generations. Heather and her mam, and her grandmother, Manon. Until the landlord took the house back. Killed the old lady off, they said. They came to the village but she was gone within six months. Olwen's sister turned up and moved in then. But she never fitted. Bethan was a townie.'

'Why do you think Olwen moved here?'

'Probably to get away from Bethan.' He tipped his cap back. 'Olwen Morgan had a reputation for being a witch, like her mam.' Dan raised his eyebrows. 'Lot of women's nonsense if you ask me. The real rumours started up then mind, what with Olwen expecting and being single. Manon was never married either. Apple doesn't fall far from the tree.' He gulped his tea. 'In the end though, it was a nine days' wonder. Some passing gypsy chap they reckoned.'

'Who didn't stick by her?'

Dan made a dismissive noise. 'That sort don't. And Olwen did all right by herself. Resourceful, like.'

'It must have been awful for Heather.'

'After her mam passed there was only Bethan, and she left again right after. Met some chap and went off with him.' Dan shook his head. 'Like I said – Morgans. Funny do all round, mind. Leaving that poor girl on her own.'

'You would have thought social services would have taken an interest.'

Dan made a face. 'We don't go in for social services much round here. And she's all right, she helps out at the dogs' home couple of days a week. Other side of the village. Mary Jones, the owner, she sees her okay.'

'Oh, she never mentioned it.' Ida picked up the mugs. 'Will you let me know how much I owe you?'

'Come by the shop and settle with Catrin. She sees to the money.'

'And the gas?'

'From Gladys at the garage. They'll work it out between them.'

'I can write you a cheque now if you like.'

Anything so I don't have to go back to that village.

'Cash be better, *bach*. See Catrin.' He winked. 'Big house for you, all on your own.'

'Yes, I suppose it is.'

'Planning on staying?'

No, not that it's any of your business.

Was it always going to be like this? No wonder her mother had hated it.

'I don't know.' She held out her hand. 'Thanks again, Dan.'

Taking her hand he nodded, and Ida decided, nosy or not, he was a lot more likeable than his wife.

Seventeen

There was no sign of Ida.

Rounding the corner at the top of the final slope, the back of the house came into view. Heather guided her bicycle between the reeds and hummocks, towards the gap in the wall where the garden began.

She had no time for thin, timid Ida with her wide, startled eyes and her too big blue coat, nosing into things that didn't concern her. Heather had always known how to pay attention. Each time she saw Ida she noticed how she weighed her words, asked questions and filed away the answers for future reference.

She's made a mistake: Miss Ida Spider. She thinks if she's nice to me she can get round me and get rid of me.

Stupid woman would soon find out her false cordiality was pointless, and letting her anger show did her no favours either. Heather wasn't afraid of Ida with her threats and letters and solicitors.

Bloody interloper.

It had been too easy to wind her up. Heather smiled to herself, remembering Ida's face when she mentioned witches.

Her mam had had spells: remedies and glamours – every wise woman did. But there was a difference between spells for good and the kind used by arrogant idiots trying to impress people.

Her mother's wisdom was in Heather's blood and bones. She knew which roots killed and which ones healed. Birds came to her, she walked invisibly, and she wasn't in the least bit faint-hearted. Her mother taught her to leave a window open for the white moths; they knew the way to the woman who lived in the moon and her blessing was all Heather would ever need.

These things were Olwen's gifts. They'd kept her strong and since her mother died, Heather had managed her life well enough. Not like Ida Spider with her money and her inheritance.

I'm sorry for her loss but what's her unhappiness to me? I have my own sorrow and it's more than enough.

Standing by the low stone wall where the black birds came to peck for snails, Heather had waved goodbye to her mother.

'It's cold enough for snow, Mam,' she'd said, trying to keep the concern out of her voice.

With her back to the door, Olwen waved too, her other hand held to the tightness in her chest. 'Don't fret, *cariad*, you get off. There's people waiting for their remedies.'

'I don't want to leave you. You have the 'flu too, Mam – a fever.'

'I'm fine. I'll rest and you'll be back in no time.'

'Keep warm and take your own medicine.'

Olwen had laughed and waved again, stayed where she was, smiling and watching as her daughter cycled down the track, not letting her know how, from the moment she left, she would wait for her to come back.

Out on the hinterland, the weather could shock you. It changed in a heartbeat and the wisest of women might miss the signs, not least one whose seeing was blurred by fever. By the time Heather reached the village, a snow spell the like of which the village had never known had taken hold.

Within hours it lay in a thick, shining shroud, inching over each garden and rooftop until the entire village was buried. It erased roads and obliterated landmarks. Telephone lines went down and small birds froze in the trees, their wings turned to ice.

Due to the weather, the landlines were out everywhere, and although her Auntie Bethan told her not to worry, Heather watched uneasily from the window, the dead telephone in her hand. Snow layered the land and the sky turned to the colour of tears. Heather closed her eyes and listened for her mother's heartbeat.

By first light it was barely audible and she ran to the garage, woke Gladys and begged to be driven to Ty'r Cwmwl.

Gladys turned her away. 'Nothing will get through this. No point.' Her voice had been terse and edged with the inevitability of fate.

'You have to at least try!'

Olwen Morgan had known everyone in the village, most of their business and more besides, which meant people had been wary of her. They made use of her when it suited, creeping up the track to Ty'r Cwmwl at midnight, troubled and desperate, begging for her help. And the next day, meeting her in the village in broad daylight, giving her less than the time of day.

It was hard to trust a person who knew your secrets.

Once, after a woman left the house, Heather had heard her mother crying as if her heart would break. When she asked what was wrong, Olwen said that sometimes the only magic that worked was the truth. All the charms in the world weren't a match for men's lies and broken promises.

Heather stood her ground with Gladys and resorted to manipulation. 'You don't want a witch's death on your conscience.'

Reluctantly Gladys agreed to try and as they drove through the dark and the drifts, the sound of her mother's heartbeat faded until Heather no longer heard it.

She knew exactly when her mother died because every clock in the house had stopped at twenty-five to four.

Olwen hadn't been the only person to find herself stranded; she was the only one too ill to do anything about it. In the end, not even her knowledge and spells had been able to save her. Bethan took Heather away, to the claustrophobic cottage, but within a month she'd left, and Heather was more alone than at any point in her life.

She no longer tried to please, or use the word unless it was necessary, unless what she wanted was vital.

Through the window, she watched the moon rise, saw her eyes reflected in the glass. 'My eyes are on you, Ida Spider and yours are as blind as a bat's. Even so, I reckon you're up to something.'

Heather was her mother's daughter; she sang to birds and danced with bees. She had no intention of being part of whatever Ida had planned. And in the same way her mother had once believed – at a similar age – whatever Heather wanted, she thought she could have.

She didn't want Ida.

Heather wanted things to be how they were before skinny, selfish Ida arrived.

If she couldn't have her mother back, then Heather would make do with the life that was left over. Ty'r Cwmwl was the only real home she'd ever known. Heather knew she couldn't claim rights to a rented house and she was old enough to understand what might happen if she trespassed. But if she couldn't live there, at least she could have access.

She would whisper to her mother's memory and elicit her help. Brown leaves would fall on Ida's silly head and she would know what it was like to be haunted. Olwen wouldn't stand for her.

People who angered Heather's mother didn't sleep well at night.

I don't make the rules, and I don't follow them.

My mother had the right idea: don't make rules, make sense. Dress in earth colours, she said, they'll disguise you. Wear green boots, they'll make your footprints invisible. Keep a grey cat rather than a black one, it will fool the neighbours. And most importantly, don't let anyone hear you talking to the birds.

Once upon a time, when the woman from the Wild Edges bid them follow me across the moor, the black birds heard my song and knew it was made of trust. They took care of me. Blinking and nodding, comparing notes, they watched over me, and how I took care of myself. Caught the spells I made, before I knew I was making them.

As moons rose and set and rose again, they never ceased their vigilance, guarding my childish magic, guiding it as the knowledge passed.

They're patient, these generations of blue-eyed, see in the dark, shadow-black birds. Tonight, woman in a too big coat, while the rain falls, I'll make you a sleeping spell from skylarks' songs, and the dust of moth wings.

Moths and mothers know the way to the moon.

Eighteen

Ida stared at the taps.

Tentatively she turned the cold one and to her delight, water tumbled out, clean and pure.

'It works!' She grinned like a child.

The other one worked too, the water still warm. She'd left the boiler on for hours and before she went to bed, indulged in a deep bath. Curled under the primrose bedspread she'd slept like a baby.

'Goodbye Primus stove and good riddance!' She shoved it back in the cupboard, boiled the electric kettle, and made strong coffee. The caffeine went straight to her head and the rush brought her surroundings into sharp focus.

Dan had instructed her how to use the robot heater and the kitchen was now much warmer. Casting her eye around the room, something about it bothered her. Not because it was dirty. Ida had to admit, thanks to Heather, it was clean and neat. It was layered in something less tangible than dirt: a patina of someone else's past.

Olwen's.

The arrangement of the furniture was wrong. Ida didn't like the table set against the wall. The table in the kitchen of Wisteria Cottage had sat in the centre of the floor.

Ida dragged it across the flagstones, set the chairs on the four sides. She grabbed hold of the chair Heather had told her not to touch and shifted it into the space. The sofa may as well stay where it was. It was comfortable and it fitted.

Rearranging the kitchen was a small defiance in the face of her uncertain future.

And it's my kitchen, for now, not Olwen's.

Not Heather's.

Pouring a second mug of still hot coffee, Ida unlocked the back door and stood on the worn slate step. In front of her, the barn glowered. She wasn't sure she believed Dan's assurance. One good shove and surely the structure would collapse.

The morning was fresh and damp, filled with cold and a trace of pale gold. Unsure where the cloud ended and the mist began, Ida shaded her eyes. Under the faltering sun, a few black birds crouched on the roof of the barn, their bright, prescient eyes watching her.

Draining her coffee, she rinsed the mug and the cafetière, pulled on her boots, wrapped her mother's coat around her and made for the barn. She needed to make sure she'd remembered what Dan had said, and that his instructions, in the event the generator stopped working again, made sense.

Her eye was drawn again to the overgrown garden and on the other side of the fence she glimpsed Heather, like a trick of light. She was pushing her bicycle up the slope, from the hidden track, for all the world looking as if she'd grown, like a weed, out of the earth itself.

What was she doing here, every day, reinforcing her crazy claim?

It wasn't only that her moorland-coloured clothes meant she merged in – she was alive with the place: untamed brown hair and flying feet, her secret red petticoat and eyes that saw everything.

Ida dodged into the barn, watched from behind the half-open door. Heather propped her bicycle against the fence. She took a bunch of flowers from the bicycle basket, and a small garden fork, tucking it under her jacket.

What on earth is she up to?

Heather took off down a slope, away from the house and garden. Picking her way, Ida followed, puzzled by the girl's covert behaviour. The ground was slippery and Ida stumbled on roots and rocks, biting her lip against a stab of pain.

Heather's feet were steady; she knew exactly where she was going. She disappeared behind the lee of a low rocky outcrop and when Ida rounded it, in a dip she saw a sheltered circle of trees. They cast shadows across the ground like figures stitched together with mist and lichen. Unlike the blackthorns, they were tall, more substantial and unbothered by the wind. They had a spectral look and Ida wouldn't have been surprised to see them dance in her direction.

Swinging in the lowest branches, wind chimes chinked together, twisted, tarnished cutlery, hollow bird bones, bells and pieces of broken mirror. As the breeze caught them, it created eerie, off-key music.

It was exactly the kind of place Ida imagined witches might hang out.

As Heather stepped into the circle of trees, Ida peered from behind the outcrop, stepped on a twig, heard it snap under her clumsy foot. She froze, watched as Heather knelt down under one of the trees. She set to work, easing up weeds with the fork, picking off dead leaves and bits of debris, casting them to one side, smoothing the mossy grass.

Ida was reminded of a grave. Was it possible that Olwen was buried here? She felt a sudden and overwhelming sense of guilt. She shouldn't be here. Whatever ritual was playing out, whatever secret Heather was hiding, it was personal and nothing to do with Ida.

The girl sat back on her heels, patted the ground one last time, and exchanged a bunch of dead flowers for the fresh ones. In amongst the shifting shadows she looked like a wraith and Ida had the oddest notion: if she blinked, Heather would vanish.

Getting to her feet, the girl tied something round the stems of the dead flowers and reaching into the tree, hung them from a low branch next to several others, their heads dried and faded.

Ida realised she was holding her breath.

This close, she saw how the slender tree trunks belied their true age. They rose out of the bank. The soil was too shallow to contain their old roots and they ran away like ancient fingers. Other things hung in the trees: ribbons and scraps of cloth, black feathers. Small bundles, folded and fastened to twigs, swung in the breeze.

Something made a whispering noise and Ida trembled, until she realised it was the last of the leaves on one of the trees she didn't know the name of.

'Oak and beech,' Heather said, for all the world reading her mind. When she laughed, the spell was broken. 'Scare you, did I?'

You want me to be scared.

'You'd make a rubbish burglar, Ida Spider. I heard you coming a mile away.'

Exposed and feeling foolish, Ida took a few steps down the patchy grass. Under her feet the ground felt uncertain. At any moment she might be pulled down into the dark, shabby earth.

Heather wiped bits of dirt off her skirt, her hands moving like birds. There was something feral and unfettered about her. Ida noticed her light-littered hair, calculating eyes, and the bone necklace. Energy surrounded her. She looked like she was about to catch fire.

'You didn't scare me,' Ida said. 'But even if you had, is it any wonder, sneaking round...'

'Sneaking?' Heather made a noise of derision.

'Well, what would you call it?'

'Look, you may own the house, you don't own bloody Wales. And it was you followed me, remember? Think I didn't spot you, crashing around like an old ewe?' Heather looked down. 'What's up with your foot anyway?'

'Nothing.'

'If it's bones, you need comfrey.'

110

Unnerved, and determined not show it, Ida took another step. Heather grabbed her arm. Her fingers were like a strangling vine. Framed by two of the trees, her face took on a luminous hue; only her hair and her startling eyes looked real. She tilted her head backwards in a gesture of defiance. 'I suppose you want to know what I'm doing here.'

Ida hesitated. Heather was like a wild animal; suspicion marked her and red spots appeared on her brown cheeks. Her lips flattened into a line. She narrowed her eyes, daring Ida to challenge her.

'My mam's ashes are buried here. You got a problem with that?'

Fear, like damp, had a way of creeping up on a person, and when it found purchase it clung. Ida shivered and she heard leaves rustling like old paper, the faint sound of the wind in the chimes. Heather hovered like a camouflaged ghost and Ida had the same notion: if she blinked, the girl would vanish.

'This was where she was happiest. And sometimes it's like she's still here.'

There was a tone to her voice Ida found deliberately aimed at putting Olwen at the centre of things. She had the uncomfortable sensation this strange girl and her dead mother's memory had more right to be here than she did.

More right than my mother…

'I'm not afraid of you, Heather – whatever you think.'

And I am such a liar.

Heather brushed a brown leaf out of Ida's hair.

Ida lifted her hand, palm out like a shield. She didn't want this strange girl touching her.

'Is that a fact?' Heather whispered. She twirled the leaf between her fingers, like a conjurer with a penny. 'A dead leaf falling on your head is a sign of a restless ghost.'

Ida shrank back. 'I told you, I don't believe in ghosts.'

'So you keep saying.' Heather's face said she didn't believe a word Ida said. 'Well there's one here seems to believe in you.'

'Nonsense.'

Heather spread out her hands, letting the brown leaf fall to the ground. 'You think everyone who dies is ready to leave this world?'

Don't talk to me about dead people.

Heather carried on. 'Don't sleep with your mouth open is all I'm saying. An angry ghost will try and live off your breath.'

'Now you're being ridiculous.'

Ida gazed down at the brown leaf, resisting the urge to crush it with the heel of her boot. Trying not to appear as scared as she felt, she searched for a tangent. 'These trees. What are they?'

'Oak and beech. I said. They're witness trees.'

'Sorry?'

'Some trees are for seeing. They keep secrets. The things we aren't meant to forget.'

'I suppose that's something else your mother told you.'

Heather turned back to the spot where her mother's ashes lay buried. 'She told me lots of things. Things you wouldn't understand in a month of Sundays.'

'Tell me about her,' Ida said.

For a second Heather looked indecisive. 'Now all of a sudden you're interested?'

'I'm trying to understand, Heather. Honestly, I am.'

The girl leaned back against one of the trees, spread her hands behind her and touched the bark. 'All right then. But you have to listen and not make any stupid comments.'

Ida nodded. 'I promise.'

Heather pulled off her hat and her hair erupted in tangles as wily as she was.

'Then you better sit comfortably, Ida Spider.'

Nineteen

'Mam didn't want to be cremated,' Heather said. 'No one listened when I tried to tell them. Bethan said I was a kid and what did I know about anything? She ought to have known better, and she can go to hell.'

The light was changing and Ida noticed how long the shadows were becoming.

'Next to finding her,' Heather went on, 'the cremation was the worst day of my life. I got the better of them all in the end though. After that apology for a ceremony, they gave the ashes to Bethan. I waited until she thought I'd forgotten.' She let out a snort of derision. 'Like that was going to happen. Bethan didn't care anyway. I brought them here and buried them under this tree, the way Mam would have wanted.'

A wave of guilt overwhelmed Ida. Goosebumps erupted all over her body.

I am not like you…

And yet she carried her own dead with her. The plastic urn was in the boot of her car.

Was it unlucky to hold onto their ashes? Not to have some sort of ceremony and create a suitable final resting place? Ida didn't know and now, gazing at Olwen's, it suddenly seemed important.

In the depths of grief, Ida hadn't been able to decide where her mother would have wished to be laid to rest, or if her father would have wanted his ashes brought back to Wales. Under her mother's roses would have been the likeliest place. The discovery her father hadn't owned Wisteria Cottage put paid to that plan. In the end, still undecided, Ida had brought them with her to Wales.

In all likelihood, it wasn't even them. People will say anything to placate you, and everyone knew there was no proof that what ended up in an individual urn was the actual remains of the dead person.

High above the trees, a great flapping began. Several birds, charcoal smudges calling across the late afternoon sky, flew down. Ida watched as they settled in the topmost branches of the tallest tree. For the first time she became aware of their instinctive, inherent grace, setting them apart from any earthbound creature.

'Why are there so many birds here?'

'Because this is where they plot their best spells.'

'What?'

Heather grinned. 'Oh my god, you're dull, and so easy to wind up.'

'And what about all of this?' Ida pointed at the charms hanging in the trees.

'There's three kinds of magic, Ida – good, rubbish and symbolic.'

A slice of broken mirror hanging on a green thread caught Ida's reflection. Her eyes looked like saucers and she turned away.

'There's no bad magic here, Ida. No poppets or pins or pointy hats.' Heather touched her finger to one of the little bundles and it twirled. Round and round and she grinned. 'No wicked *enchantments.*'

The way she said the word sent a quiver through Ida's body.

That's exactly what you want me to think it is.

Heather shaded her eyes and stepped forward, stood next to Ida, looking up. 'What do you *think* the birds are doing? They come here to roost, that's all.'

Ida licked her lips. 'Yes, of course.'

'They came in the first place because my mother did. And because she was smart and wise and so beautiful they couldn't stay away.'

Ida stared, and her mouth dropped open.

Heather's face softened. 'It's true. They followed her from the place she was born, out on the moor, to the village, and they left songs for her to learn. And they came back to listen, make sure she'd learned them right. Then, when she came here, she said they came too, left new songs for her. Spell songs.' Heather smiled and her face lit up in a way Ida hadn't seen before. 'She left food for them in winter and in the fiercest storms she came out here to leave seed and fat balls. In the garden, she grew the kind of plants they liked to eat. And in return, they sent rain so soft that when she died, there wasn't a single line on her face.'

Ida's heart was beating so hard it pressed against her ribs.

'See the big one?' Heather pointed into one of the trees. 'Up there?'

To Ida, all the birds looked enormous.

'She's a raven. Flown down from the crags to check on things. See how the other birds make way for her? She was my mother's favourite. Her and the magpie.'

'What? Like pets?'

The scornful look returned to Heather's face. 'Don't be daft. You can't own an animal – especially not a bird. Any creature come to that.'

Once again she left the comment hanging and Ida's head filled with images.

'Creatures?'

'You'll see them – when you start looking properly. If they decide to show themselves.'

'You're doing it again aren't you – trying to spook me. The only creature I've seen creeping round here is you.'

Heather's eyes shone, bright as diamonds. In them Ida saw the sly intelligence again and she told herself to stay alert.

You don't have to trust her, just because you feel sorry for her.

'Listen,' she said, trying to sound more rational than she felt. 'It's all right about the ashes – about your mother, I mean. Do whatever you need to. I understand.' She paused. 'My mother…'

'Yes.' Heather's face had regained its indifferent demeanour.

Her voice was quiet, the combative edge gone. 'Your mother.' She stared at Ida.

'Was yours really a witch?'

'I never said she was.'

'You did!'

'No, Ida. I told you she was a wise woman.'

'What's the difference?'

'Witch, wise woman, hag, crone? But all right, if you want, she was a witch – only not the way you think.'

'You don't know what I think.'

'Same as the rest of them? It doesn't take much, Ida. A thing doesn't have to be true; it only has to be believed.' Heather sighed. 'One too many black frocks, rain every day in August. No husband and a baby in her belly. And you know what used to make me really angry? They still came looking for her when they needed her help. For the *spells*.' Her voice took on a sarcastic edge. 'Best go at dark moon when they're strongest.' Heather gave a snort of derision. 'Morons.'

Ida stayed silent, sensing any response would be the wrong one.

'Mam never made a charm for anyone at dark moon – she knew its power. Let sleeping crones lie.'

'So—'

'They're old fears, Ida, and deep rooted. My hypocritical village neighbours – they go to chapel and pray with their mouths instead of their hearts, read their Bibles *and* the tabloids.'

Ida wanted to smile and see the joke only she could see how serious Heather was. She heard Catrin Jones again, and the woman in the brown coat.

We've been expecting you…

'You don't have to listen.'

'Is that a fact?' Heather's expression turned to a sneer. 'Like you'd know.' She pulled on her woollen hat again, eyed Ida from under the rolled edge. 'And why am I'm telling you this anyway? You're the same as the rest of them.'

'That's not fair.'

'You think words can't hurt? I'd rather have sticks and stones, at least they're honest.' Heather shook her head. 'If they're whispered wrong or spat at you, you better believe words can hurt. People can't resist them: gossip to brighten up their nasty, narrow lives.'

'You make it sound awful.'

'It's ignorant.' Heather began collecting her belongings. 'But you better believe it – if my mother wants to—'

'Stop it.' Ida's patience began to slip again.

'Dead mothers everywhere. Ghosts too.'

The shadows were falling fast now and all Ida wanted to do was get away – away from Heather and her crazy talk. She turned and began walking towards the house. Behind her, she heard the hollow bird bone wind chimes shifting in the breeze, and Heather's voice, soft as snow in April.

'Keep your eyes peeled, Ida Spider.'

Out on the hinterland, if you blinked, you could miss twilight. The change was a flicker in time as the day became invisible. Watching at the kitchen window through the falling light, Ida saw a straggle of black birds drifting down in the direction of the grove. She closed her eyes, and when she opened them again, the dark had devoured the house.

Before she fell asleep, behind her eyelids she saw an image of Heather, in her eccentric clothes, with her wild brown hair flying like a murmuration of starlings.

In the morning she could have sworn she'd dreamed a woman in grey, dancing out on the moorland. Under her bare feet, purple heather formed a cushion, held her as she moved, poised like a hare in the moonlight.

Olwen Morgan or Anna Plessey?

Then Ida remembered, she never dreamed. She hadn't dreamed since her mother died and it was nothing more than a trick played on her by the night and her fears.

And the ghost of the wrong mother.

Washed up on the morning, Ida let the tear in the corner of her eye trickle into her ear. Little by little, as she came fully awake, she knew the safest thing was to lie as still as a star, until she returned to herself.

Twenty

From the cottage window, Heather watched the night gather, and the pearl moon as it rose.

Dead mothers everywhere…

Had she really said that? It crossed her mind she'd been cruel, only she didn't want to care about Ida or her grief. There wasn't room – it was too hard.

She hadn't meant to scare her. Not really. Or if she had, only enough to let Ida know she couldn't take liberties.

She's not the only one with a dead mother.

A moth, lured by the light's possibility, played around the lantern on the windowsill. Heather did nothing to save it. Her misery made her heartless and she could summon no remorse.

She hadn't been there when her mother died – no one had. Not a single person to hold her hand or comfort her. There were no rules to death and Heather had been left without directions. Her sorrow was too heavy to bear, let alone make room for anyone else's.

At first they'd tried to keep her away from the body. Heather had screamed and pleaded until they allowed her a few precious minutes. Her mother's hands lay on the sheet. When Heather had touched them, they were cold. She kissed the waxen face, took the bird-bone necklace and slipped it under her jumper.

Her blood turned to ice, her skin became as cold as a lizard's, her limbs light, as if they had been replaced by air. From that day on there weren't enough clothes to keep Heather warm.

When they tried to make her leave Ty'r Cwmwl, she fought

them, fierce as a cat. They were too strong and dragged her away, took her down to the cramped cottage in the village, into the care of her aunt.

In spite of Bethan's public insistence her niece was welcome, Heather knew she resented her.

'You can have the back bedroom,' Bethan announced. 'It's small but you'll have to manage.'

Bethan had most of Olwen's personal belongings brought from Ty'r Cwmwl to the village, leaving behind anything that didn't interest her.

She took a cardboard box filled with letters, bills and receipts out to the back garden and burned the lot, watched the grey flakes turn to ash. She rifled through clothes, fingered frocks and found them wanting, picked through her sister's jewellery, checking each ring and pair of earrings. Heather held her hand over her jumper, tight around the bird-bone necklace. When Bethan wasn't looking, she took her mother's red petticoat and hid it under the mattress.

When her auntie found Olwen's journal and began reading it, Heather protested. 'It's private and it's not yours to go prying in.' She snatched the book out of Bethan's hand and got a punch on her arm for her trouble. She didn't cry and refused to let go of it, and in the end Bethan gave up.

'None of this belongs to you,' Heather said, her face battered by grief.

'That's the thing though, it does,' Bethan replied. 'I'm the eldest and the legal next of kin, so I get the lot.'

Heather didn't believe her – Nain and Mam would have meant anything they left to be fairly shared.

'I can do whatever I like. But have it if it means that much. It's a load of witchy crap anyway. Talk about the weird sister.' She scanned the clothes, discarded on the floor. 'Load of god-awful tat. My sister never did have any taste.'

Few people came to offer condolences. Catrin Pritchard

brought pies and pity, doorstep eyes that curled around corners and set Bethan sneering.

'Bloody vultures.'

Heather agreed, although nothing would have induced her to say so.

The experts in death showed up too, accomplished mourners: a funeral director equipped with platitude-laced sympathy, and the local vicar declaring the cemetery full.

No wise woman with half her wits courted fire but in the face of the man's implacability, surrounded by the impassive conformity of the village, Heather found herself overruled.

Regardless of her quiet pleading, her mother was cremated.

Even if Bethan hadn't decided to leave of her own accord, Heather swore, in spite of her mother's disapproval, she would have cast the best banishing spell she could conjure. Once the funeral was done, Bethan packed her bags and told Heather she was going to Swansea to be with a man she'd met on a dating site.

'You got money?' she asked.

'There's Mam's account. I've got her card. I know the pin number.'

'How much is in it?'

Heather shook her head. 'Not as much as you think and I need it. A few hundred quid, that's all.'

'You've got that job, haven't you? With the scabby dogs?'

'It's only two days, and only twenty quid.'

'Well, here's a few more.' Bethan threw a handful of twenties onto the table. 'Make it last and with what's in the account, it'll keep you going for a while.'

Heather stared at the pile of cash and said nothing.

Bethan refused to meet her niece's eyes. 'You'll be fine. You're your mother's daughter.' She flashed Heather a brief smile made of false kindness. 'You may as well have this place too. I won't see you out on the street. I'll sort the paperwork. Keep it and good luck.'

The next day she boarded a bus. It was the last time Heather had seen her.

'Good riddance more like.' Heather took the red petticoat from beneath the mattress and put it on under her dowdy skirt. And as soon as the coast was clear, she pulled the bird-bone necklace free and never hid it again.

With Bethan gone, Heather couldn't bear to sleep in either of the bedrooms. She moved a mattress downstairs and slept in front of the fire. Her mother's belongings made shadowy memories and Heather made shrines of them all.

The cottage grew darker and dustier. Jackdaws made a nest in the chimney and bats took possession of the rafters.

If the villagers didn't actively shun Heather, they pretended not to see her. It was hard to decide which was worse. Occasionally someone would risk a smile, a quick, fixed facsimile because old superstitions stuck. (If the witch hadn't been able to save herself, what hope for the rest of them? Like mother like daughter; bad luck sticks and bad magic was contagious.)

Heather had no idea about tenancy law. Afraid of the authorities, scared that if she drew too much attention to herself before her eighteenth birthday, she'd be taken into care, she rationed her visits to Ty'r Cwmwl, made herself as invisible as she knew how. She rode her bicycle over the moor and it soon became apparent, no one cared what she did. If anyone saw her, they didn't try to stop her.

As the days lengthened and the light lingered, she found herself drawn back to the house again and again, letting herself in with one of her spare keys, often staying overnight, and some nights, sleeping under the stars in the grove, watching for a ghost.

Certain she wouldn't survive the loss of her mother, she waited for death. It didn't once occur to her to kill herself. Heather believed all she needed to do was be patient, her lizard blood cooling, convinced she wouldn't last long beyond the bitter winter that had taken Olwen.

She lost weight and her eyes dulled and she looked for ways to be in pain. Making her way through the silent rooms she walked into furniture, deliberately, so bruises as big as storm clouds bloomed on her legs. She held her hands in front of steaming kettles, walked barefoot down the garden path to leave food for birds that no longer came, until the stones cut the soles of her feet.

Each time she went back to Ty'r Cwmwl, she dreamed her mother crooned bird songs to her, and they were so beautiful, she cried as if her heart would break.

Then, one day, without warning and in spite of herself, the black birds came, trailing spring and hope, with wild flowers in their beaks.

At first Heather resisted, until she pricked her finger on a thorn in the garden and saw her blood was red again and when she licked it, it tasted warm. Creeping outside, she felt the sun and the silky air on her face. Still she resisted; she didn't want to be happy or notice bluebells and green leaves clustered in pale buds.

She didn't want to be brave, but the black birds flew down into the grove and set the bells and bones and broken mirrors ringing. Heather took the urn from its hiding place in the cottage and buried her mother's ashes in the grove beneath the witnessing trees.

Closing the curtains, Heather lay down on the mattress in front of the fire. Flames set the soot on the back plate ablaze, making red-gold fire stars.

You won't keep me away, Ida Spider. The birds followed my mother and they came for me too.

She thought of Ida, listening to the birds as they settled on the roof of the house, or flapped down to the grove and the tall trees. How the sound of them would keep her awake for hours.

When no one, save for a ghost and a girl with no directions, knows where you are, anything is possible.

Twenty-one

'Ida?'

Liz's voice at the other end of the phone, echoed: disembodied and far too cheerful for eight o'clock in the morning.

'Do you know what time it is?'

'I do. And you can stop whinging. I've been texting you for days. You've been gone a week and—'

'Six days. I know, I'm sorry.'

'So what's up?'

'Nothing. It's the back end of nowhere and I want to come home.'

'That bad, huh?'

'It's so remote. There's nothing, for miles.'

She made no mention of the gate-crashing girl and her ghostly mother. Didn't say anything about the black birds. She made light of things, told Liz about the village shop and the odd women, the generator and Dan, and how the sooner she sold the house the better.

'You're going ahead then? With the sale?'

'Of course. Why wouldn't I?'

'I don't know – it sounds like an adventure.'

'It's a bloody nightmare. I hate it.'

They talked for a few more minutes – Liz's boyfriend wanted her to go to Japan with him, on holiday.

'I know we talked about going somewhere.'

'Go to Japan. You adore travelling. You'll love it.'

'You can come here, if you come back and don't fancy your place. I'll leave a key.'

They chatted for a while, about inconsequential things and when Ida promised to keep in touch Liz rang off, satisfied.

Glancing at her watch Ida saw she'd only had a few hours sleep. She forced herself out of bed. Underneath her feet the boards were cold. Pulling on her thick cardigan and a pair of socks, she made her way to the kitchen.

The heater sent waves of warmth into the room. Ida made coffee, relishing the scent and taste of it, the heat of the mug in her hands. Checking the cupboard and the fridge, she saw how low on provisions she was. After almost a week eating up the last of the food she'd bought with her, she was desperate. She'd even resorted to the ghastly tins from the shop: corned beef that tasted like cat food, and peas, their colour so virulent they made her queasy.

Ida wasn't much of a cook and her mother had been the same. Next to dress shops, Anna's favourite retail outlets were florists, delicatessens and patisseries.

Ida could just about rustle up an omelette, spaghetti bolognaise or a stir fry.

This is what happens when you don't leave home until you're twenty-five.

Her coffee finished, Ida wiped the table clean. From the window, the day looked bland and in her head she began making a new shopping list. She opened the window and somewhere she heard the cry of a bird. Immediately she was reminded of the black ones with their sea-coloured eyes and wondered how many of them might be gathered on her wall this morning.

They came because my mother was smart and wise and so beautiful they couldn't stay away.

Witch, wise woman. Ida wasn't interested in semantics. She thought about a dead woman's ashes under the earth in the grove. In spite of telling Heather she didn't mind, Ida knew the assurance for a lie. It was creepy. And surely, Olwen deserved a more suitable resting place.

125

A churchyard perhaps. Out in the middle of nowhere struck Ida as bizarre. She thought of her parents' ashes again, still in the boot of her car. Equally unsuitable and she felt a pang of remorse.

'I'm sorry, Mum,' she whispered. 'I'll make it right.'

Anna's face wavered behind Ida's eyes. Another unpredictable moment of missing, tripping her up like invisible strings across her path. She recalled Heather tending the patch of grass – a treasured resting place marked for remembrance, and felt another stab of guilt. But she wasn't like Heather. The idea she might dispose of the ashes in some kind of pagan ritual horrified her.

For now, she should at least remove them from the car, bring them into the house and make a decision about their disposal.

The word made her flinch. She couldn't think of a better one. Release?

Would releasing them free her from this hollow grief? She doubted it.

Upstairs, she dressed in jeans and a jumper, dragged a brush through her hair and peered out of the window. There was no sign of the black birds and she wasn't sure if this was a good thing or not.

Just because she couldn't see them didn't mean they weren't around.

Out on the landing, she paused at the bedroom Heather insisted had been Olwen's. On the other side of the door she thought she heard a scratching noise.

Mice?

Please don't let it be mice.

Ida didn't want to go into the room and yet something drew her towards it. She leaned against the wall to steady her nerves.

What was happening to her? A few months ago she'd been an ordinary woman living a normal life. In an instant, a rift had appeared in her universe, laughing in her face reminding her she couldn't depend on anything. There was no point in plans or dreams or notions of happy ever after.

Taking a deep breath, Ida threw open the door. The room was silent and she paused, jittery and filled with unease. It was cold enough to freeze her breath in her lungs. She allowed her head to move, a fraction of an inch, enough to see there was nothing, only the pulsing air and an empty room.

Creeping cold formed a sour spot around her.

Ida had never experienced pure terror before. Fear was the ring of the doorbell when you've been trying to contact your missing parents for two days. The precise knock at the door when the only reason for it was as the harbinger of horror. Fear was the hairs on your skin stiffening as your heart dipped into despair.

This was on a different level. Whatever inhabited the room was feral and even though it had no shape, Ida could smell it, thick with rotting apples and something horribly corporeal.

'I know you're here. What do you want with me?' Her voice echoed off the walls, cracked and ineffectual.

Now she sensed it: energy and the air alive with—

What?

She didn't have the word. All she knew was a moment freighted with knowing, and that she wasn't alone.

The knowledge passes, like blood…

Whatever Ida may have thought before – about the reality or even the foolishness of ghosts and witches – here in this room she knew she was in the presence of a woman who had been dead for a year. Dread took root in her stomach and beads of sweat broke out on her brow. Whirling on the spot, Ida looked and looked, wide eyes with fear and still she saw nothing.

'Where are you?' Her voice was ragged with panic.

Silence.

There was no one in there, even so, regardless of what her eyes told her, Ida sensed someone else occupied the room. Flinging herself at the door she wrenched it open, tore down the stairs, not caring when the pain in her foot stabbed like a knife. She threw open the front door, ran out slamming it behind her.

Nothing!

Sinking onto the step, Ida held her arms tight around her body, her bones trembling. Against her back the door felt solid. And in front of her, the black birds, shaking themselves off the roof, swooped low and she felt the hairs lift on her head. Veering off again, they made for the grove.

Ida huddled on the step, waiting for something to happen.

Twenty-two

A brief rain shower in the night left a glisten on the world making it look unreal.

Light fell on puddles creating silver ripples on the water. In the kitchen doorway, Ida watched as heavy, stratocumulus cloud overlaid the house. The memory of the previous encounter in the empty room refused to leave her. When she'd closed her eyes last night and tried to sleep, it was as if an image of a woman she'd never seen had been implanted inside her eyelids: a wild looking woman clothed in unruly mist and guile.

Ida had lain awake for hours and only fallen asleep as dawn broke. She woke, bleary-eyed, watching dull light float between the curtains.

Coffee only partially revived her. The cupboards were still bare and Ida knew she must go shopping. She dressed quickly, buttoned up her mother's blue coat and pulled on her beret.

Stepping outside, a strip of wind snatched her breath away, the fresh air making her eyes water.

Clean air. A clean escape.

After a week of doing little more than sleep and read – and pander to her imagination – the need to get away was now intense.

Nothing would induce her to return to the village. Consulting her map, Ida worked out that another village lay about ten miles from the house, in the opposite direction. She drove away from Ty'r Cwmwl, remembered she'd left her shopping list on the kitchen table, and made a new one in her head.

It was a plain, unassuming village, and on the uncluttered main road Ida was able to park outside a non-descript Spar. Inside there were few people and no one took any notice of her. Ida filled a trolley, filled the car with petrol at a nearby garage and in just over an hour, she was back at Ty'r Cwmwl. She unloaded her groceries: more coffee, bread and milk, fresh fruit and vegetables, eggs and butter, bacon, cheese and a selection of ready meals.

Closing the refrigerator, she nodded in satisfaction. With luck, she would be out of here within a week, and once her bill for the work Dan had done was settled, she wouldn't need to return to Catrin's dismal shop ever again.

As if to add to her momentary sense of well-being, a pale sun emerged from behind the cloud, played against the window, and Ida smiled.

'May as well make the most of it.'

She put on her coat again and avoiding the puddles made her way across the yard, past the barn and the tangled garden. Beyond it, a rough stile stood between fallen stones, scattered like bones making the stile obsolete. Ida placed her hand on the rotting wood, her foot on the bottom step.

Did she remember it? Had her father brought her out here, had he helped her over this stile, when the wall was still intact?

However hard she tried to remember, only a semblance of memory surfaced.

There were two paths after all. Ida guessed one must lead to the village – the direction Heather kept appearing from. Sloping off and at an angle, a narrower path meandered out across the shimmering moorland and more than anything, Ida wanted to believe it was one she thought she remembered.

So long as she kept the house in sight, she was unlikely to get lost. Despite the pull of her injured foot, Ida was determined not to allow it to hold her back. Stepping over the stones, she set off down the path, taking her time.

Ida had little faith in her sense of direction because she'd never needed it. Where she came from, streets were marked, buses knew the way and until now she'd always been surrounded by familiarity. Out on the moor, as far as the eye could see, there were no landmarks to steer a course by, only the scarred remains of walls and here and there, stunted trees caught in the wind's path.

She smelled fresh, damp soil and rotting leaves. In places, red-brown bracken spread like a blanket, clumps of heather, still bright with colour and draped with spider web.

Ida Spider...

She stopped and peered at one of the webs. As far as she could see, there were no spiders.

Like you'd know. You know nothing...

She turned, caught a glimpse of the house, leaning away from her. In the blink of an eye, cloud circled, the fragile sun disappeared and moments later the roof and chimneys disappeared.

Stubbornly hunched into her blue coat, Ida trudged along the path. Small dips and hollows threatened to trip her. The wind whipped her hair into her eyes and she pulled her beret lower. The barely discernible path began to slope upwards and she soon became breathless, the ache in her foot only serving to remind her how vulnerable she was.

The path, which had seemed bent on confusing her, all at once reappeared through a break in the mist. To her right, a ridge of rock rose, overlooking a long, undulating slope. She made her way to it, sat down in a dip in the rock, resting her foot. The wind dropped and Ida clamped her hands between her knees, peering into the shredded mist.

The screech of a bird made her jump. She turned, got to her feet, searching for the house, for anything familiar. It was all gone, and she tried not to let her mind get the better of her. She'd been walking for less than ten minutes and couldn't possibly be lost. All she had to do was wait until the mist lifted and she would be fine.

A gap in the mist and for a second, she saw a ragged tree. The air cleared and Ida saw the path again. This fast-changing weather was unlike anything she had ever experienced, and although it was now better than the blind mist, she wasn't a bit reassured. In seconds there was more sky than land, and it moved in confusing swathes, as if it and not the cloud was on the move.

Retracing her steps to the best of her recollection, Ida thought she recognised a chunk of rock and breathed a sigh of relief. As she did, another curtain of mist fell, engulfing her once more. Her teeth chattered in her mouth like dice and unable to move, Ida held her body rigid, her hands fisted into tight balls and the air began to smell fetid and the earth seemed to rise up around her.

She heard a harsh cry and out of the gloom, a huge bird swept across the murky ground. There was something frantic in its call, like a wild whistling. Distracted and terrified, Ida realised she had wandered off the path. And to her horror, a few feet from where she stood, the land dropped away, this time, into an abyss of mist. Trembling, she backed away.

Keeping the precipice on her right she followed her nose, careful to keep a few feet between her and the terrifying drop. As she descended, a shallow gully running with brackish water trickled across the path. She stepped across it and the ground became slippery and sodden. Petrified of falling, with no sense of being anchored, Ida stood as still as a post. As the mist became heavier, she could barely see a yard in front of her hands. Everything drifted, grey and chilly and as she took a tentative step, keeping the drop at her back, it was like walking into cloud. There was no way of knowing if she was going in circles.

The sound of flapping came again, loud as thunder, and the huge bird reappeared, its wing feathers fanned like knives.

Ida screamed.

Chilled to the bone, she made herself move, hardly caring if she fell or not. The wind turned the cloud to rags and Ida saw a slit in it, a tree she thought she recognised, and she shook with relief, convinced she must be close to the house.

It was short-lived. The only thing in front of her were more folds of mist and the sky hanging so low she feared it might fall on her The wind whipped into a frenzy, abruptly as if ordered, hurling dead leaves into wild spirals. Ida lost her balance, held her arms out to steady herself. There was a buzzing in her head, her throat was dry and she jerked her head from side to side, frantic and desperate.

Fear made her careless. She struck out, down the slope. To her left, on a rocky outcrop she glimpsed a group of enormous dark birds and a chill ran down her spine. The sight was momentary, a string of cloud rearranged the crag and it vanished.

The birds were still there though and they'd seen her. Ida knew it and now, she really didn't care if she fell. As she ran, her foot screamed with pain. Behind her she heard them, shouting and flapping and she held her hands over her head, staggered and groaned in fear as the birds gained on her.

Twenty-three

'What the hell are you doing, wandering out here by yourself?'

Once again, like a mirage, Heather materialised: a wild fairy godmother. Her hair, freed from its woollen hat, blew boldly around her head.

Ida wailed. 'Oh god! Get them off me!' She hurled herself at Heather.

'There's nothing there, you idiot.'

Ida was sobbing now. Panic-stricken, she pulled away and made to run. Heather grabbed her arm and Ida stopped, snatched at the girl's hand, terrified she would disappear. 'Don't leave me.'

'I wasn't planning to.'

'Have they gone? Did you see them?'

'Calm down. They're birds, Ida, they won't hurt you.'

'They *attacked* me!' Ida's voice came out in a strangled moan and she shook with fear. 'Didn't you see them?' She clung to Heather as if her life depended on it. 'Why would they do that?'

'They didn't attack you, you stupid thing. They were warning you.'

'What?'

Heather unpeeled Ida's fingers from her arm. 'Look.' She stretched out her hand.

Still shaking, Ida followed Heather's pointing finger. They were standing less than three feet above the lip of the precipice. A small tree, barely a branch, growing close to the edge of the drop, was the only thing that might have broken Ida's fall. She stepped back so quickly she nearly lost her footing again, sank to the ground, her hands clasped over her head. Cold, wet mud seeped around the hem of her coat. Her jeans were soaked and her ankle pulsated with pain.

'Bloody hell, you were lucky. If the birds hadn't warned you, chased you from the edge, you'd have gone right over.'

'I must have gone in a circle.'

'Not a magic one though.' Heather let out a sharp laugh and to Ida's horror, took a few steps down the slope, as easily as descending a staircase, stopping in front of the tree that looked like a branch.

'Don't!'

Heather grinned, turned away and held her arms out, threw back her head and let out a cry, half song, half howl.

Mesmerised, Ida held her breath. The girl inhabited her body the way an animal did, as if she shook herself out each morning, like a pelt, and smoothed her creases until she hung right. The wind pressed against her body, flattened the layers of her skirt. Ida caught a glimpse of red petticoat again, saw the shape of Heather's legs, sturdy and planted on the slope, nothing fazing her.

Crouched in the mud, she felt her own awkwardness more acutely than ever, carrying her body like an encumbrance. 'Please, Heather, don't. Come away, it's too dangerous.'

Heather snatched up her skirt and bounded up the slope. 'Only if you're an idiot.'

'Yes – and it's exactly what I am – a complete idiot. If you hadn't found me, I could have died.'

'Or worse.' Heather took hold of Ida's arm again. 'You could have landed on the rocks and broken your back and been paralysed for life. There's no one comes by here. And there's no phone signal either.'

'Say what you mean, why don't you?'

'Oh give over and get up. I've never met such a scaredy-cat in my life.'

'All right, I'm a scaredy-cat. I can't help it. You should have met my mother.'

Heather threw Ida one of her looks. 'She must have loved it here then.'

'I told you—'

'Yes, I heard you the first time. She hated it. Whatever. Come on, I've better things to do than chase halfway across the moor rescuing you.'

'How did you know where I was?'

Heather didn't answer.

'Were you following me?'

'Not exactly. I told you, it was the birds. I heard them.'

'How did you manage to find your way?'

'I know the way.' Like magic, the mist evaporated and the path came into view again. 'Let's go.'

Heather grabbed Ida's arm and hauled her along, and within minutes, sure enough, there was the house. In the pale light, it looked supernaturally beautiful and not the brooding grey façade it usually presented.

Ida turned and looked back over her shoulder, down the long incline.

There's no one comes by here…

The air tasted of loam and damp, and it coated Ida's throat. She had a flash of the edge of the precipice again, the drop into a chasm. She felt sick. Looking up she saw Heather, waiting by the back door, her expression giving nothing away.

Ida hesitated.

'Would you like a cup of tea?' she heard herself asking. 'I have electricity now. I need coffee and—'

Heather pushed open the door and slipped inside, her sense of ownership leading the way. 'Yes, but what you need is tea: sweet, for the shock. I'll make it. You better hang up your coat, it's covered in mud.'

Ida draped her mother's coat over the back of a chair and sat down, pulled at her muddy bootlaces.

Heather filled the kettle, found teabags and a couple of mugs.

'You got a gas bottle then.' She lit the robot heater. 'Can't stand these things, they stink. You need to get the range going. You need proper warmth.'

136

Why this sudden concern for my well-being?

Heather opened the fridge, whirring now and useful, filled with food.

'Been shopping then?'

'Yes.'

'Not in the village, I see. That'll boil Catrin Pritchard's blood.' She grinned and grabbed the milk. 'There's plenty of wood in the barn, you know, for the range.'

'Yes, I saw it.' Ida pulled off her boots and damp socks, rubbed her throbbing instep. 'And thanks again, for before. I mean it. If you hadn't come along—'

'And I told you, it's no big deal.' Heather dropped a teabag into each of the mugs. 'Don't go off again though, okay? I'm not bringing you back lost every day.'

What did that even mean?

Ida smiled and lowered her head in case Heather thought she was being mocked. 'Why *did* you come looking for me?'

'I told you—'

'Yes, yes, I know what you said, about the birds. It was more than that though. You knew I was in trouble before the birds came and you knew exactly where to look for me.'

'I told you, it wasn't far and I know the moor.'

'You certainly do.' Ida shuddered. 'How can you bear it? It's so bleak and unforgiving. Dangerous.'

'You think that because you don't see it. You're wrong. It's beautiful.'

Out there and alone, Ida had seen only wildness and harsh, brutal loneliness. Heard the wind bending and beating, herding the clouds.

'I don't understand it,' she said. 'I live in a flat, Heather, in the middle of an ordinary town, with street lights. This is completely different from anything I've ever known.'

'Isn't that the point? The difference is what makes it beautiful.'

'I suppose it's because I'm not used to it.'

'You don't remember anything about being here? From before?'

'Heather, I was barely five when I went away.'

'I remember being born.'

Ida didn't believe her. Not for a moment. It sounded like another of the outlandish things her mother must have encouraged her to believe. In the silence, Ida realised there was very little about this strange girl she wanted to know. Heather disturbed the air. Even in their common language, when she spoke them she made her words sound other.

Ida pulled on a pair of dry socks. 'The woman in the shop. Catrin. She said the locals don't call this place Cloud House, or even by its Welsh name as far as I could tell. They called it, the old house.'

The kettle came to the boil and Heather poured hot water into mugs. 'You don't want to go taking any notice of her.' She placed the mugs on the table, pushed the milk carton towards Ida. 'You got any sugar?'

'No. And I hate it.' Ida reached for the milk. 'It's the right name though, isn't it? Ty'r…'

'Cwmwl.'

'Yes. It's on the deeds.'

'There you go then.' Heather took the chair opposite Ida. 'Superstitious and thick, most of that village.'

Ida said she could see why the house would have invited its name. 'I never saw so much cloud in my life, not day after day like this.'

Heather didn't say anything. Ida felt the heat from the girl's body, her knees under their layers nudging her own.

'So why *is* there all this cloud do you suppose? You must admit it's weird, like some kind of weather phenomenon.'

'Mam called it a concealing.'

She leaned closer and Ida caught the scent of her hair: violets and rain and bracken. Her pupils sparked, and Ida drew back, pressed her hand where her heart was beating.

138

Heather stared back for a long moment, drained her tea, as if the heat of it was nothing. She rinsed her mug under the tap and picked up her jacket. 'I best be off. Things to do, you know?'

Ida didn't, and she knew Heather knew it too – she was playing another one of her games and the rules were a moveable feast.

'I'll drop by tomorrow – show you the garden. Collect some apples.'

It was a statement rather than an offer and Ida was helpless again, gratitude making her incapable of protest.

'Okay,' she said. 'And thank you again. I mean it.'

As Heather left, each atom of energy in the room went with her. Ida crossed to the window, needing to see her leave, make sure she was gone. There was no sign of her. How did she manage to move with such speed and disappear so effectively?

The sky turned liquid and rain began to fall in tiny, furious shards, drenching the ground.

She'll be soaked.

Ida realised she minded, although she half-suspected Heather would be quite capable of conjuring some kind of concealing spell of her own, ensuring she arrived home as dry as a bone.

Ida felt the chill of her wet jeans seeping under her skin. The lower half of the window was open and rain spattered onto the sill. She wrestled with it, tried to pull it down and the rain beat a tattoo, as if it came for her. She was reminded of the black birds and how, in spite of what Heather said, out on the moor it had felt the same.

No... They were warning you...

The window frame groaned.

'Close, why don't you, you stupid thing!' The window slammed down with such force, Ida had to snatch away her hands. 'I've had enough of this dump.'

No one heard her and she was more alone than at any time since she'd arrived. The sooner she sold the place the better.

In her bedroom she undressed, pulled on her pyjamas and

139

cardigan. Her head was full of the cries of birds and she smelled rotting apples and dead leaves.

Ida's fist curled around the tiny diamond on the gold chain. Certain she would be awake for hours, she curled into her pillow. Even with the sheets so chilly they felt damp, she was fast asleep in seconds.

Twenty-four

By mid-morning the next day, Ida decided Heather must have forgotten about the garden and she crossed her fingers.

Still shaken by her experience on the moor, she had no desire to see the girl again. She didn't want to be reminded of her own vulnerability. At the same time, she reluctantly owned a myriad questions milling in her head.

What had Olwen's life been like – isolated out here with only her young daughter for company? She recalled Dan's words – how Olwen had kept herself to herself. How had she lived? Paid the rent and fed her child? If it was true, and she had been some kind of witch, it wasn't exactly a job description.

Ida wondered how Heather lived now. Two days a week in an animal shelter wouldn't pay much, in spite of what Dan Pritchard thought. Did she claim benefits? Technically, as she was only seventeen, someone still had a duty of care.

At the barn, Ida paused. Behind her the new day's cloud clung to the roof of the house. It was petulant weather, more like midwinter than early autumn. She heaved open the door and eyed the neatly stacked pile of wood. It rose several feet in height. A few split logs lay on the ground around a stump of wood.

Would Olwen have been strong enough to chop her own wood? Ida decided Olwen, and her daughter if they were minded to, could fell whole trees.

Picking over the split logs, Ida saw how the bark on them was rotting, leaving green slime on her fingers. She doubted it would burn. She spotted an axe leaning against a sawhorse. It looked heavy and Ida knew, even if she managed to pick it up, she wouldn't be able to swing it. A ballet dancer was only as strong as her last class, and Ida hadn't stretched her muscles for thirteen years.

She dragged the axe across the floor, ran her hand up and down the curved handle. The wood was smooth and worn, the metal head dull and pitted.

'Morning.'

The axe clattered to the ground. Heather's trick of manifesting out of the blue was becoming tiresome.

'Bloody hell, do you have to?'

'I didn't see you.'

'Yeah, right,' Ida muttered. 'You always see me.' The amused look was back in the girl's eyes. 'It isn't funny, Heather – you nearly gave me a heart attack. I could have cut my foot off.'

'So, not content with flinging yourself into a ravine, you're going in for a bit of self-mutilation too?'

It was her obsession … her demise…

'I didn't, and you aren't funny.'

A stab of pain jabbed at her foot. A chill ran down Ida's spine and she had the horrible feeling Heather could see through her skin to her badly healed bone, to her secrets.

The girl scuffed the toe of her muddy, unlaced boot in the dirt. 'You're hilarious.'

'Well, I'm glad you find my misfortune amusing.'

'Oh chill out. For someone who has the look of an old soul, you're well weird.'

It was another one of her talents: the ability to make mincemeat of a conversation and head it off on a cryptic tangent.

'What on earth are you talking about now? What's an old soul?'

'It means someone who's been here before. Only I'm not a hundred percent sure about you.'

Ida was tempted to sarcasm; to tell Heather she'd been here twenty-four years ago. Only she knew it wasn't what the girl meant.

'An old soul can walk between the worlds,' Heather said. 'It's a gift.'

'I haven't got the slightest idea what you're talking about.'

'I can show you if you like.'

You know you're safe because you know I won't agree.

This raw, rooted belief of Heather's made Ida nervous. She had no faith, orthodox or otherwise, and supposed this made her an atheist. It wasn't something she'd ever thought about. And Heather, she suspected, wasn't talking about religion.

'There's a lot of wood,' she said, determined to change the subject.

Heather kicked a few of the logs. 'Mam had this load delivered a month before she died.' She reached for a piece of sacking and placed it on the floor, sorted through the wood, choosing the driest pieces. 'There's probably some kindling in the cupboard and then all you need is firelighters. Next to electricity and tampons, Mam reckoned firelighters were way the best magic.' She grinned, rolled up the wood in the sacking, and dumped the bundle by the door. 'We can pick these up later.'

Paused in the light, she became a silhouette. Once again Ida thought it was deliberate. This girl knew exactly how to make herself appear both powerful and ambiguous.

'Are you coming?'

'Sorry?'

'The garden? I said I'd show you.'

Her eagerness was infectious. Ida told herself it wouldn't hurt, even if she wasn't planning on becoming a gardener. She wasn't planning on becoming anything. And what she knew about gardens could be written on the back of a seed packet.

The weight of the grey sky, the bland intensity of it as they emerged from the barn, was oppressive.

'I still don't understand this cloud,' Ida said. 'And there's no colour to it.'

'The colours are there if you look properly.'

'I'll take your word for it.'

Heather led Ida towards the garden, lifted the wooden gate and propped it open. It was greener than Ida expected, striated with flashes of colour darting like dragonflies. She stopped, uncertain before this oddly out of place garden.

Heather glanced back. 'You look scared stiff.'

'Well, I'm not.'

'So why do you look like the devil himself is after you?'

Ida ignored her, wrong-footed again and caught out. She was nervous and this strange girl not only knew it, she was enjoying herself. By the gate, Ida fought her reluctance. This wasn't her mother's garden, it was Olwen's. Ghosts went wherever they chose and what was to stop Heather's mother following them into this strange, forbidding place?

'You coming or what?'

By the time Ida would have been old enough to follow her mother outside and play in this garden, Anna had already been planning her escape. Had she ever thought it magical, inhabited, perhaps, by fairies?

If you left your memories alone for too long, they disappeared.

'This garden is the only place round here where twilight happens,' Heather said. 'It's why you think you can see ghosts.'

On either side of obscured paths, plants grew in muddled confusion.

Ida kicked a bramble out of the way.

Heather narrowed her eyes. 'Do you wish you could see the ghost of *your* mother?'

'I don't want to talk about my mother.'

'Even if you wanted to, you probably won't. I bet your mother never even came out here. Anything she left behind is in the house.'

Ida knew this wasn't true. However hard she searched she would find no trace of her mother inside Cloud House or out here. Heather didn't know what she was talking about.

144

'See them?' The girl pointed to a scattering of pale yellow and orange flowers. The leaves were shaped like lily pads. 'Mam planted them from seed when I was a kid, and they've spread like a river. The flowers won't be completely gone until midwinter and I've never seen anyone able to make them last that long.'

'Nasturtiums,' Ida said.

'Well, get you, townie.' Heather picked off a leaf, handed it to Ida. 'Ever eaten one? Go on – they're delicious.'

'I—'

'I'm not going to poison you, Ida Spider, why would I?'

Because you hate me and you see me as an intruder, and your mother was a witch and she's haunting the house and this garden and...

Ida put the leaf in her mouth and instantly the taste of sweet pepper overwhelmed her.

Heather grinned. 'Lush, isn't it?' She moved away, through the weeds and raggedy plants: lolling pale yellow roses, reluctant to give up on summer, and lavender, still with a few soft blue spikes, bent over the invisible paths. Clumps of small lily-like flowers in shades of peach and green mingled with stands of fading Michaelmas daisies.

'What's that?' Ida pointed to a large bushy plant close to the wall.

'Buddleia. Gorgeous come summer. For the butterflies and bees.'

A long time ago someone had planted an apple tree in the centre of the garden. Over time it had grown twisted, bark peeling, the fruit wormed and bittersweet. Underneath it, a curved wooden bench leaned into the trunk. On the ground lay dozens of windfalls, pitted and dried out. And in the branches hung more tiny wind chimes, fashioned from bird bones and feathers.

Out here, the scent of apples was different, less pungent. Ida breathed in and the sweetness caught in her throat.

Heather patted the seat, inviting Ida to join her.

'One thing I do recall,' Ida said, 'is my mother complaining how the ground was too stony to grow anything.'

Heather picked the head off a dandelion. 'Goes to show how much she knew.'

'Quite.' Ida wasn't going to rise to the bait.

'Mam knew which plants were best suited to the soil. She said it was about understanding what it wanted. She had plans to turn this into a physic garden.'

'Sorry?'

'For medicinal plants. Like in medieval times.'

Something fluttered past Ida's cheek. A brown leaf landed on her shoulder.

A dead leaf falling on you is a sign of a restless ghost…

Ida flicked the leaf away, hoping Heather hadn't noticed. She focused on the garden. It didn't matter how well you cared for it, once you stopped tending a garden, it reverted to doing exactly as it pleased. It was easy to believe this one would last forever, minding its own business, like the sky and the oblivious moorland.

'It might not look like it to you,' Heather said. 'I do take care of it. And Mam's spirit does too. Most of what she ever needed is planted in here – for her spells and potions.'

Ida didn't like the way the conversation was going.

'You're doing it again,' she said.

'Doing what?'

'Trying to scare me.'

Heather flicked the dandelion head away and it hovered, a bright yellow disc on the air before falling to the ground. 'Doesn't take much, does it?'

'Listen,' Ida said, 'I can see for myself what needs doing out here.'

'I know what needs doing!'

'Perhaps, it's not the point.'

'Are you telling me not to come out here anymore?'

'No, not exactly. And in any case…'

'In any case, what?'

'I…' The words stopped in her throat and Ida swallowed them. She knew Heather was beginning to feel safe again. If she told her the truth, that she was going to sell the house, she could only half-imagine the fury it might unleash 'Nothing. I mean, well, there's no need for you to come here is there?'

'You're a piece of work, and no mistake,' Heather said, her face tightening. 'No need to come to the house, no need to see to the garden. Nothing sinks in with you does it?' Her eyes were reckless as lightning. 'There is *every* need.'

It wasn't hard to fight with her.

Ida had never met anyone quite so confrontational. The most innocuous words seemed loaded with contention, turning a simple exchange into a dispute.

'Oh, don't, Heather. Please don't make this something it isn't. I'm trying to find my way – by myself, if that isn't too hard for you to understand. It's how I do things.'

Heather glared. 'Well you know best, Ida Spider. Whatever you say.'

Again, Ida refused to retaliate. 'I mean it, Heather. There's no reason for us to snipe like this. I understand, about the house, about how much it means to you. And I feel responsible.'

'Well don't. I'm responsible for myself.'

Ida sighed. 'That's as maybe. What you need to know is, just because I prefer being on my own, it doesn't mean I don't want to get to know you.'

'Meaning?'

What did she mean? Once again Ida was wrong-footed. Heather had as good as let her off the hook and here she was, flinging herself back on it.

'Well, you've told me about your mother, what about your father?'

'Don't know anything about him.'

147

'What? Nothing at all?'

'Didn't know him.' Heather shifted her feet, as if to slide the conversation away.

'I'm sorry about that.' Ida's foot was aching and she sat down again. 'I can't get anything right can I?'

Heather pulled on a branch of the apple tree, picked a yellowing leaf and stared at it. 'Mam didn't talk about him. Why would she? He was nobody. Some random bloke from nowhere.'

'She must have told you something.'

'I don't even know his name. And I don't care. You can't hate a person you've never known. I don't need to look for a part of me I wouldn't have liked. A person I might have hated.'

The Welsh bit of you … see if it remembers…

'It must have been hard on your mum. On both of you.'

'No, it wasn't,' Heather said. 'Mam was tough. She wasn't ashamed about having me. She said she'd never get married anyway. Called it slavery.' Heather stared at the leaf, still caught between her fingers. 'I don't suppose she liked it that he left her. Who would? But what kind of a man dumps his pregnant girlfriend? Better off without him. And I told you, Mam was tough. We managed.'

'Yes, I can see that.'

'He wasn't important.'

Ida thought about her own father, how he had loved her mother so much it was little short of devotion.

'Men, eh,' she said, for want of anything else.

Heather gave her a look. 'Mam didn't need a man. She had me. And I had her. I didn't need a father.'

Ida shivered. 'I'm cold. Can we go?'

'You don't like me talking about it, do you?' Heather faced her down. 'You ask your questions and as soon as I start telling you stuff, you wish you hadn't bothered.'

Once again, it was like having her mind read.

'I'm going inside.'

Heather didn't reply.

'You can come in if you like,' Ida heard herself say. 'Have a cup of tea.'

She stopped and Heather was at her shoulder. Close up, she smelled of marigolds, dew and derision, and Ida thought how strange it was that a person's scent could change so completely from one day to the next.

'I thought you wanted to be by yourself.'

Ida said she did. 'It's freezing though, and quite a ride back to the village. At least have a cup of tea before you go.'

As she spoke, one of the black birds landed in the apple tree and Ida flinched. It bent its head to one side and its visible eye scanned her. She looked away and saw Heather watching her with an odd, covert look.

Tell her to go and not to come back...

'I'm used to it. But okay, if you like.' She pulled down one of the tree branches, picked three apples. 'Here, take these in. I'll get the wood.'

Ida cupped the apples in her hands. They were yellowy green and smelled fresh. She watched as Heather made her way across the yard to the barn, scooped up the bundled wood.

'You can collect the deadfall from the trees around the house too you know,' she called. 'When it's dry it burns lovely.'

'Thank you, I'll remember.' Ida hugged the apples against her chest with one hand, held open the back door with the other. Still maintaining the pretence of staying at Ty'r Cwmwl, she said, 'You're right – I need to get sorted before the nights draw in. Some days are barely light enough to see.'

'It's the season, changing. Come winter, the frosts will kill the bugs, keep the colds at bay. It's what Mam used to say.'

They didn't kill them all though did they?

Ida kept her unkind thought to herself.

'And you wait until spring,' Heather went on. 'If you stay that long you'll see some wonders.'

149

Spring played no part in Ida's plans. If she had her way, she wouldn't be there for more than another couple of weeks.

Twenty-five

The moment Heather came indoors, it was as if the room expected her.

She had an easy way about her and Ida thought it must come from having been born and brought up there. It gave her an advantage Ida found hard not to resent.

'You can put the apples in the bowl,' Heather said, and Ida did, reluctant to start an argument by reminding the girl, yet again, whose house it was. Heather stacked the logs, neatly, by the range and Ida left her to it, busied herself making tea.

'It draws nicely, this range,' Heather said. In the cupboard housing the boiler she found a box of dry kindling and a pile of old newspapers. 'There you go, and look, I told you there'd be some.' She held up a crushed box of firelighters. 'If you can't start a fire with this lot, there's no hope for you.'

She didn't offer to do it and Ida sensed another challenge. Setting the mugs on the table, she allowed herself a smile.

I'll do it or die in the attempt.

Heather pulled out a chair, plonked herself down and drew the blue bowl to her, smoothed the three apples.

'Pretty, isn't it?' Ida said.

'Mam made it. She did a pottery class only she got bored. Said they were a pretentious, posh lot. This was the only thing she made. She always kept her apples in it.' Her voice became deliberate. 'On this table.'

As Heather spoke, Ida found her eyes drawn to the apples, and she could smell them, ripe and sweetly pungent. Swallowing, she turned to the fridge for milk, and changed the subject.

'Do you ever think about leaving?' she asked. 'And don't get defensive, I'm not meddling, I'm curious, that's all.'

'Why would I do that?'

'Broaden your horizons?'

'Like you, you mean?'

'Touché.' Ida smiled. 'You must have ambitions though – a bright girl like you.'

'I like it here.' Heather paused. 'And out on the moor. I'm not so keen on the village mind.'

'You must know a great deal about herbs and stuff.' Ida sat down opposite Heather. 'You could study it – get away from the village and go to college. Become a proper, medicinal herbalist.'

'Mam was a proper herbalist.'

'I only meant—'

'I know what you meant.' Heather pushed the bowl to the centre of the table.

'Tell me more about her.'

'She was beautiful. Fearsome.'

'That's an odd thing to say about your mother.'

'Is it?' Heather shrugged. 'Well she was. She was brave. Nothing scared her. She wasn't afraid of anybody.'

And you want me to know that more than you want me to know if she was clever or kind or in any way talented.

'I dream about her most nights.'

'I never dream.' The words were out before Ida checked them.

'Everybody dreams.'

'Not me.'

'You don't remember them, that's all.' Heather stirred milk into her tea. 'Dreams make us powerful.'

Ida didn't want power. She wanted to be left alone and once again, here she was, allowing herself to be pulled into this crazy girl's fancy.

Heather persisted. 'Dreams are signposts.'

'Well, I'm sure they are and remarkably – considering I'm such

152

a townie – I managed to find my way here in spite of the weird Welsh signs and a lack of dreaming. And for now, I'm not planning on going anywhere.'

Mentally, she crossed her fingers, avoided Heather's gaze.

'We're all going somewhere, Ida: one way or another.'

There was so much meaning behind her words, Ida was at a loss to try and unpack it.

'If she'd known about the snow,' Heather said, 'she wouldn't have sent me away.'

'What?'

'You asked me to tell you about my mam.'

'Well, yes, I did.'

'Story time again, is it?' Heather's face changed, softened slightly as if she was fixing it in place. 'She was ill. There was 'flu everywhere and of course, they all wanted a remedy, even the ones who pretended they didn't believe in them.' A soft shrug and she sighed. 'Mam sent me to the village with medicine for Auntie Bethan and another lady – Mrs Williams – her husband was bad with his chest. Her boy too.' Heather stared into her tea. 'The snow had been in the air for days, biding its time. It was starting when I left and I didn't want to go but Mam made me. And then the snow came on hard, like a curse.'

'What do you mean?'

'It was a blizzard and I couldn't get back. I don't know why she hadn't realised. Except she probably did. She was always more concerned about other people than herself. Maybe it was the fever getting worse, I don't know.' Heather paused and the lights in her eyes shone like tears. 'She should have watched the stars. Snow stars are bright and they glitter. Only she didn't, or if she did, she took no notice.'

Ida wasn't unmoved by Heather's words; she was perturbed and deeply unsettled by them.

I don't need a confidante and I don't want to be hers.

They had drifted into one another's lives like litter on the wind and now Ida felt uncomfortably trapped. She forced herself to listen, even though she no longer wanted to hear another word of Heather's story, sensing that knowing it would somehow bind them even more.

The girl was tapping her foot on the floor, a nervous movement she appeared oblivious to. 'Mam waited for me, see. She died, but her soul held on until I got here, so I could watch it leave. And I did, and I saw what stayed behind too. I took hold of her hand… ' Heather's voice cracked and she swallowed before carrying on. 'It was cold as ice, but I watched the little lines around her eyes melt away. I pushed open the window so the free spirit part of her could escape. I knew she needed to be able to come and go. Still be about her business.'

When Heather stopped talking, Ida didn't know what to say, only it didn't matter. The girl laughed, the sound sharp as knives. Her face changed again and in an instant the guarded arrogance was back.

'You look a right idiot.'

'What?'

'Your face. It's only a story. About how my mam died. I'm sure yours is every bit as tragic.' Her face was a mask again, her emotions coiled into a ball, daring Ida to challenge her. 'Remind me to ask you about it sometime.'

'Are you for real?' Shocked and furious, Ida stood up so fast the chair fell backwards, clattering to the floor. Before the threatening tears welled up, she told Heather to leave. 'I'm sorry about your mother, Heather, only you can't keep messing with my head like this. I can't deal with it any more. You need to go.' She turned away, placed her hands on the sink and bowed her head. Bit her lip to stop more words forming.

When she looked up again, Heather had disappeared the way she arrived – silently – like she had planned it that way.

With the shade of Olwen Morgan hovering at her shoulder, Ida sat on the front doorstep.

There was less light than usual. She could barely see and it was easy to imagine it a ghost house inhabited by Olwen and Heather. Ty'r Cwmwl was redolent with their presence.

Heather's story horrified her. What a dreadful way to die. Holed up in a snow storm with no form of communication. Freezing to death. Ida was surrounded by death and it confused her because the only person who had died here was the one person who felt most alive to her. Since arriving at Cloud House, Ida's sense of her own mother had been quietly diminishing, overwhelmed by the ubiquity – real or imaged – of Olwen Morgan. She wrapped her arms tightly round her body. Olwen wasn't real and Ida needed her parents' memory to unseat her.

'I need *you* to be real, Mum. And Dad too… Are you turning into a ghost as well?' Her whispered words drifted into the gloom.

She recalled Heather saying her mother had been fearsome – how Olwen hadn't needed a man, and she hadn't needed a father.

We all need a father of some sort.

Ida had no idea what to do about Heather, only that she must either let her in or make sure she couldn't have access to the house.

In the intermittent moonlight she imagined footprints down the track and a sense of being observed overwhelmed her. There was nothing, no birds or moths or ghosts and yet still, she felt surrounded. The sky turned to indigo, low enough to seem within reach. The air smelled of soil and wild animals, the witch trees bent and creaked and Ida could barely breathe.

It was as if she had swallowed stones.

It's all in your head of course, this idea you have, that if you look hard enough you'll see a ghost.

Lonely people think they see more than they do – they have too much time on their hands.

I'm too quick for you; the caught thing at the edge of what you imagine. Witches don't shape-shift or fly, not outside of fairy tales. The ghost of a wise woman can make you think she's doing both these things, and more, if she chooses. I don't. If I did, I'd be the witch you think I am: appear as a crow or a badger or a bat. I'd wrap myself in moonlight and show you – for want of a better expression – a real live ghostly witch.

My mother disdained ostentation however, and told me no one liked a show-off.

Visibility upsets the balance and unless there's a reason, I don't care to be seen. There are quieter ways to make my presence known and you already sense me.

There is hurt inside you – I sense it the way you sense me – and not only in that badly healed bone of yours. Which, by the way, I'd have mended in no time.

Heather's right. (You ought to take more notice of her.) The old ways, some of them at least, are still the best. Knitbone – that's the stuff. It grows in my garden. You'll find it if you look hard enough.

And don't be offended when my girl calls you "spider". It's a compliment. A spider has more eyes than you'll ever find use for. And magic too – spider is a wonder – resolute and tenacious. She's a repairer and she'll spin and wind and bind the good spells.

It really is all in your head.

The thing is though, until I'm at peace, I'm tricksy.

I'm the tick of that old clock and the wordless whispers in your cobwebbed sleep. I'm the scent of apples and soot and feathers. I slip through open windows, in and out on your whim now, not mine. I drift through woman-shaped keyholes. Slip and smile and you taste me on your bitten lip.

It isn't my job to make things easy for you. You have your own decisions to make.

Stay or go?

That is the question, girl with no feet, and who knows how many answers there are?

Twenty-six

A deeper sleep than any she'd had since arriving in Wales left Ida groggy, exacerbating her anxiety.

A vague unease sat like a ghost-hand on her shoulder, the certainty that at any moment, Heather might turn up, unannounced and unfazed by Ida's pathetic attempts at hostility.

Unless she hid, there was no way she could pretend not to be at home. Ida didn't imagine there were any hiding places in Ty'r Cwmwl unknown to Heather.

Dwelling on the girl, on her snooping and her disclosure about her mother's death, threw Ida back into the reason why she was here in the first place. Unlike Heather, she felt no sense of ownership. Ty'r Cwmwl may have been her birthright, but it was a burden.

Checking her phone there were only text messages from Liz, which she didn't answer. From the solicitor, there was nothing.

Aimless, and with the shreds of Heather's story still nudging, Ida wandered through the house, peered into the room Heather still hadn't cleared of her belongings.

Bloody cheek.

Ida supposed she could do it herself only she wasn't sure she wanted another face-off. Closing the door, she paused outside the room Heather still insisted had been Olwen's.

You better not have touched anything.

Heather had been far too proprietorial about the room and in particular, the bureau. Ida wondered where the key might be.

Downstairs, she made a desultory search, exhausted all the likely hiding places. Scrabbling in the dresser drawer for a second time, she found a screwdriver.

It occurred to her she could prise the bureau open.

It was hers … from the day she came here…

In which case, not hers. It had been borrowed.

Armed with the screwdriver, Ida made her way back to the dingy room. This time, as she opened the door, instead of apples and dust she caught a whiff of candle wax. On the windowsill, in the battered tin holder, the candle glistened and soft wax pooled round the blackened wick. When she touched it the wax was still soft and barely beginning to solidify.

Had someone lit it? Impossible. It must be the warmth from the sun.

Ida didn't need to look out of the window to see there was no sun.

'Then it's my imagination.' Deliberately, she spoke out loud, summoning a mote of defiance. 'Nothing more than a flight of fancy.'

The screwdriver hung in her hand like a gimmick. She turned to the bureau, poked the end of the screwdriver under the lip of the fallboard, above the lock. Wriggling it around, she swore as it slipped, and a small scratch appeared on the wood.

'Damn, you stupid thing.'

She tried again, prised the tip of the screwdriver up and down to no avail knowing it wasn't going to work. The bureau was solid, and it would take more than a bit of metal to break it open. Without the key, other than taking an axe to it, there was no way Ida was going to open the thing. And in any case, she didn't want to damage it.

'*Ida…*'

It was little more than a whisper. She whirled. The room was empty.

A breath stroked her ear.

'Who…?' Trembling, she clutched the screwdriver, and a chill ran down her spine. 'Hello?'

Nothing: other than her absolute conviction someone else was in the room with her. Another sound, a swish and a thud. 'Is that you, Heather?'

'Well, it's not the Free Wales Army is it?'

The screwdriver clattered to the floor. 'Jesus Christ, you nearly gave me a heart attack.'

Heather hovered in the doorway, leaning against the jamb, arms folded; her face animated with provocation. Too alarmed to be angry, Ida stood with her back to the bureau, trying to conceal it.

Will she be able to tell I've been tampering with the lock?

'Oh, sorry, did I scare you?' Heather raised her eyebrows. 'You need to get a grip on your nerves.'

'Was that you – before – calling out to me?'

The girl let her arms drop and came into the room. 'Me? No.'

'Are you sure? I thought I heard—'

'More ghosts, Ida Spider?'

'Can you *please* stop calling me that?' The words came out in a strangled shout.

'Touchy or what? It's only a bit of fun.'

Ida swallowed. Her anger mounting, she took a step closer to the girl. Heather side-stepped, looked right through Ida, stared at the bureau and a small hiss of rage escaped her mouth. Her eyes fell on the screwdriver and her expression clouded.

'You wouldn't bloody dare.' Snatching up the screwdriver from the floor she waved it in Ida's face. 'Tell me you haven't. Oh my god, you have though, haven't you? You've been trying to break into my mam's bureau.'

Ida backed away, shaking with fury and guilt. 'How many times? It isn't your bloody *mam's* bureau! And it's none of your business what I do – this is my house and—'

Heather flung down her disdain the way she might scatter birdseed. 'You think you're something, don't you? But you know what, Ida *Spider*, you're pathetic. You've no respect and if you'd half a brain in that stupid *English* head of yours, you'd stay out of things that don't concern you.'

160

She dropped the screwdriver, held back her mass of hair with both hands, exposing her face in such a deliberate fashion Ida was unable to move. She stared, at the star-coloured eyes, and she was seeing someone on the edge, as afraid as she was enraged.

'What do you think you're looking at?' Heather let go of her hair and it fell like an overblown flower. She met Ida's look and it was bold and uncompromising again. 'Cat got your tongue? You're unbelievable, you are.'

Ida was the first to look away. 'I want you to leave,' she said, her voice shaking. 'And I want any keys you've got: for both doors and the one to this bureau. Because I know you have them and if you don't give them to me – all of them – I shall take the necessary steps.'

There was something incredulous in Heather's expression now. 'Necessary steps? Are you threatening me? Again?'

'Just hand them over, Heather.'

The girl let out a disdainful laugh and it was as unnerving as her arrogance. 'Mam was *very* careful about keys. And I told you, if there's one for that bureau, I don't have it.' She fished in the pocket of her jacket. 'As for the house keys, you're welcome.' She dropped a small metal ring holding two keys onto the floor. 'Have them. Take more than a key to keep me from anywhere I want to be.'

Ida ignored this. 'If you have spares, I want them too.'

'Well, if I did, I've lost them.'

Ida held her gaze. 'You've never lost anything in your life.'

As she said this she knew it was true and the look on Heather's face confirmed it. Pushing past her, Ida stamped down the stairs.

'I have to go out,' she said, having no idea where, only that she wanted to be away from the house. 'So I want you to leave, and this time I mean it. No more trespassing, Heather. If you want to come and pay your respects to your mother, that's fine, but you have to stop treating this house like you own it.'

'Don't pretend to be interested in my mother.'

It was as if yesterday's conversation had never taken place.

Ida kept a hold on her temper. 'I'm doing my best here, Heather. Trying to be reasonable and understand.'

'Understand what?'

'For god's sake, I'm not the enemy.' Ida wrenched open the front door, gestured through it with her arm. 'Now, please. Go.'

'Whatever you say, *Ida*.' Heather's quicksilver eyes flashed and she turned on her heel, strode through the door and across to the gate to where her bicycle lay propped against the wall. 'If you're going to the village, can I have a lift? I've got a puncture.'

Utterly taken back by this fresh tangent, and the audacity of the request, Ida was lost for words. She stared at the wheels of the bicycle, unable to tell if Heather was lying or not.

That's how stupid I am – I can't tell a flat tyre from a hole in my head.

Once again, Heather caught her thoughts. 'It's a slow one; it'll burst if I ride it.'

'You better get in then. I'll drop you off.'

It occurred to Ida to offer to somehow tie the bike to her car. It would need rope and more time and the logistics floored her. Heather slid into the passenger seat and Ida turned the key. The engine groaned and faltered. She tried again and the same thing happened.

She banged the steering wheel with her fist. 'Shit, shit, shit. Stupid bloody car.' Ida hadn't sworn this much in her entire life.

'You need a mechanic,' Heather said.

'I need you to shut up!'

'I know one. That's all I'm saying.'

Ida sighed and slumped back in her seat. 'Okay, do you have a number?'

'Phone the garage, ask for Roni. Parry's. It's in the book.'

'Thank you.'

'I'll be off then.' Heather slammed the door and picked up her bicycle. 'May as well push it home.'

Ida slammed the car door. 'You'll survive.'

Heather stared at her and it was there again: the scornful light in her eyes.

Without waiting for a reply, Ida returned to the house, slammed the door firmly behind her and dropped the latch.

In the kitchen, on the windowsill under a pile of cookery books, she found a well-thumbed telephone directory, and the number for Parry's Garage.

Her phone was devoid of signal and reluctant to go outside again, she went into the hall and tried the landline. It was still working and she tapped out the number.

'Yes?' A brusque, impatient voice answered.

'Er, may I speak to Roni, please?'

'No.'

'Oh, I—'

'She's not here.'

She? A woman mechanic. The place was full of surprises. Ida could only hope she was friendlier than her aunt or her neighbours.

'Right.' Ida coughed. 'When will she be back? It's my car you see and—'

'I'll tell her. What's your number?'

'Do you have a pen?'

'Just give me the number. I don't have all day, I got customers.'

I'm a customer. Or at least I might be.

The woman was shouting now, loudly, and with the telephone receiver still clamped in place Ida was deafened. 'Be with you now, Aled. Someone for our Roni.'

Ida didn't know the landline number so she recited her mobile one.

'There we are. She'll call you.' And the line went dead.

Twenty-seven

Rain didn't bother Heather.

Her jacket was lined with fleece and her mother had sewn feathers between the layers. Bird feathers were waterproof.

As she pushed her bicycle up the slope Heather smiled and stamped through the puddles, enjoying the sound her boots made, sensing the vibrations. The ground thrummed beneath her feet and changed key. The rain on her face was cool and sweet. There was no such thing as bad weather. Some of it was wild and if you weren't careful you'd be caught up in it.

Just like Ida Spider.

Rain like this was gentle and refreshing. Looking up, she spotted several black birds circling against the sky, calling. Heather loved the sound of them, singing songs with no words because they didn't need them. Shading her eyes, she watched as they moved in time with the cloud. Remembering how they had flown through the mist and cloud to save Ida, she smiled. If she was too stupid to know the difference between a bird attack and a warning, she had no business living here.

The birds rose higher, shaggy and graceful, circling and flapping their sail wings.

She'll pay for her meddling. I saw those scratch marks on Mam's bureau and I don't care if I scared her. She has no respect.

Heather didn't have the key to the bureau. If her mother hadn't wanted it to be found, it wouldn't be. As for her precious house keys, Heather had several and Ida was welcome to them all.

I'll keep her guessing mind – it's a game and it's fun.

If you didn't say words out loud, no one could accuse you of doing wrong or telling lies.

At the top of the slope, the ground fell away and Heather jumped on the bike, freewheeling down the familiar path, not caring if she ruined the tyre. There were plenty of tyres. If she wrecked this one, Roni would find her another.

Heather flew along the path, knowing exactly where she was going, avoiding the dips and rocks with skill. She was made of her mother's glamours and nothing could harm her.

She doesn't like her nickname one bit, Miss Ida Spider.

Heather grinned. Well tough, it's what she was, a meddlesome spider and Heather wasn't in the mood to placate Ida's sensibilities. Ida thought she could get the better of her – get rid of her. Heather didn't care about that either. It would take more than a bit of shouting or daft threats to make her leave.

I can see right through her.

Heather already knew a lot about Ida: how she didn't like surprises and the family tree she came from had as few branches as her own. How she wore a gold chain with a tiny diamond pendant under her jumper. How she was scared of ghosts and witches, and no matter how much she liked to kid herself, she believed in them too.

The village appeared at the bottom of the hill. Heather slowed down, the uneven thump of the tyre harsh against the metal frame. She'd have to get it fixed. She needed her bicycle or how else was she going to get around? Get up to Ty'r Cwmwl.

If Ida thought she'd frightened Heather away she had another think coming.

'Dream on, lady.'

She said she didn't dream. Heather didn't believe her. Her mother had said, if you didn't dream you became a hostage to your imagination. And it would get the better of you until it drove you mad.

Maybe that was it then, and Ida was going mad.

Part Two

Twenty-eight

Restless and impatient, Ida sat on the edge of the sofa in the parlour, trying to ignore the ache in her instep.

Still smarting from yesterday's run-in with Heather, Ida realised that without her car there was no escape. Until she rested her foot, walking further than the barn was, for a day or two at least, out of the question.

A single bar of service flickered in the corner of her phone screen. Glaring at it, she willed it to ring. It wouldn't surprise her if the woman at the garage hadn't bothered to pass on her message.

She tried her text messages and caught one from Liz.

Not funny. Not clever. Call me or I'm coming to Wales x

Ida tapped out a reply, an apology and a promise to call. She clicked send but it failed and the phone died. Flinging it to one side, her eye caught the clock on the mantelpiece, stalled at twenty-five to four.

It did that when she died...

The altercation with Heather sat heavily. The previous evening, Ida thought she'd seen her near the garden. It had turned out to be nothing more than shadows and skeins of mist. If the girl had come back, she was making herself scarce – wandering in the grove perhaps, and Ida tried to tell herself she didn't mind. Nevertheless, she found herself watching from windows, scanning the garden and the moorland beyond.

She wondered how Heather had managed, pushing her bicycle all the way home in the rain.

Not my problem.

Ida was under no obligation to the girl and frankly, after what

169

had happened, she didn't see why she should care about her. If she never saw her again it would be too soon.

She didn't like herself one bit. She liked Heather even less.

Her mother would have been shocked. Kindness cost nothing and Ida knew she hadn't been kind. She was twelve years older than Heather and ought to know better. And it was ridiculous to allow herself to be intimidated by a teenager. She told herself to get the car fixed and have a proper day out. Forget about Heather.

The truth was, Ida found herself thinking about her all the time. She thought about her the moment she woke and remembered where she was. Each time Ida touched something in the house, moved a chair or straightened a picture, she was aware of Heather's presence.

And Olwen's.

Had the clock really stopped the moment she died?

Curious, she stood up and lifted it down. It was heavy and elegant, the frame curved and made from dark wood. An oval face under a convex glass was adorned with slender black hands.

Ida turned it over, searching for the winding mechanism. A single brass key protruded from the back. She began turning it, waiting for the click as the ticking began. When it didn't, and when after a few turns the key stuck, the silence was unnerving. She tried again and this time the key refused to turn at all. She peered at the back plate and noticed a second key hole – presumably, the one to move the hands. Irritated, she jiggled the key. It was stuck fast.

Thrusting the clock back onto the mantelpiece, Ida tried not to read anything into the fact it might have stopped at the time Heather said her mother died. The clock was old and more than likely hadn't worked for years.

All the clocks except for this one…

Other than the longcase clock in the hall, Ida couldn't recall seeing any others. In the hallway, she thrust open the door to her father's empty study. There were no clocks in there. She went into the kitchen and scanned the room. On the wall next to the back door, a small clock set in a cheap plastic casing hung above an out-of-date wall calendar. If Ida had noticed it before, it hadn't registered.

Now it did.

The hands stood at twenty-five to four precisely. Unable to take her eyes off it, Ida told herself it was a coincidence. Either that or another of Heather's tricks.

A shrill ringing sounded in her ears – loud and urgent. It took Ida a few seconds to realise it was her mobile phone. She ran back to the parlour and snatched it up. 'Yes?'

The voice at the other end of the line was warm, Welsh and laconic. 'Is this Ida Llewellyn?'

'Yes, it is.'

'Roni Jones. Hi. My auntie said you have a problem with your car?'

Relief flooded through Ida. 'Oh hi, yes. Ida Llewellyn. I rang.'

'Yes, I know, *bach*, that's why I'm calling you back.'

'Right, of course. Sorry.' Flustered, Ida cleared her throat. 'It won't start. The car. I didn't have a chance to explain to – er, your auntie. She was a bit…' The connection faltered. 'Are you still there?'

'Just about. Keep going. And don't mind Auntie Gladys. She's rude to everyone.'

'Is it a thing, round here?'

Oh god, please tell me I didn't say that.

When Roni let out a low laugh, Ida nearly wept with relief. She made her way to the front door, walked a few paces from the house.

'You've met the locals then?'

'I'm sorry, how incredibly rude of me – it's just—'

'It's just that everyone *is* rude, even when they don't realise. Let me guess – you got the third degree in the shop; Brenda Lewis stared you out and Catrin Pritchard knew all about you, palmed you off with a load of out-of-date food and you've decided you're never going back there again.'

'Something like that. How did you know?'

Roni laughed again, and the sound of it faded and returned like a lulling wave. 'Wild guess?'

'I really am sorry. I hope I haven't offended you.'

'Not at all. Don't worry about it. You have, for some reason best known to yourself, decided to come and live in the back of beyond. And frankly, the last time anyone round here welcomed strangers, they were still burning witches.'

Ida's mouth dropped open.

'I'm joking.'

'Of course you are.'

'So, your car won't start.'

'No. And I don't know the first thing about them.'

'Well that's a relief. If everyone knew how to fix their car, I'd be out of a job. Right, when would suit you?'

Ida wandered down the track, the phone clamped to her ear. 'Oh, whenever's best for you. I don't need to be anywhere urgently.'

'Right you are then *bach*, I'll be over first thing day after tomorrow. That do you?'

'That's fantastic, thank you so much…' Another dead spot and Ida thought they'd finally been cut off.

'Still there?'

'Yes. Yes, I am. Thank you, Roni.'

'No problem. Have the kettle on, all right?'

'Of course.'

'See you. Ta-ra.'

The line went dead and a grin spread across Ida's face. Roni Jones sounded so normal, she half-thought she must have imagined her. At last, a straightforward conversation with a sensible person. And one who appeared to have some sympathy for her situation.

Ida retraced her steps to the house, walked into the kitchen and made a face at the clock on the wall.

'Stay stopped. See if I care.' She unhooked it. It was a cheap, battery-operated affair and turning it over Ida saw the battery was missing. No wonder it had stopped. Dead as a dodo. Ida would bet money on Heather having removed the battery herself, and fixing the hands at three thirty-five, to spook her.

'Either way, if you don't work, what's the point in you?'

Marching outside, Ida heaved the lid off the black dustbin and dropped the clock inside.

It landed with a thud and she slammed the lid down.

'Tick, bloody tock, Heather.'

Her supper dishes washed, Ida made coffee and with a steaming mug in her hand, opened the heavy front door. The moon was pale, a paring off full above a bank of cloud. A few stars stabbed the sky. When the cloud shifted, the moon lit up the track, dotting it with silver specks like flowers. Ida walked into the shine of them; imagined picking a bouquet, arranging them in a vase. At the end of the track, she turned and the house loomed, its windows blank and black.

Save for one.

In the window of the room inhabited by the ghost of the wrong mother, a shred of pale light wavered.

Candlelight.

Ida's coffee mug slipped from her fingers, landing with a dull thud on the grass. A deep sense of foreboding gnawed at her and she tore back along the path, fear and adrenaline fighting for precedence. She pounded up the stairs and flung open the door to the room she was, despite herself, beginning to think of as Olwen's.

Moonlight shifted in the shadows. Ida saw the bureau, with its tell-tale scratch, the grubby cushions on the floor. And on the windowsill, a stump of yellowing, unlit candle. When she touched her finger to the blackened wick it was stiff, and the greasy wax was icy cold.

Twenty-nine

Ida woke late, sat bolt upright, and rubbed her hand across her face.

She could still smell the dead candle, the stagnant wax. She thought how she had imagined silver flowers on the track. Was it too much to imagine the flame had been an illusion too and what she had actually seen had been a trick of moonlight?

Her foot ached and she flexed it. She'd run like a wild thing along the track.

Like the devil himself is after you.

'Stop it.' Admonishing herself out loud was becoming another device aimed at maintaining her sanity.

Sitting up, she pulled back the covers, ran her fingers across the bony ridge of her foot. She thought how deformed it looked, and how no one would ever find a foot like that anything other than ugly.

Concentrate…

Falling…

Chaîné *turns unfolding like heartbeats…*

Pulling on a pair of socks, Ida shook off the memory, stood at the bedroom window, the curtain held to one side. She followed the lines of the witch trees, the bent shape of them. In the distance, the land was intransigent and solemn and she wondered if she would ever become used to it. Get to know it, the way Heather clearly did.

She let out a sigh. It wasn't in her nature to be insensitive or callous. She reminded herself how sad Heather must be, how lonely. Was it even legal for her to be living in the village by herself? Ida thought not, and recalled how Dan Pritchard had dismissed social workers. It was no life for a teenage girl. What would become of her?

The girl's overt hostility – to say nothing of her rudeness – meant Ida had been struggling to find a thread of understanding, and few if any words of consolation. She needed to do better, behave like an adult and make allowances.

Startled out of her thoughts by a loud noise, Ida dropped the curtain. For a second, she thought it was thunder. It wasn't raining though and when the noise started up again, she recognised it. A loud flapping: a bird must be trapped in one of the other bedrooms. Opening her door a few inches, she listened again. More frantic flapping sounded and a harsh, alarmed cry.

It was coming from Olwen's room. Ida crossed the landing, grasped the door knob and as she did, immediately knew an echo of her previous disquiet. Gathering her courage, she flung open the door.

There was no sign of a bird.

On the windowsill, the candle sat inert and cold. Air swirled with dusty soot, and light dimmed to a fogged smear, green and opalescent. It reminded her of swimming underwater.

The scent of apples wafted around her. A sudden taste – tart the way mature cider was – filled her mouth and Ida gagged, unable to move. She had no idea how long she stood there, her mouth open until the inside of it began to dry out. She swore something in the room moved, only when she blinked the space was empty and silent.

Ida saw fallen flakes of plaster patterning the floor. She noticed the scratch on the bureau, raw and pale, and filled with guilt put out her hand to touch it. As she did, from behind the bureau a large bird erupted into the air: a frantic burst of feathers and a raucous screech.

Ida shrieked and for a second she was tempted to turn tail and run. The flapping slowed a little and she released a long, shaky breath.

She may have known little about birds, she did recognise a magpie when she saw one. In the garden at Wisteria Cottage, they would congregate in the branches of a silver birch tree and she remembered their noisy, chattering black and white presence and how her father had called them scavengers and thieves.

Her mother told her to salute them, to ward off bad luck.

The bird landed on the bureau, its black bill opening and closing like shears. Close up, Ida saw how mistaken she was in believing a magpie was black and white. This bird's feathers were iridescent, flashing, prismatic shades of blue, green and purple.

She stared and the bird stared back, its eyes ruby red and feral.

'It's okay,' Ida said, her voice low and she hoped, reassuring.

Not that the bird looked afraid. It looked as hostile as the black ones, as if it too had a plan. Keeping her eye on it, Ida crossed to the window, fumbled with the stiff sash and staggered as the window shot up. The noise sent the magpie into the air again and Ida ducked as it flew round the room screeching, for all the world as though it were cursing her.

Ida threw her hands over her head, her courage gone. Backing up against the wall she kept her head down. A whirl of air, the touch of a wing tip as it swept past her, and the bird found the open window and was gone.

In the grate she saw a pile of soot and several shimmering feathers. The soot was fresh and it was scattered across the floor like dusty ink blots. Kneeling down Ida rubbed it between her fingers. It was moist, as if it had only recently fallen. As the window had been closed, the only way the bird could have accessed the room was down the chimney, dislodging the soot in the process.

There was a rhyme about magpies and she tried to recall it.

One for…

Sadness? Sorrow?

'Who *cares?*' Ida held her hands over her ears. She was sick of birds and could happily spend the rest of her life never seeing another one. Wrenching down the window, locking it shut, she left the room, found a dustpan and brush in the kitchen and made her way back upstairs.

'*My* mother's room. Anna's room. You hear me, Olwen?'

Crouching in front of the hearth Ida's head began to spin, and the air in the room thickened. She let go of the brush, set the pan to one side and sniffed. Over the pungent aroma of the soot, she smelled apples again, putrid and rotting. This time as she left the room, she slammed the door behind her.

The whole house repelled her.

Ida huddled by the back door, rubbed her upper arms, trying to warm herself up.

It doesn't mean anything. It was a bird trapped in a room. It's what they do – they're stupid and fall down chimneys.

Each atom in Ida's body told her this wasn't true. Heather had said something about a magpie. Olwen's favourite. And the last thing any of the birds at Ty'r Cwmwl were, was stupid. They were clever and cunning and she was sure they hated her.

Already the day was dimmer, the ubiquitous cloud gathering fast, making it seem like late afternoon rather than mid-morning. The tang of damp earth was strong, preferable to the smell of soot and rotten apples, and Ida wandered across the yard to the garden, paused, wanting to be brave.

She lifted the gate and walked in.

Ida knew nothing about the kind of gardens that weren't trimmed and tidy. She was used to lawns and hanging baskets, flower beds filled with well-behaved roses, and sweet scented lilies. What strange things occurred out here in this curious, out of place garden with its brambles and poisonous berries, its guardian black birds hovering like note-taking nuns?

And yet Olwen had clearly made good things grow here too. In amongst the weeds, there were sweet flowers: obstinate ones unwilling to give in to an impending winter. A stray breeze caught

Ida's hair and as she lifted her hand to straighten it, the wind brought the scent of decayed apples again and with it a memory of the little room. The sensation of being watched was so acute, she stopped, wanting to turn, but wary.

Unable to resist, when she did turn round and there was nothing to be seen Ida told herself she'd known there wouldn't be. Why was she unable to ignore these irrational feelings? It was her imagination working overtime again, along with whatever childishness she still associated with ghosts and witches.

Ida shivered and it was as though the ghost she couldn't see, did too. And Ida sensed, she couldn't be seen either. Whatever connected her to Olwen was more fundamental than a random haunting. There would be no apparition, no ragged clothes or ravaged face and it was more disturbing than if the dead ghost of Heather's mother stood in front of her.

'I'm sorry.'

Another version of sorry, only Ida wasn't altogether sure what she was apologising for.

Being a rubbish friend? Making a hash of her life?

'It's all right.' Liz's voice sounded close and normal. When she'd called, that evening, Ida had given her the number of the landline. She'd discovered it, written on a strip of paper and sellotaped to the base of the phone.

'Except it isn't,' she said. 'You deserve better.'

'Well, yes I do and you better buck up.'

Ida heard the smile in Liz's voice.

'It's a virtually non-existent signal for the mobile,' she said. 'I have to wander out onto the moor or hang from the bathroom window to text you.'

Liz laughed. 'You best come home then, as soon as possible, before you fall out.'

It was dusk and Ida was tired, curled on the little sofa in the kitchen, the extension cord of the telephone stretched to its limits from the hallway. She picked at the remains of a cottage pie from the freezer.

'So, any news?'

And Ida fobbed her off with irritations about the solicitor, the impossibility of getting anything done and how the house was far too big.

'That's the back of beyond for you. I did say.'

'I have managed to find a mechanic to fix my car. And she's a woman.'

'So not all bad then?'

'No, she sounds nice.'

'Not as nice as me though.'

'Obviously! And as soon as I hear from the solicitor, make the arrangements, I'll be back,' Ida said, 'I promise.'

She couldn't explain what was really going on because she didn't know.

Thirty

Opening the curtains the following morning, to see what the day brought, Ida was taken aback by a sight so spectacular it looked as if the sky was bleeding.

In little more time than it took to blink, the molten red disappeared, giving way to a weak sunlight threading through the grey cloud.

Ida peered out across the mosaic of low hills. The moorland was patterned with shadows and moss, episodes of light making the rocky outcrops blink. There were no other houses for miles and the only roads so narrow, in the distance they looked like the ancient trackways they'd begun life as.

It was as though she'd landed in someone else's life. As it was, she'd driven across the tall, pale bridge, slipped out of her old self and become a woman with no identity, the sort of woman who mistrusted everyone and everything.

Including a band of calculating birds.

Her thick cardigan folded itself around her, like a pair of empty arms enhancing her loneliness, exacerbating her sense of disconnection from the person who had arrived here less than two weeks previously.

It occurred to her there was no one to care if the hills evaporated, if the black birds dropped out of the sky and pecked out her eyes, or even to be pleased for her because, for a few moments this morning, the sky had begun with such vibrancy, for a moment it had eclipsed the relentless cloud.

Her eyes caught a spark of reflected light and down on the ribbon road she saw a car. From where Ida stood it was impossible to tell the make, only that it was small. As the road dipped, she lost sight of it. And now it reappeared, bickering and noisy, sounding more like a motorbike than a car.

At the end of the track, the car slowed and the driver expertly negotiated the gateway. A pale blue Citroen 2CV lumbered towards the house. The rattle of the engine, and the sound of loud music, sent a trio of birds into the air. As they rose in a clap of protest, Ida's heart flipped.

Roni Jones!

The car pulled in behind Ida's Peugeot. A woman with spiky hair the colour of peonies stepped out. She wore heavy boots, worn jeans, a Siouxsie and the Banshees T-shirt and a sardonic smile made of red lipstick.

Ida went out to greet her.

'Ida? I'm Roni, good to meet you.' She held out her hand. The nails matched the lipstick and Ida wondered how you managed to fix cars and keep your nail polish that neat.

Tall and slender, with dark eyes heavily outlined with smudged black, Roni Jones was as far-removed from Ida's idea of a mechanic as a cat from a caravan. Her age was written on her face in invisible ink, daring you to guess it and not caring if you did.

'Hi.' Fascinated Ida took the proffered hand.

'Sorry about the noise.' Roni leaned back into the car and switched off the music. 'Gotta love a bit of *Train in Vain*.'

'It's fine.'

'Don't tell me, you're a Clash fan?'

'Well no, I won't, but it's still fine.'

'Good – I already like you. Other than beer and cake, the only thing I spend real money on is real music.'

'Gosh.'

Roni grinned. 'What's your musical pleasure then?'

'Oh, I don't know. Kate Bush? I'm a bit behind the times.'

Roni nodded. 'Best stay there, *cariad*. There's far too much shite being passed off as music these days. Not that a bit of Kate

181

doesn't go down well.' She eyed Ida's car. 'Well, that's a good start.'

'What is?'

'French car.' Roni stroked the bonnet of the old Peugeot. She turned and grinned at Ida and it was infectious, impossible not to smile back.

'You can fix it?'

'Don't see why not.' Roni heaved a battered metal box from the boot of her car. 'Keys?'

Apologising, Ida ran into the house, returned with the car keys. It was the work of minutes.

As she pottered under the bonnet, Roni talked Ida through the process. 'Damp, see – the damp up here will kill a car as soon as look at it. It's why WD-40 was invented.'

Ida quickly found herself won over by Roni's vibrancy, and her questioning eyes that didn't ask direct questions.

Roni wiped her hands on a piece of rag. 'How long since you had this old girl serviced then?'

Ida said she didn't know. 'My father took care of the cars.'

'Well, not to worry, we can talk about it later.' She sat in the driver's seat of the Peugeot and started it up. Leaning out of the window, she nodded. 'There you are, you're good to go.'

Ida grinned. 'Wow – thank you. Amazing.'

Roni threw the rag into the toolbox, heaved it back into the boot of her car. 'Don't thank me, *cariad*, put the kettle on.'

With the range working, the kitchen was cosy. Roni washed her hands at the sink. 'I love this room. It was Olwen's favourite. She said the parlour was too cold in winter and this was the easiest one to keep warm, so long as there was enough wood.'

So long as you weren't too ill to plough through the snow to fetch it in.

'Tea or coffee?' Ida asked as she filled the kettle.

'Oh, coffee, if you have it.'

'Good coffee.' Ida smiled, rinsed the cafetière, and Roni nodded approvingly.

'Woman after my own heart,' she said. 'Can't be doing with tea.'

'Oh, I don't mind tea now and then, but you can't beat a decent cup of coffee.' Ida reached for the packet. 'Heather, Olwen's daughter, she prefers tea.'

'Ah, you've met our Heather then.'

'I certainly have.' Ida paused. 'How well do you know her?'

'As well as she'll allow.' Roni smiled. 'Since she was a baby. Olwen and I were good friends. I liked her a lot. We had a lack of men in common.' Her laugh was bold. It took no prisoners and Ida was reminded of Liz. She thought Roni's laugh could make most bad things better.

'Isn't she rather young to be living alone?'

'She is but don't be fooled. Heather Morgan can take care of herself.'

'Oh, I don't doubt it, the question is, should she? She's only seventeen.' Ida hesitated, chose her next words with care. 'She's been up here a few times. Seems overly attached to the house.'

'Well she would be, seeing as she was born here.'

There was no criticism in Roni's voice and Ida risked another comment. 'The grounds too, there's clearly a connection. The grove in particular.'

'I know – she nicked her mother's ashes off that bloody bitch Bethan and buried them down there.'

'You know about that?'

'Oh yes.' Roni accepted the mug of coffee Ida held out to her, sniffed it appreciatively. 'Thanks. Lush.' She looked up. 'Does it bother you? Olwen's ashes being here?'

'It did, at first. Only because the idea of it wasn't anything I'd ever heard of before. I told Heather it was okay though. And I said she can come here any time she likes – to see to the grave. Or whatever she wants to call it.'

'That's generous of you.'

'Not really. Although to be honest, I feel odd about the whole thing.'

'And you don't want her in the house.'

It wasn't a question.

'What makes you say that?'

'It doesn't take a genius to work out how Heather must be feeling, about you being here. And vice versa.'

'It is my house!' Ida protested.

'Of course it is and don't get me wrong, it must be very weird for you.'

'It is.'

'The thing you need to remember about Heather is, she isn't led by reason. Olwen was the same – pure instinct. When her mam died that girl folded up her loss like it was an old jumper. If she looks at it, it'll be like the moths got in.'

'That's some metaphor.'

'It's true. Still, strange for you.'

'The whole thing's strange. It's a mess, frankly.' Now she'd said it, Ida realised how true it was. 'What do you know about this house, Roni? The history of it.'

'That it isn't a happy place?' She grinned. 'But don't worry, it's isn't haunted.'

Oh, I think it is.

'It's a lonely house.'

Roni leaned forward and Ida saw how dark her eyes were – how small specks of green dotted the irises.

'There aren't any scandals, no horror stories or anything like that, just a litany of leaving. People have died here – naturally – of course they have. It's an old house and old folk like to die in their own beds.'

'That's pretty much what Heather said.'

'She's right. Like I said, there haven't been any murders or suicides. Nothing spooky.' Roni raised her eyebrows. 'Not that I know of.'

'Until Olwen died.'

Roni sighed. 'Bloody waste.'

'What do you know about it?'

'Has Heather said anything to you?'

'In lurid detail. She made is sound incredibly dramatic and of course, for her it must have been.' Ida blocked the other images trying to get in, pushed away a sudden picture of the crematorium, the huddled mourners. 'She told me about the snow storm and how her mother died because no one could get to her.'

'No one could.' Roni's voice softened to a whisper. 'Olwen's death was a tragedy.'

Ida wasn't sure she wanted to hear another word.

A slight frown grazed Roni's forehead. 'It was like something out of a Victorian melodrama to be honest. Sick to her bones she must have been, poor thing. The 'flu came on like a tornado that year. Loads of people went down with it. And Olwen didn't drive and wouldn't learn.' Roni sighed again. 'She didn't have a mobile phone either, daft woman, not that you get much of a signal out here.'

'Tell me about it. There's the landline though.'

'Out, because of the snow.'

'Heather said no one knew how ill she was.'

'Including me. I was away over the other side of the mountain anyway, fixing a Land Rover. I was gone two days. I've felt guilty ever since, even though I couldn't have done anything.'

'Did Olwen ever talk to you about Heather's father?'

'Not a word. When she wanted to be, Olwen Morgan was the most secretive person I've ever known. She had a bloke, some secret lover she refused to talk about. She didn't discuss her men, unless it was to regret them. Only with this one, it was like pulling teeth.'

'So you've no idea who he was?'

'Married I would have guessed, if she'd been anyone else. Only it wasn't Olwen's style. She was principled – she liked things to be proper. Not because she was a prude or anything – heaven's no!' Roni's laugh rang around the room. 'Olwen was honest to a fault, and she hated disloyalty.'

'I see.'

'Whoever he was, she kept him to herself. She'd go off to meet him, although she never told me where.' Roni poured herself another mug of coffee. 'She had odd taste in men, did Olwen. Went for the unsuitable types – the hippies and the kind of men our mothers warned us not to get involved with. At least mine did. But whoever took any notice of their mother – where men are concerned?'

Or told their mother they preferred women…

'My guess is,' Roni went on, 'he was some random sweet-talker. Possibly one of the gypsy guys we used to get round here, looking for work.' She sipped her coffee. 'Anyway, next thing, Olwen's pregnant and he's gone. Bastard skedaddled, the moment she told him is my guess.'

'And she moved here. Do you know why?'

'Olwen grew up on the moors, with her mother and grandmother. When Manon lost the tenancy they moved into the village. Bought the cottage for a pittance. It was a dump. Still is. Manon didn't like it – too many people but needs must I suppose. But it was the end of her. Manon was a moors woman to her bones.'

'And Olwen inherited it?'

'Yes. Her and her sister, Bethan. They were as different as chalk is from cheese, those two. Bethan thought too much of herself. Even her mother said so.' Roni sipped her coffee. 'Anyway, not long after she fell pregnant, Olwen found out this place was for rent and next thing, she'd moved in. Like I said, she was a private person and minded her own business. Liked folk to mind theirs too, which of course they didn't.' Memory was written all over her face. 'Gossip's the life-blood of a Welsh village, Ida. It was a

186

lonely house and it suited her. Out of sight out of mind, although Olwen wasn't the kind of woman you easily forgot.'

'No, I can imagine.'

'People said there was something about her. Not always meant as a compliment. And there was. She was crazy about birds – an old magpie would come visiting, right inside this kitchen, scary bloody thing. Olwen said she was her familiar. With a glint in her eye so you weren't sure if she was kidding or not.'

'A magpie?'

'Yes. Have you seen it?'

'I've seen the black ones.' Ida hoped her abrupt reply hadn't given her away. 'They're everywhere. Like they own the place.'

'Well they don't,' Roni said. 'They're only birds – rooks and crows mostly – noisy beggars. Don't let them faze you. Olwen loved them though and I believe her when she said they loved her back. She was all about love and life, was Olwen. And knowing.' Roni have another great sigh. 'And it was part of the problem – she was too much: too knowing and people are afraid of what they don't understand.'

Ida folded her hands onto the table. 'Thank you for telling me all this, Roni. I appreciate it. And it helps me get a better picture. You see, I haven't been particularly nice to Heather if I'm honest. She unnerved me that first day. Several days actually. Going on about how her mother was a witch and wouldn't want me here.'

'Did she call her a witch?'

'As good as.'

Ida didn't say anything about the empty bedroom, the bureau or the magpie, or the sensation she experienced each time she went into the room. She didn't mention getting lost on the moor or how Heather had come to her rescue. In the presence of this level-headed, practical woman, the last thing Ida wanted to sound like was a hapless fool.

'You don't want to take much notice of Heather – she's grieving.' Roni smiled. 'As are you I imagine. If I'm not intruding.'

'You aren't. Not at all. My parents died six months ago.'

'Catrin filled me in.'

'I bet she did.'

Roni paused, gave an imperceptible, shrewd nod. 'So you do understand?'

'Sort of.' Once again, Ida chose her words carefully. 'It's like Heather inhabits a realm of her own invention, if that makes sense.'

'It does. She did that from when she was a *dwt*.'

'What?'

'A little thing – a child?'

'Ah.' Ida paused. 'Even if I could help her, even if she'd let me, I wouldn't know where to begin.'

'Don't be too quick to want to know stuff, Ida. You don't always find things you like.' Roni pushed back her chair. 'Do you mind if we go outside. I'm gagging for a smoke.'

'Of course not.'

They settled onto the bench by the back door. From a dented cigarette case, Roni took a small black cheroot, lit it with a Zippo lighter. 'Terrible habit.' Her smile lit up her face again and Ida saw how much younger it made her look.

'You should smile all the time,' she said.

Roni didn't answer and offered Ida the cigarette case.

'Thanks, no,' Ida said, 'I gave up years ago.' She paused. 'Not that I haven't been tempted recently.'

'Don't be – nasty habit. Buy some gin instead.'

Now it was Ida's turn to laugh. 'I might just do that.'

'What will you do for a job, now you're here? Or should I mind my own business?'

'I'm not planning on staying.'

'Really? But I thought—'

'I'm not sure this is where I'm supposed to be. But I'd be grateful if you kept that to yourself.'

'Of course.' Roni blew a perfect smoke ring. 'What did you do before you came here?'

188

Buried my parents...

'Worked in a bookshop.'

'Cool.'

'It was – I loved it only the place closed down.'

'Pastures new then?' Roni inhaled again. 'They say we come up against choices in life – paths to take, if we're brave enough. And who knows what's round the corner? I haven't always lived here you know. Haven't always been a mechanic either, although I could fix a motorbike before I could bake a cake.'

'Am I allowed to ask?'

'About the cake?' She laughed. 'I can bake.'

'I'm sure you can.'

'I went off once or twice, when I was young. Went mad – drank too much, had a laugh, had my heart broken. You know.' Roni gave Ida a rueful smile. 'In the end it didn't suit, or make me happy and I wasn't up for being wasted all the time.'

Ida didn't know what to say. She'd never been wasted in her life.

Roni grinned. 'So, here I am, where I belong.'

'How do you know you belong?'

'Ah, now there's a question. This is home. I was born here.'

'I was born here too, but it doesn't feel like home.'

'How old were you when you left?'

'Five.'

'Well, there you are. You escaped!' Roni laughed. 'Who knew I'd be nearly fifty and still living in my auntie's annexe?'

Ida wanted to ask her why she'd left, if she'd gone alone and more importantly, what had drawn her back. Who had broken her heart? What, or whom, hadn't suited?

What did a woman like Roni Jones do to fill the gaps when she wasn't mending people's cars? In a place as isolated as this, there had to be a limit to the number of vehicles in need of a mechanic's ministrations. Ida wondered if she ever took herself off to Cardiff or Swansea, to buy cool jeans and cooler music.

'Now you,' Roni said, 'must find something to occupy yourself, at least until you've made up your mind about the house. It's good walking country, if that's your thing.' She grinned. 'Not that I'm much of a walker. Rather drive.'

'I tried it. Nearly got lost in the mist.' Ida left out the detail.

'I guess you're screwed then!'

Now it was Ida's turn to laugh. And she realised this funny, wise woman's opinion of her mattered.

'I'll think of something.'

She walked with Roni to her car.

'It's good to know you, Ida.' Roni gave her a brief hug. 'You could do a lot worse than stay here.'

As Roni drove away, her blue car rattling down the track, Ida waved her hand. 'Don't be a stranger!'

She wasn't sure if Roni heard her.

Ida sat on her bed, ran her fingers through the frayed ribbons of the worn red ballet shoes.

She wondered why she hadn't told Roni she'd been a dancer.

Because you don't want anyone's pity. You don't want her *pity.*

When night fell and the black birds sought shelter in the tall trees, Ida found her thoughts invaded by the insistent, settling call of them. She thought about the magpie, how it had seen her.

Sprawled in her tumbled, undreaming sleep, feathers like black ribbons tied up her unquiet memories so that when she woke, Ida thought she'd dreamed, for the first time since her mother died. As a glimmer of light fell across the wooden floorboards, the black birds woke too. Their songs were slung together: *kraa* and grumble, laced with sharp, sweet grace notes.

When Ida got out of bed to go to the bathroom and looked down, she found three black feathers on the floor.

Don't call it a haunting.

I linger in the old things because I'm part of them. I line the walls and blister the paint. I come and go as I please. Time runs softly for me — I fall in and out of it, paying only enough attention as is required.

Do you really want to dream, girl with no feet?

I'll bring you some, made of your raggedy red shoes and the feet that stopped you dancing because you cut them off yourself.

There are other dances to be danced — made of steps you and your mother never dreamed of.

Thirty-one

Wandering into the room opposite the parlour, Ida noted the bare bookshelves.

What kind of a house had no books?

Thinking of her own, she regretted not bringing more with her. Limited funds didn't mean she couldn't spare money for a couple of new books, to keep her going. And braving a bookshop wasn't a bad idea either. She may have lost her job, but she hadn't lost her love of reading. It was the only thing currently making any sense.

Collecting her coat and bag, Ida locked the front door behind her and when the car started, grinned like a cat. 'Thank you, Roni Jones.'

Buoyed by her resolve, she drove off the moorland and onto the main road leading to the town. The further from Ty'r Cwmwl she travelled, the wider the roads became and the thinner the cloud, until it vanished altogether, revealing a sky as blue as forget-me-nots.

Forty minutes later, cresting the brow of a hill, the town spread out before her, houses the colours of ice-cream, castle ruins, a harbour and the ocean. The light on the sea glittered and Ida saw white birds, clean and pure and unconcerned by her.

It was called The Bookshop on the Corner.

Wandering through the aisles, instead of feeling wistful, Ida was oddly at home. Fifteen minutes later she'd found two books: a novel about suffragists and a crime thriller, both set in Wales and written by Welsh authors.

'Do you need a bag?'

'Do you have one with the name of the shop on it?'

'Two pounds okay?'

Ida paid with her card, nervously, half-expecting it to be declined. She hadn't checked her bank balance in weeks. 'It's a good name.'

'I think it's a bit weird.' The girl slid the books into a cloth bag, rang up the sale, handed Ida her card and receipt. 'You on holiday then?'

'Not exactly.'

'No – odd time for a holiday I suppose. What do you do then?'

Ida didn't say anything, irritated by the girl's casual familiarity, imagining Gina's disapproval. She left, muttering thanks under her breath.

Back on the main street there were far more people milling around. About to check her balance at an ATM, someone bumped into her, moved on without apologising. It was all it took: a careless stranger on a crowded street and once again Ida was small and alone. She clutched her bag of books to her chest, walked away, darting along a street at random, head down in case anyone saw her.

Who would see her? No one knew her.

The road began to slope upwards, away from the town centre. Ida kept going, wanting to be as far from the crowds as possible. The pavement changed, the neat patterns of the main street giving way to older, less well tended slabs. Ida watched them, carefully, and still she managed to trip.

'Steady!'

A hand touched her arm, the lightest of touches, and she flinched, heard a concerned voice.

'You okay there?'

Ida stopped in her tracks, stared at the thin hand on her arm. 'I'm so sorry.'

'No worries. I thought you were going to faint.'

A woman with red hair tied in a loose bun stared at her. She was leaning back against a low wall in front of a large detached Victorian house and wearing legwarmers and huge fluffy slippers. A black woollen cardigan lay draped across her shoulders and underneath it Ida glimpsed a leotard.

A dancer?

'It's nothing. I wasn't paying attention, that's all.' Ida looked around. 'Goodness knows where I am.'

'Here?' The woman waved her hand and behind her Ida saw a brass plate attached to the wall next to an imposing door.

Lowri Lloyd Dance Studio.

'You *are* a dancer.'

'A teacher, for my sins.'

Ida froze and she thought the whole world must hear her heart beating.

The woman didn't appear to notice. 'I come out here between classes to recharge my batteries.'

She was older than Ida. Thirty-five perhaps and she looked lean and fit and Ida wanted to run.

No more bloody dancers!

'You remind me of someone,' the woman said. 'You're not a dancer by any chance are you? You've got a dancer's body.'

How the hell could she tell? Although the sun was shining it was still cold and Ida was bundled in her mother's blue coat. 'I used to be.'

Was this how it was going to be from now on? Each time she met someone in this godforsaken place, her innermost secrets would leak like water?

'I knew it. Takes one to know one.' The woman held out her hand. 'Lowri Lloyd.' Her fingers were long and elegant and Ida wondered why so many dancers possessed beautiful hands. 'This is where you tell me yours?'

'Oh … Ida Llewellyn.'

'Llewellyn?' Lowri's eyes widened. 'You're not related to Anna

Plessey by any chance? I knew you looked familiar. She married a Welsh chap called Llewellyn.'

'My mother.'

'Anna Plessey was your mother? Oh my god! She's my absolute icon!'

Stop. Please stop.

'She died. Not recently – well, a few months ago.'

'Oh, crikey. That's about as recent as it gets. I'm really sorry. I can't believe I didn't know. And I must sound like some crazy fan girl.' Lowri frowned. 'I can see I've freaked you out, and you don't even know me. Look, why don't you come inside for a moment? The least I can do is offer you a cup of tea.'

What was it with all the tea?

Lowri was clearly contrite and Ida wanted to trust her. Everything about her was direct: her eyes, her voice, and the way her mouth moved when she spoke, each thing revealing kindness.

'I'm so sorry if I've made you sad,' Lowri said.

Still Ida hesitated. She didn't want anyone, least of all this red haired, dancing woman, picking at the edges of her past.

'You haven't. I'm fine.'

'Will you come in, then? Please?'

'Thanks. Okay. Only, coffee if you have it?'

Inside, the house was a revelation. The ground floor had been opened up to accommodate a spacious studio. Barres and mirrors lined the walls. An upright piano sat at an angle in the corner.

Ida smelled rosin and sweat and she held her breath.

Upstairs, in an airy kitchen filled with house plants, Lowri made Ida a cup of instant coffee. It was the colour of mud, but the scent was sweet and subtle. She took a sip. It tasted better than it looked.

She looked around. 'It's so spacious.'

'There's two other floors above this. It's vast.'

'I've just inherited a house,' Ida said. 'Also huge.' She gave a wry smile. 'In the middle of nowhere though. About thirty miles from here.'

'Whereabouts?'

Ida told her the name of the village.

'That is remote! How are you finding it?'

'Weird. But then I've only been here two weeks.'

Lowri laughed. 'I was born here. Couldn't wait to leave mind. I ran away in fact – to London.'

'And trained to be a dancer.'

'Yes. Came back though. Can't take the girl out of Wales.'

'Where did you train?'

'Nowhere famous. Small place in Islington.'

'And now you're a teacher.'

'London's a very tempting place, especially if you have no willpower. I realised pretty quickly that teaching was as good as it would get for me. And I'm lazy too; I wasn't ambitious. That was my mother. She thought I was the next Margot Fonteyn.'

'Mine too.'

'Yours was Anna Plessey! You must be pretty good!'

'I wish. She was my mother. It was her job to tell me I was amazing. And she did because she was lovely. She wanted the best for me. I wasn't as good as she believed though. And in any case, I had a stupid accident.'

'I'm sorry.'

'Don't be. You know how it goes. One wrong *chaîné* and … well, you know.'

'Ouch.'

Ida shrugged. 'If you don't use it, you lose it.'

'Not necessarily.'

Ida wished she hadn't said anything. Her foot was ruined. What did this stranger know? 'It's fine. I'm over it.'

There was an awkward pause.

'Do you have plans?' Lowri summoned a smile.

'Not sure.'

Not sure I want to tell you.

'Sorry, I don't mean to be rude. There was a girl just now, in a bookshop. Nosy. I'm quite a private person.'

'Nothing wrong with that. I'm far too public!' Lowri laughed and Ida was reminded of Roni.

'It's nice to meet you, Lowri,' Ida said, and realised she meant it. 'I need to meet people. Other women.'

'Well, I'm one of those!' She held Ida's gaze and her pupils shone like new ink.

Ida found she had lost the ability to speak.

It was Lowri who broke the spell. 'Would you like to look around?'

At the top of a second flight of stairs the house touched the sky. A large room at the front overlooked the ocean.

'In here.' Lowri opened another door, to a bedroom, and stood aside. 'Have a proper look. Through the door.'

Ida crossed the room and stepped out onto a tiny metal balcony, looked down an iron, scrolled spiral staircase. Lowri's arm brushed hers and they were close.

Too close.

Ida leaned forward, made a wisp of space, her hands on the rail. Below lay a garden, and a tree she was sure was a cherry. Her eye took in a swathe of wildness and when she looked up, she was inexplicably rendered speechless. There were no heavy clouds here, only the sky and a mirrored ocean of space.

'Wow.' It was all she could manage.

'I know.'

'A secret garden. Why don't you rent this part out?'

'I ought to but I never have time to fix it up.' Lowri glanced at her watch. 'Listen, I've got a class in ten minutes. Why don't you come again – I'll make us lunch.'

'I'd like that.'

Lowri tapped at her phone and handed it over. 'Put your number in and I'll send you a text, then you'll have mine.'

Ida Llewellyn was the last woman in the world to act on impulse and yet here she was, remembering how it was the scent of a woman's skin, and the curve of her, that made her heart lurch and sent her into a spin.

And caused her to hand over her telephone number to Lowri Lloyd as easily as if it were a spare tissue.

Ida lay on her bed. She closed her eyes and all she saw was a woman with red hair.

Somehow, another dance had begun, eclipsing her certainty. She listened and there were no black birds, only the ebb of the wind, so otherworldly they might have come out of a dream.

Only Ida never dreamed.

Thirty-two

The sash window in the kitchen had been left open again.

This time, Ida didn't bother to question it. She knew she hadn't opened it, which left only Heather. And it meant she had lied about having a spare key. Had the girl been again while Ida was out?

She was in no mood for games.

Moisture clung to the glass chimney of the oil lamp and the corpses of a few moths lay on the windowsill in a shrivelled halo. Ida slammed down the window, swept up the dead moths in a dishcloth and rinsed them away down the drain.

'Rest in pieces.'

She took her coffee outside, sat on the rickety bench by the back door and checked her phone. Nothing. No missed calls, not even a text from Liz.

Or Lowri.

They'd barely met – a day ago – and Lowri had been friendly, nothing more. And just because she was single didn't mean she was gay.

You know she is.

Ida didn't do gaydar. Her reticence about admitting her preferences meant she'd avoided any kind of analysis of her instincts, and in any case, she thought it was a silly, contrived word.

Nevertheless, she knew…

Her foot still ached from the previous day's walking and Ida thought about what she'd said to Lowri. What she'd left out.

It had been a stupid accident, only Ida would never be

completely over it. It was another grief: her small ambition – made brighter by her mother's extravagant one – forever marred by a moment's lack of concentration.

Of all the streets in town, what were the odds she'd stumble – literally – on the one with a dance school? She was livid with herself. Once again, she hadn't been paying attention, and not only to where she'd been going. She'd tripped up in other ways too, babbling her private business like a rambling fool.

It was stupid and unsettling.

She switched off her phone.

Determined to find Heather, explain her plan to sell the house, and demand her spare keys at the same time, Ida set off for the village. It wasn't far – Heather had said it was less than half a mile across country.

She buttoned up her coat and wound a scarf around her neck. Stuffing her beret in a pocket she let the wind blow through her hair. The air was fresh and fine, the turf beneath her boots springy with moss. Nothing stirred, save for a single black bird which flew down to the stile and landed on the post.

'Go away!' Her voice sounded thin and the bird was clearly unimpressed. Ida waved her hand in dismissal and resolutely turned left. If she lived here until the end of time, nothing would ever tempt her to walk out on the moor again.

The wind dropped and the silence struck Ida as unnatural. There were no cars, no human voices, not even the bleat of a sheep. She wondered about the skylarks. Perhaps Dan had made them up. Plodding on across the field, she followed the ruts which must have been made by Heather's bicycle.

The girl had been right – it wasn't far. Even so, by the time she arrived at the brow of the hill Ida had a stitch and her foot was smarting. In the distance she noticed the river running under the half-moon bridge, and the huddled houses.

The track petered out and became a dusty path running

alongside a high wall surrounding the chapel. Ivy and brambles climbed over the coping stones and large overhanging trees created a tunnel. As Ida approached the end of the path, she saw the oddly triangular shape of the village ahead of her. A stray bramble caught on her coat. She stopped to unpick it, heard it spring back behind her. Somewhere a dog barked. Ida was about to step onto the pavement when she heard voices.

'No, not a peep.' A few words in Welsh, and then, 'She must be running out of basics by now.'

Catrin Pritchard. The voice was unmistakeable – husky and laced with cigarette smoke. Ida pressed herself into the wall, grateful now for the overhanging cover.

'Hoity-toity,' a second voice piped up. 'If you ask me.'

Ida recognised this one too. The blonde woman in the brown coat. Brenda somebody, Roni had said. Brenda muttered in Welsh before reverting to English. Ida would have found the shifting between languages fascinating had the words not been harsh, and clearly aimed at her.

'Probably gone off to town for her shopping,' Brenda continued. 'Her father was the same. *Saesneg*. Bit of a toff with it. And the mother never showed her face.'

'I heard that Heather one's been up there again,' Catrin said. '*Be mae hynny ambiti te?*'

'No idea, *bach*. It isn't right, living by herself, running wild across the moor like a gypsy and up to goodness knows what.'

'Someone ought to report her.'

'And the state of the place.'

Ida risked a peek. Both woman had their backs to her, heads inclined towards the smaller cottage set apart from the row. Even more dilapidated than the rest, peeling, once whitewashed walls, framed windows filmed with dirt.

'*Ych y fi*! Disgusting.'

Ida ducked back against the wall.

'Sneaky little thing too,' Catrin said. 'Morgan blood.'

'Gypsy blood too – the father was one of them, I'm telling you.'

'Which would make her a thief into the bargain.' Catrin lowered her voice. 'I swear she's had stuff from my shop she's not paid for. *Lleidr bach.*'

'Like mother like daughter. Father too. And the sister was no better than a tramp.'

Catrin Pritchard coughed and it sounded like gravel. 'Blood see – it doesn't lie.'

Furious, and against her better judgement, Ida stepped out of the shadows. 'I don't think it's very nice to gossip about someone behind their back.'

The two women whirled on the spot, almost crashing into one another.

'Gossip?' Catrin Pritchard glared. 'Who said we were gossiping? That's a very strong word.'

'I don't think it's nice to *gossip* about a person when they aren't around to defend themselves.'

Why was she defending Heather?

Catrin's nostrils flared. 'And I don't have much time for people who go round eavesdropping on other people's conversations.'

Brenda sniffed. 'I should think not.'

'In which case you ought to watch what you're saying.' Ida's skin burned. She hated confrontation but this was a step too far. 'Accusing someone of being a thief without proof is slander.' She didn't care if it was true or not – these ignorant women were unlikely to know. '*Lleidr?*' She stumbled over the pronunciation, sensing the word meant "thief".

'If you say so.' Catrin didn't even try to hide her disdain. 'But there's no smoke without fire.'

'There *is* no fire, Mrs Pritchard.'

'What's it to you anyway, *Miss* Llewellyn?'

'She's seventeen-years-old! And alone in the world. Where's your humanity?'

'Where's your common sense?' Catrin scoffed. 'I heard you

were entertaining her up at the old house. You want to watch that.'

'And with respect – you want to watch what you say about people.'

The other woman turned as if to go.

'Not keeping you am I? *Mrs* Lewis.' As the woman's surname came to her, Ida allowed her voice to rise.

Catrin glowered. 'Is there anything else? No? Then I'll thank you to get out of my way.'

Dismissal was Catrin Pritchard's forte.

At the end of the dark path Ida turned. It ran away behind her like a burrow, and she waited in case anyone followed her.

Her heart was racing. The village became smaller and smaller until Ida was out on the moorland once again. By the time she found her way to the top of the hill, she was limping hard.

She thought about Heather, in the crabbed, grubby cottage, the butt of vicious tongues and a shocking level of unkindness. Heather was a pain. She was rude and arrogant and wily. Ida didn't trust her as far as she could throw her. It didn't mean she was prepared to condone nasty gossip.

And in that moment, Ida realised she wasn't ready to tell her, about selling the house. Not yet. It would break her heart.

'What is wrong with me? I have to tell her at some point.'

The wind blew chilly and Ida hugged her coat close. Twigs and dried bracken crackled under her feet. Thinking she was walking in a circle, her heart beat faster. She wasn't about to get lost again.

A sound made her jump. It was only a sheep, staring at her, immobile and curious. Her heartbeat rose. Her imagination was becoming a liability. Five minutes ago she'd felt emboldened enough to stick up for a girl she didn't even like. The truth was, this hinterland, with its shifting shadows and impregnable secrets, alarmed her.

'And I haven't got the guts to tell her the truth anyway.' She addressed the sheep and it turned away, as disdainful as Catrin Pritchard had been. 'Suit yourself.' Ida walked on, head down, watching each blade of grass, rock and thistle.

The silence was interrupted by a high, sweet sound. A flash and a small brown bird rose into the air and as quickly, disappeared. Ida caught a glimpse of a white-sided tail. In seconds, the sounds multiplied and although she couldn't see them, she knew they were there.

Skylarks.

Smiling, she made her way down the last stretch of path to the house.

Before she went indoors, Ida stopped at the garden gate. She lifted it out of its rut and made her way along the path to the apple tree. A breeze stirred the yellowing leaves, and the brown ones Heather had insisted, if they fell on her head, were ghosts.

Ida caught one between her fingers, crushed it in her fist and watched as the fragments fell like brown ash. Tiny bits of broken leaf stuck to the palm of her hands and she brushed them away.

My mam's ashes are buried here.

Ida thought about making a grave for her parents – finding the perfect spot, standing barefoot on cool grass, scattering their ashes.

And she wanted to cry because her mother wouldn't be there to gently chastise her for ruining her feet.

Thirty-three

Kicking off her muddy boots at the back door, Ida heard a sound in the room above.

A scuffle, and something moved across the floor. Leaving the door open, she stepped into the kitchen. Now she heard a footstep, as if someone stumbled.

A burglar?

Hardly. Her heart thudded against her ribs; she tip-toed across the kitchen. The door was ajar and she slipped into the hallway and up the stairs.

'Hello?'

In spite of knowing it was Heather in her bedroom, when Ida saw her, a scream rose in her throat. She swallowed it.

Heather stood in front of the window. Backlit again. It was her superpower; she was in league with the light and it prevented Ida's eyes from focusing. Heather was so much a part of the outside, when she came indoors she brought it with her. This time she smelled of soot and soil and there were tiny twigs in her sky-larking brown hair.

The scream inside Ida turned to anger. 'What the hell are you doing in my house? In my fucking bedroom!'

The interior of the room flickered like the broken mirror reflections in the grove. Another trick.

'Stop it!' Ida pushed the door closed behind her, cutting off Heather's escape.

'Stop what?' The girl's face was alight with bravado.

'Whatever it is you're doing!'

Ida took in the room. The bed was in disarray. The pillows

205

pushed aside, her pyjamas unfolded and Giselle, sitting at an awkward angle, her legs splayed.

Heather hovered by the bed. In her hands she held the red ballet shoes, the ribbons trailing and frayed, like dead flowers.

'Give me my shoes.' Ida's spoke the words slowly, with emphasis, her voice quivering with rage.

The girl didn't move.

Ida found her voice and she shouted. 'Put them down!'

Heather shrugged and with a flick of her wrist, tossed the shoes onto the bed.

'What is wrong with you?' Ida pressed a hand to her face to contain her rage, spoke through clenched teeth. 'Each time I think I've got through to you, each time I try to be nice, you repay me like this. Intruding and prying and taking liberties. I've had enough, Heather, do you hear me?'

'I didn't mean any harm. I was—'

'You are *trespassing*! Breaking and entering only, hey, no you aren't because somehow you still have a key. To *my* house. Which for some bizarre reason, in spite of the fact this is my house and you don't live here anymore, you still seem to think means you can come and go as you please.'

'I was curious.'

Incredulous now, Ida threw up her hands. 'Curious? What the hell does that mean? This isn't curiosity, Heather, this is intrusion. It's beyond snooping, going through my belongings. It's outrageous.'

'I haven't been going through anything. I was just looking at the doll and I found—'

'You didn't *find* anything. Those shoes were under the pillow. You came sneaking in here and you nosed through my things, messed up my bed and now you've been caught in the act, and I am *done*.'

'I'm sorry.'

'Oh, please.' Ida snorted her derision. 'You're impertinent

and… And totally bloody aimless. Why the hell can't you find something useful to do with your life instead of intruding in mine?' She folded her arms. 'I could have you arrested, you do realise that, don't you?'

'You wouldn't.'

'No, you're right, I wouldn't. I'm not a monster.'

Outside the window, mist hung like cobwebs. The sash was open and Ida guessed it was down to Heather again; she would have left it like that: to listen out for Ida, hoping not to get caught.

Too bad, Heather, caught in the act.

A black bird slid across the sky, letting loose a stark shriek into the air.

Ida slammed the window shut.

'I mean it, Heather,' she said. 'I'm done with this – with you and your creepy witch mother. With those damn birds and this bloody house.'

'You're a coward.'

'What did you call me?'

'I said, you're a coward. You call me sneaky and aimless, you insult my mam, and who are you? Some stupid townie scared of her own shadow, who can't stick at anything.' Heather's startling eyes glittered. 'You may as well be dead.'

'That is unconscionable.'

'Listen to yourself. Tripping over your fancy words same as you do your stupid broken townie feet. Showing off, showing how nasty you are because you know I don't always understand what you're on about. Looking down your nose like I'm ignorant.' Heather sneered. 'My mam will make mincemeat of you.'

'Your mother is *dead*!'

'Shut up!'

If Heather had been a child, Ida might have been more inclined to put her claim to a ghost mother down to invention. Children believed impossible things, fantasy was second nature to them. Heather was seventeen and too old for pretend.

'Now listen to me, Heather—'

'No one's listening to you. Don't you see? There's only me and I don't care. I may not be clever like you – but I know things you haven't dreamed of.'

'You don't know to keep your nose out of other people's belongings though, do you?'

'What? A stupid doll and a pair of old ballet shoes looking like they ought to have been binned years ago?'

'Those things were gifts from my mother!'

'This *house* was my mother's gift to me.'

Heather's misery filled the room, daring Ida to feel sorry for her.

'No, Heather, it was my father's bequest to me, but I know—'

'You know *nothing*.'

It was true. Regret hung in the air. They were both too angry for rationality. Neither of them had anything the other wanted. Even their grief was different.

'I know this – I'm selling the house.'

'What?'

'You heard me. I'm putting the house on the market, at the first opportunity.'

'But, you never said—'

'We'll, I'm saying it now.' Ida lifted her head, to make herself taller. 'I think we're done here, Heather.'

The space was too small and the scent of rotting apples filled the room.

'We never started,' Heather said. 'Not you and me at any rate.' She stared and her eyes glittered like shards of glass. 'I can't speak for Mam.'

At the window, another bird appeared. Ida saw it, hunched on the sill, its feathers gleaming.

Heather laughed. 'Scared are you? Ida Spider?'

Impotent rage finally gave way to impulse and Ida's arm swung out, the flat of her hand slapping Heather's face. The blow sent the girl reeling against the bed.

'And don't you dare,' Ida hissed, 'tell me I'll be sorry.' She stood rigid as a stick, her hand smarting from the impact. 'Now get out of my house.'

One hand held to her burning cheek, Heather regained her balance, and like lightning, moved to the window. Before Ida could stop her, she lifted the sash again, called out, her voice a guttural howl. One after another, more birds flew down, nudged themselves into a ragged row on the sill and Ida shook with a mixture of fury and fear.

'Close it!'

'Why should I?'

Ida grabbed her arm, pushed her away. 'Fuck *off*, Heather!' She screamed at the birds and they rose up in a pandemonium.

The look on Heather's face was contemptuous. She held her hand to her cheek. 'You'll pay for that slap.'

Ida scrabbled at the window, desperate to close it in case the birds returned. 'You need to leave.'

Behind her, she heard Heather move to the door, the knob rattling as she turned it. 'My mam doesn't take kindly to anyone who hurts her own – human or animal.'

'Your mother is *dead*. They're both *dead*.' Ida felt her nerve going, tears welling in her chest. She turned and Heather's strange eyes were on her. They'd changed again and now they were the cold colour of mercury.

'Yes, but mine's still here.' She gave Ida a last disdainful look and left the room, a small, hostile figure in her swirling skirt, hands folded together across her chest as though she was hiding her heart.

Ida followed her, out onto the landing, watched as she flew down the stairs and vanished into the hall.

Silence fell, drifted in slow motion, and Ida heard the front door slam. She stayed by the window, one palm on the window pane, saw Heather running like a stray fox, swift, sly and silent.

Her hand made a faint print on the glass and she waited until the girl disappeared round the edge of the house.

Heather's words stung like wasps.

Mine's still here…

The other mother – the wrong mother – taking what didn't belong to her.

Ida listened and the only thing she heard was the echo of the slamming door; all she saw through the window was the vast brushstroke of a slate-coloured, seamless sky.

Thirty-four

When her mother died, Heather heard her heart break into a million tiny pieces.

They still floated in her veins, shards as sharp as razor blades, making tiny cuts inside her and she felt them: bleeding like tears through her pores.

I know this – I'm selling the house…

Heather had been born at Ty'r Cwmwl. It was her heart's home. Although she wouldn't have admitted it in a thousand years, the future frightened her. If Ida meant what she'd said about selling the house, it changed everything. It was one thing for her to leave, another entirely for her to sell it to someone else. To people who might not be as accommodating.

There was no love lost between them, but until now, even as Ida had seemed to dig herself in, and Heather sensed herself being edged out, she imagined she'd brokered a small deal with Ida. Ty'r Cwmwl wasn't out of bounds, and her mother's grave was safe. And hadn't Ida said she had nowhere else to go? Whatever future she had in mind for the house, Heather could have sworn, Ida Llewellyn intended to be part of it.

Until today, and now it seemed as if they would both be going.

Shaking, she grabbed her bicycle and pushed it towards the stile. How could she have got it so wrong?

Her face burned. The blow Ida had inflicted still stung.

Who knew she had it in her? Ida bloody Spider.

In the end, we all pay our dues.

Heather remembered all the words her mother had ever spoken to her. Each day was a gift from fate, she had insisted. There was no future – not until you arrived – what mattered was the present, making the best of it, until it became your past.

I'll make sure she pays, Mam.

She bit down on her lip. Heather didn't cry in front of people and after her mother died she'd turned into a liar. The biggest lie she told was to the people who asked her how she was managing. She said she was fine, when what she'd wanted was to weep, explain that she was lost and needed her mother. Apart from Roni, they'd hated Olwen and the last thing Heather needed was their pity. She hadn't shed a single tear in public and few in private.

Leaning against the stile, too shaken to ride her bicycle, she brushed a treacherous tear off her stinging face. Her mother would have soothed the skin with aloe vera, given her a glass of brandy for the shock.

She would have made everything better.

A few hot tears slipped between her fingers and Heather rubbed the heels of her hands hard into her eyes, sweeping them away. 'I won't cry, Mam, I'll get even. I'll kill her before I let her lay a hand on me again.'

Heather didn't care about the doll. Or the stupid red shoes. She cared about her mother and what Ty'r Cwmwl had meant to her. Before she'd gone into Ida's bedroom, she'd looked again at the bureau in Olwen's room, seen the scratches on the wood and they had made her angry.

'Not yours to break into, town girl.'

Sitting on the bed, the golden-haired doll had looked like a princess. Not the Disney kind – Ida's doll had a look of the fae. When Heather gazed at her ethereal face she'd seen love and moonlight and mist. As her fingers stroked the doll's silk gown, the hairs on her arm stood on end. When she found the ragged red ballet shoes underneath the pillow, a pain had run through her fingers, like the sadness of a broken, torn up dream.

'I wasn't going to take anything, Mam – she just makes me so mad.' Heather straightened up, fastened her jacket and rubbed a cold hand on her cheek.

I could have you arrested…

'Like that's ever going to happen. Try it, Ida Spider and then you'll see what my mam can do.'

Ida was everything Heather had suspected. It was money that mattered to her. People like her: privileged, with property and money to spare, hung onto it.

Heather stared down at the grass and moss, as if the patterns they made could be a map or a set of instructions. Unprepared for death, weakened by fever, her mother had made no plans and left no directions. Not even a note to say goodbye.

Heather straddled the bike and kicked up the pedal.

I hate her but we have to make her stay, Mam. And if we can't, you have to mend my heart so I can't feel this sadness anymore.

The grass swished under the new tyre Roni had found for her. She steered the bicycle along the track and down towards the village. The wind caught her thoughts, and in particular the one that however hard she tried to make it go, clung like a net of cobweb.

Heather knew the only way to mend a heart as broken as hers was to find someone else who knew what a heart sounded like when it shattered.

Thirty-five

The staircase creaked under her feet and Ida wondered if it was the house, warning her.

She placed her hand on the windowpane again, over the visible patina of her palm print. The impact still tingled. Blinking, she saw Heather, tottering against the bed.

The surface of the glass was slightly sticky and Ida flinched.

You hit her.

Heather already considered her to be little more than a useless townie and a superstitious fool. Why not add violence to the list of her crimes? Even Roni had managed to make her feel slightly inadequate. The village women clearly despised her. As for Lowri – her silence spoke volumes. Everyone she had met since she'd moved here had written Ida off as some sort of a loser.

An intruder.

Returning to her bedroom, Ida ignored the mess, slumped in the chair by the window. She wouldn't cry – and in any case, she wasn't sure she could conjure a single tear. Her insides were as dry as sandpaper.

Anna's photograph stared at her.

'Mum?' Speaking to her mother's frozen image seemed absurd. 'This isn't part of the plan. She isn't.' Ida touched the enigmatic smile. Sighing, she turned her attention to the bed, righted the pillows, refolded her pyjamas and set Giselle in place.

And looked around for the red shoes.

They were nowhere to be seen. Heather, she knew, hadn't thrown them across the room or done anything dramatic with them. After Ida shouted at her, she'd dropped them onto the bed.

214

Puzzled, Ida leaned down, poked around underneath the bed in case they'd slipped to the floor. She lifted the edge of the bedspread, peered into the darkness. Dust skimmed the floorboards and the empty, echoing space.

Ida snatched Giselle up and sat her on the chair. Turning back, she ripped the bed apart, harried the pillows, flung the duvet and sheets to the floor, and dragged the mattress halfway across the metal base.

There was no sign of the shoes.

Next, she turned her attention to the chest, opened drawers, tipped the contents onto the floor. She pulled the bedside table away from the wall, felt in the space, the back of her hand scraping against the wall. Inside the wardrobe, she rooted through her few clothes, knelt down and ran her hands along the baseboard.

It was as if the shoes had been spirited away. Impossible and yet they were gone.

Giselle watched, her bland face giving nothing away.

'If she's taken them, I'll kill her.' The doll slid to one side and Ida clutched at her. 'I will, I swear it on my mother's life.'

Tears of rage welled up inside her. Was it possible Heather had taken the shoes, when Ida hadn't been looking? Would she have done that?

Yes – she was sly and she'd been angry enough. She would have risked it, taken advantage of the smallest opportunity. The moment when Ida had tried to shoo away the birds: a second's sleight of hand and the shoes would have been tucked into her jacket.

Like a shoplifter.

Lleidr.

Were the women right and she was a thief after all?

And she still had a key! All the keys that had ever existed at Cloud House or so it seemed.

You're a coward.

Heather's voice, inside Ida's head still, made her wince. It was bitter and accusatory and a bubble of hysteria began to churn inside her.

A pair of old ballet shoes looking like they ought to have been binned years ago...

'If I count for so little, why am I here?' Spoken out loud, into the mute chaos of the room, Ida knew, in spite of the certainty of her intention, regardless of the threat she'd articulated to Heather, a rearrangement in her thinking had occurred. Being lost had become a habit. Ida was tired of it and it wasn't as if she hadn't been here before.

I'm a bit Welsh...

Right then, Ida knew she wasn't going to leave – not yet. Not after this latest outrage. Nothing would induce her to back down, or be forced out of her own house.

That said, in the light of her declaration to sell up, Ida could only guess what Heather might do next.

You don't mess with witches...

In the short term she needed to make sure the girl couldn't gain access to the house. Downstairs, she shot home the bolts on the front door. The sound echoed and when it faded, in the silence Ida realised the longcase clock had stopped.

Had someone else died? Some other mother, close by – this was the place for dead mothers, after all.

Chiding herself for her superstition, Ida decided there was nothing sinister about it. The clock simply needed winding. Opening the glass front she saw there was no key.

She allowed herself a wry smile. Had the house conferred an accolade on Heather Morgan: keeper of the bloody keys? No matter where Ida looked, there was the damn girl with her quicksilver eyes, her sense of entitlement and her collection of keys. And each time Ida had attempted to gain some ground, make her point and assert her authority, she had failed.

She knew she ought to take the initiative. Go to the village again and confront Heather. Demand her keys and her shoes. She hesitated. What if she was wrong? What if she'd made a mistake and the shoes were here somewhere. What if the crazy witch-ghost of the wrong mother had whisked them away out of revenge?

Because you hit her…

'Stop it.' Ida clenched her hands into fists so the nails dug into her palms. Heather was a nightmare and a thorn in Ida's side; she was also a grieving child. Buying into her fantasy would help neither of them. Being angry simply placed Ida at a disadvantage.

The fact remained, the shoes were gone.

She closed the glass on the clock face and went into the kitchen, intending to bolt the back door too. It was open and she saw the day was bland. No hint of trauma or raised voices remained. She was tired of being afraid. Weary of the house and its gloating presence, Ida slipped on her boots. As she walked across the yard, a few black birds shouted at her. This time she refused to be intimidated.

'Bugger off.' She didn't bother raising her voice. These birds would hear her even if she whispered.

The light shifted as a thread of wind caught the cloud. It was high, a great pale canopy tinged with citrus. It would drop later and perhaps there would be rain. For now it was wide and calm and unexpectedly beautiful. Ida stared at it, willing it to stay that way. She lifted the wooden gate out of the rut, slung it to one side, tramped along the overgrown path, spotted a clump of the flowers she'd seen when Heather had first brought her here.

Nasturtiums.

Ida picked a few. A marigold plant, leggy and tenacious, offered up a few last blooms as bright as suns. She picked a fading yellow rose, some spikes of lavender. And a handful of the tiny lilies.

Her phone rang.

Liz.

Her finger hovered over the delete button. How the hell was she supposed to explain herself to her best friend?

I lost my temper and slapped a child.

217

She ignored the call. Later, she would send a text, make something up. Looking up into the branches of the apple tree, Ida dared the hovering brown leaves to fall on her. Instead, she felt a splash of rain. The sky, which seconds before had been benign, now darkened. Something passed through the trees, cold and insistent. Ida clutched the flowers and walked quickly to the gate.

'Bloody Welsh weather!'

The words flew away. The rain began to fall faster and head down, she couldn't recall shutting her car window. If it was open, and she left it, the seat would be soaked. She made her way round to the front of the house, closed up the car and turned to go inside the front door.

Above her, a light glimmered.

The window of Olwen's room was tight shut. This time there wasn't a breath of a breeze, and the candle flame rose straight and still.

Thirty-six

Ida had come looking for Roni, hoping to accidentally run into her.

In her head she'd made up a reason – the car was misbehaving – because the real one was feeble. From her car, she watched a pile of leaves skitter across the road. Her gaze shifted, to a figure leaving the village shop. An elderly man walking with a stick.

She breathed a sigh of relief. Not the creepy women. Not that they wouldn't see her. Everyone, she suspected, saw her.

It was mid-morning and she was already regretting the impulse to drive to the village. Her former resolve was in danger of crumbling and she couldn't stop thinking it might be better if she returned to England after all. Start again from scratch in a small flat, or a house on the south coast near the sea; fill it with books, with house plants and her mother's lovely belongings.

Still reeling from the sight of the burning candle – which this time she'd refused to investigate – feeling stupid again and no closer to making a decision about her future, Ida knew she needed another viewpoint. She sensed Roni wouldn't be sentimental and could be relied upon to say what she really thought. She had seemed like a rational woman; if Ida decided to tell her about the candle, she didn't think Roni would mock her.

And Ida was at a loss as to what to do about Heather.

Each time she thought she'd made a decision, made up her mind to be understanding, try and work out some kind of compromise, the girl threw everything into chaos. Roni was the only person who knew Heather in a way that made sense, without the judgements other people appeared to level at her. Not that Ida wasn't judging. She was still angry, convinced the girl had taken her shoes.

Heather had played her. Since the first day, when she walked into the house for all the world as if she owned it, Ida had been at a disadvantage. Thwarted at each turn, by a wily, scheming creature armed with an unconstrained sense of entitlement and what amounted to terror tactics. And each time, Ida had found her own strategies overthrown, what little wisdom she possessed, questioned, and her sanity challenged.

Parking by the bridge, Ida pulled her beret low, crossed the road to the garage, trying to remain invisible.

'You looking for our Roni?'

A thin woman with her hair tied in an old-fashioned turban stepped out from behind the solitary petrol pump. Ida decided there was no point in trying to fathom how this grapevine worked. It was like a giant web with the likes of Catrin Pritchard, Brenda Lewis and Roni's Auntie Gladys at the centre.

'I am. Are you—?'

'Round the back.'

The woman vanished into the garage.

Behind it was a wilderness – wilder even than the garden at Ty'r Cwmwl. Roni stood at the end of a short path in the open doorway of a single story, stone annexe.

The strains of something classical threaded through a window. A cat the colour of apricot jam eyed Ida from the sill.

Roni waved from the doorway. 'Come on up, Ida.'

Inside, the small space resembled a greenhouse. Plants grew everywhere and briefly, Ida was reminded of Lowri's sunny kitchen. The room held the contents in a stylish imperfection. Black and white photographs covered one of the walls: Marilyn Monroe, Elizabeth Taylor, Grace Kelly and several faces Ida didn't recognise. She spotted books, a camera and a pile of magazines.

An entire wall was lined with vinyl records and in a corner a vast stereo system sat as though it grew out of the floor.

Ida turned and turned again, on the spot, taking in the colour and patterns, the mixed scents of plants. 'It's amazing.'

Roni nodded her thanks. 'Coffee?'

The kitchen was a miniscule extension, the counters crammed with mugs and pans and Kilner jars filled with jewel-coloured, dried foodstuffs.

'Thank you.'

'Sit – make yourself at home and tell me to what do I owe the pleasure?' She turned down the music.

Ida stared at her hands, turned them over like they were the most fascinating things about her. 'Well—'

'Yes?'

Ida laughed, embarrassed now and struggling for words. 'My car's been making a weird noise.'

'You and I both know your car is fine, Ida. I'm delighted to see you and if you hadn't come I'd have invited you at some point. So what's this really about?'

'I need someone to talk to, if it's okay.' The words came out in a rush.

'No problem.' Roni placed an old-fashioned tin coffee pot and two mugs on a low table in front of the sofa. 'Are you okay? You're very pale and those circles under your eyes look like hammocks. Not sleeping?'

'On and off.' Roni's straight-talking manner was comforting. 'Being here – it's on my mind. Once I commit it's so final.'

'Because then you'd live here.'

Ida nodded. 'Like a local.'

'I wouldn't go that far.' Roni laughed. 'And you're not sure it's where you want to be?'

'Are you a mind-reader?'

'Hardly. That was Olwen's province. All I do is listen and take notice. Which is all she did to be honest. With a few more whistles and bells.'

'Well, whatever it is, you're right.' Ida leaned back against soft cushions. 'I came to Wales thinking I knew exactly what I wanted and now…'

'Now you're confused. Do you know why?'

'Oh, pick a reason… I'm not used to so much quiet for one thing. But I suppose you can tolerate anything if you put your mind to it.'

She was prevaricating and sensed she wasn't fooling Roni.

'And your mind is telling you what?'

'My mother tried to like it here and didn't manage it.'

'And?'

'And I don't know how to cope with Heather.'

'What's she done now?'

Ida picked out her words. 'I've … lost something. Mislaid maybe? I'm not sure. A pair of ballet shoes.' She hesitated. 'I think Heather took them.'

'Why?'

'Instinct.'

'Okay.'

'She had ample opportunity, Roni. And before you ask, there's nowhere left to look. She was in my bedroom, messing about with my things, mocking me about the shoes.'

'In your bedroom?'

'Yes, I caught her.'

'No wonder you're pissed off.' Roni poured coffee for them.

'My mother bought the shoes for me when I was a child,' Ida said. 'They're very precious.'

Roni frowned. 'Of course, but are you absolutely sure? Heather's a lot of things, I wouldn't have her pegged as a thief.'

Ida thought about the girl, with her strange eyes and her arrogance. Recalled the arc of her own hand as she'd reached out to slap Heather's mocking face.

'Oh, Roni,' she said, her voice a whisper, 'I've done something terrible.'

'How terrible?'

222

'I hit her.'

'You did?' Roni raised her eyebrows and made a face. 'Oh.'

'She stood there, smirking and taunting me, with her mother's curses and those awful birds, and I lost it.'

'Wow.'

'You have to understand, Roni, it's been going on ever since I arrived. She won't leave me alone – it's relentless, like she's on a mission to get rid of me. The shoes, well, they were the last straw.' Ida bit her lip to hold back the tears. 'I can't bear the idea she might have thrown them away or destroyed them.'

'She wouldn't.'

'How can you be sure? She's devious and she tells lies and she hates me.'

'Yes, perhaps, and no.'

'She does. You haven't seen her – the way she looks at me, the way she sneaks around trying to scare me.'

'Ida, listen to me. I would probably have done exactly the same in your place. Heather's clearly been behaving atrociously, but I honestly don't believe she would have stolen your shoes. Not permanently. She'll give them back when she thinks she's made you suffer enough.'

'And how is that okay?'

'It isn't. And when I see her I'll make sure she knows it.'

'And then she'll have all the proof she needs. She already thinks I'm pathetic. You can't say anything.'

'If that's what you want.'

'It is. I have to deal with this myself. I just needed to offload. Sorry.'

'I'm flattered.' Roni reached for her cigarette case. 'Let's sit outside.'

Another door led from the room, out back to a patch of grass, sitting like a green tablecloth. It was open to the moorland and other than a few hardy shrubs, as bland and bare as the front was a wilderness. They sat on faded canvas chairs; Roni smoked and Ida watched the clouds.

223

'Tell me about your mother,' Roni said.

'I can't. If I do I'll cry. Everything's too raw, and it's as if she doesn't matter. Like Cloud House isn't anything to do with me or her.'

'What made them leave?'

'That's the irony – Mum hated the place, and now Heather wants to claim it for herself and *her* mother – like mine didn't exist.'

'Were you very close?'

'Oh yes.' Ida sighed. 'I adored her. She was remarkable.'

'And talented?'

'Yes. It set her apart and meant everyone wanted a piece of her. My father and I … sometimes it felt like a competition.' Ida pretended to be engrossed in the pattern on the coffee mug so as not to look directly at Roni. 'I'm not sure how I'm supposed to go on without her.' As she hoped, Roni made no reply. 'And your mother?'

'She died when I was a baby. Gladys took me in. She's been good to me.'

All the lost mothers…

'I'm sorry, Roni.' Ida sighed. 'I was a better person with my mother around.'

'And now you need to be yourself.'

'I don't know what that means.'

'You're like two people, Ida, and one of them is sharing her space with the imagined ghost of a dead woman. It isn't healthy. It's weird and you have to get to grips with it. Tell yourself there are no ghosts.'

'I keep trying.'

And yet there are candles lighting themselves, and a witch's voice in my head.

Roni carried on. 'The thing about Heather is, she doesn't do self-pity.'

'Meaning you think I do.'

'No. I mean she's resilient. I'm not excusing her, but you know as well as I do, when you lose someone you love, it's like you lose the world too, for a while. But eventually, one day you wake up and what's outside the window is exactly the same as it was before, and the world's still there.'

'I can't bear what I see from those windows. The damp and the dark and the cloud. And most of all I hate those wretched birds.'

'And Heather?'

'No, I don't hate her. I agree with you; I want to feel sorry for her.'

'You don't have to, you don't even have to like her.'

'I know.'

'We've all got a sad story, Ida.'

'I miss my mother so much.'

'And Heather misses hers. Have you thought about that?'

Ida sat still as stone. If she let go of the breath she was holding, would it stop or would it flow out of her until each atom of air was expelled and she collapsed from the inside out, deflating like a balloon?

'Tell her you're sorry for slapping her,' Roni said. 'You can sort the rest later.'

'I'm not sure I know how to apologise to her. I'm too angry. And I'm not sure this can be sorted.'

Thirty-seven

A week passed and as the nights drew imperceptibly in, to Ida, it was as though the dark moved in on her, sidling around the edges of the house, a little earlier each day.

She called Liz and managed to sound normal. Liz wasn't fooled and said she didn't know what was going on but it was clearly odd. 'You sound weird. I'm worried about you.'

'I'm still waiting, Liz. The solicitor, you know?'

'You need to sack him. It's ridiculous.'

In fact, Mr Caterpillar Eyebrows had called, assured Ida the papers were in the post.

Ida tried to read one of her new books but found her concentration slipping. It was the crime thriller, and could have been set right on her doorstep.

The road snaked across the bleached moorland, a dark grey slash slicing the hill in two...

The words blurred and Ida realised however good the story was, she couldn't keep up.

Surprised when the day disappeared, it was as if the night was an ambush aimed at catching her unawares. Each evening, in spite of having the electricity connected, she lit the oil lamp in the kitchen, liking the light, becoming adept with the wick. She found another, smaller lamp which she cleaned and placed next to her bed. Staring up at the flickering ceiling she saw cracks in it, spidery lines and imagined them, through the decades, spreading like plaster scars. Some were wide and dark suggesting cavities and hidden spaces.

Hiding places.

The loss of the red shoes was a physical pain. She searched everywhere, even went to the grove, half-expecting to see the shoes hanging in a branch like a bizarre offering. There was no sign of them and no question in her mind: Heather must have taken them. Either – as Roni suggested – as a joke or, more likely, as Ida believed, an act of deliberate spite.

She watched the gaps in the ceiling, how they appeared to move and she closed her eyes, feeling stupid and guilty. How could she have lost control?

She asked for it...

No she hadn't. No one asked to be hit.

Ida turned into a peeping Tom, watching from windows, expecting Heather to turn up, scared she would, desperate to ask her what she knew about the missing shoes. And she knew she had to offer an apology. Slapping Heather had been an awful thing to do.

Still she did nothing.

In between her fruitless searches and random reading, Ida attended to the house. She cleaned and sorted, folded up the musty throws and put them away in a cupboard. Out in the barn, she tried her hand at splitting logs, found a more manageable axe and it made the job a little easier.

Every day she checked her phone and still there was no message from Lowri, no invitation to lunch. Ida began to dread the days, trying to find things to occupy her mind. There was money to worry about but once she considered how little she had, that line of thinking was done.

Resolved to stay at Ty'r Cwmwl, for a while at least, how she would live there was the biggest puzzle. Without a job, her finances would be precarious. And there was the loneliness. What had her mother done for four years? How had she coped with the isolation?

She hadn't of course, which was why they had left.

It was just over a week since she'd seen Heather. Still desperate to locate the red shoes (and with an apology burning a hole in her gut), Ida decided it was time to confront her.

As she rinsed the cafetière, she heard a knock at the back door. Drying her hands, taking her time, she beseeched her thudding heart to quieten.

Heather was here, stealing Ida's moment of courage the way she had the ballet shoes.

She stood on the doorstep, hands at her sides. She looked feral. Her hair was caught in a tangled knot at her neck, tied with something blue. A different jacket – dark as old wine – hung open, the pockets sagging with secrets. Her skin was rose-blushed by the wind and she was breathless, as though she'd been running.

The particulars of her were becoming more distinct and Ida noticed freckles, what the layers of her clothes were made of: linen and velvet, a hem of something red and soft. Pockets and folds, pleats and tucks.

Close up, she was a shabby work of art.

'What do you want, Heather?'

The girl smiled, a lopsided, unreadable affair. 'I'm on my way to the grove. Unless you've changed your mind.'

'No, of course not.'

The air reverberated with the absence of apologies. The one Ida knew she owed the girl, stuck to her tongue like a dead leaf.

'Can I come in?'

The fact of her asking rattled Ida. Once again Heather set the pattern of the conversation, as if she had an aim in mind. As if it was a competition she had to win.

'All right if I sit down?'

'I suppose so.'

Ida watched the girl out of the corner of her eyes, sizing her up, trying to decide whether to accuse her or ask her question.

Or say she was sorry.

Heather shifted in her seat. 'Here, this came for you.' She

228

pulled a thick envelope from one of her pockets. 'It needed signing for.'

'I didn't sign for it.'

'No, Catrin did. I said I'd bring it up, seeing as I was coming anyway.'

'She had no right.'

'She does it all the time.'

'What? Forges people's signatures?'

Heather's shoulder's shifted, as if a full-blown shrug was too much of an effort.

'Unbelievable.'

'Get over yourself, Ida. It's a long way for the postman to come, for one letter.' Heather slapped the envelope onto the table. 'At least I bothered. Knowing Catrin Pritchard it could have been the last anyone saw of it.'

'It's not the point.'

'The point is, you got your precious letter. And after what you did, you're lucky I didn't set fire to it.'

Ida cleared her throat. 'Yes, about that – I'm sorry I hit you, Heather. It was unforgivable.'

The girl's face gave nothing away. She held out the letter and Ida tried not to snatch it, any thanks lying dormant. Was Heather really not going to offer an apology in return?

'I told you, I was coming up anyway.'

Clearly not.

Ida ran her fingers across the embossed name in the corner, aware of the girl's scrutiny.

'Important, is it?'

None of your business.

'Papers. My solicitor.'

Heather laughed. 'Well, there you go. Lucky I decided to bring it then, isn't it?'

'It's just business, Heather. Nothing of importance.'

'Looks fairly important to me.'

Ida stared at the thick envelope, guessing it contained the documents she needed to sign in order to make her the official owner of Ty'r Cwmwl.

Heather was still smiling and Ida wanted to slap her all over again – wipe the nosy grin off her face.

'Heather,' she said, 'I have to ask you something.'

'What's that then?'

An edge of arrogance again and Ida's indignation stirred. 'When you were here, before, did you take my shoes? The red ones?'

'What?'

'My ballet shoes. I can't find them and you were the last person to see them. You had them in your hands, then you threw them on the bed. I certainly didn't touch them and after you left, they were gone.'

'Are you accusing me of stealing?' Heather was on her feet, her eyes bright with anger.

'I'm not accusing you of anything. I'm asking.'

'Oh, right, so me being the last person to see your precious shoes, and you asking me if I *nicked* them, means something else in your fancy version of the English language?'

Her emphasis was loaded and Ida flinched. 'I'm not saying that, only if you didn't take them, where are they? I've looked everywhere. What happened to them after you put them on the bed?'

'I haven't *stolen* your stupid bloody shoes!' She aimed the words like poisoned darts.

Ida shook her head. 'I don't believe you.'

'And I told you, I'm not a thief and I don't tell lies.'

'Oh stop it!' Ida shouted. 'Give it up, Heather. I know you're lying, it's written all over you.' They were eye to eye and her voice rose, full of fury. 'Where are my shoes?'

Heather held her gaze. 'I'm warning you, don't call me a liar!'

'Oh, and if I do, I suppose you'll curse me.'

'Don't joke about things like that, Ida. I've never cursed a living soul in my life and neither did my mam.'

'It's not what you said before.'

'I know exactly what I said. You don't listen. Cursing will come back on you threefold, and most spells too.' Heather's eyes blazed. 'Unless you know what you're doing.' She paused. 'Unless it's *allowed*.'

The girl was perfectly still, her pupils dilated and Ida's skin crawled.

She can't do anything. She's a thief and a charlatan...

'You're bad news, Ida.'

'*I'm* bad news? You are joking?'

Heather folded her arms. 'Well, let's see shall we? Are you the one accusing me of stealing or not?'

Was she?

'Okay.' Heather narrowed her eyes. 'Here's the thing. I'd rather wear a pair of Dan Pritchard's smelly socks dipped in sheep shit than your ripped old ballet shoes. I wouldn't be seen dead in them.'

'So where are they? Taken by a ghost I suppose?'

'You're obsessed.'

'And you are rude and obnoxious and I don't believe a word you say.'

Heather shook her head. 'You know what? I feel sorry for you.' She turned to go, paused and glanced over her shoulder, her eyes fixed on Ida's face. 'If you ever accuse me of being a thief again, you'll regret it. And what you don't realise is, she's heard all of this. Mam I mean, and she won't ignore it.'

'You're talking nonsense again. And you don't scare me.'

'Is that a fact?' Heather spat air.

'Heather—'

'Leave me be, bitch.'

Ida was shocked into silence.

Heather carried on. 'It doesn't matter what you do, you won't get rid of her, not until she's ready to leave. My mam belongs here. She loved this house and it knew. It still knows.' Her voice was sly and she said the words again. 'You won't be rid of her. Or me.'

Ida opened her mouth to speak but Heather cut her off.

231

'Don't you see, Ida Spider? No one wants you here. So go ahead, sell your precious house, chuck me out, try and chuck my mother out. For all the good it'll do you!'

Ida concentrated on keeping her temper. 'I want you to leave.' She ran the flat of her hand into her hair. 'Keys as well, before you do. All the keys. I know you have them.'

Heather fished in her pocket as if she too was bored with the fight. She threw something to the floor and the sound of it hitting the flagstones ricocheted.

Ida leaned down and picked up a key to the front door.

'You can have this one too.' Heather threw another key across the room. 'And this!'

Ida ducked as a key flew past her ear.

'And for the last time, no, I didn't steal your shoes.' The girl reached into her pocket again and Ida flinched. 'You're so stupid,' she said, throwing down yet another key. 'You can't see for looking. How many *times*, Ida.' She gave a crooked smile. 'I swear you'd miss the bloody bus if it *stopped* outside the house.'

Turning on her heel, Heather left the kitchen, slamming the back door behind her.

Ida felt the fight go out of her. She sank into the chair. Under her fingers, the thick, creamy envelope reminded her of what she was trying hard to ignore. If she opened it, the edges of the paper would cut her like knives.

Perhaps she would tell the solicitor to put the house on the market sooner rather than later after all, go away where no one knew her.

The words, 'running away' ran in her mind again.

The truth was the house didn't want her. No one did. Lowri had forgotten her, Heather hated her and the ghost of the wrong mother was on a mission to destroy her mind.

The right mother's ghost was nowhere to be seen.

Ida's previous conviction that she ought to stay and stick it out, stick two fingers up at Heather, now struck her as pathetic.

What had she been thinking?

Thirty-eight

She hadn't closed the curtains.

The bedroom window stared, a smattering of queer light in the room, picking out the cane chair, her discarded clothes and the dressing table. Ida swung her legs over the edge of the bed, and shivered. The cloud was so low it felt like an attack.

She made her way downstairs, saw the range had gone out, the supply of dry wood reduced to a few sticks, and cursed her foolishness.

You have to remember to bank it up.

Heather Morgan, fount of all knowledge.

Pulling on her boots, and her coat over her pyjamas, Ida set off across the raw patch of yard, enveloped in misty cloud.

There was no escaping it. It clung in patchy folds, overlaying the house like smoke: fat plumes, curving and breaking apart, cold against her hair. As it touched her it became invisible, which only added to its freakish nature.

At the barn door she shoved it open, gathered an armful of wood and scuttled back to the house.

When her phone rang she jumped. The screen glowed – the tiniest glimmer of a signal and an unfamiliar number.

'Hello?'

'Ida? Hi, it's me.'

'Sorry?'

'Lowri. It's Lowri.' Her voice was different. She was talking quickly, explaining how the time had flown, how she'd remembered her promise to call and something about exams. 'I'm up to my eyes – I've too many classes, it's crazy.'

'How did you get my number?'

'You gave it to me?' Her voice faded and came back.

'Oh yes,' Ida said. 'Of course I did. Sorry.'

'I'm really sorry too – that I didn't call sooner – it's been nuts here. Some of my pupils are doing their first grade on pointe. It's a stressful time. Well, you know.'

The smell of rosin was all at once everywhere. Ida was thirteen-years-old, her hair tied back so tightly it made her head hurt, wearing a black leotard and her first pair of pointe shoes: pink (not red) with the ribbons sewn in the correct way, meticulously, by Anna the ballerina. The years of toil behind her, technique perfected, bones hardened and ready.

'You have the ideal foot for pointe,' her mother had insisted. 'You'll be fine.'

Until she fell and dashed both their dreams.

Merde…

'Are you still there?' Lowri's voice crackled down the line.

'Yes, sorry.'

'I was wondering – do you fancy a day out? Well, an afternoon actually. The morning's half-gone.'

'You mean today?'

'Why not? Unless you're busy.'

Ida was a stranger to spontaneity. 'I suppose so.'

'If it isn't convenient…'

'No, it's not that, Lowri – I'd love to. You've taken me by surprise, that's all.'

'So you'll come?'

'Yes, I will.' Ida glanced at her watch. 'It'll take me about an hour though.'

'Brilliant. Park on the prom and I'll look out for you. Buy you some chips and an ice-cream.'

They were nervous with one another, walking, not quite side by side, eating fat chips laced with salt and vinegar.

Ida, careful not to make eye contact, watched the sky.

'The clouds are different here,' she said.

'Are they?'

'There's something about cloud out on the moor. When it falls it's like a curtain – it obliterates everything. There's nothing gentle about it.'

'Wow.'

'Wow?' For the first time that day, Ida smiled, caught Lowri staring at her and looked away.

'You make it sound spooky.'

'It is,' Ida said. 'It's uncanny. The house is named after it.'

'Really?'

'Cloud House.' Ida hesitated. 'I'm still trying to get my tongue around the Welsh.'

'Ty'r Cwmwl? I like it. It's mysterious. Like a ghost story.'

Ida wondered what Lowri would say if she told her she believed the house might be haunted. By a ghost as invisible as air.

They stopped near a bandstand, sat on the sea wall their backs to the sea.

'Finished?' Lowri tapped Ida's chip paper.

'Yes, thanks.'

Lowri strolled over to the bin, and Ida watched her, recognising the dancer's walk, the turned-out feet and arched back. Her hair, freed from its classroom severity, fluttered, fine and wavy and as red as old port. Ida watched how she dropped the crumpled paper into the bin, laughed at a gull pecking on the ground for scraps. And quick as a sylph, she was back, swinging her legs over the wall so she faced the sea. Ida did the same and Lowri shifted, stared at her.

'You have startling eyes,' she said.

'I do?'

'Yes, they remind me of rain.'

'Oh.'

'In a good way.' Lowri smiled. 'I like rain.'

'You do?'

'I'm Welsh.' A smile graced her face and her gaze was unwavering.

The inside of Ida's chest burned. An introvert by nature, she wasn't comfortable with this level of intimacy. Time stopped, like a broken film reel. The sand and pebbles evaporated until she felt herself floating, thought about desire: how it surfaced, unbidden, when you least expected. Again she sought to deflect the conversation. 'May I tell you something?'

'Sure.'

'There's a girl.'

'Ah, I see—'

'No, you don't. It's nothing like that.' Ida blushed. 'A girl who lived at the house. My house. Ty'r … Cwmwl?'

Lowri's smile broadened. '*Da iawn.*'

'Her name's Heather. Her mother was my father's tenant. She died, last year, I think. Then he did. They did, I mean. My mum and dad. And the house came to me.'

'Yes.'

Except for the incident with the red shoes, Ida skirted the detail. She alluded briefly to Olwen's ghost – to Heather's absurd claims for her. And she owned the slap. Lowri listened carefully and without interrupting.

'I feel dreadful,' Ida said.

'If she'd nicked something that precious off me,' Lowri said, 'I'd have punched her lights out.'

'No you wouldn't.'

'I might have.'

'Don't make it sound acceptable, Lowri. It was a terrible thing to do. And I don't feel good about accusing her of stealing either.'

'Even though you think she did?'

'Yes.'

'She sounds like a nightmare and a bit of a fantasist.'

'I don't know about that.'

'She says her mother's *ghost* is going to make you leave?'

'I know. That is crazy.'

No it isn't…

'You're staying then.'

Once again, Ida realised she might be. Somehow, in the midst of the chaos and drama, and like a human version of a revolving door, she thought she might have rethought her decision yet again.

'Yes. I think perhaps I am.' She shook her head. 'Oh, who am I kidding? This week, I've changed my mind as many times as there've been days. But yes, I think so. Maybe.'

'Do you mind if I ask why you came back? I mean, if there was a choice.'

'There's always a choice, only where else would I have gone?'

'I suppose if it feels right—'

'I wouldn't go that far.' Ida managed a wry smile. 'I was curious, all right? There's a part of me that's Welsh. The part of me I left behind? If that makes sense.'

'Of course it does. I did the exact same thing.'

'I just wish Heather would leave me alone – give me space to settle things one way or another. But she's relentless, and I'm responsible for her.'

'I don't see why.'

'Because she's young and alone. And she misses her mother.' Ida stared out at the horizon, at a line between the water and the sky, straight as a thread. 'We both know what that's like.'

'You miss Anna a lot, don't you?'

Ida gave an imperceptible nod.

'Do you miss dancing?'

Ida flinched. 'Where did that come from?'

'Do you want to tell me?

'Not really.'

'Okay.'

'It's hard.'

'Yes, it must be. Why don't you start at the beginning?'
Because no one does.

Only fairy stories began with once upon a time. The real ones were a melting pot and people picked out the bits best suited to their audience.

'I had a fall. I told you. It happens and I was unlucky. Game over.'

'Are you sure?'

'Of course I am!' Always the same anger. 'What do you think?'

'I don't know. I can't see how giving up is the answer.'

'I didn't give up – it gave me up.'

'And one ricked foot makes you a cripple?'

The word hung on the air like a stink.

'Jesus, I'm sorry. That was awful.' Lowri touched Ida's arm.

She flinched and pulled away. 'Don't. You've known me for five minutes; I've shared something deeply personal, and you think it's all right to attack me?'

'I'm sorry. I only meant—'

'Where do you get off picking on me?'

'Is that what you think I'm doing?'

'Aren't you?'

'I'm trying to work you out, Ida. I like you.' Lowri held her hand to her head, pushed back her hair. 'You can carry on believing you're washed up, or you can change things. You're right – we have only known each other for five minutes but I don't have you down as someone who gives up.'

Ida pressed her lips together. Crying would make her look pathetic. But Lowri was wrong. Her analysis ought to be flattering, instead it was ludicrous.

You can't give up something you never had.

She had never been brave. Or had many friends. Other than Liz, everything she cared about was gone and nothing could fill the space. Least of all a woman with an uncanny way of seeing her heart, albeit with a knack for tactlessness.

'Ida, I mean it, I like you. I want to see—'

'See what? You don't know me.' Ida gazed at Lowri's earnest, hopeful face and thought how little anyone knows about another person. Thought back to all the times she'd passed on opportunities to be included: how refusing had become a habit. She had no aptitude for friendship, and certainly not for anything more.

Lowri wanted more. Ida knew it. And Ida saw her own desire reflected back from a pair of languid green eyes.

Thirty-nine

As Ida parked her car, the house greeted her, implacable and stern.

Inside, it creaked and whispered. She listened, trying to sense its character. It struck her as taciturn, reluctant to give up its secrets. The smell of apples was stronger than ever, like sap, and it was everywhere.

Removing her coat, she slung it over the newel post. Her eyes scanned the scarred stair treads, worn bare of wax and the attention of anyone who cared. The longcase clock was still silent and Ida wondered again, why it had stopped. She ran her hand down the satin-smooth cabinet.

Because Heather hadn't returned to wind it?

The internal workings of fancy clocks were a mystery to Ida. She guessed there would be a pendulum and weights, but that was the extent of her knowledge. Curious, she looked closer, and saw a neat keyhole in the narrow wooden door.

With a key.

Ida turned it, heard a gentle click as the key turned and the door swung open. Inside the dark interior, the dull gleam of brass workings greeted her. Weights and a heavy pendulum, inert and perfectly still.

And the reason became immediately apparent. Wedged in the workings Ida saw her red shoes. The ribbons were caught in the mechanism, twisted like red snakes, the ends more frayed than ever. She sat back on her heels, lost for words, her hand to her mouth. For a second the hallway shifted and she went with it. Her head spun and she touched the wall to steady herself.

It took a few moments to untangle the ribbons and free the shoes. As she did, the pendulum shuddered and various bits of brass clunked, a hollow sound, before stopping again, leaving only a truncated echo.

The shoes lay in her hands, as fragile as broken butterfly wings. The red of them had long ago bled to a pale imitation. They seemed more vulnerable than ever, as if they might disintegrate at any moment. Ida held them to her heart, closed her eyes and waited until she was sure the dizziness had passed.

Not stolen.

Don't call me a liar…

When Ida stood up, her knees buckled. The scent of apples wafted round her, so strong it made her gag.

More cunning than a liar, Heather was a trickster – a game player who had deliberately hidden the ballet shoes, stuffed them inside the clock, in the dust and grime, not caring if she destroyed them. Left them to rot or worse, to be eaten by mice.

Technically, Heather had told Ida the truth. This in no way mitigated the enormity of what she had done. Hell-bent on making mischief, she had deliberately played the unkindest trick she knew, knowing it was possible Ida would never discover the hiding place of her precious shoes. And to add insult to injury, she'd dangled a childish, pointless clue.

You're so stupid … you'd miss *the bloody bus if it* stopped *outside your house.*

Ida stared at her phone. Next to it, on the kitchen table, the shoes lay side by side, the ragged ribbons wound with care, holding them in place.

Still stunned, she placed her palms together, set the edge of her index fingers against her lips. She was uncertain what to do – unsure how to deal with the potential fallout; a confrontation with Heather could go anywhere.

You have to.

Her heart pounding, she picked up her phone. Digits shifted like insects, and Ida realised she was nervous.

Scared of a teenager.

She was being ridiculous. How many times had she told herself over the last weeks that she was a grown-up? It was time to bring this ridiculous situation to an end.

The screen showed a flicker of connectivity and Ida listened as the number rang out. When an automated answerphone voice finally kicked in, she was near to tears.

'It's me, Heather. Ida. I need to talk to you. When you get this message, please call me. It's urgent.' Her voice wobbled. 'And don't ignore me. I found my shoes. You need to explain.'

When her phone rang, twenty minutes later, Ida snatched it up like it was alive. 'Heather?'

'What's so urgent?'

'I told you. I found my shoes and I know you didn't steal them. I do know exactly what you did.'

'Well, aren't you the clever one then?'

Her voice faded and Ida went to the front door, walked away from the house, holding on to her temper. 'We need to talk.'

'All right – if you like. I'll come by the house. Now – if you're in that is.' She laughed, and the echoing, intermittent phone connection made it sound artificial and mocking. 'But you're always in, aren't you? Mostly.'

The phone was hot against Ida's ear. Did the wretched creature know everything about her? Did she know Ida had been out yesterday?

'I'll expect you.'

This time Heather's hair was a wild brown halo and with the light behind her – a trick Ida was determined to ignore – sparks flickered in it. She had the look of a petulant child, scorn in her startling eyes, her hands spread in a question. 'Am I allowed in then?'

'Don't play games, Heather, I'm sick of them. Just come in. And shut the door, you're letting in the cold.'

As Heather closed the door behind her, the light was gone, the spell diluted. Ida saw how her eyes glanced over the red ballet shoes.

'What do you want, Ida? I don't have all day.'

'Well, you can at least do me the courtesy of pretending you give a fuck.'

'It was a joke.'

'No it wasn't, it was spiteful and you could have destroyed my shoes. They were caught in the clock's mechanism.'

'If I said I was sorry, would you believe me?'

Ida flung herself onto a chair. 'Why would you do something like that?'

'You hit me.' Heather's eyes flared. 'I was pissed off with you. And I gave you a clue.'

'What?'

'I told you to look properly.' She sidled into the chair opposite Ida.

'And that was supposed to tell me you'd hidden my shoes inside a *clock*?'

'I thought you'd guess. You're supposed to be the smart one.'

'I'm in no mood to indulge you, Heather. There are rules. About privacy and personal space. And you have abused mine big time. Can't you even try to understand how what you did was unacceptable?'

'All right, all right – keep your hair on.' Heather chewed the side of her finger. 'I'm sorry, okay?'

'But do you mean it? Do you understand why I'm so upset? Those shoes, Heather – my mother bought them for me when I was seven-years-old. The doll was her last gift to me. And between them—'

'There's history.'

If Ida was startled by this apparent level of understanding, she kept her face non-committal. She was still furious and in no mood to placate.

'Yes,' she said. 'Exactly. Memories and love and a sense of her and me.' She paused. 'You know what I'm talking about, don't you?'

Heather nodded. 'I didn't mean any harm.'

'And I want to believe you. But you can't—'

'It's hard not to be here.' The words came out in a rush.

'I know,' Ida said. 'I get it. It's hard for me too. Being here.' She searched for the right words. 'Our lives have collided and it's not our fault; it's a mess. But you fit Heather, and I don't. I'm the stranger, the one people are talking about, making fun of.'

'No they aren't. Believe me, the only person giving you a hard time is me.'

'So you admit it?' Ida allowed herself a brief smile.

Heather rolled her eyes. 'They're too up themselves to be bothered about you. Believe me, you'll know when you're interesting. The sky will fall in.'

Recalling the look of contempt on Catrin Pritchard's face, Ida thought the woman was likely in league with the entire firmament. 'Stop changing the subject.'

'I'm not, I'm just saying.'

Ida waited. The desire to argue had dissipated like smoke up a chimney. She had no energy for another fight.

'I mean it,' Heather said. 'I'm really sorry.'

'I know.'

'So what are you going to do?'

'About what?'

'Everything.'

'Work on a new life?'

Heather considered this. 'Some life, eh?'

It was the first time Ida had detected so much as a hint of vulnerability in the girl. 'How do you manage, Heather?'

'What do you mean?'

'For money?'

'I have Mam's – the money meant for me.' She gave a brief smile. 'I never told Bethan the full amount. It's not much mind – a few hundred a month. Until I'm eighteen.'

'So he wasn't all bad? Your father?'

Heather shifted in the chair. 'I told you, I don't know anything about him. It was guilt money. An afterthought by the sounds of it. He was a coward and he owed us. He disappeared when he knew I was on the way. But if it was good enough for Mam – if she hadn't thought it was immoral to take it – why would I turn it down?' Her mouth twisted. 'Fathers are meant to take care of their children, even wasters. Only when did money ever make a person happy? Mam had nothing and she was the richest person I ever knew.'

'And social services? What do they have to say?'

'They came once – sniffing around, asking questions. I told them I was eighteen and there's no papers to prove otherwise. Mam made sure of that. They soon got bored. I was either too much trouble or not enough.' Heather shrugged. 'You choose.'

'That's tough.'

'It's the life you're dealt.'

'Heather, can I ask you something else? About your mother?'

'If you like.'

'Do you ever see her?'

'You mean her ghost?'

Did she?

'I suppose that's what I mean.'

'It either is or it isn't, Ida. Make up your mind.'

'Yes then. Her ghost.'

'She left her spirit here.'

Ida thought Olwen must have left a lot of other things too: anger and resentment and grief.

No wonder I think I'm being haunted.

'It's hard to explain, you wouldn't understand. About her leaving.'

'Stop saying that, Heather. Stop assuming I don't know what you're talking about.'

'You don't light the candle though, do you? Like I asked?'

I don't need to – Olwen lights it for me.

'When a person dies, there's more to it than the dying. I told you – Mam still needs to come and go.'

Ida thought about open windows that had nothing to do with her.

'When people die,' Heather whispered, 'there has to be a true leaving, when they find peace and their soul's set free.'

Ida couldn't stop the image coming – the broken wall, the brick dust and the crushed bodies.

'And I'm waiting, see,' Heather said, 'for her true leaving.'

Dying and leaving – making a thing of it – is human business.

My black birds can take it or leave it. It doesn't mean they don't notice.

Twilight brushes against dusky night and a thin moon knifes a tear in the cloud. We draw the dark, me and my lovelies, watch my girl walk away, hear her bruised heart beating in tune with my shimmery one.

I see you, girl with no feet, falling into your fretful sleep.

The birds nod to each other, mutter and murmur, quiet as moths.

This moment?

Oh, would you look at that? The black beauties see my old magpie, with her still keen eye, and they make space. They know her business is part of the story, still in need of telling.

Look again, how they pause, shoulder-roll and confer, nod as my raggedy favourite flies up to the high chimney.

Part Three

Forty

Ida skimmed the second of her new books, half-listened to a play on the radio, not concentrating on either.

It was when she put down the book she heard a noise somewhere above her. In the hallway, she stood at the foot of the stairs. The sound came again – from Olwen's room – a slide and a dull thud, as if something fell to the floor. As quietly as possible, she made her way up the stairs. Pausing at the door, she pushed it open, slowly, slowly.

The first thing she noticed was the open window. And on the sill, the candle stump in the tin candle holder.

Alight.

The flame flickered, a thread of smoke curling from the tip of the flame.

It was illogical and impossible. Once again, Ida chided herself for a fool. She was on edge, anxious and exhausted and this was some kind of fallout: a trick or an illusion, and there would be some reasonable explanation.

Heather must have come back, to wind her up again.

Ida knew she hadn't. When Heather had left the previous evening, she'd been subdued; she'd said goodbye quietly and it was sadness, not hostility that surrounded her.

The candle fizzed and it sounded like bees. A wave of heavily scented air, thick as dust and smelling of withered apples, engulfed her. Ida felt a jolt of fear. She shook her head to clear it. The flame guttered and a gust of wind played with it for a second before extinguishing it. Soft wet wax pooled in a greasy mess and the remains of the wick hissed. The stink obliterated the smell of apples, intensifying until all Ida smelled was burning wax and soot.

Soot.

As she watched, a small feather spun on the air before settling on a pile of fresh soot spilling out of the hearth like a stream of black lava.

Something metal glinted in the black and Ida crouched down. With her index finger she touched the ornate head of a thick, heavily tarnished brass key. She picked it out of the mess and brushed off the soot. The shank was short, the bit neat and perforated with a small star.

Ida laid the key on the palm of her hand. She felt it at once: a tingle that set her fingertips on fire and she knew exactly what it would unlock. How the key to Olwen's bureau had ended up in this second soot fall was a mystery, and for now she didn't care. What mattered was she had found it.

Wind sighed down the chimney as if the outside wanted to get in. The scent of apples came again, stronger, making her head spin.

Ida knew this was no random discovery. Nothing connected to Olwen Morgan involved chance. None of the events of the past few weeks were down to happenstance. She stared at the key, examining the detail of it. It was neither misplaced nor lost. It had been hidden. And Ida was meant to find it. She knew this, the way she knew the detail on her birth certificate or the lines on her face.

The key cooled and Ida's heartbeat slowed. She got to her feet, slowly, in case she fell. In the corner of the room, the bureau looked bigger.

You don't get to touch anything…

Heather's voice insinuated again, telling Ida, if her mother had locked the bureau it meant she hadn't wanted anyone poking around inside it.

And if you do … it won't end well.

Ida snapped her fingers around the key. 'We'll see about that.'

Outside the open window, a bird called – a loud, familiar *kraa* – and for the first time since she'd moved to Cloud House, Ida wasn't afraid.

The key slid into the slot in the fallboard as if it were oiled. *Click*.

A satisfyingly coherent sound and the fallboard tilted forward on heavy brass hinges. It settled into place revealing a dark leather writing pad, pigeonholes fretted with more carved decoration and beneath them, a row of drawers.

It was a work of art and once again, Ida wondered why she had only the dimmest memory of it, how she had forgotten what it looked like inside.

Why would I remember? I was a little girl. Uninterested.

Furniture had meant a comfy bed, a sofa to curl up in with her mother, and places to keep her books and toys.

The bureau appeared to be empty and a wave of disappointment engulfed her. Ida's fingers grazed the smooth wood of the empty pigeonholes. She didn't know what she had expected: spell books and more tattered charms like the ones hanging in the grove? Something more mundane perhaps – private correspondence, bills and receipts?

One at a time, Ida opened the drawers. They were shallow, seven in all: five small ones and bookending them, two wider ones. One by one, they opened and each of them was empty.

The final drawer – the long one on the left – moved an inch and stuck. Ida jiggled it, trying not to be heavy-handed. It refused to budge and in the dark cavity she glimpsed something wedged and impeding the drawer.

Paper.

Ida eased her finger into the gap, forcing the paper down. Now the drawer slid open, revealing a single folded sheet. Released from the confines of the drawer, it half-opened, enough for Ida to see it was a document of some sort and handwritten.

A letter?

The paper was pale blue, folded in three, the creases well defined as if someone had run a finger along them.

Ida hesitated. She had been brought up to respect other people's privacy. Reading a letter meant for someone else was a taboo. And this letter was unlikely to have been meant for her. Yet there was no envelope, suggesting anyone who found it might read it.

And who else but Ida, or possibly Heather, would?

The page fluttered, the edges opening slightly, and before Ida could decide otherwise, words began leaping out at her.

David.

Her eyes darted to the signature.

Olwen…

Ida slid to the floor, her back to the wall, soot dusting her jeans.

Olwen? Why would Heather's mother write a letter to her father and lock it away?

It was written in ink with a fountain pen and only slightly faded. The hand was elegant, the words touched with delicate flourishes. They lit up the page, their wait over, and they demanded attention.

Ida dragged her eyes back to the beginning.

…you are a thief. You stole my heart … when you left me, I soon stole it back…

In her shaking hands the page trembled. The words blurred and she blinked.

…your true heart was never mine. It was bound to her … how swiftly you ran back … once the consequences of adultery became clear…

She stared at the word – *adultery* – and it stared back, an ugly word made of treachery. Ida knew she ought to stop. This letter wasn't hers to read and yet it was. It was written to her father.

By Heather's mother.

If these words – suggesting an outrage Ida barely comprehended – weren't hers to read, whose were they?

Your weakness for beautiful women marked you…

A cold chill slid down her back. The meaning eluded her – at the instant its clarity choked her. She saw him – her handsome father turning heads, heard other women's comments, which her mother had always dismissed with a smile, indulgent and trusting.

'Such a charmer.'

Such a liar.

I try to imagine your face as you read this ... the appalled one you showed me when I told you ... pregnant.

Ida felt physically sick and her throat tightened.

When I found you out in your lie ... the tawdry bargain...

She clamped her lips together, looked away; looked back, unable to stop reading.

Daughter ... the word shines and bleeds into the paper ... This other daughter – this sister ... eyes the colour of rainlight...

Sister? *Sister.*

'Oh, Christ—'

I'll keep my side of the bargain ... take your money and your house for her sake ... keep your dirty secret hidden.

A secret, hidden from his wife. Money paid for a love child.

A sister...

The words hurt her head – rang off-key and Ida thought her brain would burst. Her eyes flicked back and forth...

This letter won't be posted of course ... you made sure I can't find you...

Instead it had found her. Found them both.

This sister...

She checked the date. Olwen must have written it around the time Heather was born. After he'd found out, had David abandoned her? It certainly looked that way.

Or had Olwen, discovering he was married, given him his marching orders?

When I found you out in your lie...

Ida's heart thumped inside her chest. And now the memory locks were clicking open, the pictures coming into focus.

Her mother, gently questioning. 'An extra night? Oh, David, must you?'

'Only one, my darling. Some things need attention at the house.'

'Get the solicitor in Wales to send a man.'

'It's easier if I go myself. Just a quick detour. I'll be back before you know it.'

Before you *know*...

What was it Roni had said? Olwen had had a secret lover she refused to discuss.

Married I would have guessed, if she'd been anyone else...

If she'd known.

An attachment. Had *he* known? Mr Caterpillar Eyebrows? At the very least he would have had his suspicions.

It looked for all the world as if, once he knew about Heather, her father hadn't set foot in Cloud House again. Which meant he certainly wouldn't have found the letter, written after Heather's birth and locked away.

Bound to her...

On his flying visits to the house, would her father have ever looked in the bureau? Unlikely. He hadn't violated Anna's privacy when the bureau had been hers. Why would he do so when Olwen took it over? And he would never have broken into it.

The way I did...

Her father had been a fastidious man too, respectful of beautiful things.

A collector of beautiful women...

The one thing Olwen hadn't bargained for was her premature death. Had she been too ill to retrieve the letter? Or had she wanted it to be found by Heather? Her last act of revenge on the man who had betrayed her? She couldn't have known he too was going to die before his time, and revenge would be a dish served up to absent diners.

To me.

Ida had no idea why Olwen had cleared the bureau or why she might have felt the need to do so. One thing was for sure, she'd emptied it of everything, save for the letter, guessing Heather would find it.

But how had the key ended up in the chimney?

She thought about the magpie she'd surprised in the room. The key would once have been shiny and a treat for a bird known for thieving. On the day she disturbed it, had the magpie been in the act of hiding the key? Or had it been there for years?

Some strangeness – chance or whatever spell Olwen had cast – meant the key had ended up in the chimney, until a random soot fall – if random it was – dislodged it.

And the letter had lain hidden too, waiting to be found.

By the wrong sister.

'Me.'

Ida felt another wave of nausea.

Fierce in her determination to protect her mother's privacy Heather had been telling the truth. She'd had all the keys except for the one that mattered. And unknowing, Olwen had had her revenge.

Serendipity was a powerful player and Olwen had always known her business.

It was the third bad thing.

I never did care for bills.

Box up the bits for disposal, and lock away the truth.

That was the plan. (I knew Bethan would pry and poke and take; make my business hers.) And it would have worked sooner, had my magpie – my pioden *– not taken a fancy to the key.*

Always after the glittery, that one.

I was too clever for my own good. She took the key, hid it away and didn't tell me. Not that I could have done anything about it.

(She kept an eye too. Made you jump, girl with no feet!)

There's nothing like your own death on the doorstep to stay your plans. All I could do was summon the last of my energy and cast a finding spell, hope it was strong enough.

That crazy bird flew away when I did.

And then you *came … and she came back, to finish the magic because I hadn't been able to.*

The trouble is, the weakest spell can be as tough to conjure as a ghost is thin. Who knew? You're the wrong sister, but you'll have to do.

I didn't mean to scare you – well, perhaps I did, but needs must.

And now I must hurry. Time, for me, runs softly and it runs out again…

These words are the before; I'll leave them, and what lies between the lines, in your dreams, for dreams you will surely have now. Dreams made of truth.

A dream for you.

And one for your sister.

Are you sleeping comfortably…?

We met in town one bright afternoon. He came out of a newsagents and I stumbled in front of him. The heel on my shoe had broken.

'Are you all right?' he asked. 'May I help?'

Reaching for my shoe, I eyed him. A tall, spare man, a lock of inky hair falling over his forehead. His eyes were blue as blackbird's eggs and I liked the look of them.

'I expect so. A broken heel's a nightmare. Is there a cobbler nearby?'

Later, the shoe fixed, and paid for by him, we sat on the prom, watching the ocean, and he fell under my spell.

'How can I ever thank you?'

'There's no need. It's my pleasure.'

'No, I mean it. I'd like to do something for you.'

My vitality mesmerised him.

'It isn't necessary.'

I held his gaze, breathed a small apple-scented spell into the space between us.

'Would you care to have dinner with me?'

Even as he spoke he hesitated, and I saw how the words struck him as both thrilling and foolhardy. He was helpless by then, the weakness in him.

The next time, he took me to the smartest hotel in town. I wore a frock scattered with tiny green apples. When I asked him to tell me about himself, before he could, I laughed and said, 'No, let me tell you about me.'

I didn't of course – I gave him a version. And I didn't bind him as I might have done. I wanted him at least half-willing, only a bit entranced.

Still – to make sure when we parted I brushed his cheek with a kiss, and slipped a skylark's feather into his pocket.

Forty-one

Ida knew what shock was.

How, at first, you didn't feel a thing. How, when you cut your finger the shock penetrated, numbing it and then, when the pain hit, how it rocked you.

Motionless, her hands still in her lap, the letter hovering like a blue bird, there was nothing: no curiosity, not even any disbelief. Stupidly, all she could think was how the spilled soot would tread through the house and make a mess.

You have another…

She didn't try to move, knowing she wouldn't be able to, not until her blood began to flow again because it had surely stopped.

Her name is Heather…The sibling bond is as strong as spider silk…

Sisters…

For the third time in her life, a moment of chaos tilted Ida's world. A misstep, a wall falling – a wall of words…

She didn't have the slightest idea what to do.

It was after midnight and although she was tired, her head rattled with thoughts, and a sense of Heather like a physical weight pressing on her.

Sister…

Too restless to sleep she wandered down to the parlour, the small oil lamp in her hand. The curtains hung open. She set the lamp on the windowsill, and its mirror image wavered in the black window. Ida thought about the letter, replaced in the drawer of the bureau because she didn't know what else to do with it.

Yes, you do.

The dark lay like a blanket. Ida couldn't see further than the edge of the front wall and the wooden gate. Night animals would be abroad and she blinked away half-imagined shapes. It struck her how there were no new nights, only recycled ones and even the days, if she examined them, held the familiarity of the previous one, practising for tomorrow.

Decades of the same old night, centuries, millennia old, surrounding the house, showing the cloud how it was done.

The lamp flickered. If anything was out there, would it see her? Would bats and spirits be drawn to the light's danger, along with the moths? Heather had told her she would get used to the dark. It was caught in the trees like black dew, and Ida knew she wouldn't.

However much she told herself there were no ghosts, only the dark making her small and insignificant, it was no comfort. She was utterly overwhelmed and with no idea how to process the cacophony inside her.

It was cold in the parlour. Ida thought about Heather in her bleak little cottage. Was she warm enough? The idea made her uncomfortable. Pulling her phone out of the pocket of her jeans, she sat with it balanced on her palm, gazing at the screen.

Phone her, you have to. You have to tell her.

Ida wondered what her father had told Olwen when they first met. That he was single, divorced, or worse – unhappy and misunderstood? These were the stereotypical lies men told, to cover their tracks, and put their lovers at their ease. Was this what her father had done?

Clearly, one of these was exactly what he'd done. And then he'd been found out.

Your lips as they revealed the existence of your wife and other child … the bargain concocted…

The sin of omission.

Ida had thought her father invincible, selfish sometimes, self-centred, certainly, but good-hearted and, above all, trustworthy.

And Olwen had been a witch – she had surely spellbound him, cast a dark hex on him. Even though common sense insisted this was impossible, a part of Ida wanted it to be true. The need to blame Olwen was intense because the likely reality appalled her.

When she thought about the nature of love, Ida knew there was more than one version. Her mother's eyes had been like a looking glass, the kind you stepped through. On the other side, her love drew you in, its purity revealed. And Ida had loved her mother back, deeply and inexplicably.

For the first time, it occurred to her that she had never felt that way about her father. She had admired his intellect. And he was her father – irascible and often remote; but of course she had loved him. Now he was diminished. Had she not found the letter, he would have remained respected and held in regard.

He may as well have ripped open her ribcage and torn her heart from its moorings.

She tried to piece the odd things together. His absences, on university business, and her mother's moments of distraction. The occasional arguments, standing out because they were so rare. The extravagant making up.

The second honeymoon…

Anna had wanted Ida to go with them. Why? Because she couldn't bear to be parted from her daughter. Or had she doubted him? Had she guessed?

The lamp's flame wavered and Ida carried it upstairs to the dusty room, retrieved the letter from the drawer. Sitting on one of the old cushions, she read again the words Heather's mother had written to her father and not posted. Searched between the measured recriminations, for a clue to the man she remembered.

Your weakness for beautiful women marked you…

Undoubtedly, her father had worshipped her mother – he raved about her talent and her beauty to anyone who would listen. They had loved one another with an insane devotion that often excluded Ida.

Forever. Or so everyone believed.

In the margins of the night, shadows gathered and if Olwen's ghost was in the room, she was keeping quiet.

And what of her mother's ghost? Where was her place to be remembered? Not here, that was for sure. Was there nowhere for Anna's memory? In Wisteria Cottage perhaps? But it would soon be someone else's home.

It had never been hers either, it was another lie. And the first clue. Had there been others?

You made sure I couldn't find you...

Roni said he was a mystery man who Olwen had kept to herself. Ida didn't believe Roni knew the truth. She'd been fairly sure about the unsuitable hippy.

Had no one in the village guessed? Ida felt sick. There was no way to keep the truth hidden indefinitely, and when they did find out, the gossips would feed on it forever.

The bastard sister and the cuckold mother. The deceived wife and daughter.

Unless her mother had known? Was it possible? Once again Ida banished the thought as inconceivable. Anna would have been broken by any infidelity on David's part. Most of the stories she told Ida about her life began with him and concerned his achievements, his devotion to her and her pride in him.

Her love.

Ida knew this above all: her mother had adored her father. He had been her life, and Ida her cherished daughter. They were a family – a unit.

Growing up, Ida hadn't been affected by the lack of siblings. Her mother had been her world and Anna's was the theatre, full of fascinating people only too happy to play surrogate sister or aunt to the child of their star turn. Ida had been cosseted and spoiled, and on her birthdays taken out on grown-up evenings, to premieres and first nights. As a child, she hadn't wanted more than she'd been offered, because it was enough.

And now this – words cutting like daggers, making her head pound.

Making the word.

Daughter.

Sister.

How was it possible for her to be related to a contrary, halfling girl with windblown hair and startling eyes?

You have strange eyes…

It was cold now and Ida shivered, dropped the letter to the floor. Getting to her feet, she crossed to the window. The moon appeared and Ida saw how it seemed to shift, when it was the cloud rearranging itself, creating yet another illusion, and she thought how quickly a life can change.

A moment's distraction and a girl dressed in her mother's dream falls. A falling wall, a brown ghost leaf falling on her head. A soot fall.

Ida stared at the dark reflection of her face and it was less like her than it had ever been.

She wondered how many times Olwen must have rewritten the letter before she decided it was done. Before she placed it in a drawer for the daughter of the wrong mother to find.

In the presence of Olwen's words, Ida was more cut off from language than it was possible to be. She longed for her mother so fiercely, her heart shivered with the pain of it.

'Mum,' she whispered. 'Forgive me, but right this moment, I'm glad you aren't here to know the truth.'

…your blood runs in her veins.

A tear rolled down Ida's cheek.

I have a sister…

It didn't mean a thing to her and yet Heather's sense of entitlement no longer looked either arrogant or misplaced.

It was almost October. A petulant month at the best of times.

It made no difference to the birds. The sky above the old stone house moved to its own rhythm and the birds echoed it.

The sky was filled with them, so black and wild and wilful not even the sharp wind could blow them off course. They carried the pieces of a ghost-woman's promise, flew down to Ty'r Cwmwl and in through the open bedroom window; stepped across the pillow, dainty as wrens, snicker-whispered to one another, and left the dream morsels dancing on the sleeper's trembling eyelashes.

Winking and bobbing, the black birds feather-stepped across the room and flew away.

Forty-two

It was the noise that woke her.

A loud, swaggering clatter and Ida slid away from the edge of her new dreaming.

There were too many damn crows. They weren't meant to gather in such numbers. That was rooks, she was sure. Ida staggered from the bed, shivering in the chilly morning, moving the curtain to one side.

This close, the birds felt more predatory than ever, wings like sails, opening and closing as they pecked at gaps in the wall. One of them threw back its head, a snail caught in its beak. It nudged its way along the wall, knocked the snail against the stone, breaking open the shell.

'Bloody show-off!'

As Ida looked away, on the other side of the window she saw it: a black feather on the sill like a ragged quill. It was long and thin and the colour of spilled petrol. As she ran a finger along the edge of the vane it moved against her skin, keeping its shape.

She flicked it, watched as it whirled away. 'Bloody *birds*.' She slammed the window shut.

In the bathroom, brushing her teeth, Ida caught her reflection. There were shadows under her eyes, the eyes themselves brilliant with comprehension.

The same eyes.

How had she not seen it? Was she so disconnected she didn't know what colour her own eyes were? And how like Heather's? The truth was, she hadn't looked properly. Everything about Heather's appearance had bothered her. And she'd stopped looking at her own eyes the day her mother died.

I have to tell her.

The letter, back in the bureau, haunted her. Ida toyed with the idea of telling Roni first – ask her advice about how to approach Heather. Roni was kind and wise, but would her loyalty be to Olwen's memory? And by default, to her daughter? Roni would say she must tell Heather. And she would be right.

The longer Ida put it off only added to her sense of panic. Ashamed of her timidity, she was angry too. This mess was not of her making and yet here she was, left with the debris, with Olwen's words and her father's lies.

Her mother's grief?

Before this, Ida believed she had known everything there was to know about Anna. If she'd looked more carefully, would she have seen a suffering, betrayed wife?

There was too much in her head. How was this meant to work? She had spent twenty-nine years being an only child and now, out of the past, came this crazy, inconceivable revelation.

She could walk away now – pretend it wasn't happening. She didn't owe Heather anything and she had no obligation to her father either. Had he still been alive, it would have been for him to atone for his wrongdoing. But he was dead and Ida knew there was no question of not telling Heather – only the impossibility of the words and how to shape them.

I found a letter, she could say, and keep it simple. We're sisters. And Heather would ask her if she was kidding. Then, without missing a beat, she'd add, 'Of course you aren't, who would kid about a thing like that?'

Don't be too quick to want to know stuff, Roni had advised. You don't always find things you like.

And now she had, and Roni was right.

An hour later, in search of fresh air, Ida followed the line left by Heather's bicycle on the other side of the garden. Watching her boots, tramping awkwardly and favouring her right foot, she plodded across the rutted ground. A bee buzzed, loud in the heather, and Ida wondered how it survived, exposed to the cold. Her breathing slowed, the buzzing ceased and she realised it wasn't a bee at all, only her blood pumping close to her ear.

She sat on a rock, her foot resting on her thigh. Walking too far would be a stupid, self-inflicted punishment for a crime she hadn't committed.

I have whispered my truth to the birds…

Words from a dream? It no longer mattered; Ida's dreams were filled with Olwen's words now and chances were, they were all true. And if she didn't tell Heather about the letter, it would be another dirty secret. It would make Ida as bad as him.

'Sod off, Olwen. Don't you think you've caused enough trouble?' Ida had always preferred not to trouble her intuition. And yet here she was, shouting at a ghost she'd never seen. 'I can't argue with the written word though, can I?'

Tugging at a piece of heather, Ida saw how, although the purple had begun to fade to dusty brown, it was still in flower.

Tough.

I'll say that for Heather – she's tough…

If it were the other way round, if Olwen had been able to hide the letter in the cottage in the village for her daughter to find, would Heather have run like the wind, up the track to Ty'r Cwmwl, the news flying in her wake?

Ida thought she would. Heather was fearless and in spite of her childish tricks, staunchly truthful; exactly as Roni had claimed.

I'm not ready.

Her resolve plummeting, Ida got to her feet, brushed the back of her coat and began retracing her steps. A fine drizzle began to fall. As she approached the house she saw how the cloud spun round the chimneys, trying to scoop it up – like Dorothy's house – and dump it somewhere else. Only this wasn't Kansas, and this house was going nowhere.

All her previous decisions – the indecision of them – had

crumbled to dust. Ida was stuck here now, stuck with Olwen's ugly secret.

Inside, the house was as cold as the moor. Ida rattled the wood in the range, watched as sparks flew up and the wood began to burn, bright as copper. Her stomach was hollow and she knew she ought to eat something. She'd had no breakfast.

While the kettle boiled and bread browned in the toaster, reluctantly, once again Ida fetched the letter from the bureau. She buttered the toast and with her coffee made, sat at the table, Olwen's words scurrying like ants.

Everything she knew about her father was a lie. As she read and reread the letter, she tried to reinterpret him, examine him like a set of instructions discovered in the bottom of a box after you thought the thing you'd made was complete.

There had been times when Ida thought her father arrogant and overbearing. He had loved her, of that she had no doubt, but she wondered at times if he'd liked her. When she'd finally left home, it had been his idea.

'You need to be independent, Ida.'

He'd given her money for the rental deposit on a flat, helped her move, and dispelled her mother's objections.

'We aren't doing her any favours, darling. She has to stand on her own two feet.'

My broken foot...

Ida had felt superfluous to requirements, had known he was being economical with the truth, and it was Anna's undivided attention he'd wanted, not her independence.

Her father had liked his own way. If Ida had ever wondered what his life was like in Cardiff – immersed in academia and university life – she'd never thought to suspect him of deceit or an affair.

Because she knew where she came from it hadn't occurred to Ida to ask where she belonged. She belonged with her mother who, if only she hadn't come to Wales in the first place, wouldn't have been betrayed by David Llewellyn. But then Ida wouldn't have existed. And for a fleeting moment, she thought how she would have been content to be nobody: never born and no one's sister.

Heather broke into her thoughts again, with her hair flying and her rainlit questioning eyes.

What's the matter, Ida Spider?

Ida didn't know. The madness was happening to another woman, another Ida, free-falling between where she had expected to be happy for the rest of her life and here, where there was no connection and no affinity. Her memories weren't linked to this house. It was the way street lamps at midnight transformed a wet street to a glittering stream she wanted to remember, not how dark moorland night stole the shape of everything.

Sitting in the shadowy kitchen in a dead woman's coat, Ida's memories shattered. This new Ida – *the sister* – was an unknown woman, and utterly alone. Nothing would be the same again and there was a lifetime of it to get through.

First, she had to tell Heather. There had been too much hiding in lies.

Forty-three

Dreaming, there were no limits and Ida woke with a sense of foreboding.

It was deep, middle of the night, dark.

Trust the truth...

It was the simplest of dreams: a voice she didn't recognise, yet knew belonged to Olwen Morgan.

My father betrayed my mother.

The lie he'd told Olwen, meant he'd sold her down the river too. And the truth belonged to all of them – including Heather. For that reason alone, Ida resolved to call her as soon as it was daylight. She fell back into sleep and in the morning, the dream stayed with her, as clear as if Olwen had been in the room, dictating it.

My vitality mesmerised him ... he fell under my spell...

Ida no longer dismissed anything as a possibility.

'Well,' Heather said. 'More messages than you can shake a bloody stick at. What's so urgent this time it wouldn't wait?' Standing on the back doorstep, a band of light dissecting her face, she rearranged the air. 'Make up your mind, Ida Spider – one minute you're telling me to stay out of your hair, the next you're phoning me before the birds are barely out of bed, making out it's a matter of life or death. I can't keep up with you.'

Heather's words ran on like water over stones and Ida allowed them to. Anything to stay the moment, because she was here, this watchful girl, with her careless nature and her slow-blinking eyes.

Can she read my mind?

A silence settled in the space between them.

Heather at innocent ease, Ida unnerved, because the only words she had were in a dead woman's life-changing exposé.

The girl took off her woollen hat, releasing her hair and it billowed, a dark dandelion, revealing her face. And for the first time Ida took notice of her eyes, the way you looked at a real painting rather than a postcard impression.

Our eyes aren't the same colour at all.

Heather's were lighter: brilliant and piercing, like shards of glass. Eyes that held you, startling eyes making you nervous, reluctant to return her gaze. Ida could see radiating lines of blue in the clear, liquid irises and there it was.

The same blue as his.

'Well?' Heather's voice had a combative edge again.

'What?'

'You said, to come – you've got something to tell me.' She arched an eyebrow.

'Yes, I did. Come in.'

The letter floated in the centre of the table, its ends overlapping and Ida half-hoped Heather's nosy curiosity would get the better of her. Instead, she didn't take her eyes off Ida. She watched her fiddle with the lid on the near-boiling kettle, take mugs out of the dish rack, and a box of teabags from the cupboard.

'Getting a taste for it?' Heather asked.

'Huh?'

'You're making tea.'

'Oh, yes, why not?' Ida dropped two teabags into the mugs. 'Biscuits in the tin. If you want one.'

The tin, bright red and embossed with gold, sat next to the letter.

Heather ignored it. She was still watching Ida.

Hot water spluttered from the kettle into the mugs. Ida flinched and dropped the kettle back on the counter.

'Steady,' Heather said. 'You don't want to go scalding yourself.'

Ida licked her hand, dumped the mugs on the table. 'Listen, Heather, I have something important to tell you and it's—'

'What?'

'Can you please not interrupt? Just this once?'

'All right. Don't go on.'

'I've no idea how to tell you this, but, well – I found the key.'

'What key? You've got keys on the brain, you have.'

'The key to the bureau.'

'Where?'

'Heather, please. Stop interrupting. This is hard enough—'

'Did you open it?'

'Yes, I—'

'You had no right!' Heather leapt to her feet and Ida snatched at her wrist.

'No,' she said, 'it's not what you think and you have to listen to me. Please, Heather, you need to sit down. Yes, I opened the bureau only there was nothing in it.'

Heather tugged her arm away and frowned. 'Nothing?' She paused. 'Well that would explain the box.'

'Sorry? What box?'

'There was a box of stuff – bills and the like. Mam must have cleared the bureau out, goodness knows why, and Bethan burned the lot.' She frowned. 'Empty then. You sure?'

'Yes. I mean no; there was one thing.'

A massive thing.

'What thing?'

Ida patted the letter. 'This. I found this.'

Heather's frown became a question; her eyes slid over the letter and back to Ida. Her head tilted to one side. 'What is it?'

'A letter.'

'Well yes, I can see that.'

Ida shifted her gaze; there was only so long you could stare at someone you hardly knew before appearing rude. Searching Heather's enquiring face, her eyes that could change from mist to mischief in a second, was like seeing beneath her surface. 'Your mother wrote it.' Ida slid the letter closer to Heather, to the edge of her motionless hand. 'To my father.'

'What are you talking about? You're not making any sense.'

'It doesn't make sense. It's massive. It says—'

The page fluttered up, a millimetre away from Heather's fingers. 'Says what, Ida. You're starting to freak me out.'

'How we're related?' Did she make it a question in order that the truth might still be contradicted? The real word sat in the back of her throat like a stone.

Sisters…

Heather's face was unreadable. A single finger stretched out, the dirty, nibbled fingernail touching the edge of the paper. 'Related? Don't be daft.' She stared at the letter as if she feared it was contagious. Cautious as a cat, she picked it up, opened it out and began reading.

Ida watched her eyes, darting back and forth along the lines, her hands gripping the page.

It wasn't hard, afterwards, to recall the moment when everything changed, when their separate pasts became an enforced, incomprehensible and conjoined present. The room was so quiet it seemed even the wood in the grate had stopped snapping and outside, the wind dropped to a lull.

When she finished reading, Heather stared at the page, clearly unsure what she was supposed to do with it. She held it at arm's length as though it might burn her. 'I don't get it. What does it mean?'

'It means he was a liar. My father.' Ida swallowed. '*Our* father.'

Heather scrutinised the floor. She appeared to be concentrating, her body tense. When she looked up, she had become more visible, eyes fearful and as bright as stars.

This was her real face, Ida thought, the one she kept hidden for fear people would see how young she was, take over and ensnare her in their rules and regulations.

As they stared at one another, Heather's face changed yet again and now Ida couldn't be sure what she saw. She felt ridiculously guilty. And furious because although none of this was her fault, she knew it was probably how Heather would want her to feel.

Heather moved her shoulders and it was less a shrug and more a gesture of dismissal. Her face was mute now, without any trace of curiosity, the prettiness subdued. Ida saw how they both held their unimaginable thoughts close, unwilling to share them.

Ida and Heather. Heather and Ida. Shocked into silence like two stopped clocks, only now they had a key.

It was Heather who spoke. 'Welcome to the house of fun, eh, Ida?' In the dim light, she visibly drew herself up and now she looked older.

Ida thought about the day she'd arrived at Ty'r Cwmwl, and how the figure in the garden had disturbed her, how she had sensed something out of kilter, on the edges. Now she saw exactly what it was. A dark, dirty secret, drawing them towards one another.

'He cheated them both, Heather – both our mothers. We're all his victims.'

Heather shook her head, not in disagreement and Ida understood. They were accomplices now, even if neither of them wanted to be.

When Heather handed the letter back to Ida there was an honesty to the moment. Her hand was steady.

'I don't want this,' she said. 'There's nothing in it for me. It isn't about me.'

'It's about both of us.'

'Oh no, Ida, it's about him.'

Once I began it, he couldn't stop.

'Take me or leave me David, this is who I am.'

He took me, knowing it would be impossible to leave me, and said so.

A shiver of pleasure ran through me. He was like no other man I'd ever known. I knew the risk I took, and that he assumed I wasn't taking any. (Men, especially entitled ones, are easy to dupe.) A child with this man would be perfect. A girl child, as intelligent as she was magical.

In the darkness, in the hotel bedroom, his heart beat beneath my own, hot as a fire and impossible to put out. He inhaled the scent of apples on my skin, and we seduced one another, daredevil moths, dancing at our respective flames.

Stunned by my passion, I saw a moment of panic in his eyes. He placed his hand over my cries.

'Don't trespass,' I whispered into the dark, pushing his hand away.

And I sensed he longed to know the private part of me I would never allow him to touch.

I was yet to discover the truth of him – the part I wasn't privy to.

Listen with your hearts – both of you. The story is nearly done.

Sweet dreams, dear girls…

Forty-four

She knew something terrible had happened, the moment she'd heard Ida's voice on the telephone.

For a second it had crossed her mind that Ida had decided not to sell the house after all. And then a fault in her voice told her it was something other.

Sister.

The word hovered like a hungry kestrel, ready to strike.

Dumbfounded and too exhausted to make a fire, Heather crouched by the window in the cramped cottage, chilled to the bone, watching stars pour out of the dark sky. Her thoughts were like seeds, waiting for the light. She thought of all the perilous plants, the ones used in the kind of dangerous magic her mother had eschewed.

Heather's world was small and it had always been that way. Hiding had become a habit – the loss of her mother, her isolation, had made her distrustful of people. The fire that defined her as a child had diminished and become an act of deliberation. Fire to order – when it was required. Lighting the blue touchpaper of Ida's insecurity and running away, feeding her fear of witches, had been a game. Now it was anything but. Now the fire was out of control and Heather smelled a conflagration.

No matter how hard she tried to deny them, the words in the letter reeled across her brain. She went over and over them, until she had each one by heart.

Like it or not, your blood runs in her veins.

And there were older words too, from older conversations.

'Did my dad love me, Mam?'

'He didn't know you, *cariad*. If he had, he would have adored you.'

'Why didn't he know me?'

'He didn't want to – he didn't want to know either of us.'

'Why not?'

'We were too good for him.'

He'd been nothing to them, her mother insisted: a myth Heather had grown to accept.

Now she had a father, albeit a dead, deceitful one, she could think of nothing else. For seventeen years there had been none but the most basic questions, and answers her mother had provided that satisfied Heather's childish curiosity.

And here was Olwen, telling the rest, filling in the detail, in a secret letter scratched in bloody ink.

Liar. Cheat. Betrayer.

Daughter of a charlatan: a man who deceived his wife and lied to his lover. What kind of a person did it make him? A man who hadn't wanted to know his own child, and whose twisted loyalty disguised his innate weakness.

Heather's eyes were hot with dammed-up tears. If they fell, they would turn to acid and burn her skin. She pressed her lips together to hold them at bay. Her head was filled with questions, and the rage inside her was directed in part at her mother.

How could she have kept something like this to herself?

You don't deserve this daughter the way you didn't deserve me…

She didn't think that was good enough. A mother's love was a pact. It was part of you, like your blood and bones. When you looked into the eyes of mother love, you saw the honesty of the moon.

I'll keep your dirty secret…

Is that what she'd been? Heather felt ill with grief and confusion. Her mother had taken his money, lived in his house and made a life for them both, all of it built on a lie.

As a girl wandering the moor, wrapped in Olwen's magic and love, Heather had thought her life idyllic.

An idyllic lie, because now it was all wrong. Heather squeezed her eyes closed, tried to rid herself of her mother's image: how her voice sounded when she sang Heather to sleep. She wanted rid of Ida too: her pinched pale skin, her limp and above all, the colour of her eyes.

It was her eyes that had deceived Heather. Downcast and wary of contact, occasional flashes of silver mixed with the blue even Heather's sharp ones had missed. Now they gave her away. Now Heather saw her, really saw her. And she knew it was the same for Ida.

Sisters.

Heather didn't want to be identified. Once she became visible, it was dangerous. No one must see her, especially not the interfering busybodies with their clipboards and false concern.

Being invisible was a woman's best trick, or so her mother always told her.

Earth-coloured clothes to disguise you, green boots to make your footprints invisible…

Heather ran her hands down the fabric of her skirt, the muted tones of it merging like a muddy stream. The hem of her red petticoat looked like a bloodstain. She stood up and ripped it off, stuffed it under the mattress.

No clues. No hints for the do-gooder village women who thought they understood her and especially not the social workers with their box-ticking exercises. Heather didn't want any of them, didn't want anything they had to offer. And she certainly didn't want a sister.

The cold, hard place inside her expanded. She wanted her mother And what she had, was a dead father and a live sister.

I was happy just being my mother's daughter.

Damn Ida Spider and her prying. If she'd never come here, kept her nose out, there would have been no key and no revelation. There was nothing Heather wanted to share with this woman, least of all a father. Who did she think she was, with her pseudo-concern?

Does she think she's done me some sort of favour?

For two pins Heather would banish her, summon every shred of her mother's magic, including the hidden, harsh kind no wise woman ever considered, and be rid of Ida forever. She would make a spell out of ill-tempered wind and wormy oak apples, and tie it up with wasp stings.

Those kinds of spells were dangerous and Heather knew it. Wise women left them well alone. It was a dark path – and no coming back. Magic of that kind was risky – like walking out on blue ice into the middle of a frozen lake.

'Mark what I tell you, *cariad*,' her mother had cautioned. 'Wayward is a lonely life at the best of times. You don't want to go messing it up by adding poison.'

Heather didn't care. Her mother was a liar too.

'I could steal one of Ida's scarves,' she whispered to the cold, unforgiving hearth, 'fold it up, make a poppet, and take hair from her comb to stuff it.'

Heather could, if she chose, stick pins in the place where Ida's heart would be.

That night she cried herself to sleep and tears soaked into the pillow, leaving silvery stains that burned holes in the slip.

Sleeping, the voice weaving through her dreams belonged to her mother.

His eyes were blue as blackbird's eggs and I liked the look of them.

...a small apple-scented spell in the space between us ... brushed his cheek with a kiss ... slipped a skylark's feather into his pocket.

Forty-five

Once the dreaming began, there was no holding it back.

Ida's mother danced into her dreams too, light on her feet, a whirl of white and footlights. The pirouetting went on and on and her mother began to jerk like a marionette. There were blue flowers in her hair and her fingers pulled at them, frenzied and snatching.

No flowers before a curtain call – and never anything blue…

As the stage darkened, Ida heard her mother's voice call out.

Last one to go … leave the light on… Merde…

The wild dancing continued. It was too fast and her mother would fall and now it wasn't her mother, it was her – Ida – eyes blank, her feet moving in torn shoes, red as congealed blood, the tattered ribbons unravelling.

You're much too young … you'll ruin your feet…

She was dancing in the garden, the soft red kid of the shoes turning to rags, her feet blistered and the pain scalding…

Her pyjamas, damp with sweat, cooled as Ida threw back the duvet. Her foot burned with cramp. Out of bed, pushing it hard into the wooden floor to relieve the pain, Ida swept aside the curtain and was greeted by a slate-tinged sky, inevitable and needy, wanting something to happen.

Something has and it's my fault.

Leave well alone, her mother had always told her. (Roni too.) No good came of prying. Ida watched as thin cloud parted and the milky sun broke free. She fingered the gold chain at her neck, the little diamond reflected in the ghost-mirror window, and gazed at her blurry face: eyes as big as eggs and ringed with smoke. As she stared, the image changed and Heather took her place, her face white with bafflement, rumpled like a rag, her silver-blue eyes as she read the letter, darting like fish.

Dragging herself from the room, the cramp in her foot still tingling, Ida paused at the open window on the landing, barely questioning how the sash came to be lifted. When Heather had gone upstairs to use the bathroom? It didn't matter. All the ghosts of everyone who had ever died in Ty'r Cwmwl could be abroad – Ida no longer cared.

Up on the ridge tiles, out of sight, the black birds muttered.

'You have no manners, you horrible things. Shut up and leave me alone.' Ida slammed the window shut. Stupid birds, what did they know?

If Olwen was to be believed, they knew it all.

Birds aren't scared of anything, least of all the truth…

The truth was, the letter changed everything. The life Ida had known was unravelling at a pace now, the old faultless memories and the faulty ones alike, blemished by her father's deceit. In one shocking disclosure she had ceased to mourn him. She would rather lose all her memories than remember a single thing about him.

What a god-awful mess. And she had handled it so badly. Every word she'd said to Heather now appeared inept. Too much, not enough? Ill-judged? All of the above? She couldn't remember. The only things in her head were Heather's face, and the details of the letter – exposing and sharp as nails.

Before, Ida had been afraid of Olwen. Now she hated her and her selfish seductions, almost as much as she despised her father.

When her phone rang, Ida jumped out of her skin.

'Hey, it's me, Lowri.'

'I know. Sorry. Hang on, bad signal, I have to go outside.'

She grabbed her cardigan and pulled on her boots. It was cold. She walked to the end of the track where the signal was stronger.

'Are you still there, Lowri?'

'Yes.'

'Right, that's better. Start again?'

'Bad timing?'

'Terrible.'

'Ah.'

'I'm kind of kidding,' Ida said. 'Only I'm not. I'm—'

She couldn't speak.

'I thought, after the last time…' Lowri's voice faltered and Ida realised, they were about to have an entirely other conversation. One that had nothing to do with fateful letters, deceit and betrayal.

'It's okay,' she said.

The words for what had happened between them the last time they'd met had been made of hesitation, with only the vaguest shape, written in pencil that could be erased in a moment. It had been awkward and Ida had made her excuses; they'd said their goodbyes on the prom with the gulls shrieking and the boom of the sea as the tide came in.

Ida had said she would call; Lowri had replied, only if she wanted to.

Now, her voice sounded normal and friendly, as far removed from Ty'r Cwmwl and its secrets as it was possible to be. 'Do you want to come here? I can make us lunch.'

'Yes,' Ida said, without a moment's hesitation. 'That would be amazing.'

She dressed quickly, found her car keys, put on the blue coat and locked the front door behind her. The roads were clear and in no time Ida was in town, parking outside Lowri's house, wondering what on earth she would say to her.

Lowri was standing in the doorway, a green turban hiding her hair, the black cardigan draped over her dance clothes. Several tall, chattering girls swooped out through the front door, out of the gate in the low brick wall. They had an air of collective confidence and Ida knew they were Lowri's star class. With their hair freed from constricting buns, flying down the path on long legs, they reminded Ida of flamingos.

'Bye, Miss Williams!'

'Bye, girls.'

They were gone and Lowri was laughing. 'Free at last!'

'My goodness, it's like the *corps de ballet* sprouted wings.'

'Aren't they though?' Lowri's smile broadened. 'Hi, Ida. We meet again. I'm so glad to see you.'

'Me too.'

'Sit down here,' Lowri said, indicating an iron bench with a scrolled back placed under the window. 'It's nice in the sun. I'll make coffee. Hang on.'

Ida sank into a yellow cushion, shaded her eyes against the sun. This high up she could see the sea – mottled with silver waves.

Lowri reappeared, with coffee in earthenware mugs.

'It's instant again. Hope that's okay.' As she handed a mug to Ida, a look of concern crossed her face. 'You look awfully pale. Has something happened?'

I have a sister… One I didn't know about… I like you and I fancy you, even though we've only met a few times, but I'm terrified and a mess…

'I'm fine,' she said. 'I'm always pale.'

'Okay.'

'I am – it's the place, the house. It's like living in a Brontë novel.'

'Charlotte or Emily?'

'Both.'

Lowri laughed, then stopped herself. 'Only it isn't funny?'

'Not really.'

'I am sorry about the last time, Ida.'

'Don't be. It's me. My life's weird right now, Lowri. I'm not dealing with anything very well.'

'I don't want to pry.'

284

'You aren't.' She sensed Lowri watching her, taking her in. She changed the subject. 'Have you lived here long?'

'In this house?'

Ida didn't mean that. It didn't matter; she was already regretting coming.

'When my mother died, in France,' she said, 'I wasn't there and I ought to have been.'

Lowri bit down on a retort.

'I don't know why I told you that.'

So you wouldn't be tempted to tell her what was actually on your mind.

Sister.

'My mother died too,' Lowri said. The words fell like two small birds, into the space between them.

Ida barely had enough energy for her own sorrow. Was every woman she met motherless?

'Suicide.' The word was blunt and harsh. 'It was years ago though. I hardly remember her.'

'I…' Ida stopped, empty of words.

'It's okay. And now I'm making it about me.'

How can any of this be okay?

Ida wasn't in the mood to be helpful. 'Is that supposed to make me feel better? I didn't realise it was a competition.'

'Ida…'

'Don't.' Ida hated herself; she knew perfectly well Lowri hadn't set out to hurt her. Her misery meant she couldn't stop. 'You think a mother who killed herself trumps a mother you may as well have killed?'

There was so much silence the air froze.

Lowri was the first to find her voice. 'I'm going to pretend you didn't say that.'

'Sorry.' It was a whisper. 'Honestly, I am, but why do you care so much, Lowri? You don't know me.'

'No, but I want to.' Lowri tucked her hands inside the sleeves of her cardigan. 'I do know what it's like. And I'm deeply sorry about your mother.'

'Me too. Yours. I didn't mean—'

'It was a long time ago. I was a kid. I didn't understand it and I'm not sure I do now, although it's better than it was. I do know it wasn't about me.'

'I've been horrible to people, made everything about *me*.'

'Grief's a bastard,' Lowri said. 'People can't cope with it. Not if it isn't theirs. It consumes you. It's supposed to – like a safety blanket. While you wait for it to pass, you need a friend. A friend who won't judge.'

Her eyes were gentle and Ida saw her miniature self in the mossy-green reflection of them. She knew Lowri wanted to kiss her and she wanted that so badly her lips burned.

Instead she turned her head away. She knew what would happen if she faltered and allowed this generous woman to fall for her. Ida's grief was vast and if she let it, it would smother them both.

It was too soon, the wrong time and Ida had no idea how to be the person she was turning into. A ripple fluttered round her stomach and her knees tensed, the one pressed against the other.

Lowri smiled and it was sweet with understanding, as if she read Ida's thoughts, which was another reason not to be kissed. She took Ida's hand and Ida stared at it, folded into the elegant fingers and a tremor ran between them, charged and dangerous. Ida didn't know which one of them had let it loose and alarmed, she pulled her hand free.

She didn't want Lowri in her head, seeing her sorrow. More than that, she liked her too much to drag her into her chaotic life.

'Don't be scared, Ida.'

'I'm not.'

The lie lay between them, bruised and lame.

Lowri nodded, tipped the last of her coffee into the undergrowth. A child appeared at the gate, a pink rucksack slung on her shoulder.

'Hello, Miss Williams.'

Lowri jumped up, checked her watch.

'Goodness,' she said. 'Hello, Amy.' She turned to Ida. 'Listen, why don't you come in?'

'Oh, no, I don't think so.'

'Go on.' She shooed Amy in through the door. 'Just watch for half an hour – it would please me so much. Then we'll have lunch.'

More girls arrived, and Ida found herself caught up, swept through the door like a breeze.

Forty-six

In the studio, small girls swarmed like pink butterflies, tender and eager, pulling on soft ballet shoes.

Pink for class, darling...

Once again Ida caught the smell of rosin and faintly, a trace of sweat. The windows let in light making the studio look larger than it was. She settled into a plastic chair at the edge of the room, trying to be invisible. It was impossible, and the little girls couldn't take their eyes off her. They giggled and nudged and whispered and Ida wanted to run.

A woman with a toothy smile appeared through a door at the back of the studio. 'Morning, class, morning Miss Lowri.'

Catching sight of Ida, the woman looked startled and Ida's sense of discomfort increased. She was on show and she hated it.

'Ah, Stella, there you are.' Lowri smiled. 'This is my friend, Ida. She's going to sit in.'

Stella gave a small nod. 'Pleased to meet you, I'm sure.'

Ida didn't think she looked pleased at all. She sat at the piano, shuffled music scores.

'Okay, class,' Lowri said. 'Now, before we start, I have a lovely surprise for you. A guest.' She turned to Ida. 'This is Ms Ida Llewellyn, and she's the daughter of Anna Plessey. How many of you know who I'm talking about?'

One hand went up and Lowri laughed. 'Well, goodness me, what are you lot like? Anna Plessey was only one of the greatest ballerinas in the country.'

'I know who she is.' The girl who'd raised her hand spoke. 'My nan saw her dance. She's always going on about her.'

'Yes, Ruby. I remember you telling us. Lucky Nan!'

Ida swallowed and because the room seemed to pitch, she held onto the piano to steady herself. And she saw how Lowri noticed, how she immediately knew it had been the wrong thing to say.

'Ida—'

A sea of small faces were fastened on hers and Ida conjured a smile and said, 'I'd love to see you all dance now, if that's okay.'

Lowri threw her a smile of apology mixed with embarrassed gratitude. She clapped her hands together. 'Right, places please!'

The girls scurried to the barre, lined up, eyes still on Ida.

'Eyes, front,' Lowri said. 'First position and *plié*.'

One by one, the children worked though the positions. Most of them danced competently. They were clearly well taught and as Ida watched, in spite of her misgivings, found herself drawn in.

Pliés, tendus, dégagés…

The piano thumped and Ida winced. Stella's playing was terrible.

Ruby hadn't taken her eyes off Ida and she lost her concentration. Ida smiled and without thinking, made her way to the barre.

The piano stopped. Lowri stopped too and watched as Ida placed her hand on the child's back.

'Like this,' she whispered. 'Now, lift your spine – imagine you're attached to the ceiling by an invisible thread. That's it. Perfect – well done.'

Ruby's smile split her face.

Every eye was on Ida and she was acutely aware of each one of them, and it was as if she was held, spellbound in a good dream gone bad.

She blushed and the room wavered. She was in the old studio again, alone, surrounded by mirrors, practising early in the morning and her feet were careless, her shoes too soft.

Make sure you change your shoes, Ida…

She was turning and turning. Falling. Walls and leaves and words…

How could you, Ida…?

'Ida?'

Drawing a sharp breath, she was back in the room, Lowri in front of her, frowning. Ida tried to say she was okay and couldn't because her jaw felt stapled shut.

'I'm fine.' Her voice sounded tiny. She found a smile and the little girls looked up at her and smiled back.

Their faces were like roses, and Ida wanted to cry.

'You were amazing.'

'Was I?'

'You really were incredible. Ruby's a bit of a show-off – a baby ballerina. You know the kind. You made her day.'

Tears welled in Ida's eyes and she forced them back. Above the ocean, the sky was falling and the space where it joined the sea moved and blurred, so she couldn't see where one began and the other ended. Her edges were blurring too and she thought she might faint.

'You looked right in there.'

'I'm not though. I'm out of my depth, Lowri, and it isn't my world. Not anymore.'

'Why not? I don't understand.'

'I'm broken. I thought I didn't mind, but all today has taught me is how much I do.'

'You've lost your connection. It was bound to happen.'

'Because I lost my *concentration*. I got complacent, messed up and fell, like a stupid beginner.'

'It's just the luck of the draw.'

Ida shook her head. 'You really were last in the queue when they handed out the tact, weren't you?'

'Oh god, my mouth's running away with me again. It's because you were impressive in there. And just because your foot's—'

290

'Horrible.'

'All ballet dancer's feet are horrible.'

'Mine's ruined!'

'Just because you foot's *ruined* then, doesn't mean you can't heal from the other stuff.'

'The other stuff.' Ida sighed and realised she was almost out of words.

'There's more than our bodies need healing, Ida. Lots of ways to heal too. First of all you have to learn how to feel again.'

Ida found it impossible to imagine being that far down the road. Right then she knew if she thrust her hand into a fire she wouldn't feel the flames. She swallowed, and the thing she didn't mean to ask spoke for her. 'How?'

'How do we heal?'

Ida nodded.

'Slowly. By speaking to the elephant in the room.'

You have no idea…

'Most people can't say the word death,' Lowri said. 'So they share hope for life. They tell you time heals when it obviously doesn't. Not for ages anyway. They tell you to take care like it's a thing you can physically pick up.'

'I'm sick of it.'

'Yes. Of course you are.'

Yes? Perhaps this woman does know…

Only they still weren't talking about the same thing.

'Are you listening to me?'

'No. I don't think I am.' Ida shook her head. 'Sorry, I don't mean to be rude, I just—'

Her words finally deserted her.

People were unreliable and love was dangerous. Ida didn't want to be close to anyone. She knew what happened when you did. You lost them. She was a jinx. She had a sister no one else knew about, and a father who had been a deceitful liar. And Lowri – with her innocent, sweet solicitude – didn't deserve to be dragged into the mess.

'I have to go,' she said. 'Sorry about lunch.'

'It's okay.'

Lowri pulled her into a loose embrace. Ida's hands flapped, stiff and awkward. Both their hearts beat in unison, too big, too loud. When she pulled away, her shoulders were warm where Lowri's hands had touched her.

She turned away, walked out, got into her car and drove away without a backward glance.

Forty-seven

As Ida approached the house, the noise from the car's engine scattered the black birds.

She hit the horn, deliberately, watched as they flapped above the wall in a complaining clutter. The house presented itself differently: a parody, cold and insubstantial, the walls on the verge of dissolving. And if they did, she thought, she would be left, stranded and alone on the bleak hinterland. She brought the car to a halt, her misery draped like a shroud.

The kitchen was still warm. Opening the door of the range, she broke the hard layer on the log and it flared, shifting some of the shadows, making a few more.

Faces.

Lowri's, and those of the little girls. Ida shook her head, shook them out. Lowri was the wrong kind of distraction.

She squeezed her eyes shut and conjured an image of her mother – deliberately – to anchor herself. Not the crazy, spinning woman from her dream, but the smiling, sweet-faced one with uncomplicated, pure blue eyes. So long as she still saw this version of her mother, she wouldn't disappear.

But now Heather's face intruded again.

In every sister story Ida recalled, one was always prettier, or smarter. One was spiteful as a thorn, the other, gentle and kind. No one could deny how beautiful Heather was, or that she had an undeniable contrary streak, which sometimes got the better of her.

It ought to have made Ida the nice, plain sister, but anyone who looked inside Ida would see her wicked heart. She was as mean as Heather, only her animosity was unforgivable.

'Go away.' Crouched in front of the fire, Ida whispered into her hands. 'I don't want you in my life any more than you want me in yours.'

She thought about other sisters she'd known. There had been some at school – a pair of identical twins who played tricks on teachers. And two at university, as unalike to look at as it was possible for sisters to be. Yet still, devoted – indulging in normal sisterly behaviour: finishing one another's sentences, sharing clothes, sharing secrets.

Ida couldn't imagine sharing anything with Heather. The thrill of discovering things to like about her, to be intrigued by her rather than irritated, would be like betraying her mother.

Heather was a whirlwind of evidence: David's infidelity writ large in her mother's hand, palpable and alive.

How long before everyone knew? Village gossip had a life of its own. No secrets, Roni had said.

Oh, but there was.

A years-old secret, magpie-guarded until Ida had stumbled upon it. And how it would leak. Pass, lip to lip: each one of them claiming to be sole privy to the truth. Ida already saw them: invisible and alert, listening and spying, raking around for the detail, tentacles of inquisitiveness drawn to scandal.

People are afraid of what they don't understand...

Step outside of what passed for normal and you would soon find yourself unsuitable.

Ida slept and a kaleidoscope of dreams now assaulted her: little girls with faces made of roses, her mother and father, blurred lines, falling bricks and muted voices, recrimination and birds screaming. And unedited and random: Olwen's story, imprinting like blood seeping through a bandage.

Once I began, he couldn't stop...

She fought the bedclothes, woke and raised herself on her elbow, searching the dark. The wind blew hard against the house and Ida thought she heard a window or a door bang open somewhere. Perturbed and unable to go back to sleep, she rolled back the duvet, rubbing her eyes.

Stumbling from room to room, up and down the stairs, she saw how every window and door was shut tight, impervious to whatever the wind hurled at the house. She was safe.

Safe as houses.

Ty'r Cwmwl was impregnable, and for a moment Ida wanted doors flung off their hinges, glass imploding. Anything to counteract the intractability of a house too lonely to be a home.

And what about her?

Ida, giving herself airs. How long before they worked out who she really was? Who they all were? Ty'r Cwmwl's sordid *ménage à trois* where only one person understood the rules.

Olwen.

And her father, wilfully allowing himself to become entrapped, making his own rules as he went along, lying to his wife.

To all of us.

The liar and the betrayer: a man Ida now realised she had only ever glimpsed. It had been like looking at a fading film reel. As she replayed it – a home movie in her mind – she wondered if he had ever loved them. Loved Anna? Ida ran him through an imaginary filter; if she looked again, might she make a different kind of sense?

Time passed too slowly and it was overlain with a mute silence. Ida spent the day dithering between her bedroom and the kitchen, at the windows overlooking the garden. She wanted to know when Heather returned, knowing she would.

She listened for Olwen too, sensing it was pointless. Olwen was now an absence. The house was silent too, uncannily so, as if it waited.

Ida waited for Heather and her misery deepened.

Her father's betrayal seemed to her like a crime for which some kind of reparation was required. He wasn't there to answer though and as the day passed, the question unravelled to a loose end. And the more Ida tried to rid herself of his face, the clearer it became. She saw him, out on the town, peacock proud, wife and daughter on either arm.

She pinched her eyes shut and the face changed and it was no longer his. It twisted, merged into that of a stranger and dissolved, like a reflection in a still pool disturbed by a stone, the bits of him breaking into cold atoms.

Her naivety shocked her. She had loved him and he was nothing more than a traitor.

Overwhelmed, as the long day drew to a close, Ida was terrified to go to sleep, for fear the dreams she had longed for and that now assailed her – page after page of Olwen's story – turned into nightmares.

Holding Giselle close, she thought how she and Heather were in different versions of the same shabby story, their words unheard and indistinct.

At best, they were footnotes.

The doll's face lay against Ida's upper arm and she turned to look at it, make its inanimate muteness real. Giselle's blank eyes stared back and Ida turned away, buried her face in the pillow.

The face she sought, the only face she wanted to see belonged to the one person who might help her make sense of the chaos.

Her sister.

Forty-eight

The black birds fell silent and the space they left disturbed Ida as much as their raucous shouting once had.

She wasn't fooled; they were still around, just less vocal, and she imagined it was because they no longer needed to be heard. Olwen's secret was out and the birds knew it.

The air in the house was deathly still. Each person who had ever lived there had deserted it. It was no longer Olwen's house either. Finally, it belonged to Ida.

To me and to Heather.

In the morning dimness the kitchen was shadowed as a woodland. Only a muted wire of light from the open door fell across the floor, enhancing the silence. If Ida had ever longed to be alone, be rid of Heather's presence, she no longer did. Although she wanted to see her, she was unwilling to pre-empt another showdown. If the present was now thrown into disarray, the future was equally unsettling.

Needing to be outside, unwilling to go anywhere she might have to talk to people, Ida made for the garden. When Heather eventually turned up, she would see her coming.

She began clearing weeds, piling them into a wheelbarrow she found in the barn. She made a bonfire. The dampness of the weedy debris mixed with soggy leaves sent up smoke signals, slow grey hints and Ida poked at the fire, making it crackle, watching the plume of smoke as it rose to meet the incoming cloud.

She wondered if Heather would see it – translate it into a message.

Rain took her by surprise: thin, restless rain and an insinuating wind, sending her scurrying for the house. In her bedroom she stripped off her damp jeans, pulled on a pair of sweat pants. Inertia overtook her and she lay on the bed. Within seconds she was asleep, woken only by a knocking at the backdoor.

Her watch said ten to two. She'd slept for hours.

Frowning, Ida made her way downstairs. The knocking sounded again. Not insistent, a polite tapping.

'Heather?'

She stood on the step, motionless, waiting: finally finding her manners. In barely three days Heather had become insubstantial, no longer courting attention. Her face was bleak with misery.

Looking at her, Ida knew a moment of pure compassion. 'Are you all right?'

'I don't know.'

'Come in, out of the rain.'

Heather stood inside the door, far enough into the room to allow Ida to close it.

'Do you want anything? I can make tea.'

Heather ignored the question, countering with one of her own. And although her gaze was without a shred of confrontation, it still sent a shiver down Ida's back.

'Why did you come here?'

It was a simple question. It hovered, each word neat and precise. The same question she'd asked before. The one Lowri had asked. With the same answer, and Ida shrank from it.

'Where else would I have gone?'

Heather lifted her chin. 'You don't belong here.'

'That's as maybe. But it's my house. I had to come, at the very least to settle things.'

'Everything was all right before you turned up. No one cared what I did. Now, when they find out – about *him* – I'll be *seen*.' Her voice was almost a moan. 'I don't want to be seen.'

'Heather, even if I hadn't come, eventually, the solicitors would have discovered who you were and that you were hanging out here. You wouldn't have been able to come and go indefinitely.'

'Yes, I would. I'd have made sure no one found out.' Even in her still belligerent certainty, there was something helplessly vulnerable about Heather now. She began crying, a small, choking sound. 'I hate you.'

'No. You don't. You can't.'

'Yes I can! Your family – *yours* not mine – people like you, you think because you're rich and educated it makes you special.'

'We weren't rich! Whatever gave you that idea?'

Heather spat her reply. 'It's obvious.'

'How?'

Ida realised Heather was no longer listening.

'My mother wasn't just a tenant, she was a custodian. She loved this house, took care of it. He abandoned it. Abandoned *her*. When she died, no one came. She was braver than anyone. Braver than all of them.'

Ida opened her mouth to say something.

'Don't talk!' Heather's hands were clenched in tight fists, anguish etched on her face. 'Mam was clever and wise and she helped them all. No one helped her though, did they? Not when it mattered.' She broke off, her voice cracked with despair.

'I—'

'No, Ida, don't. Let me say it. All that energy and wisdom and when it came to it, she couldn't save herself.' Tears ran down her face. 'She was unique. Nothing scared her.'

'That's what Roni said.'

'Did she? Well, Roni was the one person Mam trusted.'

'She didn't tell her about—'

'Don't you dare say his name. He's no one. And nothing to me, which makes you nothing as well.'

'It makes us both victims. You aren't the only one.'

Mutual hostility was making them careless with their words, and though they saw one another's grief, they couldn't untangle it.

Ida couldn't let go of her animosity, despite the girl's obvious distress. 'You aren't the only one who's scared, Heather.'

'You think I'm *scared*? Well here's a thing, Ida, everything's scary if you let it be. Life, death, the moors at night! Cars and flying and crossing the bloody road.'

She stood like a cantankerous child and Ida didn't know if she wanted to hug her or slap her again.

She's your sister.

Ida found herself questioning this new process, wondering how much she could trust it, listening to the gaps between the words, a new language neither of them were yet conversant with.

'It's called, "*life*", Ida.'

And it was – life made of moments. The one when you're too lazy to change out of your dead ballet shoes, the one when you give in to your father and not your mother and stay at home. The moment when the damp soot in a chimney dries, shrinks and loses its grip, falls in a messy, revealing heap and gifts a key.

And in that moment, you unlock a sister…

'You can go to hell, Ida.'

And now the words they weren't saying lay between them like accidents waiting to happen. Heather's eyes had turned cold and the blue shards flickered. Her pretty face was ugly now; her hair shook, the light behind her making it wild and monstrous, like snakes.

She looked dangerous.

As she turned on her heel and strode off, Ida shivered.

Forty-nine

Ida walked across the moor, down the path to the village, hints of winter accompanying her.

The village struck her as more unwelcoming than ever. Smoke coiled out of chimneys: lazy smoke with no hint of heat. The silence was unnerving. Hunched, making herself small, Ida scurried down the side of the garage track to Roni's cottage.

Before she could knock, Roni opened the door.

'Am I that obvious?'

'No, *bach* – I heard you coming.'

You'd make a rubbish burglar ... I heard you coming a mile away.

Roni made coffee, found biscuits and settled Ida into a comfortable armchair.

'I hardly know where to begin.'

'Anywhere you like.'

Ida dipped in and out, knowing she was telling the story out of order, but guessing she must be making sense since Roni didn't interrupt. She ground to a halt and waited. 'Some story, eh?'

'Just a bit,' Roni was rooted in her chair, her face stunned. 'Wow. I wasn't expecting that.'

'You and me both.'

'And Heather's read it. The letter.'

'Yes, and now I have no idea what to do. It's like we've reached an overemotional stalemate.'

'Yes, I can see why you might think that.' Roni let out a long sigh. 'Well, it's quite a story. You must be in shock.'

'Something like that. And Heather – well, I can't imagine.'

'You haven't seen her?'

'Briefly, yesterday. Didn't go well. And when she'd read it, she refused to take it. Said it wasn't about her, it was about him.'

'She's not altogether wrong though, is she?'

'I know. But it feels wrong for me to have it.' Ida hesitated. 'I've been wondering, do you think Olwen could have forgotten about it? Because she was ill?'

'Maybe. Seventeen years is a long time.'

Seventeen years ago, Ida had been twelve. Did she recall anything she'd written down so long ago?

'Heather said there was a box of papers – Bethan burned it. Bills and bank statements, stuff like that. It looks like Olwen cleared her desk before she died, except for the letter.'

'So not forgotten then.' Roni poured coffee. 'And she'd lost the key to the bureau?'

'Aren't magpies supposed to be thieves?'

'They are.'

'Then that crazy bird could have stolen it.'

'You're making it very spooky.'

'It is spooky! The whole thing's nuts.'

'So, what are you going to do?'

'I was so hoping you weren't going to ask me that. It's like a mantra and my head's splitting,' Ida said. 'What do you think I ought to do?'

'It's not down to me, lovely.'

Ida pulled the letter from her pocket. 'Damn thing's turned both our lives upside down. Last night, I thought I'd decided – about the house. From being so certain about selling it, I'd come round to the idea of staying. But when Heather told me to go to hell, I thought, why not? What's the point? I can't see any alternative.'

'Sell it after all, you mean?'

'Yes. Back to Plan A. It must be worth a fair bit. I could buy a flat and give Heather some money. She could go to college. She's clever. She already has an amazing knowledge of herb lore. Trained, she'd be formidable.'

'How much do you think you'd get for the house? Out there in the middle of nowhere. With no land.'

'Who knows? God, what a mess.' Ida fiddled with the letter, making more creases in the paper. 'She doesn't want to know me, Roni. You didn't see her. She hates me.'

'She's confused.'

'She hates him even more – any mention of him.'

'And you? It isn't only about the house, Ida,' Roni said, 'or even what it represents now. It's about a different kind of ownership.'

'What do you mean?'

'Out of the blue, Heather's having to share everything with you. House. Father. That letter's as much about her as it is about you, or your father.'

'I could kill Olwen.' Ida turned the letter over. 'It's all her fault. Sorry, but it is. Even though she never sent it, she intended the bloody thing to be found. It's like grand opera.'

'It's a story, Ida.'

Just a story… Your face…

'You're very kind, Roni.' She stuffed the letter back in her pocket.

'Just not particularly helpful.'

'Oh, you're helping, believe me. Giving me this space to vent. I'm grateful. You hardly know me.'

'I like you though. Will that do?'

I like you, Ida…

'Yes.' Ida smiled. 'Thanks. I like you too.' She sighed. 'I still don't know what to do though and I have to make a decision.'

'Listen to me, Ida, you're both in shock. You need time to work out what you feel instead of trying to second guess each other. And it's too soon to think about helping Heather. She doesn't want help. Never has. Goodness knows I've tried. I helped her as much as she would allow, after Olwen died and Bethan left. She's a tough ask. Always has been. She was more like a wild animal than a little girl.'

'No change there then.'

'Don't let it fool you.'

'I'm not. It's why I want to do more for her. Sell the house, set her up, away from here, somewhere she can blossom.'

'Too far away from here, Ida, she'd die.'

'That's a bit dramatic don't you think?'

'It's true. This place is in her blood. I don't give two hoots for the witchy stuff, I do know this: Olwen's blood runs in that girl's veins every bit as much as your shared father's does.'

'More so.'

'Exactly.'

'In the short term then, I suppose I better be patient.'

'Do I sense a hint of empathy?'

'Don't go mad, Roni – we have a way to go. And I do wonder what I'm getting into.' Ida was unsure if she was ready for any of it – for this unsought, potentially fraught relationship and its consequences. 'I have nothing to compare it with. I'm a spoilt, only child.'

'Do you think it would make a difference, if you'd grown up with other siblings?'

'Perhaps. Someone in the same boat to share this new one with?'

'You can still talk to her, Ida. Let her know you care.'

'Yes.'

'It's her birthday soon.'

'Is it?' Ida looked up. 'She'll be eighteen. When?'

'End of the month.'

'Excellent.' Ida smiled. 'Thanks for this Roni. I made a hash of yesterday. Too many days. It helps to get some perspective.'

'Ah, you're welcome. And why don't you try again? Say hello.' Roni jerked her head and her peony hair shook. 'She's only round the corner.'

Fifty

Outside Heather's cottage, Ida tapped the door.

Behind her, she sensed watchers, refused to react and give whoever might be spying the satisfaction of knowing how unnerved she still was.

Heather opened the door, stared at Ida.

'I ought to have phoned. I'm sorry. This is an impulse. Sort of.'

'In other words, you planned it.' Heather folded her arms, her face impassive.

'May I come in? Please? People are watching and you don't want that any more than I do.'

They sat opposite one another, at a tiny table in the cramped room.

A small fire burned in a leaded grate. The letter lay between them. A lamp softened the gloom, disguised the dull corners and the shabbiness. What appeared to be boxes stood in corners, draped with blankets and Heather caught Ida's drifting eye.

'Mam's stuff. It wouldn't look right here.'

Ida nodded. 'Are you all right?'

Heather's mouth twitched. 'I guess.'

'We do need to talk about things.'

'What things?'

'This?' Ida flicked the letter.

'No.' Her voice was adamant.

'All right.' Ida perched on the edge of the chair. 'Listen, I think I might be going after all.'

'Going where?' Heather asked.

Ida saw how pinched her face had become. 'I don't know, but it's probably for the best.'

Heather avoided looking at her. 'Did you drive down?'

'Walked.'

'You don't want to go leaving it too late, getting back. It'll be dark before you know it.'

'I've only just arrived.'

'No, you haven't,' Heather said. 'You've been to see Roni.'

Ida didn't ask how she knew.

'So, get on with it, then. Go where?'

Heather turned and Ida saw the flash of hostility in her eyes, too like her own for comfort.

'So, don't derail the conversation.' She kept her voice calm and was rewarded by a faint smile. 'This thing between us, Heather, it makes everything different.'

'Inconvenient.'

'*Important.*' This time, Ida wasn't going to be undermined.

'I suppose.'

'We've been given something shocking. We didn't ask for it and it isn't our fault—'

'You're saying it's Mam's fault.'

It wasn't a question.

'No. Absolutely not.'

'His then.'

'Yes. And the fact of it – the bald, bloody truth of it – has stolen something from us.'

'I don't know what you mean.'

'I think you do.' Ida placed the palm of her hand on the letter. 'He stole our certainty. What passes for normality and a normal life? Don't you see?' Ida quelled her welling anger. 'Our belief that both our mothers were happy.'

'Mam was happy.'

'No, Heather. She made a life – for her and for you. One that appeared to be happy. On the surface. The same way my mother did for me.'

Heather's eyes widened. 'Are you saying she knew? Your mother?'

306

'I don't know. Maybe. I have to allow for it. Most of me doesn't believe she did because I think I'd have known.' A smile graced her lips. 'Mum liked a bit of drama and she was someone who was easily hurt – her emotions were fragile. I don't think she would have been able to hide something this enormous, not from me. But she didn't like it that he wasn't always with her. I think he hurt her and she covered it up. For me.'

Heather held her gaze.

'But I know.' Ida flicked the letter. 'So do you. We both know he betrayed them. He betrayed *us*. And I don't want him to win. That's why I don't want this any more than you do. Only I think one of us ought to keep it.' She hesitated, knowing the fragile equilibrium of their relationship lay in the balance. 'I don't want either of us to be weighed down by this, Heather. Because I don't know about you, but I'm on the edge of a massive black hole and I do not want to fall in.'

When Heather nodded Ida knew, their fear was the same.

'Is that why you're leaving?'

'I haven't said I'm leaving. I don't know. I'm thinking aloud, but it's something we need to discuss because it affects you too.'

'Does it?'

'Of course it does. The house – it doesn't feel like mine. And in spite of what I said before, it's much more yours anyway. Can we talk about that?'

'You keep saying the same thing: talk, talk, talk. You don't stop, even when there's nothing to say.'

Heather's voice had lost its animosity. She looked like who she was: a girl still in her teens, her world thrown into chaos. However hard Ida tried, she couldn't put herself in Heather's place, access her feelings about a faithless father she believed she hadn't needed. It didn't matter how equally Ida was caught in the nightmare – their backstories were too different for any points of reference. They were both pretending to be fine and in control, when the truth was, they were isolated with a secret neither of them had asked to know.

'If I sold the house, I could help you.'

'How would that help me?'

'I could give you some money.'

'Why would you do that?'

Ida paused, weighing up what to say next. 'Because it's the right thing to do. And it's only an idea. You could find somewhere nicer to live. Me too.'

'That's it, is it? Your big plan?'

'I don't know yet, I—'

'So be quiet.'

'Okay.'

'Don't you see, I don't need to think? In fact, I don't care. About the house. About any of it. I've decided. There's no need for you to leave, because I'm going. I'll be eighteen soon and no one will be able to tell me what to do.' The words came out in a rush. She already looked older, determined.

'Heather, that's ridiculous. You're in shock – we both are. You can't make decisions on a whim.'

'Not like you then?' Heather fixed Ida with a derisive stare.

'We have to discuss what's happened—'

'Why? I was okay before you came. So were you, in a way. We'd both lost our mothers but we were coping.'

'We can cope better. Have a future.'

'What? Like *sisters*?' Heather's face hardened. 'Oh, I don't think so, Ida Spider.' She gave an aloof shrug. 'It's all yours. And you're welcome to it.'

Heather, who not so long ago had clung to her claim to the house, now eschewed it. It was as if she detached herself, deliberately, from her pride. There would, Ida knew, be no more bad behaviour, no tricks. In spite of her youth, the enormity of what she was dealing with, Heather had somehow found a kind of wisdom. Even her features were different: her cheeks sharper, lips fuller and her eyes less guarded and more confident.

And Ida, who was supposed to be the grown-up, knew she had

possibly ruined everything. Unintentionally and with no malice, she had come here and Olwen's shade had sensed her, pulled Ida into her old revenge, and forced her own daughter to be part of it too. If Olwen had suddenly materialised and stood in front of her, Ida would have happily killed her.

Keeping her tone measured, she asked, 'If I say we still have things to discuss – legal things – will you bite my head off again?'

'If I say no, will you go away?'

It was almost a moment of conciliation.

'Of course.'

Heather leaned over and poked the fire. 'I go to the grove when I want to think about serious stuff.' She said it quietly as if she'd forgotten Ida was there.

Because it's where your mother is.

'Okay. Drop by the house, whenever you're ready.'

'I'll see.'

'Do you promise not to do anything hasty?'

'Okay.'

'And the letter?'

'What about it?'

Ida held on to her exasperation. 'What do you want to do with it?'

'It's not up to me. Do you want to keep it?'

'I told you, no.'

'Me neither.'

'It's her handwriting, Heather – your mother's.'

'I've got her journal.' Heather kept her back resolutely turned away.

'I thought you said it was full of recipes.'

'It is – spells and remedies. All sorts.'

'The letter's the truth. Proof.'

'We're the proof.'

'The letter's her heart, Heather.'

'He broke her heart.'

Fifty-one

A splash of rain against the windowpane and Ida was awake.

A pipe clanked. Her dream left her, left something unsettling. She came down the stairs, rubbing the back of her neck, cricked from lying awkwardly.

In the hall, Heather stood in the front doorway.

'Holy hell, you scared me.'

'Back door's bolted. You left this one open. You want to watch that, Ida, anyone could get in.'

Ida tried a smile. 'What's up?'

'I decided you're right. There are things we need to talk about. May as well get it over with.'

Heather tramped across the hall into the kitchen, slumped in a chair. She was wearing a different jacket, black linen with sagging pockets, heavy with whatever they concealed.

Dead bats and hemlock? A shrivelled mouse or two?

Ida chided herself for her bitchy thought. The truth was, despite urging Heather to talk, she was afraid to trigger more drama. Ida bit her lip, held her breath. Let Heather instigate a conversation. She was better at it in any case.

'I'm here because you asked me, Ida. It doesn't mean I've changed my mind.'

'Fine. Tea?'

'May as well, but I'll do it. You make terrible tea.'

Once again, Ida was overwhelmed by her, only this time, she let the feeling settle, turn into something she could manage. She watched as Heather busied herself, at home.

It was her home for twelve years longer than it was mine.

310

'Before either of us make any decisions,' she said, 'we need to be sure we're doing so for the right reasons.'

'Yes, that's sort of what Roni said.'

'Oh.'

'She came to see me, last night, after you left.'

'I see.'

'Do you?' Heather dumped mugs of tea on the table. Liquid slopped over the edges. 'Can't say I do. I told her I didn't want to talk about *him*, so what was the point? But Roni's not stupid and she cares about me. More important, she cared about my mam and I trust her.'

Ida knew better than to ask what Roni had said.

The room hung with unsaid words.

'Can we go outside?'

Ida said of course they could. 'Do you want to go to the grove?'

'No.' Heather was silent for a moment, as if she weighed one thought against the other. 'But I don't feel right in here. Not anymore.' However hard she tried to hide, Heather's eyes gave her away.

'The garden, then,' Ida said. 'Come on.'

At the gate, they stood together, cooling mugs of tea in hand, stared into the morning shadows, neither of them speaking. Heather's arm brushed against Ida's. She drained her tea, dropped the mug into the grass and with a swift jerk, lifted the gate and took off, letting the gate sag back, barring Ida's way.

'Don't mind me.' Ida drank down her own tea and set the mug next to Heather's.

At the centre of the garden, the girl sat under the apple tree, waiting. 'Sorry. I didn't mean it.'

'*Plus ça change.*'

'Don't be clever, Ida, it's boring.'

Ida laughed.

'And don't laugh at me.'

'I'm not, honestly.'

There wasn't a lot of room. They were close enough to touch and when they nudged one another Heather tensed and made space. 'Roni thinks I ought to take my time.'

'Sensible.'

Heather gave her a sideways glance. 'Don't rush me and I'll stay. I mean, we can talk, about whatever it is you think we need to talk about. Legal stuff.'

Her eyes were fixed and resolute and Ida knew she had to keep her tone light. 'Whatever you want.'

'You've been weeding?' Heather pointed to the wheelbarrow, piled high with limp nettles and dock leaves.

'A bit.'

'You shouldn't leave the barrow out. It'll rot in the rain.'

She strode across the garden, heaved up the wheelbarrow and made her way to the corner of the garden.

Ida followed.

'Compost.' Heather dragged on a piece of rotting carpet. 'This one's for weeds. So long as they haven't gone to seed. Otherwise, you have to burn them.' Heather picked at the pile in the barrow. 'Maybe burn this lot, be on the safe side.' She tipped them into a small metal bin, with holes punched in the side. 'I'll see to them later, if you like.'

Ida nodded. 'Great. And can you show me?' Ida asked.

'What? How to burn weeds?'

'The difference. Between weeds and – not weeds?'

Heather raised her eyebrows. 'Okay, townie.' She pointed at a wild leafy plant, dark green with a hairy stem. 'Comfrey. Definitely not a weed.'

'What? That ugly great thing?'

'It's one of the kind plants.'

'Kind?'

'Healing. Mam called them kind.' Heather ran her fingers over one of the leaves. 'It would work on your foot.'

'My foot?'

'I'm not blind, Ida, I've seen how you limp sometimes.'

In the silence, Ida waited, not trusting herself to speak.

'What's wrong with it?'

'I fell – damaged it. Broke a bone and it didn't heal well.'

'That's what I thought.' Heather fished in one of her pockets. 'I've been meaning to give you this.' She handed Ida a small brown jar. 'Comfrey ointment. It'll help. And I can make you a poultice if you like.'

It sounded far too witchy. Ida stared at the brown jar on her palm and it reminded her of a toad. 'There's nothing can be done.'

'Rubbish – there's always something. Mam called it knitbone. It's one of the oldest medicinal plants. It's medieval.'

Ida thought about Olwen – clever Olwen who called birds. She thought about spells and trickery and how Heather's mother had believed she was entitled to have any man she wanted.

'You have to be careful with it mind,' Heather said. 'Know how much to use.'

'You see, you do know about this stuff. You could make it into a career. Train to be a medicinal herbalist.'

'And I told you. Mam trained me.'

'Your mother knew who she was. She would have wanted you to have a chance to be who you could be.'

Heather pushed her hair out of her eyes. 'Let's just garden, eh?'

'If it was your garden,' Ida said, 'and you could do whatever you liked with it, what would it be?'

'Mam always wanted to make a physic garden. I told you.'

'Sounds like a plan.'

'There you go again – making plans for me, when it was my mam's idea and you don't have a clue what I want.'

Ida thought perhaps she did.

They stayed in the garden for a couple of hours. Ida pulled weeds, watched Heather wander in the gathering of autumn, tending to the remnants of the season, to the plants that would keep going into winter.

As the afternoon drew on, and a quiet blue light edged its way into the garden, they both slumped on the bench, exhausted.

'Are we getting somewhere?'

Heather made a face. 'In the garden, or you and me?'

'Both?'

'The *garden* needs years.'

'Same as us.'

'Are you leaving?'

'I don't know, Heather. I'm saying perhaps I need to wait. Maybe we both do. Let the world do its thing and relax?'

'I suppose. I can't see how it can get any worse.'

Ida didn't think the world would take Heather by surprise. She might be naive, she was no one's fool. She was brave and she'd look the world in the eye, both of her own as bright as rainlight.

Heather would make everything a question, until she found the right answer.

Fifty-two

By tacit agreement, Heather came every day and Ida suggested she stayed over.

Heather brought her night things, and not much else. She slept early and rose at dawn. Before Ida was down in the kitchen each morning, fixing coffee, Heather was off, doing whatever it was she did. Ida didn't question her. They made food together, worked in the garden and now and then, talked, still edging around the things they were avoiding.

They were kinder with one another and Ida made a surreptitious study of this new sister, wondering about the missing years: the child Heather – wishing there was a way to discover them, and know her.

Now and again – with her guard down – Ida saw how, beneath her wild exterior lay a fierceness that was nothing to do with belligerence and scornful criticisms. Heather had survived a lot in her seventeen years. Her unconventional upbringing, the derision of the village, and the loss of her mother.

And now she was doing her best to withstand her dead, redundant father.

Given a chance, Ida suspected Heather would blossom. She had a talent for life – a knack Ida envied. All at once she felt protective and at the same time, wondered about her own future and what she needed.

Not this flawed house. It represented a wrong turn. Ida had believed in her father, given herself up to trust the way children do.

The way daughters do.

Ida took a risk.

'This house,' she said. 'Morally, it's as much yours as it is mine.'

'How do you work that out?'

'Come on, Heather, don't pretend you don't know what I mean.'

They were in the kitchen and Heather was tying the last of the rosemary into bundles. Ida decided not to interfere although she had no idea what she would do with it. 'Because he was my father?'

'Yes. You're his daughter too.'

'I don't have to be. I don't want anything to do with him.'

'Even though you are?' Ida started again. 'My mother never criticised him and neither did I. Not really. It's hard, accepting she was little more than a gullible fool. I used to tease her for missing him the way she did, when he went away.'

'To see Mam.'

'Yes. I suppose so. But for work too. At the university. He had a room at the college. Sometimes he was away for days at a time. Said it was more convenient. I'd tell her to make the most of it and we could be girls together.'

And it had seemed ideal. Now, Ida saw the lie, how her mother had possibly chosen ignorance. 'I'm finding it hard too – having his memory entwined with hers. I want to mourn her separately.'

'I hate him.'

'I know.'

'No you don't. He's spoiled this house for me. And now, he's driven Mam away too.'

'She did that herself. From the moment she wrote the letter.'

'Don't say that.'

'I didn't mean it in a nasty way. But she must have known what could have happened, if he'd read the letter.'

They sat in silence, each one laden with impossible thoughts. Ida was too weary to order hers. They were bewildering, as if they belonged to someone else. She wondered what was going on in

Heather's head. There was something diminished about her, her confidence wavering, her face drawn – too young for the burden.

Why haven't I noticed?

'The secret's out,' Heather whispered. 'And I can't feel my heart.' Her voice was thinner too, like the rest of her. Her shoulders drooped. 'Mam always said a secret was a burden.' She leaned forward, her elbows on her knees and Ida thought she was crying. 'I'm sorry, Ida.'

'For what?'

'Everything?'

She wasn't crying. Her voice was heavy with knowing. Whatever they now shared – *a liar for a father* – Ida knew their thoughts were in equal disarray. And Ida was helpless. If Heather turned to her, she would have nothing to offer.

Her sister's anger was rooted in the fact of an unforeseen sibling.

The fact of me.

For Ida it was the deepest betrayal. The denial of her sister. A relationship built on a lie. Lies and secrets: the cliché made real.

'I'm afraid I'll forget what Mam looked like.'

'Don't you have a photograph?'

Heather shook her head. 'She didn't like cameras. I've only got one.'

'Do you have it with you?'

Heather fished in her pocket, brought out a small wallet.

The image of Olwen lit up the paper it was printed on. A mass of brunette hair framed a smile giving nothing and everything away. Her eyes were half-closed, against the light. Ida guessed the photograph had been taken out of doors, possibly on a beach somewhere.

'Oh, Heather, she's beautiful. I mean, astonishingly lovely.'

'No need to go overboard.'

Ida smiled, held out the photograph. 'You look like her in this. What did you look like when you were little?'

'I don't remember – I told you, Mam didn't do photos.'

'My… *He* only took pictures of my mother.'

'No photos of either of us then?'

'There's a few of me, in an album. It's mostly Mum.'

'Can I see them?'

'Do you want to?'

'May as well. See what all the fuss is about.'

Ida hid a smile. 'Hang on.'

She fetched the album, set it on the table. It was filled with pictures of Anna, the ballerina. Posed and dazzling. A few snaps of Ida linked them.

Heather turned the pages, found one of Ida aged about fourteen. 'You've got the same hair as her. Why did you cut it?'

Now it was Ida who shrugged, reluctant to admit it was because there was no longer anyone to brush it.

'Do you think they would have liked one another?' Heather asked.

'Mine would have been scared of yours.'

'Mine would have hexed yours.'

Ida laughed. 'Well, spells notwithstanding, we both look like our mothers.'

'Do we?'

'Oh yes.' She glanced at Heather, at the photograph of Olwen. Looking at her mother's face must have been like looking in a mirror. 'You're her. She's you.'

'I don't feel like me anymore.'

Ida was getting used to Heather's illogical tangents. This one, at least, made a kind of sense. Ida hadn't felt like herself for so long she wondered if she might mistake her reflection for some other woman. There was a part of her she could no longer touch, crucial and cut out. What she was left with was a hurt place inhabited by the stranger she'd become. 'If you feel anything like I do—'

'I don't.' Heather's retort was brutal. 'And don't compare us. At least he loved you. He *chose* you.'

Ida didn't know how to respond. Heather was wrong. He hadn't chosen any of them; he'd chosen Olwen. And imagined he could get away with deceiving Anna. He'd betrayed them all, but Ida knew, this hurt girl was in no frame of mind to hear it.

'We're all broken, Heather.'

'My mam told me to hold on tight, that way I wouldn't fall and break.'

Concentrate, Ida…

Ida dismissed the memory. 'Mine told me not to walk on the cracks, and never wish her good luck.'

'What? Never?'

'Nope. Dancers say, shit – in French.'

'*Merde.*'

'That's right.' Ida grinned, ridiculously pleased.

'See, smart-arse, you're not the only one who knows French.'

'Touché?'

Heather managed a smile, said she remembered Olwen's voice. 'It was low, like an old bell.'

Ida touched her hand, the gesture tentative. She squeezed Heather's fingers, once, twice, unsure if she would be rebuffed. Heather didn't pull away.

'Do it again,' she said.

'Do what?'

'Squeeze my fingers?'

'Why?'

'Make it odd. Mam had her superstitions too. She didn't trust even numbers. Said the odd ones were feminine and went in circles.'

Ida thought about odd numbers and began counting in her head. How many odd years made up a lifetime? Twenty-nine? Did her mother's smashed powder compact, returned with her meagre belongs, the mirror shattered into spidery slivers equal seven years bad luck? Or forever? Nine stunted trees, three black birds and one old house secreted behind a cloud-spell.

And before she could stop herself the words were out. 'Two sisters? Two mothers?' Ida's irritations were falling away like stones in an avalanche and she saw only Heather's vulnerability and her unassailable eyes. 'He lied to both of them, only I don't believe his love was a lie. Not entirely.'

'He loved your mother best.'

'No. He loved her *differently*.'

'There you go again. Saying stuff when you don't know what you're talking about.'

'What if I'm right though? He loved Olwen when they made you.'

'I was a mistake.'

'So was I!'

'What do you mean?'

'It's why they married in such a hurry. My mother was pregnant.'

Heather sighed. 'I thought we'd decided it isn't a competition.'

From the back of her mind, Ida heard Lowri's voice, and her own, filled with rancour.

You think a mother who killed herself trumps a mother you may as well have killed?

The skin on her cheeks caught fire and she grabbed at her interrupted words. 'That's not what I mean and you know it. I'm only saying, there was honesty. In some of it.'

'He tricked them both!'

They were sparring again: awkward kindnesses masking something beneath the surface that still threatened. Heather made Ida think of an animal again: wary, like a hare ready to run. And at the edge of her words, unsaid ones Ida knew were waiting to hurt.

Heather's look was unwavering. 'Don't think because we're some freaky version of sisters it means anything.'

'Whatever you say.'

'What I say is, he was a liar and a bastard, and nothing you say will make me care about him.'

320

Oh, the lies he told! (The sin of omission has never mitigated a lie.)

When I found him out, his lies went through me like a winter wind. I was already carrying and the second I told him, and he confessed his deceit, I knew there would be nothing for me.

Or my child.

The weight of my scorn burned holes in my skin. I bathed in the pool, near the crag where the black birds watched, for fear I would set my furious heart on fire. For two pins I would have thrown myself off. The birds barred the way and saved me.

He wasn't worth dying for.

Instead, I sent him dreams made from cobweb snares, misty manacles designed to stop his wickedness. He woke and found his mouth bound by gossamer stickiness, trapping any lies he might have left.

I had a daughter to live for.

Listen – is that the sound of consequences colliding?

Fifty-three

Heather had finally decided she was ready to go to the grove.

It was raining – a light drizzle and Ida cast a mistrustful glance at the sky. 'It's a bit damp.'

'Don't be such a wuss,' Heather said. 'It'll stop in a minute.'

Pulling her beret low over her hair, Ida picked her way, trying to place her feet in Heather's footsteps. The ground was soft, padded with leaf litter and the trees slid out of a mist as thin as vapour. They made their way toward the trees, each with her arms folded across her body, as if to hold onto her thoughts.

Ida noticed Heather had abandoned her concealing skirts. She wore a blue frock – dark, with green flowers appliqued to the hem – and the black linen jacket.

The rain stopped and in an impossible instant, the sky was rinsed with silver.

'Told you.'

They sat on the grass, on a rug Ida had insisted on bringing with her. Their shadows stretched behind them in the afternoon light. Heather left a hand-space between them. Through the dripping branches, sky glimmered like blurred glass and for once there wasn't a cloud to be seen. It wouldn't last. Cloud, Ida knew, was as inevitable as dawn.

A fairy wind rustled in the trees, unsinging birds waited, curious to see what was planned.

Or that was how it felt to Ida.

'Is she here? Olwen?'

'Why are you whispering? Scared she might be?'

'Stop it, Heather, I'm trying to understand. This place still freaks me out. It's older than time.'

'Wow, we'll make a witch of you yet.'

'Don't say that. I don't want to be a witch. That's your heritage, not mine.'

'No – all women have the witch in them.'

'You think?'

Heather's shoulders lifted, slight and non-committal. 'Sit out on the moor with me when the dark's gathering. Watch the stars light up the night.'

'Do you think if my memories were in amongst these stones and trees I'd recognise things better? See what you see?'

'I told you. It's a bloodline, so maybe not.'

So how Welsh are you? … It's bloodlines…

Heather pulled a sprig of heather from her pocket, poked it into the softened ground where her mother's ashes were buried. 'The day she died, I didn't say a real goodbye to her.'

Ida waited. The brittle sound of hollow bones, the chinking of mirror slices, sounded above them.

Have the best time! See you soon!

'She must have thought I didn't love her.'

'No. Never.' Ida swallowed a tear. 'I can't begin to imagine what this is like for you.'

'It's the same as it is for you.'

'No, Heather, it isn't. I knew my father, or at least I thought I did. I mean, I had him in my life.'

'It doesn't matter.'

'Yes it does.' Ida tried to keep her voice calm. 'I'm no good at this – talking about my feelings. Personal stuff.'

Heather gave a thin, cracked laugh. 'I'm no good at anything.'

'That's simply not true. You're the most confident person I've met in years.'

'Mam said if you believed you mattered then you did.'

Ida eyed the place where the ashes of Olwen Morgan lay, returned to the earth and unlikely to physically exist any longer. She resisted the idea it was sacred, even though it was the only word that fitted. 'I do respect this place, you know. I respect her. Your mother.'

'You're whispering again.'

'Am I?'

'Yes.' Heather grinned. 'No one's listening, Ida.'

No one was. Not even Olwen.

'You could scatter her ashes here. Your mam's.'

Ida thought about the ugly plastic urn in the boot of her car. 'How do I know it's the right place?'

'It's about how it feels. And why I brought Mam's ashes here. Because it was right.' Heather paused. 'Remember what I told you, how the smallest part of a person can attach itself? Maybe a bit of Anna's here after all.'

'You've changed your tune.'

Heather ignored her. 'Enough to make it count?'

'No. Mum hated it here. You were right the first time.'

'No, I wasn't. I was being a bitch. No one could ever hate a place like this, Ida.' Heather's gaze was miles away, like she was the only person who saw how faultless the landscape was. 'Your mam hated what it represented.'

The wind picked up again and Ida hugged her arms to her body. 'Can we go now? I'll even drink tea.'

Ida eased off her boots and out of habit, bent to rub her foot. Over the past few days, after several applications of Heather's brown ointment, a small miracle had occurred. At first, the smell and the dark, greasy look of it had disgusted her. Ida wrinkled her nose and rubbed it in, massaging it the way Heather instructed.

She peeled off her sock.

'Better?' Heather asked.

'A bit.'

'Told you.'

Ida made a face. 'Listen, I've a favour to ask you. Will you help me clean up – in Olwen's room? There's soot everywhere.'

If the request pleased her, Heather gave no indication. 'If you like.'

It didn't take long. Heather dealt with the hearth, sweeping up the soot, tipping it into a bucket. 'Mam had a special compost heap for soot. Only you have to leave it for a year. I'll show you.'

'Okay,' Ida said. 'You're the expert.'

'I just know stuff.'

'No, you have authentic skills, Heather. You could turn them into a career.'

Heather shrugged and Ida carried on, cleaning the windowsill, wiping away the bird droppings, throwing bedraggled feathers out of the window.

'Leave it open.'

Ida acquiesced, no longer afraid a ghost would get in.

'The fresh air will sort the stink of soot and bird droppings.'

It was such a practical statement, Ida laughed. 'Good plan.'

Heather came over to the window.

'What?' Ida frowned.

'Our eyes.'

'They're sometimes the same colour.'

'I know.'

This time Heather smelled of rosemary and fate and Ida had to swallow the lump in her throat. She thought of all the harsh words she'd spoken to Heather, how she'd raged and railed and told her she wasn't wanted. But any remorse or weakness in her would have to wait.

You're the eldest.

There had to be a way to make it up to her.

She's my sister.

Gazing at Heather, at her chewed fingernails and haywire hair, Ida saw a creature who belonged on the moor, who slept under the stars and sang to birds. 'Heather, can I tell you something?'

'Go on.'

'The ashes – they don't just belong to my mother.'

'I guessed that.'

Ida wiped the last streaks of dirt off the windowsill. 'In that case, what you said, about scattering them in the grove. I could, I suppose. If you don't mind that is. And do it properly?'

'You mean like a ritual?' Heather grinned. 'I told you we'd make a witch out of you.'

'*You're* the witch, Heather. Like your mother. I want you to promise to think about what I said. About doing what she wanted. Make her proud, and show them all.'

Ida walked her sister out to the edge of the garden. Heather said she needed to go to the cottage and Ida suspected she wanted some space. They were too new, and the atmosphere constantly verged on the brink of volatility.

After Heather's bicycle disappeared into the mist, Ida wandered across to the crag, looked down toward the grove. Diaphanous light dripped through the trees, making patterns. She thought again about scattering the ashes – how they would look, as she let them go. Would they sink into the ground or float in the air, an ephemeral moment with no more significance than the trappings of a belief system she disdained?

Would releasing them, release her?

Fifty-four

Ida was eating porridge in the kitchen when Lowri called.

'I've been wanting to … apologise.'

'Again?' Ida let out a sigh. 'What for this time? For being insensitive and cruel?'

She heard the catch in Lowri's voice and instantly regretted her words.

'Wow. Harsh, but okay—'

'Damn, now it's my turn to apologise. Forgive me. I'm—'

'No, Ida, it was me. I can't believe how out of order I was. Put it down to excitement. You saw how the girls reacted. But you were right – I shouldn't have outed you. Not without asking.'

Ida couldn't speak.

'Was it so awful?' Lowri's voice faded on the faltering signal. 'Ida? Ida, are you okay?'

No.

'Yes.'

Oh, the lies…

'I just thought—'

'You thought what? You'd alert the press? Famous dead ballerina's daughter moves into area?'

'That's horrible.'

It was.

'Hell, I don't know what's wrong with me,' Ida said. 'That *was* horrible. It was a shock.'

'I know and I feel like a right idiot and can only apologise again. For letting my excitement run away with me. For not respecting your privacy.'

'Okay.'

The line buzzed.

'Am I forgiven?'

'I can't hear you.'

Lowri shouted. 'I said, am I forgiven?'

'Of course.' Ida hesitated. 'To be honest, Lowri, I've got other, weird things on my plate right now. It's not you, honestly.'

'Sounds ominous.'

'Try life-changing.' Ida hesitated. Her normal reticence was unravelling and she knew she was on the edge of disclosure.

'Are you still there? Ida?'

Ida was outside now, walking to the edge of the yard. The sky stretched like a grey ocean. 'Lowri, can I trust you?'

'Of course you can. I know I natter for Wales but I swear, you can trust me. Cross my heart and hope to die.'

Ida smiled, charmed by Lowri's words. 'Okay, whatever. I trust you.'

'Only if you want to.'

'I do.' Ida took a deep breath. 'What would you say if I told you, the girl – Heather – the one who's been hanging around here, is related to me?'

'What, like a long-lost cousin or something?'

'Not exactly.'

'What then?'

An impulse pushed Ida and she let the last of her resistance go. 'She's my sister.'

'You're kidding?'

'Hardly.' Her ear was hot. She held the phone away from her head. 'Ida?'

'Yes, I'm still here.'

'How did you find out?'

'It's a long story.'

'It's Sunday, I've got all day.'

The telling made it sound as if it had happened to someone else.

Once upon a time…

The version Ida gave Lowri was trimmed and sparse, punctuated by the idiosyncratic signal. It sounded bleak, like the synopsis for a Gothic novel.

'Bloody hell,' Lowri said, when Ida trailed to a stop. 'It's like something out of a book.'

Ida gave a sharp laugh. 'Isn't it, though? And that's only the bare bones. It's beyond complicated. She's my sister – my blood sister. Which means the house is half hers.'

'Not legally though, surely?'

'Morally. And yes, legally she might have a claim. I don't know, I'm not a lawyer. And in any case, she's a kid. I feel responsible for her. I'm almost her next of kin.'

'I thought you couldn't stand her?'

'Hardly the point. And she's not that bad. It's different. Now…'

'I'm not trying to make light of it, Ida.'

'I know you aren't.'

'You have to look at it for what it is though. I mean, if you hadn't found the letter—'

'I would have.'

'What do you mean?'

'I was always going to find it and even if I hadn't, eventually someone would. Heather herself, most likely. The truth would have come out one way or another. I'd have had to do something about her. Her mother was my father's tenant, which means I'm at least accountable.'

'I suppose.'

'I am and I'm horribly conflicted. Can't decide what to do. About the house, which frankly, I can't stand. About Heather, about anything. And if I'm staying, I need a job.'

'Come and work for me.'

'What?'

'With my classes. I told you, I'm overwhelmed, what with the exams on the horizon.'

Ida thought about the tall, intimidating swans. 'Those girls were terrifying! No way.'

'Not with them, with the little ones. You were amazing, Ida. They loved you. They haven't stopped talking about you. And you say you need a job. I've been thinking of employing someone for a while. It's the perfect solution.'

'Lowri, stop—'

'If I can concentrate on my seniors, I'll get the passes. They're worth it – those girls work so hard for me. And I need the passes, Ida.' Her voice had an excited intensity to it now. 'Parents like results. You'd be perfect. You're patient and—'

'Lowri, please, stop talking.'

'Why? What's the matter?'

'Didn't anything I say last time sink in?'

'I don't understand.'

'Have you forgotten? I can't dance.'

'Oh, Ida, not that again. You don't have to *dance*, not as such. Not to be a teacher. You guide them and deal with the minutiae.'

'The *minutiae*.'

'It's only a foot, Ida, not your whole body. The rest of you is who you are. The rest of you is perfect.'

'You aren't listening, Lowri.' Ida was holding on to her temper – and her tears – by the skin of her teeth.

'Yes I am. I'm trying to make it sound like what it is – a good idea. There's a flat here too – or there could be. You saw it. You liked it. You could bring your things.'

Ida thought about her belongings, gathering dust in her flat. Clothes she had probably forgotten she owned, rugs and lamps and books. Her mother's lovely things in Wisteria Cottage still to be sorted. She saw them in the light airy rooms at the top of Lowri's house, and a lump came into her throat. 'It's too soon.'

'I'm offering you a job, Ida, not a marriage proposal. You have a gift. Don't waste it.'

'You think it's that easy? I just up sticks – *again* – move in with you?'

'Not with me, it would be your own private space.'

'I—'

'Ida, you just said you can't stand your house. And we usually end up where we're meant to be. Ty'r Cwmwl obviously isn't it. Sometimes it takes a few goes to find home, and it's the last place we imagine.'

Ida stared into the darkness. She was cold now and the room clung to her. She felt nothing. Not a flicker of belonging, in this dark house on the moor, only a sense of wanting to be gone.

'Ida?'

Lowri, Lowri, lovely Lowri … slipping into her consciousness like a sweet and unexpected gift…

Ida started. No, first she had to fix things with Heather.

'I can't, she said. 'Can't make plans until I've worked out this stuff with Heather. It's massive.'

'Yes, I see that. I hear you only isn't it another reason to say yes? Sell the house, give her half or whatever you think's best, and—'

'Lowri. You're trying to making me run and I can barely walk.'

'Listen to yourself, will you? Can't? Won't, more like. That's the word you're looking for.' Lowri's exasperation rose to the surface. 'There's more than one way to abuse yourself, Ida. If you cut off your own feet, you have no one else to blame when you find you can't walk. Or dance.'

The silence quivered between them.

'Oh, Christ, I—'

'Fuck off, Lowri.'

Ida slammed down the phone.

331

Fifty-five

The price for pride – cutting off her own feet.

Ida lay against the pillows in the morning dark, her misery weighing her down. Even before they'd begun, she'd ruined things with Lowri, by her extreme reaction to what was essentially, kindness.

And if you don't care, you can't be hurt.

Ida did care, and already, an affinity was being forged with Lowri, far simpler and less complex than the one that existed with tricksy, irascible Heather.

But Lowri talked too much, and her taunt had lodged.

You have no one else to blame when you find you can't dance…

It wasn't her fault, but Lowri had no idea what being Anna Plessey's daughter had been like.

The pressure had been immense. Not least when Margeaux staged her three monthly shows – excerpts from well-known ballets, showcasing the skills of her best students. Painfully shy and singled-out, Ida would warm up in the wings, listen for her cue, terrified of making a mistake.

In costume and make-up, dancing a character, fear of failure invariably saw her through, but she never stopped dreading it. In class, with the lesser burden of expectation, it had been easier. Sweat-stained and untidy, Ida had given a different kind of performance, often imperfect, but always her best endeavour.

Until she broke her foot and everything changed.

Recognising Lowri's inherent goodness, Ida knew there was no malice in her words. She'd heard the way Lowri spoke to her pupils, her pride in them.

They're worth it, those girls work hard for me.

Or was it, that some of them worked hard for their parents?

Lowri didn't call and when Ida tried to phone her, there was no reply, only a voicemail request. It was too important for a message. And in any case, what would she say? What version of sorry was appropriate when you had thrown their kindness in a person's face?

What was wrong with her? Lowri made things easy. It was Heather and the unwitting weight of her presence that left no room for Ida to gather her thoughts, never mind make sense of them.

She peered over the edge of the duvet, into the insubstantial morning shadows. Even the house was losing its solidity. It may as well have been made of paper. She staggered out of bed, to open the window.

Outside, cloud hung like a tattered veil.

People said the best time to view a house you were thinking of buying was at the end of the year, when the flaws showed. It was certainly the worst time to move *into* a house. Nothing compensated for the sense of being stranded beneath some version of dense, flailing cloud when what she craved was light.

And she thought how the rooms at the top of Lowri's handsome house looked out on an expanse of ocean, and sky, demanding to be seen on its own terms. She heard Lowri's voice, full of laughter, her bright humour and sweetness filling in the shadows.

Ida hadn't heard the postman. He must have left his van at the gate. She picked up the heavy envelope. It was from her solicitor. Puzzled – she already had the paperwork for the final transfer of ownership – she was taken aback by the fact of more money.

An internet account … only recently come to our notice … apologies for any inconvenience … monies to be transferred once all formalities addressed…

It was a sizeable amount and Ida had to double-check, take in the meaning of this unexpected addition to her father's legacy. It didn't change anything – it did represent possibilities.

The house was hers. It had been his and Ida was done with him. His money too, only she was a pragmatist. Money was money and her father's had been good enough for Olwen.

We all pay our dues in the end.

Ida would pay his dues for him, and like Olwen, take the money.

For her sister.

Heather had twigs in her hair and a dogged look on her face. Her cheeks were flushed and she looked younger than ever. Although the light behind her was dusty with moonlit shadows it no longer looked like concealment.

Hovering by the back door, she wouldn't make eye contact and Ida realised she was poised to run. The slightest thing and Heather would be off.

'It's late to be cycling across the moor.'

'I walked. I needed to think some more.' Her mouth twitched. 'I've thought.'

'Okay.'

'I know you're right, Ida, well mostly right, and I know I can't stay here. I don't want to now, but I need you to listen to me, while I explain.'

'Yes.'

'Don't say it if you don't mean it. I know you have my best interests at heart. But what I need to do is be the one who goes.'

'No, I thought we'd been through that.'

'I'll be eighteen soon and you said it yourself; no one can tell me what to do.'

Ida threw up her hands. 'But why would you leave? It doesn't make sense.'

If she leaves here, she'll die...

'I have to be independent. I like it at the shelter, but it's not a proper job.'

'Yes, I understand and I can help.'

'No, you can't. I can find one for myself.'

They were facing each other, stranded in the doorway, shivering with the sneaking cold.

'You're freezing,' Ida said. 'So am I. Come inside.'

'I'm not staying.'

'At least close the door. You're letting out the heat again.' Ida smiled, to soften the criticism.

'Sorry.' Heather sidled in, placed herself in front of the range. 'The thing is, if I can save up some money, perhaps I'll try for one of those courses after all. Qualify and yes, be the kind of healer Mam wanted me to be.'

Without taking her eyes off Heather, Ida reached for the envelope and the solicitor's letter. 'That's brilliant. I knew you'd work it out.' She indicated the letter. 'This came, it's from my solicitor. There's more money – real money I didn't know about, and I want you to have it.'

Heather frowned. 'What are you talking about?'

'There are opportunities out there and I can help. Make enquiries, go on the internet…'

'Money.'

'Yes. It's more than enough and it's the least he can do.'

'*His* money?'

Ida laid her hand on her sister's arm.

Heather withdrew it, fast as a snake. 'You're unbelievable.'

In a moment, the calm of the last few days dissolved. Ida understood the fragility of their relationship, how a word out of place could throw it into chaos again. And in spite of her best care, here it was, cracking like thin ice and it was her fault.

She dropped the envelope onto the table. 'No, you don't understand. Please, Heather, you have to listen.' She tried to keep the desperation out of her voice.

Heather threw her a look of such scorn, Ida took a step back. 'To you?'

Ida began to panic. Were there no limits to her ineptitude? When had she become the mistress of the clumsy, pointless intervention? First Lowri, now Heather.

And Heather threw herself at the words, as if they were alive and she wanted to kill them. 'How am I not surprised, Ida? It always comes down to money with you, doesn't it? You think it's the answer to everything. And to add insult to injury, you try and get round me with *his*.'

Ida gaped. 'That's not true. You don't understand.'

'Stop treating me like I'm some kind of idiot. I understand perfectly. You're the spoiled daughter of a spoiled, privileged mother and a two-timing father. I knew it. You've never had to work hard for anything in your life. Oh, I need money all right, only I wouldn't take his, or yours, not if I was destitute and didn't have a rag to by name.'

Ida's body slumped.

'And stop giving me fucking *letters*.' Heather flicked the envelope and Ida watched as it fell, in slow motion, to the floor. 'Stop trying to ruin my life with other people's words. Go back where you came from. Take *your* father's ashes with you, and his money and your pathetic mother's memories and get out of my life.'

Fifty-six

Before Heather could move, Ida pushed past her and the crash of the back door reverberated in her wake.

She didn't care about the wind or the screaming birds. Focusing on the ruts and muddy puddles, she ran. There were too many words: a never-ending barrage of them. One minute the dust between her and Heather seemed settled, the next it rose again, choking them both. She couldn't bear it any longer.

'Ida!' A voice, somewhere behind her, snatched away by the wind.

The black birds were everywhere and Ida yelled at them. 'Leave me alone, you evil bastards. I'm not scared of you!'

The sky grew darker, the moon limped between threads of cloud. The wind stopped, abruptly as if ordered, started again, whipped up leaves and twigs. There was a buzzing in Ida's head, her throat dried, the air stilled and she heard the birds again.

She ran faster, down the slope, toward the grove. The sky moved like an ocean, and the moon slipped from the cloud's tentacles again. Recalcitrant and wilful, the wind picked up and the trees braced themselves for the next onslaught. Ida imagined roots, black beneath the ground, deeper than the trees were tall, the better to hold them fast. And now she heard the wind chimes, the stark rhythm of them an off-key counterpoint in the wildness.

A loud *kraa* sounded and she didn't know if it was a warning or a threat. Stumbling through squelching mud, and stones like dead things under her boots, she kept going.

Where was the moon? Hidden again behind the tricksy cloud. Ida heard a loud flapping, a sweep of feathers, and she almost fell.

And the moon broke free, crazy and bright, and for a split second she saw the immensity of the bleak moorland spread before her.

The moon swelled and ripped open the cloud, momentarily lighting the way. The wind was berserk, and Ida could barely stay upright. A hysterical cry choked her throat. Nothing made sense and she couldn't tell the difference between the wind, the screams of the birds or the sound of a human voice.

'Idaaa…'

She heard Heather again, in her head or her imagination – she couldn't tell. And she was down, her foot caught in a root, the air knocked out of her. Panting, her chest painful with exertion, Ida fell forward onto her palms. Small stones dug into her flesh; her knees were bruised and she told herself to stop panicking.

Heather's outrage battered her head.

Stop giving me letters … stop ruining my life…

The balance of power was shifting again. Since the beginning, it had been about who held it. Olwen's letter, littered with revelation and old hurt: even with its best intentions, bound to create chaos. Legalities formed in grandiose language and shaped with control, guaranteed to add to the shambles.

The power of words. Her father – the Lord of Misrule, Olwen and her enchantments, her elegant, revelatory handwriting. If Ida hadn't been half out of her mind, she might have seen an irony: in some ways, David Llewellyn and Olwen Morgan had been made for one another.

The birds screamed again and Ida shrieked, only this time it was at herself. 'Get up, you pathetic idiot.'

Staggering to her feet, she tried to work out where she was. There was a tremor in her foot that wasn't a pain and she stood stock still. Beneath the skin she felt a shimmer and it was as if she saw through her boot, through skin and sinew to the bone.

'Walk, damn it.'

As she did, a trickle of fear returned. The shape of the land was wrong and she knew she was lost. The moor was cunning, the way laced with traps. Somewhere, the black birds wailed a warning. For her or about her – she couldn't tell. Each time the air shifted and Ida caught a glimpse of a rock or a straggly bush, wavering in the scarce light and she tried to patch them together, get her bearings.

Heavy mist insinuated like wet rope. Ida faltered. Skeleton trees, their stunted trunks pitted with gnome faces leered at her before disappearing. A narrow animal track appeared, and her rattled imagination conjured a wolf.

'Stop this now, Ida,' she told herself. 'Get a damn grip.'

She closed her eyes for a moment and when she opened them, moonlight, bright and terrible assaulted her again. In front of her the land fell away, lines of strata curving into a vanishing point where reality and myth merged in a valley of shadows.

She was lost and alone and when the moment came, it was small. And yet it hit her with such force, for a second she forgot her fear.

What power still remained in this wreckage was theirs: hers and her sister's.

'Who the hell are you?'

Through the dark and the rain, a girl glared at Lowri, her hair a shambles of bedraggled brown, skirt billowing around her legs.

Daunted by the weather and the track, Lowri had left her car at the gate and run up to the house. She stood on the path, batting her own wet, windswept hair from her face.

'Lowri Williams,' she said. 'I'm a friend of Ida's.'

'She hasn't got any friends.'

'Sorry?'

The girl shook her head to free it from the rain. 'It doesn't matter. She's gone.'

'Gone where?'

'I don't know. We had a row.'

'You're Heather, I take it?'

'Yes.'

'What kind of a row?'

'A bad one. She ran off, onto the moor.'

'And you let her go, by herself? In this? Whatever possessed you?'

It was raining harder now and Lowri was getting soaked. 'You do know she has a damaged foot, don't you? If she were to fall, she could lie out on the moor all night.'

'I'll find her. I know the way. It'll be okay.'

'How will it be okay? It's dark and this is a howling storm.'

'It'll blow over – it gets like this.'

Lowri saw something else in Heather's face, a moment of fear behind the bravado. 'How long has she been gone?'

'About five minutes. I'll find you a coat.'

Lowri said a torch would be a better idea and asked Heather which way Ida had gone. 'Did you see her leave?'

'Yes, sort of, she ran out like the house was on fire. I followed her, only she disappeared, and in any case, she wanted to go.'

'What's that got to do with anything?'

'She needed to get away from me.'

'But not fall into a bog and *die*!'

If Lowri meant her words to have an impact, she wasn't disappointed.

'All right! I'm sorry, okay? But I know the moor.'

'I bloody well hope so.'

'Come on,' Heather said. 'I'll find her, I promise. Trust me.'

Beneath her feet the ground fell away, abrupt and steep, and Ida saw that somehow, she'd arrived at the ravine. And below it, on the other side of the swiftly gathering darkness, the drop into oblivion.

She was strangely calm. If she stayed where she was, she'd be fine.

If you stay where you are you'll freeze to death.

The edge of the ravine loomed and she turned round, facing

340

away from it, taking a few tentative steps up the slope. It was the least illogical plan she could come up with. She took a few more steps and the ground began to rise, gently and perceptibly and vaguely safer.

'Ida!'

The sound of her name cut through the gloomy mist.

'I'm here! Heather, I'm here!'

'Stay where you are and keep shouting!'

When Lowri loomed out of the mist, Ida stared, lost for words. 'You're not Heather.'

'Well spotted. Oh, thank god you're safe. Are you okay?'

'I'm fine.'

They shared a look of mutual, muddled emotion and in an instant, Lowri wrapped Ida in her arms. 'I thought you were dead.'

'Don't be daft, I told you I'd find her.' For a moment, Heather looked like a chameleon, everything about her merging with the mist and the intermittent moonlight.

'It was her,' Lowri said. 'I mean, she found you. Heather. I just got here first.'

'Because you're mad,' Heather said, 'and when I told you to wait, you just ran off.'

'Typical townie.' Ida was crying now, shivering and barely able to stay upright.

'I'm sorry.' Heather was at her side. 'I mean it, I shouldn't have said any of that stuff. Before.'

'It's all right, honestly. And I was worse. I'm a cow. It's going to be okay. I promise.'

Heather's expression was a question, and Ida knew her sister was still trying to fathom her.

Touché. Me and you both, kid.

'We should go.' Lowri held Ida tight, her arms supporting her elbows. 'Don't argue and don't you dare fall. Just follow Heather and don't look down.'

Ida allowed herself to be led, in Heather's certain footsteps.

'I still can't believe you came out here again.' Heather said. 'I told you the last time not to go off getting lost.'

'You also said you'd make a witch of me, and it's another thing that makes no sense.'

'Did she?' Lowri started, her feet stalled. 'A witch?'

Heather kept walking. 'I did, although this wasn't what I had in mind. Bit drastic.'

Ida stumbled and clung to Lowri. 'I knew exactly where I was.'

'Of course you did.' Lowri began walking again, holding Ida tightly, her arm a protective embrace.

'Well speaking as the only expert round here,' Heather said, 'I'd have to disagree. Bloody mad, the pair of you.'

Lowri pulled Ida closer. 'She's a dancer. Dancers know the right steps.'

'Apparently, she's my sister,' Heather said. 'And according to my mam, sisters always find one another.' Her voice was like a bird and her eyes were a match for the moon.

A moth moon.

Fifty-seven

A weak sun made patterns of light on the wall.

The kitchen smelled sweet, of dried rosemary and sugar.

'Hurry up, Ida, I don't like not being able to see.'

'Shush and wait. You're the most impatient person I've ever met.' Ida pulled the curtains closed. 'Don't you dare peek.'

She'd been up since first thing, mixing ingredients, taking her time. She liked that it had taken hours, that she had crouched by the oven, willing the cake to be perfect.

With the candles lit she held the cake like an offering. 'You can look now.'

Heather blinked. 'That's mad! Amazing!'

Ida tried not to laugh. She still worried Heather might take offence, read criticism into an innocent response. 'You have to blow out the candles and make a wish.'

'Are there eighteen?'

'No, I put forty on it, seeing as you're so old.' In the candlelight, chocolate frosting glittered. 'Of course there are. Count them. Then blow them out and make a wish and don't say what it is.'

'I know how it goes, Ida.'

Of course she did. Olwen would have made perfect birthday cakes.

'My mother couldn't bake for toffees and I'm afraid I'm her daughter. I'm not kidding. This cake is not only a miracle; it may taste awful too.'

'Baking cakes and bread is spellmaking. Or that's what Mam called it.'

Of course she did. Olwen had found magic in everything.

Heather inhaled, blew the candles out in a single breath.

'Did you wish?'

'Yes.' Her mouth twitched. 'Knife?'

'I found a proper one.' Ida set a silver cake-slice shaped like a trowel next to the cake. The handle was chased with flowers and one side of the blade was serrated.

Heather picked it up. 'That's Mam's.'

'I thought it might be.'

As Heather cut into the cake, Ida grinned in anticipation. 'I hope it's okay.'

Heather took a generous bite. Her grin widened and she licked frosting from her lips. 'That's lush, that is.'

Ida took a slice too and it was: moist and chocolate-sweet.

'It's really good, Ida. You have hidden talents.'

'Speaking of which, I have a present for you.' Ida hesitated. 'I hope you don't mind; nothing's written in stone but on paper, well, it looks brilliant.'

'You're rambling, Ida.'

'I know.' She was, because she was nervous. 'It's not wrapped, because you can't wrap an idea.'

Heather's mouth was full of cake. 'And?'

'There's a physic garden in south Wales. Near Swansea. They take students. I called them and they told me they still have places, for this intake. It's mostly hands on work experience but they run courses too. They said you sounded perfect.'

She studied Heather's face, alert with query, and for a moment regretted announcing her gift as a *fait accompli*. 'It's an idea, that's all. I went to see them.'

'You went to Swansea?'

'The other day. There's only so much you can do on the phone and they invited me.'

The room was so quiet, if the lamp had been lit you would have heard the moths breathing.

'You have been busy.' Heather wiped frosting from the corner of her mouth.

'I know I've taken a risk, and probably a liberty. But you're the real thing, Heather. You cure people, the way your mother did.'

'It isn't curing, it's *healing*. There's a difference.'

'Cure, heal. Semantics.'

Heather gave her a look. 'Is that even a word?'

'I can't help it if I'm the clever one.'

Heather hid a smile behind another mouthful of cake. 'Tell me what it is you're tripping over, Ida.'

'I thought you wouldn't go. Not on spec. This way, I thought you might at least consider it.'

'Right.'

Ida pressed her hand on her midriff, and the rising butterflies, knowing her plan could go horribly wrong. 'It was incredible. There was a woman there who I swear is a witch and…'

'You met a witch.'

'Well, she was like a witch…'

'You're an expert on witches now?'

'Of course not, I mean—'

'I know what you mean, Ida. Just spit it out.'

'I've paid for the introductory course. They said the money's returnable if you say no. They were lovely, I think you should go. See what they do.' Ida gave a nervous laugh. 'Even I could see how incredible the place was. If you like it, they can make arrangements for you: accommodation, mentoring. You work in the gardens a lot, with the plants. They're keen to find the right people.'

'And that's me?'

'I know I should have told you first.'

'You already said that and yes, you should.'

'Have I screwed up?'

Heather wiped her mouth on the back of her hand. 'Let's see, you phoned up a bunch of strangers and told them all about me?'

Ida knew Heather was watching her, unpacking each word, laying it before her. It was unnerving. She nodded.

'And they've offered me a job. With the plants. And they'll teach me stuff.'

'Yes.'

'And you thought I'd be angry?'

'A bit.'

'Well I am. A bit. Then again, you're the organised one and in a million years, I'd never have done any of that.'

'Are you saying you aren't angry?'

'I'm saying I need to check it out, but it's cool.'

'It is?'

'You aren't the only one making plans for me.' Heather leaned back in the chair. 'Thing is, mine are in my head. Yours are better.'

'They are?'

'Oh give over, Ida and stop asking daft questions. Yes. Your idea's better. It's an actual plan.'

'So you'll go?'

Heather made a face. 'May as well. Seeing as how you've paid for it. Look a bit rude if I didn't.'

Ida felt the relief like a blush coursing through her.

'They've got accommodation?'

'You don't have to live there,' Ida said. 'Only I'm not sure how you'd manage, commuting. You can stay here if you like, until I sell it.'

'I don't want to.'

'No?'

'No. It isn't right without Mam. And it's too big. I didn't realise how big it was before. She made it tidy. There's too much room now.'

'Yes.'

'Yes, no, blah, blah. You sound like a right idiot, Ida.'

'Thanks.'

Heather sighed. 'I thought she'd be waiting for me.'

Another random tangent.

'Your mother?' Ida asked. 'And she wasn't?'

346

'No. She was waiting for you. But I don't hear her anymore so it doesn't matter. She's getting ready to go.'

I'm waiting for her true leaving…

'I'm sure your mother still hears you, and she thinks you're brave, because you are.'

Heather cried then and let Ida hold her. And Ida knew her sister's sorrow wasn't for the physical death of Olwen. Heather wept for herself and for the loss of her mother's ghost presence, at her shoulder, unseen and as comforting as her arms had been.

The moment when your life changes, marks you.

Heather wiped her eyes. 'Thanks, Ida.'

'What for?'

'The cake. My present.'

'It's not the only one.' Ida let Heather go. 'You have to have something to open.'

Heather's fingers caught the ends of yellow ribbon, unfolded a layer of cream tissue. 'A journal.'

'I thought you might like to start your own.'

'It's lovely. Thank you.'

'You're sure you aren't angry with me?'

'I'm sure.'

'Not too bossy then?'

'Don't you worry, I'll let you know if you're getting bossy again.'

Ida hesitated. 'I might be going away myself. Not far. Lowri's offered me a job. There's a flat.'

'And the rest.' Heather grinned and Ida laughed.

'Are we turning into different people?' Heather stroked the cover of the journal.

'We're becoming different versions of the same people. That's all.'

'I've been a right bitch, haven't I?'

'I've been a thoughtless one.' Ida took her sister's hand and little sparks of energy darted between them. 'Are we cool?'

Heather smiled. 'Well, I am.'

Heather insisted on going back to the cottage.

'Sleeping here feels weird,' she said.

Ida nodded, hugged her and waved her off into the dusk. Standing at the back door, wrapped in a blanket against the chill of evening she looked up. It was twilight and the stars were beginning to come out. The light would soon be gone and for the first time, Ida wasn't afraid.

Despite her assurances to Heather, she knew she was no longer the same person. Her heart had uncurled, she could see in the dark that no longer scared her. She knew the difference between a crow and a raven and why the leaves on some trees looked like ghosts.

Ida caught a faint whiff of apples and for a second, thought she saw a figure by the gate.

'Get a grip, Ida Spider.'

There were no ghosts.

'Liz?'

'Ida!'

'I'm staying.'

'Of course you are.'

'How did you know?'

'Psychic powers?'

With the story spilled, Liz agreed she would miss Ida. But on the other hand, it was great news because holidays were what made Liz tick.

Ida leaned against the front gate, listening to the phone signal waver. 'It's going to be odd, not seeing you all the time.'

'We'll cope. And you better start planning for the English invasion.'

'What?'

'Now you're properly Welsh,' Liz said, 'You'll have to explain us. To the locals. When we visit.'

Grinning, Ida shifted the phone to her other ear, walked out onto the track where the signal kicked in.

'I met someone.'

'Is she pretty?'

Ida stopped dead. 'How…?'

'I've known for years. So has everyone else.'

'In that case, she's gorgeous. And Welsh. And kind and a total scatterbrain.'

'She sounds perfect.'

Fifty-eight

Stars stabbed the sky and when the cloud shifted, the moon lit a path across the grass.

They took their time.

'You don't hurry ritual,' Heather said.

They knelt in front of the tallest tree, the plastic urn between them. An unlit candle stood embedded in the grass.

Heather picked up a box of matches and held it out to Ida.

'No, you do it.'

Heather shook her head and Ida took the matches. She struck one, watched as it caught and a bright lick of flame flared in the gloom.

'Mothers aren't supposed to die before we're ready to manage without them,' Ida said.

Into the silence, the shared thought: neither of them had been ready.

'Are you okay?'

Ida nodded. 'It feels ridiculously normal.'

'Magic *is* normal.'

'I don't mean just this.'

Anna, David and Olwen, touched by tainted love. Ida no longer felt the burden of their old intrigue.

'I know you don't,' Heather said. 'The magic gets in anyway, however hard you try to hide.'

'Olwen?'

'She said you can't escape your fate.'

'And this is ours? Uncannily normal when it isn't normal at all.'

Heather offered an unexpected and naked smile. 'It's crazy, how

350

we both thought we'd never endure it. I felt tricked by Mam's death.'

'And now?'

'It still feels like a trick, only I've worked it out.'

Ida didn't need to ask what she meant because it was the same for her.

'Do you remember,' she said, 'when I told you I never dreamed?'

'Yes.'

'I do now. I've been dreaming about my mother – and about Olwen too.'

A child with this man would be perfect … as intelligent as she was magical.

'I think she wanted him, to make you. I think her choosing was deliberate.'

'It's all right, Ida. Guess he must have loved her – in his own way.'

'I just wish he could have been honest with her.'

His lies went through me like a winter wind…

'Then I might not have been born.'

Startled, Ida decided Heather really was unlike anyone she'd ever known. Capricious yes, and scratchy, but wise in ways Ida doubted she would ever be.

'My dreams are like a story,' Heather went on. 'In bits and moments, like Mam's trying to tell me what happened.'

'Does it matter? That we don't know the whole of it?'

'No. I'm sort of glad.'

Ida nodded. 'Me too.'

'I'm sorry she scared you.'

'I scared myself. I've always been superstitious. Mum was terrible – far worse than me.'

'I don't think she meant it.'

'Neither do I. She wanted us to know.'

'This,' Heather said, 'what we're doing here, is for our mothers.

So long as something of them is still here, we are too. Where we both began.'

Ida closed her eyes and tried to visualise her mother. 'I don't think I want it to be about him.'

'You don't have to hate him.'

Ida caught her generosity and held on to it. 'You don't have to love him.'

Heather didn't say anything.

'What next?' Ida asked. 'How do we make the magic?'

'We don't *make* magic; magic makes us.'

'Another thing Olwen told you?'

'Yes. And we make our own ghosts too.'

Ida felt the air shiver, with the remnants of redundant ghosts and she knew she would never be afraid of them again.

'We need to say their names,' Heather said. 'Make them real.'

'You first.'

Heather's hands hovered over the candle flame. 'Mam – Olwen – and your stories, your birds, and how you loved the first sweet peas and the first bite of a fresh apple. How the sight of a new moon could reduce you to tears. How you loved me best of all.' Her face was illuminated, moonlight caught on the soft blush of her skin. 'Blessed be, Mam.' She turned to Ida. 'Now you.'

'I don't know what to say.'

'Yes, you do. Remember who your mother was, who Anna was, and what you miss.'

Ida closed her eyes.

'Anna,' she said. 'Mum, and how you never picked the yellow roses because you couldn't bear to hurt them. How you sewed stems of heather under the net of your tutus – for luck.'

'You're kidding?'

'Don't interrupt,' Ida said, and smiled. 'Mother's magic – not so different after all.' She paused. 'How you bought me red ballet shoes because I begged for them, read me fairy tales and scary tales because you said they made the best ballets. How you loved me.'

'Best of all.'

'Best of all.' A tear ran down Ida's face. 'What was that you just said? At the end?'

'Blessed be.'

Ida whispered the words and they sounded right.

'It's time.' Heather picked up the urn and handed it to Ida. 'I'll wait for you.'

'No, stay. He was your father too.'

'But not my mother. It's private.'

'Let me share my mother, Heather. You shared yours with me.' She opened the urn and held it at arm's length, tipped it sideways. The ash flew in an arc: a bird made of dust. 'Goodbye, Dad.'

Heather was silent.

'Bye, Mum,' Ida called. 'I love you.' There was a flicker at the corner of her eye, a stream of pale light in the trees.

Not a ghost, a beautiful peasant girl... *Giselle*...

Merde...

She could see her mother dancing: a series of perfect *chaîné* turns, which become exquisite *fouettés*, thinking with her body and it's as if she spins in the very air. And now she's flying, airborne *grands jetés* – until a cloud catches her and she's gone...

Ida blinked and a tear rolled down her cheek.

I'll make new steps, Mum. Do my best and make them good enough.

Heather leaned into Ida.

'*Hwyl fawr*, Mam,' she whispered. 'Bye. *Am nawr.*'

'*Am nawr?*'

'For now...'

Ida sighed. 'I wonder what they'll make of it. Laid to rest together.'

'It'll be lively.'

'Is it enough, do you think? With nothing to mark the place.'

'Headstones are creepy.' Heather looked up. 'See?' Several black birds dotted the branches of the tall tree. There was nothing sinister about them. 'I'd rather rely on the birds to remember than words scribbled on a bit of stone.'

No headstone, and no brown leaves – no restless ghosts. No more falling.

'They'll sing, for both of them,' she said. 'Every day.'

Heather's hand found Ida's. It was warm and small and it fitted. Ida imagined how the two of them would look now, to other people: sisters who didn't appear to have a thing in common. Not until you looked closer, and saw the odd things making them interesting: small hands, stubborn centres and eyes the colour of rainlight.

'I've decided what I want to do with the letter.' Heather's grip on Ida's finger's loosened. 'I want to burn it.'

'Are you sure?'

'Yes.' She let go of Ida's hand and pulled the letter from her pocket. 'It's time. We're both going. You to Lowri, me to Mam's magic, and to bloody Swansea for my sins.'

'But you'll come back?'

'You'll get bored of me, I'll come back so often.'

Ida smiled. 'Right.'

'We'll read it, and let it go. Why would we keep anything neither of us needs?'

Ida knew she was right. The ghosts were gone and at the top of a house filled with light, a real woman with green eyes waited for her. She felt the air still, the moment as it held and her old skin falling away like a chrysalis.

'Read it out loud, Ida, one last time, and then we'll burn it.'

She handed the letter to her sister and Ida took a deep breath.

Cloud House
2000

David —

Does the lack of an endearment surprise you? You are no one's 'dear' – you are a thief. You stole my heart. As you didn't really want it, when you left me, I soon stole it back.

Remember, the first time we met – me with my broken shoe and you unable to resist an opportunity for gallantry? You caught the scent of apples on my skin, hesitated a moment too long, stared into eyes already reading your mind. Your weakness for beautiful women marked you. And I was young; my folly was imagining I could have you for myself. More fool me, to believe you were sincere – and single. For forgetting my mother's warning to guard my heart.

The unkind will say I paid the price for spellcasting, however innocent, because your true heart was never mine to claim. It was bound to her – with a gold ring sealing your vow.

I try to imagine your face as you read this. All I see is the appalled one you showed me when I told you I was pregnant. When I found you out in your lie. Your lips as they revealed your betrayal: the existence of your other child. And the tawdry bargain you concocted, to save your skin once the consequences of your adultery became clear.

My pen shapes a word – daughter. How it shines, blue black on the paper. You have another child. Another daughter. Her name is Heather and like it or not, your blood runs in her veins.

This letter won't be posted of course – you've made sure I can't find you and if I'm honest, I don't care to. You don't deserve this daughter the way you didn't deserve me. I'll keep my side of the bargain – take your money and your house for her sake – in return for keeping your dirty secret hidden.

Outcomes are tricky though, and this one is in the lap of fate. But words committed to paper have power and we all pay our dues in the end.

And the sibling bond is strong. Sisters have a way of finding one another. When they do, I hope they understand.

I'm not your 'love' – I never was.

I am Olwen

Epilogue

There is a fierceness in young women: the wild spinning girls made of loss and grief and their mothers' best dreams.

Let loose it could tip the world off its axis.

Now you are both going, I'm becoming a cliché; my work here is done! (I'm torn between leaving and staying myself – I am, after all, the true custodian and the birds would miss me.)

You girls are what you will become. You have a future. Don't be in a hurry to find it. It takes as long as it takes.

They called me a witch and I didn't entirely mind. The thing is, they didn't understand, how the trick to being a proper witch – a wise woman – is easy. If they need you, they'll find you.

Show up quietly and do your work. Grow and tend and don't pretend you can control things. It will only spoil the view. Love the colour red. It's the first colour you lose sight of at twilight. You can wrap a secret in red and keep it safe. Your heart is made of red; it's where you place your truthful secrets.

There's no longer any need for disguises, for a dead woman's coat or skirts made of camouflage. Be birds and dress in feathered raiment. (Now there's a fine witchy word for you!)

Be girls for as long as you choose. Some women will always be girls too, because a sense of wonder, along with hurt, is impossible to eliminate from their lives.

Keep reaching back for the luminous moments spinning in your hearts.

ABOUT HONNO

Honno Welsh Women's Press was set up in 1986 by a group of women who felt strongly that women in Wales needed wider opportunities to see their writing in print and to become involved in the publishing process. Our aim is to develop the writing talents of women in Wales, give them new and exciting opportunities to see their work published and often to give them their first 'break' as a writer. Honno is registered as a community co-operative. Any profit that Honno makes is invested in the publishing programme. Women from Wales and around the world have expressed their support for Honno. Each supporter has a vote at the Annual General Meeting. For more information and to buy our publications, please write to Honno at the address below, or visit our website: www.honno.co.uk

Honno, 14 Creative Units, Aberystwyth Arts Centre,
Aberystwyth, Ceredigion SY23 3GL

We are very grateful for the support
of all the Honno Friends.
For more information on how you can support Honno, see:
https://www.honno.co.uk/about/support-honno/